THE WRECK

BY RALPH TROUT

Published by
Libertad Publishing, LLC

This story takes place in the lower Grenadines. Most of the places depicted are real. The characters are fictitious and not based on any individual. The events described are fabricated.

ISBN: 978-0-9992239-3-2

This is dedicated to my parents who helped me
in more ways than anyone could ever expect.
They took me to the local YMCA in third
grade where I learned to swim and skin dive.
That opened a world of adventure.

WARNING!

Caribbean Islands seem dreamlike to those
not born among them. Do not allow your
dreams to become nightmares.

FORWARD

Ralph Trout's, *The Wreck*, is a good read. The plot and characters are genuine Caribbean looney types. The Wreck is fun, explaining all the problems of finding sunken treasure. I know because I've been treasure-finding for seventy years. As soon as a good wreck is found, greed can separate even the best of partners. My experiences in the early sixties, diving among the various Caribbean Islands, are almost exactly what happen in *The Wreck*. I'd ask every fisherman if he knew where any cannons or anchors were and off we'd go to a beautiful reef that could be hiding a fortune in gold and jewels. With every find, the government had to be notified, which always slowed the project, sometimes to a grinding halt. Pirates – modern day pirates – seem to be able to smell gold and silver. In the Bahamas, while working on the Nuestra Senora de la Maravillas (lost in 1656), the pirates repeatedly tried to steal our find. And beautiful women, well, they seem to mix well with treasure - and usually lust causes more problems than greed.

I have worked with Ralph on a couple of wreck sites in the Caribbean. He's quite familiar with all the simple mistakes that can easily complicate a great treasure adventure. The main object in all treasure quests is to keep life interesting. If you are only an armchair buccaneer read this book. *The Wreck* is filled with action - and it explains the reality of what can happen when the end of the rainbow is reached.

Find your own pot of gold!

For Treasure + Pleasure,
Sir Robert F. Marx

THEN

A beach seldom changes. A storm may disturb its serenity, but usually in less than a year the beach returns, beautiful as ever. That is the timeless effect of Mother Ocean. If only humans fared as well. It was 1802 and off this beach in the Southern Grenadines a schooner lay at calm anchor. On each side of the mast were two longboats loaded with barrels, and ready for a journey.

Several loud splashes broke the quiet of the morning. The four remaining crew were on deck. Captain Zane's graying hair, tamed with a black scarf, told his age. His dark coat was appropriate for a burial at sea. Twelve bodies dropped into Davy Jones' Locker. First-mate Allsop and seaman Stricklind tossed the body of a woman overboard as the sobbing cook lay on the deck, curled in a ball.

"What's there Gunness? Don't have a stomach for your own cooking? Ha!" Zane laughed and pointed to the remaining bodies. "Neither did they."

"I never thought," the cook paused, "oh my God, you're a devil, Zane. You stole my soul."

More bodies splashed into the sea.

"Hah, boy, you traded your soul for a quarter of all the gold we was carrying for them. Now it's ours." Zane said as he opened an iron strongbox to reveal the bright yellow glitter of coins. "Yes lad, we all traded our souls, and those of these dearly departed, for this fortune. Your arsenic-spiced dinner did the deed. We may all yet drink a toast in Hell, but for now… we're rich!"

The cook slowly rose from the deck, still sobbing. "I never thought…"

"That's why I'm the Captain. I do the thinking; you do the killing." He shouted, "Now you're a rich man!"

"I can't live with it, knowing…" the cook cried.

"You don't have to!" Zane pulled out a flintlock pistol and shot the cook through the heart as the other two crew watched. He blew the smoke off the pistol.

"One more to throw in the drink, boys. You two don't have a problem with one less share, do you?"

"No, Captain! No problem at all" Allsop and Stricklind answered.

"We go along with my plan — take only one of these eight chests with us in the longboat. The load would sink us. With enough water and hardtack we'll make it easy in three days to Dutch Curacao. Then, we'll buy another boat and come back to this desolate place with some Caribbee Indian divers to bring up the gold." Captain Zane bellowed, "Live like gentlemen, we will mateys!"

After they finished the quick funeral, the two crew members set a small mast into one longboat before lowering it into the water.

"This will be just enough to blow out the bow and set the Century down easy." Zane said as he poured gunpowder into a round grenade. "Then, only we three will know where the gold rests."

"Ready to go, Captain." Stricklind reported as the longboat hit the water.

"Yes, we are," Zane responded. In one sweeping movement he pulled his sword, swung, and slashed Stricklind across the shoulder, and then stabbed him in the side. The force of the attack knocked the seaman overboard.

The captain followed first-mate Allsop, who ducked the first swing of his cutlass. The blond sailor pulled his own knife and ran to the other side of the mast. As the relentless captain advanced, slashing with his sword, the mate used the other longboat for protection.

"Come now, Allsop, you're the mate," Zane professed as he advanced. "We only have two shares now."

"Gunness was right Zane, you are the devil!" Allsop shouted. "Plenty for all and you double cross those who did the dirty work."

"Aye, dirty work, and you rummies would give the king's men the story sure enough." Zane maneuvered around the longboat. "Me, King Georgie's sailor for more than thirty years, and nothing to live on in me old age. I see no reason to share a rope because of the likes of you!"

Allsop ran to the bow. Watching Zane approach, he tripped, staggered, grabbing the figurehead. Zane caught up and slashed the mate's forearm.

"You're rot, Zane. Pure rot." Bleeding, Allsop had only one move left as the captain stepped up. The mate accurately threw his knife and stuck Zane's shoulder.

"Takes more than that, mate!" Zane laughed as he grabbed the knife with a grunt. The madman swiped his long blade relentlessly — forcing Allsop further onto the bowsprit. His blood-soaked hand lost its grip. Allsop dropped and was swallowed the same as the others by the blue Caribbean Sea.

"Perhaps this sea rock will treat you kinder? Aye, where'd you go? Sharks get you that fast?" Zane uttered as Allsop didn't resurface. The captain struggled to remove his coat. He pulled his scarf off and used it to bandage the wound. He winced, "Damn him. Who would have thought any of them to be burdened by a conscience, eh?"

The longboat swung at the side of the schooner. Very carefully Captain Zane wrapped the iron chest in a cradle of ropes. He winched the box over the side and slowly lowered it. Just as it made it into the boat, Zane's strength gave out and the chest crashed into the top rail.

Unlocked, the chest spilt a few coins into the sea before it settled to the belly of the boat.

"That's your share, Neptune!" Zane smirked, walking to the schooner's forward hatch. He found the grenade and lit the fuse. With difficulty, he climbed down the rope ladder to the boat. With a wincing chop of his cutlass, the lines were sliced and the boat drifted away from the schooner. Among the barrels he found the object of his desires. With his one good hand, he plucked a black bottle and pulled the cork with his teeth. The first gulp he swallowed - the second he spit into the sea. Zane sat at the rudder and grabbed a few of the gold coins scattered on the boat's floor. "Rum and gold make the sea worth sailing! Har!" He gulped again and gasped, "Aye boys, these are for you," flipping the coins into the water, "And that's Neptune's due. Gunness, Stricklind, Allsop – don't say I didn't share. Har!"

The breeze increased as Zane leaned and carefully unfurled the small sail. With a snap, it filled and he fell back - grabbing the rudder and steering for the passage through the reef. Just then, a loud explosion ripped through the quiet bay. Zane turned to see his ship afire, the masts splintered, and the bow slipping into the sea. "Ah, darling, I know you were a great ship, but this will be a good place for eternal rest. Arrgh!" He laughed. "And you have plenty of company."

Allsop had found Stricklind floating between the Century and the shore. The first mate crawled out of the water pulling his bleeding comrade. Burning pieces of the ship and billowing smoke masked their escape. Allsop twisted his shirt to bandage the cut forearm. He wadded up Stricklind's blouse and used his rope belt as a tourniquet. He collapsed at the mercy of the intense pain. A breeze parted the smoke just in time for them to witness Zane heading south, outside the reef. "This ain't over by a long shot, you beast. We'll see who buys the last round."

NOW

The breeze blew from the east at about twelve knots. Occasionally, a stronger gust pushed the sailboat to crest a wave, slicing through the white foaming edge. Crisp seawater sprayed across the deck — making rainbows in the midday sun. Water streamed and gurgled into the deck drains.

The sleek hull parted blue water with a luscious rushing sound, as if breathing hard during a constant mating ritual with the sea. The boat heeled over, pushed by the wind, while the rudder kept her on course.

She rode smoothly. Her planks and timbers creaked slightly as the hull twisted, squeezed between wind and water. The sails slacked in the wave troughs refilling seconds later with a loud snap as the rigging strained. The boat lurched forward again.

"How did I end up here? I sailed in yesterday. Oh you mean, 'how did I end up here in the Caribbean'?" David scratched his jaw, "You really want to know?" He rattled the cubes in his glass enough to signal the old bartender for a rum refill.

"I wasn't forty yet — but fairly certain I'd already toiled away half my life. A third of that I'd spent on miserable commutes. These islands acted as a brake, to slow my diminishing days." He continued after a sip, "More like gave me my life back. I became a new person, not an occupation."

The few old heads in the rum shop craned their ears. Perhaps he had spoken a bit too loud or, it was something they had heard before.

CHAPTER ONE

Every story has to start somewhere. This one begins on a beach on Carriacou, a small island north of Grenada. It was a bright afternoon. The Caribbean sun consumed the sky above Eastern Bay. The air was hot and shade scarce. Dark women mopped their brows with cotton washcloths as they sauntered along the sandy path known as Beach Road. Their job was to herd blue-shirted children homeward at the end of another school day. Young boys laughed, playing tag with girls coming home from school. Older men waded from the beach to bathe in the saltwater during a break from garden labor. Fishermen, who had already made enough for the expenses of fuel and beer, sprawled comfortably across the covered bows of boats. Partial evidence of their spent money was displayed in empty brown bottles.

A few palm trees further from where David sought relaxation, a teenage boy's arms encircled his current love against the smooth, gray-brown trunk of a coconut palm. David shifted his eyes from the young couple to a group of white-shirted students playing cricket — while other teams kicked a soccer ball. Every group had its own music — and the blaring racket had interrupted his nap.

Coming down the hillside, brown, bare-chested men glistened with sweat in the bright sunlight. They guided gaunt cattle toward a corral fenced with rough tree branches. David watched a Carriacou cowboy snag an errant calf. The lanky youth threw a common nylon strap with a weighted end. With a deft flick of his hand, the weight wrapped around the cow's neck and crossed itself into a cinch. The calf was too tired to cry or struggle and instead chose to be towed inside the pen.

David figured it was too warm for anything except a swim, but that would conclude his nap. It was much too hot for such serious decisions. Nap or swim, there were worse ways to spend a day, he thought. In fact, there's much worse ways to spend a life.

The moonless Caribbean night glowed by the light of a million and more stars, providing only slight visibility. But darkness illuminates more than light. The more we think we see, the more evades our eyes. But not on a night like this — one so dark that his pale blue cottage and white pickup truck were barely visible. In the still darkness, he leaned from the porch and strained to see the usual border of his yard. The beach lay beyond the silhouettes of coconut palms, just beyond the rows of parched corn. Tonight, without even a sliver of the moon in view, all were hidden. The only sound was the melodic roll of the surf.

But David didn't need light to discern the boundaries of his rental. The sandy soil retained little moisture, even after a rain. A hedge of groomed pigeon pea bushes bordered three sides of the small, four-room house. The scrubby, stunted bushes waited for a watering that would almost immediately evaporate. To the south, the starlight was obscured by Dover Mountain. Anywhere else it would be merely a hill — but here it was the highest point, making it a mountain. The steep hillside slope was only suitable for pasturing scrawny, brown, Spanish goats and lean, thirsty cattle. The onshore sea-breeze was a blessing, as it kept the odors of natural fertilizers far from his abode.

This night's darkness made little difference. David knew this place even with closed eyes. The rutted lane along the shoreline of Eastern Bay cut close to his front yard. Just beyond the road was a beautiful, wide, sandy beach that doubled as the workshop for the Eastern Bay boat builders. On that beach, the island shipwrights — purveyors of a centuries' old craft, were building David's boat with local timbers.

A Carriacou vessel is a work of art. The boat would become his parachute, the escape from the escape. His small clapboard residence functioned as an office, a hardware store, and the kitchen for the project. Within a few months his sloop would be finished. Anchored inside a natural protecting reef, David's sailboat would float in good company — along with the locals' fishing boats and down-island traders.

A moon would not rise that night. Only countless pinpoints of starlight pricked the night sky. As David stargazed, Orion disappeared, followed by Scorpio and dozens of constellations with names still unknown to him. A cloud masked his celestial view as a drop of rain splashed his cheek. A light squall drummed the corrugated metal roof for just a moment —

and then the quiet stillness returned. The darkness intensified as the cloud enveloped the starlight. He put his back to the screen door, as he realized skilled predators thrive under the dark of the moon. Who saw whom first, dictated that evening's blue plate special.

Without a breeze, there were no shifting leaves to cloak a creature's movement. Everything just sat, listened, and waited; everything, except the mosquitoes that sought to explore David's ears. He listened to his immediate world for the first time in months, unlocking memories of youth on a Pennsylvania farm. A couple thousand miles and more than twenty years separated those nights from the present. The northern stars could only be seen in winter, when frigid, crisp air grounded the factory pollutants. Those cold nights and dull skies had driven him away, far from home.

He'd toured the world for twenty and got out of Uncle Sam's Navy. In those decades, he'd lost his family and the farm. It had all dissolved, except the memories. Changing locations made no real difference, other than the climate. Seasons are a state of mind.

Blizzards and hurricanes would appear at a predictable time each year, depending on latitude. Tornadoes, earthquakes, and avalanches sneak up on you like thieves, ready to steal your accomplishments. Locating a place that's safe from nature's calamities was impossible, but David chose the southern Caribbean and its friendly ambiance. Here, life passed day-by-day, but the future promised he would have a boat.

David's present home was a beautiful blend of the blue Caribbean Sea and sky at twelve degrees latitude. Life-altering hurricanes, the fierce summer storms, usually crossed the island chain farther north. It was a small island, but some isolation could be easily found. It was a native custom not to intrude on a visitor's privacy. However, if you became too friendly, the locals could provide too much company. That is, if you permitted it. So far, David had chosen to be a loner.

Cool winds blowing out of the east made for exquisite sailing. Years ago most of the locals fished, and some still did, but now most of Carriacou's African descendants either planted vegetable gardens or raised cattle and goats. As long as it rained, life was good. Without a modern desalination plant, everybody depended on Mother Nature to fill the water cisterns from their roofs. The island was small enough to hike around in a day, but big enough to get lost for hours, exploring abandoned ruins or snorkeling the many reefs. David's plan was to get lost among the Caribbean islands, for twenty or so years.

That night was what the locals had named Lually Mogumbo, or 'dark of the moon'. From dusk to dawn islanders stayed indoors. Even the fishermen kept their boats beached and spent a night with the family. The local rum shops closed early, so those patrons without the benefit of torchlights might stagger homeward without meeting messengers of the occult. Superstitions and Obeah remained strong throughout the Caribbean chain, where natives choose to fear the not-so-easily explained. Legends were created when simple minds contemplated mysteries.

The older locals recalled times before electric lights, when the night spirits held more control. Lually Mogumbo was the spirits' special night. The jack-o-lantern would burn bright to lure tardy walkers from the road into ever-present bush, where they would find themselves fitfully lost until morning…unless the 'night jumbies' or the 'cow foot woman' captured them.

During David's time in the Navy, he'd seen a lot of horrible circumstances created by humans — circumstances too uncanny for devils to duplicate. His name's Warner, David Warner. Everybody on Carriacou called him SP, because he had spent more than a decade on Navy Shore Patrol duty. He'd come to Carriacou in the early eighties to find a local boy, Paco, who'd gone AWOL. Seems Paco had missed his Mom and the local rum too much to be satisfied with only one week's reunion. It had taken David days to make all the transport connections necessary to find the boy's remote island home. He'd studied the situation, created a viable excuse on his report, and got Paco mess hall duty — scraping pots for a month — rather than the brig, or worse. By not putting a black mark in his file, David gained Paco's friendship — and in the process, discovered a future island home. He liked the lack of sophistication, the absence of cable TV, and the low crime rate. Drugs, the real devils, had been unleashed upon rural island communities by greedy monsters, but villagers were diligent to keep their homes safe.

Whenever David had leave during the years following his introduction to this island, Carriacou became his R&R destination of preference. After several visits, the village's elite, inner-core welcomed him to fish and sail with them. His ego blossomed with the fantasy that local girls were being groomed with the hope one might become his wife.

For the past four months, he'd been renting a small beach bungalow from one of Paco's aunts. Another uncle and brother were fitting his traditional wooden sloop on the nearby beach. He hadn't decided if he wanted to settle there, or buy a piece of another rock, or just float where the breeze carried him. Decisions — life's decisions — were difficult and best when slowly-formed. The lower social strata of wayward Navy personnel had surrounded his previous life and the economic level that attracted them ashore confused his perspectives. Carriacou was refreshing. Usually after a career in the service, talented men go into private security businesses, but not David. He'd had enough of pushing papers, while detailing human slime and degradation. When his boat was completed, he would be free to pull anchor and leave at the hint of a problem. Now, he owned his time. It was his to squander on lazy beach days, and a few rum-soaked evenings.

David minded his own business and only thought with his larger head. Even though local women wanted to marry their daughters to an American passport, he generally chose solitude. On a dark night — like this night — something warm and soft to touch would have been agreeable.

He kept still. The pupils of his eyes were probably as big as coffee cups. The only reason he was standing, looking to the stars this night was because his VCR had eaten Harrison Ford playing The Fugitive. Salt air and age had taken its due from the old tape player.

He'd sworn not to replace it, and to get a real life.

The creepy crawlers in the bush became noticeably silent for a few seconds. To his left, he saw a flash of someone lighting a cigarette. It was still early, before ten, and quite probable that someone was walking home. David wondered if he could be seen. He watched as the red dot rose, fell, and then somersaulted away. Without that red marker the smoker vanished. Quietly fastening the door behind him, he went to bed and closed his eyes to another oblique darkness.

"Mister SP, Mister SP."
Sometimes dreams incorporate the sounds of this real world like a

radio combines weak signals.

"Mister SP, Mister SP."

Blackness evaporated into morning much too soon. And then the morning got louder.

"Mister SP, Mister SP!"

David opened his eyes to an early, dark-gray dawn, well before the sun had crested. The digital clock read 5:24. Everyone who labored in this intense tropical heat started early.

"Mister SP, I know you are at home. You never be anywhere else. This is Reese, Auntie Shirley's boy. I got a situation, and maybe you can lend some thought."

Groggy, David stared at the rafters and white roof planking. Which one was Reese? Shirley was the sister of Bill, who supervised the building of his boat. Reese must be the string-bean teenager who had been carving the boat's ribs.

David took his mornings very seriously. The way he woke could make or break his mood. A rude awakening usually made for a rough day. A few of the yard roosters had become stew because of their early morning cries. He wanted to, yet could not ignore the call.

"Mister SP, come on now; please wake up!"

"Okay, okay, let me pull my clothes on." David certainly didn't leap from the bed. Slowly, he rubbed his eyes and jaw, sat up and pulled on his shorts. Opening his double-entry doors, he saw the gangling six-footer, dripping wet, attempting to create parallel bars from the yard gateposts. Pushing himself up on his long arms and swinging his thin legs back and forth was as close as he'd ever come to organized gymnastics. This usually lethargic youth looked nervous, and Carriacou rarely exhibits anxiety. If you're nervous here, rum sedation is prescribed.

"So?" David said, beckoning him to come up onto the porch. "What's got you so worked up? Something wrong with the work on the boat?"

"Wrong? Yes, and no, Mr. SP. The boat's all right, but there's something wrong with Uncle Bill. He ain't come off his boat this morning, and he's usually in before five, after boiling some coffee to get us started. I swims out and bangs on the hull. He still don't come out from below, so I grabs a line and pulls myself up. Wow! Mr. SP, somehow old Uncle Bill got himself real beaten up last night. Now I knows he went to his fishing boat after we finished working yesterday late afternoon. Now he's all bloody."

"Reese, wait a minute. Is he all right now?"

"I gets him all cleaned up with some sweet water, but he ain't saying nuthin'. Not a word. So I leave him and come right here as you is the closest. I knows you and Bill get right along. You a pretty quiet guy, not really related to anybody. Things here get 'round the bend quick if the old women hear anything they think is news. Ole Bill don't need no one to mind his affairs. I think he's okay now, but please come and talk with him. See if maybe he'll tell you what happened."

"Yeah, yeah, Reese. First go around to the kitchen and put on a pot to boil for coffee. Let me clean up, then we'll take some breakfast to the master shipwright."

It wasn't easy balancing a beer crate holding the pot of coffee, canned milk, a loaf of reasonably fresh bread, and a hunk of cheese, along with the medicine kit — all resting on his knees. Reese rowed Bill's small wooden skiff, which rose only about three inches above the water. A few inches shorter than six-foot Reese, but at almost two hundred pounds David's lanky days had grown to stocky. Now, he liked a description of 'stalwart'.

The red-painted skiff was a basic square ender built of planks. It pushed the water rather than parting it. The tall boy drenched their feet with his frantic oar strokes. He was obviously worried about Bill and shouted their arrival.

David placed the breakfast crate on the deck of Bill's boat and pulled himself up, tying off the line. Reese was already at the hatch, helping a weary Bill greet daybreak. Even after a beating, Bill had a gentleman's demeanor. The older man was just about a head shorter than his nephew and still trim with no late-life paunch. Usually, he carried himself with a head-up, square-shouldered confidence. This morning wasn't usual. His gray hair had just started to recede. That, coupled with a same shade, full gray beard, fashioned him to look like a fit koala bear. Bill squinted into the morning through two swollen purplish-blue shiners. This dapper man had been transformed into an elderly, gray-bearded Rocky Raccoon.

After a quick inspection, David surmised that luckily, neither the blood vessels of Bill's eyes, nor his nose, had been broken. Someone had whacked the old boy pretty hard. Watching his slow, purposeful movements, David guessed he'd probably cracked some ribs and had very sore insides. Bill's lips were cut and streaked with dried blood. Reese poured the coffee, and then sliced the bread and white cheddar. Bill groaned and pushed David's hand away when he tried to pad a forehead cut with an alcohol wipe.

The older man coughed hard, grimaced, and then spat over the side. His voice creaked from deep in his throat, "Quit fussing, will ya? I'm still breathin'. Coffee's good, but I ain't ready for no bread. Not yet. You two are messing with me like ole women. Stop and sit."

David shook two extra strength aspirins from the bottle into his own palm and then handed the bottle to Bill. They both gulped at the same time.

Reese rowed back to get some bigger bandages and some antibiotic salve from the cottage medicine cabinet. The Band-Aids that had been brought were already plastered, and more cuts needed attention.

"Bring some more drinking water and don't talk to nobody 'bout dis. Reese, you hears me?" Bill ordered with a wincing cough.

As the dinghy pulled toward the beach, David sat beside Bill on the cabin top, facing what was left of the night. "Bill, someone put a hurting on you last evening. You got any idea who it was or why? We are alone, and what you tell me won't get repeated. You can rest at my cottage for a few days."

"Look SP, me be all right. Me never saw who it was. Hell, me might have just plain tripped, fell down the ladder, banging onto de cabin floor." Bill's head drooped onto his crossed, bare forearms.

David patiently waited for answers that didn't come. "Bill?"

He never raised his head. "Seems someone could a pushed me, but me could have tripped, conked meself on de head, and was out 'til da sister's boy woke me up last hour. Member comin' back, but after dat, me no know. I might remember later."

"Bill, don't embarrass either one of us, okay? What happened was you got beat upon last night with a board or a club. Don't try to say foolish things between men. I just want you in good enough shape to supervise my boat's creation. So, as your boss, you're sleeping in my extra room for the next few days. No argument. And I promise I'll keep the story at what you say but between us, I'd expect it told differently."

The old man's hand wobbled as he sipped at his coffee mug. He winced and shuddered as the hot brew touched a sore spot. "Might remember."

It was then that David saw the pock-mark burns on his hands

reminding him of what a cigarette could inflict. He pulled at the empty hand for a closer look, but Bill quickly pocketed it.

"Me might know later. Maybe me got ambrosia?"

"You mean amnesia, and I don't think so. No, I think you got a good dose of fear. You aren't doing anything dumb, are you? Like lending your boat to crazy people for smuggling, or squeezing the wrong bumsy belonging to another man, are you?"

"Like me says, me no know. How's 'bout me get a good swig of rum and sleep a bit. Den we talk. Just got to rest. Den we talk, SP."

The West Indian elder shielded his bruised eyes from the morning sun.

When Reese returned, David finished cleaning and disinfecting the cuts. The laceration on Bill's balding forehead might have needed a stitch or two, but a butterfly stick-um sufficed. It was almost 6:30 and soon the road would have morning traffic. They hustled old Billy ashore and into bed where he slept with a wheezing snore after a generous, self-prescribed dose of rum.

"Mr. SP," Reese whispered as they stood on the cottage porch, sipping another cup of brown energy, "What you think happened out there on Uncle Bill's boat? We ain't got no violent people living on Carriacou. Somebody might get cuffed, you know, when dey starts to run dey mouth, to get dem to hush. But Uncle, he don't go no place, but de corner shop for a nip of rum. He only work, eat, and sleep. To wake up so, my God, it could be devils dat do the deed. I read about dev..."

"Whoa, Reese, didn't you hear Bill's explanation? He tripped and fell into the cabin. That's what he said, and that's it. And we keep it just like he said, between us, three men. I don't want to hear any more about devils. And I don't want to hear this story from someone else. Bill isn't gonna say a thing, and I can keep my mouth shut. So, do you have to be killed to keep this a secret?" David smiled and patted the young man on his shoulder. "Besides, it could have happened from a fall." He didn't even think he could say it convincingly, but it might lend credence when Reese repeated the event, which would be as soon as he left. "So, you gonna finish those transom braces, or do you need a day off?"

"No, Mr. SP, I can work a lot of things in place today, since we got everything lined up and drilled yesterday. If you gots some of them long stainless all-thread rods for bolting the braces to the keel, I'll keep busy." The young West Indian pulled the necessary tools from under the porch and sauntered towards the ribs of David's future boat.

Reese was busy and had already augured and bolted all of the six ribs touching the leveling strings. After a new blade was fitted to the hacksaw, he received an explanation for the necessity of using double washers and double nuts to lock each end of every all thread. The local boat builders religiously used pieces of steel reinforcement rod, normally for concrete construction. They pounded the ends over, rather than tightening threads and nuts to secure a boat's framework. Their logic dictated a wood boat's life was just so long. The wood would have rotted by the time the rods rusted through.

To the locals, a boat was a replaceable tool. David had saved enough money to build a sweet, forty-four foot boat. It had to endure as a movable sanctuary since he didn't plan on ever working again. The boat would be named Summer Breeze. A Navy pension and benefits don't go a long way, but a few lucky investments over the years with ex-swabbies would feed the boat's maintenance budget.

\\\\\\\\\\

While Bill slept, the amateur detective inside of David decided to snoop around Bill's boat, Moriah. Even though Bill didn't want to explain the incident, David was hoping to find some clues that might help sort things out. If it were an act of random violence, it would probably happen again in the island community. A dive mask, snorkel, and flippers permitted a refreshing search. Perhaps something had dropped into the water beneath the sloop.

Rowing quietly, David first checked Moriah's attachment to her mooring and found everything secure. After climbing aboard, his snooping found three cigarette butts in the deck's drain. As far as he knew, Bill was not a smoker. Islanders usually smoked the cheapest — a local brand called 222's. Two of the butts he found were thin smokes. The other filter was thicker with stronger smelling tobacco, maybe European. He pocketed them as his only detective trophies from the top deck. The inner sanctum of the Moriah had seen better days. Bill had built it of yellow pitch pine in the seventies, giving her about thirty-five years of rot and mildew. Originally, this boat was designed to fish. Bill or a relative would sail to seasonal fishing grounds, and drift with weighted baits until they caught enough fish. Bill studied under his father and uncles, and became a respected shipwright. For him, supervising boat building was easier money than fishing.

When there were fish to be caught, the ten-meter sailboat worked under the capable direction of someone from the village.

Billy kept himself busy with boat construction. He swam or snorkeled every afternoon for a combination exercise and sea bath. The old man was married to Cecilia. He'd built a comfortable home with a view that encompassed of the eastern side of the island, and almost the entire outer reef.

The cabin was a mess. David took it upon himself to clean, sort, and organize the Moriah's interior while searching for clues. Where were the signs of at least two men? One must have held Billy while the other whacked and burned. Bill's wrists were scraped as if he had been tied with rough cord. As he searched, he realized Moriah's dark cabin was uncomfortable. Even in its early life, it was probably never very livable. Fishermen usually slept on the deck, well ventilated under the Caribbean sky. The few pots and skillets were gathered and stacked on the gimbaled cook stove. The stained foam mattresses, pillows, and dirty sheets had been tossed from the bunk frames into the center aisle. The bedding and towels were bundled for a thorough Clorox soaking ashore. The table had been overturned — no easy feat — as it had been bolted to the floor. A couple of plastic, five-gallon buckets worked as stools. Under the table, a bloody piece of nylon rope, with a monkey-fist knot braided into one end, was found. This could have been used to inflict serious pain, yet nothing hinted as to why. No evidence of money, guns, or drugs on the boat appeared.

Bill wasn't one to break the law; however, someone could've borrowed the sloop and done something stupid. Last night's deed might not have been aimed at him. Bill was in great shape for pushing sixty. Although he was a slim one-fifty, two weeks ago he'd singlehandedly began framing David's boat by setting four, heavy keel beams of Guyanese greenheart wood. His cutlass was still in its place, sheathed between an overhead brace and the deck planks.

Whoever injured Bill must have surprised him; otherwise he would've had enough warning to grab the long cane knife. Bill would never invite strangers below decks. The bad guys' search included pulling up a few loose floorboards, but they'd only discovered the foul bilge. The forward compartment, where the fish were dumped into ice coolers from an overhead hatch, was empty and appeared undisturbed.

The tool locker, opposite the galley, had its rusty contents dumped. Among the spilled contents were bigger wood screws that David used to secure the bookcase and the table. Against the main cabin bulkhead were the shredded remains of Bill's library. It consisted of three folded sea charts from Puerto Rico to Venezuela, and one battered, coverless cruising guide. Within the paperbacks were tales about seafaring pirates and shipwrecks. One thick, dog-eared reference categorized treasure wrecks by each individual island. Thumbing the pages, even Carriacou had a few entries of ships lost with valuable cargoes.

Bill's traveling papers, registration numbers, and important addresses were in a Ziploc baggie stuffed between the pages of another nautical book. After locating the batteries, the old multiband short-wave receiver functioned with the aid of a coat-hanger antenna. By the time David finished, everything had been returned to a state that was better than before the incident. The cabin could use a new coat of white oil paint. Kerosene lamps and cooking oil had faded the room to an orangish-yellow. Photos of Bill's memories were still taped to the rough planked wall. Everything was just the way he liked it.

Snorkeling around the boat cleansed and refreshed David after the long morning. He'd learned during Navy investigations to search where a boat swung at anchor by attaching a lanyard to the anchor and swimming in an expanding circle. More than a few green Heineken bottles littered the grassy bottom. A small, shiny reflection caught his eye. It was a gum wrapper; the foil folded around a yellow Juicy Fruit label held a chewed wad. Was this chewing gum even sold on the island? It might be another remnant of last night's creeps. Then again, anyone could've tossed it. The amateur detective returned to shore.

After David checked Reese's slow progress, showered, and ate a soup lunch, the day was more than half over. Bill was still asleep.

Combined, Bill's boat bedding and David's stuff were transported to the laundry outside of town. Following an afternoon of running boat-building errands in his truck, the air-dried articles were being unclipped from the outside line. It was almost five. He'd bought sufficient groceries to strengthen Old Bill enough to continue to supervise Reese. A liter of good, smooth rum should loosen Bill's tongue. Reese had finished for the day and was undoubtedly telling everybody about his uncle's misfortune. Bill appeared from the bathroom, and stood in the doorway with sagging shoulders wearing only a white tank-top and long, faded, pink boxers. He looked worse since most of the bruises had blackened and the cuts had formed scabs.

"Oh, me gots to get back to it," Bill coughed, wincing. "See you tomorrow. Me gots to get to the boat and take care of the messes. Me no wanna be trouble to you, SP."

"Bill, taking care of a friend is never a problem. I expect you'd do the same for me. In fact, you are, by building my Summer Breeze. Here's a fresh towel; get a shower and have some soup — then we'll drink some medicine." David smiled and pointed to the bottle of good rum. "You'll sleep until morning."

Bill emerged from the shower, greeted by a steaming table of chicken gumbo, cornmeal coo-coo mush, and jelly jars of iced, amber rum. They sat at the outside table where Bill could view his boat. Since coming to live on this island, David had assimilated many of its local habits and peculiarities. He no longer needed to mix liquor with anything except ice or water. Here, every part of the fish or animal was eaten. Islanders wasted nothing. Bull foot, chicken feet, fish heads, ox tails — not to mention pig snout and tail — were the base of many savory dishes. West Indians had their own cuisine and he was still an avid, hungry student. Tonight they'd suck chicken bones while Bill, hopefully, revealed more of his story.

Cleaned, combed, and bandaged, Bill took a healthy gulp of rum and slurped some chicken broth without looking up. His spoon rattled, shoveling the corn meal porridge. He cleared his throat and quietly said, "What happened wasn't 'bout bad business, it was about the baddest luck. SP, you's been all over da world, and me hear stories of you finding killers and worse for your navy. But dis ain't 'bout none of that. Me telling you, me never see those guys that got me. After swimmin, me row out, and go down below to listen to Windies cricket on the radio. Next thing, me face pushed to the floor with one of them standing on me back. Told dem me had two hundred dollars and they was welcomed, but they laugh. One kick me hard in the side of me head." Bill pointed to the worst of the cuts. "Saw stars, and when they wakes me up by splashing some water, my hands are tied behind me back with some piece of plastic, not rope. All me can say is, they weren't no locals — probably Americans by the way they talked. But they could a been from another island. Can't be sure. They beat the hell out of my sides with something like a ball on a rope."

He refilled his glass and took a long swig. "They started asking me stuff, but me couldn't hear them right. By then, me head was pounding so — then they rips out a board covering the bilge and push me face down. Me pledge to help them if only me knows what they wanted. The one that was smoking start burning me. He was doin' too good a job, and me passed out. When me awoke, they ask more questions that me didn't understand. By then, me thought they was gonna kill me and be done with it." Bill's attention turned to the rum bottle.

"Bill, try to remember what they were inquiring about. It sounds like they were serious about getting an answer. Are you certain you never saw these men before? Were they tall, fat, white, black? You must have seen something?"

"Like me tell you, me wake up with one on me back doing all the questions. The other would hit, kick, or burn, but never talk. Without any lamp light, everything very dark last night. Only time me saw anything was when the smoker lit a next cigarette. Me can say that man smoked a lot — like maybe a full pack — and when he was close, me could smell tobacco real strong. But dis don't make no sense. What me know is about fishing and building boats, wood boats. And there's men here knows more on both of those subjects." Bill gnawed on the gristle of a small thighbone with a sucking noise. The rum had begun to relax him.

"You had any different visitors in the past weeks?" David asked while refilling his bowl. "Notice any strange boats or anything out of the ordinary?"

Bill pushed his chair away from the table, burped, and wiped his mouth with his forearm. "Well, me needs to have a few more of those aspirins. Let me think real hard on that. Now, there was a stateside white man — bigger than you — but bald, shaved head like one of dose basketball players. Yeah, he come, searched me out by name. He wants me to build him a boat like what we's putting together now for yous, but bigger, 'bout double in size — a schooner rig. He ask for a price. I tells him hull and rigging 'bout twenty-five hundred American a foot, but couldn't start 'til yous done. That guy might have been a bit heavier than yous, but with weird eyes. Weird, crystal-blue eyes. One didn't seem to move quite right in his real round kind of face." Bill continued, "He talked like he knows boats, but was real white like he'd been out of the sun for a long time. Made me wonder how he'd stay out of de sun on a boat. He was dressed strange with expensive-looking white shorts, dem stretchy white knee socks, and shiny, brown, hard-leather shoes laced up to his ankles. He had a nice, bright-white button-up shirt with a big rat on the back. Me member thinking at the time, just ain't fair who gets the money and what they doin' with it."

Bill yawned and grimaced from his rib pain. "But he never come back and that was 'bout three weeks or more. Told me price was right, and he'd be back. Guess he's waitin' for yous to be floating off the beach. That guy was a real character, but why would he have me beaten if he wanted me to work for him? If me knew it was him who did this licking, me build him a boat and fix it to seep water..."

The rum loosened Bill's tongue. In the service, David had always wanted to interrogate men after giving them a few drinks. That tactic was strictly forbidden. "Can you remember anything they were asking you? There must be something you remember."

"Well, let me think. The only one who talked didn't sound at all like the man me was just describing. This guy had a deep voice, kind of like he was holding a cough inside. The other guy — the baldhead who wanted a boat built — well, he kind of used this nice-nice voice with me — like one the old woman uses, nice-nice talk in church on Sunday, but screams at the children all through the week. Honest, SP, me don't know what they was asking. The little bits of stuff me remember was 'bout the reef out there. Like me knows more 'bout that reef than anybody else did!"

"Hell, we all fish there our whole lives. But they say something 'bout an old boat." He gulped the rest of his glass, and swallowed hard, "Them ask 'bout an old boat me had heard something 'bout for years and years. Yeah, it was one of dose lost ships. Guess they figured me was an expert or," Bill laughed; pushing himself up. He stood shakily, and then plopped back into the chair. "All right with you, me gonna sleep some more. Guess yous right, SP, ambrosia's wearing off. Me might remember more tomorrow."

"Wait a minute buddy. Don't leave me hanging. What boat did they ask you about? I saw your boat's got a bunch of treasure books. You've been interested in it for some time? Are these guys after a good wreck or what, Bill?" David watched Bill's movements. Trained, he could spot a liar's mannerisms in a New York second. He knew he could expect, at the very least, a nervous foot would twitch.

Bill stayed still and looked at David squarely. "They ask 'bout the Century. Yeah, me remember that for sure. They ask 'bout the Century. Me know a little 'bout lots of things. Me know a little 'bout that story."

"Well, I never heard of it, the Century, huh? What put it on the 'big treasure' list? Pour one more, give me a bit of this sea story, and then sleep like a baby." Bill had goaded interest. David retrieved some more ice from the freezer, to finish the rum. He handed Bill two more aspirins and a glass of water with the ice. After a gulp and a water chaser, Bill relaxed.

"See, SP, this is all they had to do — some rum, man, and just chat me up. Yous knows, like we is gentlemen." Bill lifted his glass in a toasting gesture. "Ah, those skunts. If they dumb enough to ever come 'round me boat or me house again, they be sorry. Me family will eat fish caught off their asses. Yes sir, me put them boys still full of life and kicking in a fish trap. They could have kilt me. An old man like me, Hell! Me might a had a heart attack. No matter, a thing like this," Bill coughed and winced, "it takes years from a life."

"Let's hope not, buddy. You still got lots of boats to build." David topped off their glasses. "About the ship?"

"The Century," Bill rose shakily from the table and half limped, half waddled to the only piece of comfortable furniture in the rental cottage. It was a thick-cushioned plantation chair with a leg rest that folded out from the side. Bill knew how it worked; he settled in and sat his drink on the floor. "Yous see, that boat was called the Century 'because it built in 1690 to sail to de next century. She was a good hundred-plus-foot, three-masted schooner out of Denmark. They built good boats, very strong boats in them days. And men was different — more stronger than today. Real sailors. Been a long time since me see a real sailor come to this island from de east. All them plastic boats come from the North or South with pretty boys and plenty toys on board, but... ah ..."

For a short moment the West Indian's concentration drifted off course again. "Yeah, they builds some boats back then, but yous knows weather was less predictable — and put a lot of them to a wet grave. That's what happened to the Century. They was sailing her from the East, London — or no, it was sumtin' dat sounds like London." He rubbed his sore jaw. "Lisbon, yeah Lisbon. They was Englanders for captain and crew, all seasoned. Supposed to have sunk somewheres 'round here."

The rum had David sprawled comfortably on the living room floor, chasing mosquitoes with his empty hand. "So, what did the Century have on board?"

"That's the thing, SP, no one knows for sure. The records are pretty good from that time. Insurance company is still 'round and they gots all kinds of records and reports. Well, maybe thirty years ago, maybe a bit longer, there was an old, thin, frizzy-haired, white man come here in one of the first real fiberglass cabin cruisers, and he's gots all this diving equipment. Well, hell, me was almost thirty then. Knew my way 'round. Me and Cecilia already had a couple childs. This guy was looking for this Century boat out there on that reef. He was paying good US greenbacks for help." Bill rattled his ice cubes, stirring the drink. "So, me took a break from sailing and fishing, me and Raymond Dubois. Poor Raymond's been drowned dead now, more than ten long years."

If David didn't move now, he would wake up tomorrow having missed the conclusion. He propped his back against a post. "What was so important on the boat?"

"Well, this guy, let me think; his name was Dean Worely. He never did say what he hoped to find. Me and Raymond thought he had to be after gold or jewels, like in one of them cinemas. We'd go out and anchor along the outside of the reef, at a different spot each day. One of us would stay on board filling the tanks off the compressor on Worely's cruiser. Worely would usually stay up in da skiff and the other would dive. Sometimes we would tow that old white guy around all day, snorkeling and looking."

"So, you don't know what was supposed to be aboard the wreck?"

David heard his bed calling and stood up.

"Like me say, dat ole white man never told us. But later, in Miami, me bought some of them treasure books. Well, one of them say the insurance company paid out a million English pounds in 1701, a year after the boat disappeared. She was lost in one of those great hurricanes. Seemed old man Worely had more information putting the Century on Carriacou Reef." Bill rose and shuffled through the bedroom door that David held open for him. "Yous can imagine how much them million pounds are worth now. Easy Street, SP. Easy Street. Yes sir, E-A-S-Y Street."

CHAPTER TWO

Dawn arrived without any other disturbing incidents. David started his day with the usual exercises meant to keep every joint loose and his muscles tight: a hundred sit-ups, pushups, leg raises, and some stretches. A shower gave the day a good start. The number one shipwright, Bill, was still passed out in the spare room while the morning's coffee was being prepared.

David sipped a hot cup while skimming a three-week-old Newsweek, and smiled. Reading about the world's depressed economy, and the president's problems, he again realized why he'd chosen Carriacou for a relaxing home. There wasn't enough local news to even warrant a weekly newspaper. The radio news usually consisted of school pageants, club meetings, and obituaries as top stories. Reese was hard at work doing what should have been finished in half of the previous day. The other workers, without Bill's direction, had decided to take a few days off. The tall boy enjoyed his sweetened, almost-white coffee, even though it was delivered a few hours later than usual.

"How's Uncle Bill doing today?" Reese asked.

"He's not up yet. He seemed to be feeling better after he had some dinner last night. You got any problems? Need anything?" David asked inspecting the ribs fastened to the keel. He could have worked alongside them, but they had a plan and David had a 'no-pressure' schedule. If he came on as part of the crew, it might become too demanding for Bill and his workers. He picked up the few tools and wrong cuts that had been dropped and asked, "Is that hacksaw blade still good?"

"Should be, 'cause that boy ain't done much work with it that me can see." It was Bill looking dapper again. Most of the swelling had gone down. He steadied himself with a stick. He'd obviously showered, replacing some of his Band-Aids in a much neater fashion. The cut on his head was obscured by a red bandanna, ala Jimi Hendrix. He had on a pair of gray sweat pants with a matching tank top labeled NAVY and multi-colored plastic beach shoes, the locals call 'dog muzzles.' His burned hand gripped a cup of coffee.

"Now boy, get yous ass in high gear. We is gonna catch up for yesterday. Mr. SP wants to get this boat in the water while he's still young enough to sail. So..."

"Bill, you feel well enough to work today? Wait at least another day."

"Like me was saying, let's see progress. Reese, you hearing me?"

Reese never looked up, but moved the hacksaw faster cutting the rod. "Mr. SP, if yous paying us, me can't sit. If nobody sees me out here or on the boat, Cecilia thinks me slipped off somewhere and there will be more questions me can't answer. Besides, this bolting's almost done — so me gots to design more ribs for the boy to shape."

"Well, it doesn't make any difference to me. You're the boss, but if you feel sickly, call it a day."

"Me thinking 'bout that bald guy wanting a boat and his American dollars. Me not getting no younger, so me might make that the last. Then Cecilia and me could take a good, long holiday. Yous knows she's been a good woman to me for lots of years. We both deserve a holiday. If it's right with you, gonna bring a few more men to work. By next week, we ought to be ready to plank her up."

David gathered the empty cups, "Like I said, you're the boss. Let me know when you need more money and more lumber."

"Okay, Okay, no problem SP. Now, look here boy..."

He turned and walked to his cottage. As he approached the wilting cornfield, he recalled the other night's phantom smoker and wondered how those bandits got out to Bill's boat. He had used his own dinghy — and surely would've seen or heard someone motoring to his boat. With no TV playing, David would've heard even a small outboard. They must have swum out...no, then their smokes would've been wet. They had to have been dropped off, and then probably rowed Bill's dinghy to shore, or they'd stolen transport. He tried to align what had been his field of vision that night to determine where the smoker stood along the dusty lane. Maybe Bill's villains had passed this way, or perhaps they had been watching him. Nah, couldn't let paranoia snowball. There was no reason for anyone to pay attention to David's small yard on this rock.

Feelings from service in the Navy, of being constantly watched and evaluated on all sides, erupted inside his psyche, forcing a shiver. Back then, everyone was always waiting for a mistake. The criminals wished he'd miss a flight connection, or accept a bribe to lose them on the return. The bosses would make sure nothing was missed and that he stayed clean, unlike so many of his more easily tempted co-workers. The Navy is like a state, and they were the State Police. But like a state, it had its drugs, gambling, and black market. Usually sailors would get into a little trouble trying to make a bit of money on the side, leading to a lot more trouble further down the road. Over the years, bad guys had offered reasonable sums to look the other way. David had disappointed them.

No similar cigarette butts were found, but he did see another chewing gum wrapper, folded in just the same fashion as the other he'd found yesterday. If the gum chewer was tied to the smoker, this wrapper indicated they'd both stood outside his cottage. David sought the cigarettes he'd found on the Moriah.

His reflection in the almost full-length mirror on the inside of the bathroom door showed that the Navy had left him a good physique, and that most of his usually light brown hair was almost blonde, bleached by months in constant sun. He gulped a handful of vitamins and herb capsules — a habit from trying to stay healthy in various armpits of the world. His Mediterranean olive skin never seemed to burn, and its deep tan revealed many possible ancestries.

There had been a time when the prospect of going undercover to stop an evil foreign menace held a certain appeal. A gray, two-by-five-foot, desk in Annapolis, Maryland, had confined the majority of David's duties. Most of his transportation took place in a gray chair, on which he swiveled from file drawers to the coffee urn. Being single, and a loner, David got all the weekend and long overnight hauls. It led to such wonderful coastal places as Calcutta, Hong Kong, and Veracruz — over-night duty transporting offenders back to the good ole U.S. of A. for court-martial or imprisonment.

Ninety percent of David's duty was riding a desk after only two tours outside of America. The first six-year enlistment tour had taught him two things: how to use and repair modern telecommunications equipment, and that the option of coming back to an apartment every night was much better than bunking in a floating, walk-in steel closet with three other smelly guys. The only other foreign duty came after he'd been in for seventeen years on one of the ships protecting the Mediterranean. His girlfriend's father, a commander back then, had probably requisitioned him to put some distance to their romance. David had also become the commander's sounding board — a drinking buddy slash surrogate son. Lounging with the upper-echelon brass almost drove him crazy. To regain sanity, he took some work ashore in Nice.

The investigation came after a greedy young ensign had tried to remove three cases of hand-held, surface-to-air rockets from his carrier in broad daylight. He thought no one would be watching his moves, camouflaged by all the other daily activity. The cased missiles were capable of snuffing out any plane during a takeoff or landing. David was a new face on the scene, and perfect to pursue the perp. The ensign was thought to be a sleeper terrorist agent, but it turned out he just couldn't wait for the Navy's pension plan. Since it had been kept within 'the family', the story never hit the tabloids. No press meant no big brasses were hauled to a Senate investigating committee. Saving the brass from hassles made David a few important friends in Washington.

\\\\\\\\\

Driving in the Caribbean is usually a bump-and-roll mission. Hit every bump, and warily roll around the many blind bends. David's faded white pickup was perfect transport on Carriacou. The roads were so bad, the rattling truck seldom made it into third gear; the fourth and fifth were useless. All of the ex-English and Dutch islands drive on the left, while the French and Puerto Ricans drive on the right. It's a common joke that all West Indians hog the middle of the road. Taking it slow over the twisting, old, donkey-cart paths, with more potholes than pavement, was the only safe technique. You never could predict when a bus or a cow might be blocking your way. Cattle usually roam free, trying to find water, and the road drains provide a suitable source. If a cow consumed a neighbor's green garden, the owner would go missing. But God help you if you hit and killed, or maimed, a cow; then every member of the owner's family would come forward to be compensated.

The truck lunged and bucked through farms and small villages to the main town of Hillsboro. Each precipice presented another gleaming, spectacular view of the Caribbean Sea. David slowed and parked as he entered the tiny business district. Snooping for clues through the few tobacco shops that sold English and French smokes was unsuccessful. Jonas, the burly proprietor of the Side Street Café, perked his spirits with a cold beer. Jonas' place was cooled naturally by the sea breeze. One wall behind the bar separated the kitchen from an open-air deck. Rusty, thumb-tacked posters of various past sailing regattas and carnivals were the bar's only attempt at island decor. Receiving a beer, David showed the cigarette remnant to Jonas.

"Yeah, me seen them smokes before. Look close. Those spots on the filter are tiny gold Hindi symbols. All wealthy, or wanna-be wealthy, Trinis smoke them. I think they're made down there in Port of Spain with good Cuban tobacco. Something like that, I heard. But these things are about three dollars a pack." The conversation enticed the bartender to light up a local brand. He coughed, "Yeah, those things are strong like a cigar, mon."

Lunch of a conch roti arrived with another beer. A roti is a Caribbean, curried version of a burrito. During David's first island visits, he'd ordered chicken roti and couldn't understand why they'd put bones inside a dough wrapper with onions and potatoes, but it made the wrap bigger. Originally, he believed the curry's spicy flavor masked stale food. But daily, the few restaurants would quickly sell out their supply. Nothing was ever around long enough to get stale. Conch were plentiful around the island — and unless it was ultra-tough, you couldn't choke on it, like you could a crushed chicken bone.

"Yo, Jonas." David got his attention by pointing to some orange, almost painful hot sauce. He'd distracted him from admiring his newly styled, raised crew cut. "You know, you gonna get mistaken for a rapper. If these cigarettes are so good, where can I get one to try?"

"Shit, mon, see this plastic cup of loose 222 smokes? That's how we sell smokes here. Most people on Carriacou are too poor to spend for even a half pack at one time — so they just buy one cigarette when they need it. Those real expensive; I don't think you'd find them anywhere here, mon. Grenada for sure. You could have someone bring them up by the ferry."

"Tell me which shop has the best candy selection. I need a special chewing gum. You ever hear of Juicy Fruit?"

"Juicy Fruit? Nah, mon, me, I don't like no chewing gum. Bad for the teeth. Check Lois' School Shop. It's just down the street. Old Auntie Lois sells everything: school uniforms, books, and candy to them kids. You can get lottery tickets, too. Kids swarm there after school."

David paid and burped loudly as a signal of appreciation for a tasty lunch.

"Hey, you know you might be able to get some of those smokes on the next island, Petite Martinique. Them guys smuggle everything. They ain't got them; they'll get them for you. And it will be cheaper than where they were made. Go figure, huh?"

Maybe boredom was setting in quicker than he'd expected. Too many lazy, undirected days, and now David's mind had started to weave a mystery out of Bill's bruises.

Hillsboro was slower than usual that afternoon, with another of the many, unpublicized, public holidays permitting businesses to close with a credible reason. There are only seven streets in Hillsboro: East, West, North, South, Hill, Shore, and Main. Most businesses populated the last two.

The school, the public library, and two bars bordered the village square. The street was clean and recently planted with deep lavender bougainvillea, which would bloom again when it rained. No competitors threatened Auntie Lois' 'School Store' across from the middle school.

Extended families throughout the Caribbean included a lot of uncles and aunts. Often you'd know someone so nice and warm to you she'd just become your aunt. With Lois and other shopkeepers, school kids could enjoy the same affection as with a blood relative. These relationships lasted from preschool until they reached maturity. Lois would always give favors. If the family didn't have enough money to buy the necessary school uniforms, they could pay later. It was the same with books. Candy and the best treat, Lois' homemade frozen ices and custards, would be given to worthy students. Auntie Lois relished her distinctive role in the small, island community.

The school shop's proprietor wore her usual, black button-down sweater over a pale housedress. It was difficult to determine how tall Lois was, because she never rose from her padded wooden captain's chair, squeezed between the wall counter and the showcase. Beside her, within easy reach, was the fridge on the left and the magazine rack to her right. If you needed something out of her reach, and if a daughter or granddaughter wasn't around, you'd have to get it for yourself. A remote control lowered the volume on the TV set hung high against the far wall. Lois was watching an American soap opera when David entered.

"Aunt Lois, how are you? You're lucky to be inside this cool shaded store on a blazing hot one like today." David paid his respects. "You on some new diet? You're looking younger and prettier every day."

"Oh, you still on island? What happened, I thought you were sailing with the American Navy? Fall in love with one of the local girls? You keep talking that way, she might have problems with me." Lois half laughed and blew her nose, wiping it vigorously. "What can I do for you today, sailor? I got some frozen soursop custard, and you can have one to walk with."

"That sounds good," he said as she snaked her short arm into the freezer. He pointed to the small selection of chewing gum. "This is all the gum, here? You don't have Juicy Fruit in the yellow package by chance?"

"School don't like me to sell chewing gum at all. Seems that those kids never correctly put it away. It's always getting stuck on the wrong things. I sell it. Yes, it's so sweet; the kids love it. Don't have none right now. All sold out 'till a shipment comes the end of next week from Grenada. Got some cloves gum, or some cinnamon. You ought to try some of that delightful coconut fudge I got."

"No, the frozen custard will be enough. You haven't had any other men in here buying Juicy Fruit, have you?"

"Oh, I don't know. I get everyone in here from toddlers to old timers like me. Everyone gots a sweet tooth. They says it comes from us belonging to a sugar cane culture. Like that's all our slave ancestors had to eat. But everybody comes here to gets the good, old-time sweets. Lots of tourists, too," she said proudly.

"But nobody came asking for that type of gum?"

"In particular, I'd have to say no. The other thing people on this island like more than sweets, is to talk. I just hear they had some problems down by where you is living. The problem makers chewing this gum? Hear Old Bill Steward took some licks while working on the boat he's building for you." She laughed, "Guess you laid into him for dragging his tools so slow."

"The island telegraph system must be working overtime. Billy boy slipped on Moriah, fell into the cabin after finishing a hard day of work.

By the time he was done rolling around, he got some cuts and bruises. He's back to boat building today. How did you hear about it?"

"Oh my, divulge my sources?" She shifted on her cushion and leaned out over the glass case. "Wendell Cronen passed by with the story of how Billy got himself beaten in a robbery. Wendell is the brother of Katherine, who's married to Phillip. Now Phillip's renting the farm plot next to Bill's sister, Shirley, and her brood. Seems he came running when he heard Shirley scream. Guess she almost fainted when her boy mentioned it during supper. I'd guess Phillip saw Wendell at a corner drinking spot and passed the story along. Now I got it straight." She looked him hard in the eye and ran her pink tongue around her dark lips. "Bill just fell; okay, I'll tell it right."

"Yeah, Lois, it's really no big thing," David remarked. "It shook me up. The boy woke me up early. Guess Bill had cracked his head when he fell and was out cold. Thanks for the custard. It is really good." He tipped his ball cap and turned to the door.

"I knew you'd like it." She laughed, blew her nose, and said in a much softer voice, "I always know what good looking men wants."

She laughed again. "Serves Bill right if he was drinking any of that Kill Devil rum he likes. And by the way, there was two white guys in here last week buying all kinds of candy. They was both older than you by ten years at least. One bought some of everything; reminded me of a big old kid. You know what I mean. He had gray hair braided into a ponytail, and he was big and broad — hardly able to fit though the door. Wore a muscle man outfit. You know, one of them muscle shirts and tight shorts like the women wear. I couldn't forget those shorts. That guy was built strong, and had a big gray handlebar mustache. Made me think he was one of those famous wrestling guys. He didn't say too much; just pointed at what he wanted. The smaller one paid. He got upset when I made him go stand outside with his cigarette. He laid it down to come back in to pay. The big one couldn't fit no money in those tight shorts," Lois laughed, "but he bought the last five packs of Juicy Fruit. Does that help you? You want them for some mayhem or something?"

"Well Lois, things are getting clearer. No, I was expecting a friend who sails into here each year. He's always trying to quit cigarettes, and really likes sweet chewing gum for a replacement. Maybe he went back to smoking. What did the smoker look like? Maybe my friend's already here."

"I wouldn't make those two to be friends of yours. From a different cut, I'd say. They was in here last Wednesday…no, it was Tuesday, a full week past. The smoker was smaller. Had real loose clothes covering everything like he was afraid to get sunburnt, and a big straw hat, to top it off. Dressed real dark though. I think it was all maroon. I could tell he was hot, 'cause he kept wiping his face. No matter. He was short, with curly black hair and one of them fancy beards that go with a mustache, but he still shaved. You know what I mean? They was Americans like you, but they talked different."

David took his thumb and forefinger and drew a V below his mouth. "Like that?"

"Yeah, just like that," she said as he thanked her and turned again for the door. "You come around anytime to question me, you hear! It's good for business to have a handsome guy like you in my establishment."

David could feel his face reddening. The temperature of the day was at its peak as he left the shade and the mechanical breeze. The concrete sidewalks broiled under his sandals. The Immigration Department at the Police Station would be the final stop. Next to God, your fate in another country lies in the authority of an immigration administrator. Agent Richmond was the only immigration officer and a nephew of Luella, the owner of David's cottage. They knew each other slightly. If there weren't any visitors at the airport or the dock, Richmond doubled as a police investigator. He took the effort to review the entries for the last two weeks and miraculously remembered each of the almost three-hundred male visitors to the island. Whether they arrived by air or by sea, none matched the descriptions of a gray, ponytailed, big-mustached man with a smaller, goateed cohort.

"Mr. Warner," Officer Richmond spoke in precise London-trained and accented English. In an effort to impress the value of his formal British education, he never used the local phrases. He was young, ambitious, and groomed to succeed in the civil service. All Grenadine public officials take pride in their appearance. Richmond stayed fresh by showering, and changing uniforms each day during lunch. Relatives claimed he worked to secure the destiny of his name. His light brown, clean-shaven head sprouted from a starched, white collar. "I can assure you those two gentlemen you described did not seek clearance into this nation through my office. They probably entered at the main airport in Grenada, or arrived on the mother island by yacht. There is a chance they immigrated illegally. However, I have seen the bigger individual of whom you speak. I think it was mid last week when I literally bumped into the fellow as I was leaving my post on the dock as the St. Vincent ferry, the Lord's Way, finished disembarking passengers. Your fellow seemed to be distracted as he watched the ferry."

"Officer, did you see the smaller one? Perhaps he was on the ferry or on the dock."

"No, Mr. Warner." Officer Richmond pushed away from the desk and unfolded a starched, white handkerchief and ceremoniously dabbed his forehead. "I closed my small, one-window office on the pier and exited with a stack of entry papers. Locking my gate, I turned directly into that man. I dare say, he was about as tall and as broad as that booth I'm forced to characterize as an office. He was just a bit more than my six feet, but he outweighed me by fifty solid pounds."

"Did he say anything?"

"Not really. I think he nodded or performed some sort of slightly respectful gesture, and then walked off. I dare say that if our paths should cross again, I'll ask to inspect his papers. Would you mind explaining your interest in the big bloke?"

As sort of an ex-official, David disliked lying to another. His gut feelings told him that these two were involved in the melee with his boat builder. "I thought that they might be friends, or crew of a buddy of mine whose arrival is a bit overdue. I'd expected his yacht about a week ago. This time of year my buddy always brings coworkers and friends as crewing passengers on a charter through the Grenadines."

"And you think this graying hulk is in the company of your friend?" Officer Richmond neatly refolded his handkerchief. "May I ask what type of business attracts that sort of individual?"

"Movies," David stretched the lie. "You know how strange the movie types are."

"Yes, that explains it all. Perhaps I should procure the tall actor's autograph when I inspect his papers, if, as you say, he's a cinema attraction."

David rose from the hard, metal chair to make a hasty exit before his story got so entangled the island would be expecting a visit from Steven Spielberg. "No, not an attraction — only builds the backgrounds, the sets.

My friend with the boat has a company that builds backdrops for television programs." Predicting the next comment, he added, "I don't think you'd have seen any of his products."

"Yes, that California society creates some rare individuals." Primping, Officer Richmond stood as David opened the door. "I've always fancied I could be beckoned by Hollywood life, but duty to my country comes first. I'd like to meet your acquaintance when he arrives. Perhaps he knows a producer who might like a competitor for Wesley Snipes or Denzel Washington."

"I'll be sure to bring him by, Officer Richmond. Thank you for your time and attention."

A slight sea breeze curled around the municipal building as David retraced his path to his parking spot. Realizing he wasn't even treading water with this inquiry, he decided to let it go and return to his cottage — asking why he should complicate his simple life with other people's misfortunes. Whatever had befallen Bill was a product of his own bad luck. This afternoon's mission had been the combination of boredom and a slight necessity to return to a dutiful existence. The succession of brilliant blue ocean vistas eradicated that twinge of responsibility in him. David crested a parched hillside and could see his home on the east bay.

\\\\\\\\

Bill was asleep against a palm tree next to the frame of David's boat. Another six ribs had been fabricated and installed along the keel. Reese was quietly bolting the last one. "Looks like a good day's humping, huh, boss?" Reese sought favor. "Uncle's still a bit under from the bruises, but we's got a lot done today. He just placed this rib for me to bolt and sat down over there."

"No problem, you tighten that and then call it a day." He turned to Bill, whose inner alarm had responded to David's voice. "Bill, you okay? Like I said, no need to hurry on my account. I never had a sailboat, so I won't miss this one by a matter of a few weeks. You need time to recuperate."

"Where to cuperate? Me ask where?" Using the rough palm trunk for a lift, he stood up, tweaking his spine carefully. Bill spoke deliberately, "Me goes home at lunch, listen to Cecilia bawlin' 'bout these injuries, like they's aching her. Then me gots to listen to family's questions, so can't even put me head on a pillow in me own nest. Tell you this; now she sees me alive and walking, me should stay here on the boat. But you know the woman rule, and she says, 'Get home!' No matter, me finish your project. Me needs to go slow for a few days 'till some of dis paining leave."

Bill laid his hand on his rib cage and gently massaged for a few minutes. "Me no want them other boys to know me business, so in a few days they coming down to start screwing planks to de frame."

"Bill, please come over to the house and enjoy a cold beer with me. Work's over for today."

Reese was finally learning to gather the tools at the end of the day and organize them under David's porch. It was a good habit few workmen anywhere acquired — respect for another man's tools.

"Can't do that, boss," Bill replied, "but me'll give you a cold one if you rides me to my place up the hill."

For the better part of an hour, they chatted about various island boats and their good and bad features — where they sailed, their owners, and of course, who built them. David's truck climbed through the narrow switchbacks towards Bill and Cecilia's home in Top Hill. The small, thirty-house village was appropriately named. Bill's sloping lawn had a panoramic view of about half the east side of the island. Farther up his drive was a cut on a higher rise, which viewed the western half of Carriacou. Bill's home looked to the cool morning and benefited from a constant sea breeze.

"Seeing sunsets is real nice, yous knows, SP, but that afternoon heat don't drop off, making it hard for me to drop off. Me likes to see that cool sun come outs the ocean, and feel the breeze."

Bill pointed past the reef and east of the smaller populated island of Petite Martinique. Carriacou's barrier reef encompassed the two large windward bays of Eastern and Mt. Pleasant. The bright sun created multiple shades of blue as it moved across the horizon. In the evening, the reef ran from shallow's turquoise to the cobalt of the deep.

Cecilia sat on the concrete porch of their stucco house, shelling pigeon peas. The house had expanded with the births of five children. Three girls, ranging from eight to fourteen, washed laundry by hand in a series of plastic tubs.

"Well, Mr. SP, I am so glad that you dragged my old man back home. I knows he don't want to come. Bill loves that damn boat Moriah more than his family."

Cecilia was considerably younger than Bill, but she was also considerably bigger, by at least fifty pounds. A bright red scarf covered her hair rolled in big, pink curlers. Her oversized blue T-shirt showed Yosemite Sam with two drawn six shooters. She had a pretty face and a strong, shapely figure. Cecilia was attractive and in great shape, but a big woman. David thought to himself that he definitely wouldn't have wanted to get on her bad side.

The girls said their perfunctory hellos and kept at the laundry. "Bill, get Mr. SP a beer, will ya? I don't want to get up or dese snap beans will scatter. Get me one too, will ya Billy?"

Without a word, Bill entered the house. As the springed screen door slammed closed, his wife said, "You know SP, that man of mine give me such a fright. I mean Bill don't do church regular, but I'll bet this Sunday he is in the pew between the children and me. I think this bruising is making him think 'bout things. What you suppose happened? It don't seem like no fall scraped him like that. I volunteer at the clinic, and I sees a lot of beatings among the drinkers, wives, and young boys. Billy's bruises looks the same."

"Well Cecilia, it's just what Bill told you, a bing, a bang, and kaboom. Falling six feet through a hatch would surely put a hurting on me, and I'm a lot younger than Bill. Sometimes you get into a habit. You have something on your mind, and you might take an extra step."

Bill returned with three beers as Cecilia told the children to remember the fabric softener in the last rinse bucket. He sat down next to her, leaning his narrow back against her broader shoulders. It was obvious they had an affectionate union.

"So, what you think, huh? Maybe we sell this place to some rich guy and retire to Californy or Miami. Everybody say this a million dollar view." Bill gulped, and with a slight wince, wiped his mouth with his forearm. "How long we been up here, Cecilia? What is it now, thirty or forty?"

"Bill, something's wrong with your head; I've not yet made fifty! You think you've had me since I was but ten? Get real. You must be getting Alzheimer's. We come here in seventy-nine. You know SP, this was my uncle's wedding gift. My uncle wanted to marry me, but Mama wouldn't let him, so Billy got this prize." She primped and carefully draped her big arm over Bill to tickle his stomach. "Everybody was after me back then, but Bill was the luckiest. Huh, Billy? You know you was chasing me just after finishing school. I played around a few years, but Billy-boy caught me. We lived with Mama for a short while, until Billy couldn't stand it no more." Bill squirmed as she tried to tickle him again.

"Now we gots six beautiful daughters," Cecilia pointed to the laundry workers and started the introductions with the smallest. "That's Sheila, Ruth, and Deborah. You met little Darla yet, SP? She's seventeen trying to go on about thirty. I swear." She pointed again to the laundry. "If you girls give me a tenth of the trouble of Darla, I'll have a conniption fit," she shook her finger, "you hear? And our two oldest, Lurina and Laverne gave us our first grandchildren."

Night approached the distant horizon, and David realized his return trip would be slower dodging the maze of potholes in the dark. Bill pointed to the semi-circle of white froth designating the barrier reef. "Beautiful! Yous knows we was once gonna build a porch on the back, but figured kids would fall off and kill themselves. So me still just walk 'round the corner and enjoy this sight most every evening if me ain't on the boat. Wonderful! Ain't it, though?"

"Yeah Bill, you've done well. You've got a great wife and family with a fine home. No man can ask for more."

"Yous knows, SP, there was a time me wanna a lot of tings. Yous knows, like most youngans. That's how Adam get tempted. Start wanting things he don't really need. Hell, we could still get by without 'lectricity. Only had it up here for 'bout ten years. So now, we have telephone, television, stereo music, and the like. Half a life ago, things was so simple. Feed me; keep me dry, some sex, and me happy. Now me think more 'bout crazy things, like leaving here. But me knows that's impossible. Me sees those going to New York or London comes back unhappy. Unhappy, me tell you! Unhappy, but with lots of money. Me like to see some of that money and stay here. Me no know?"

"Well you can do that, Bill. You got lots of years left."

Bill sat gingerly with his legs flat on the ground. "Yous sees, wanting more than me have might have got me in this mess? That guy years ago thought there was a rich wreck outside the reef. We look the entire length. Twice, mind yous. Up and back. Nuthin' found worth much. Couple of anchors, and lots of fish traps. Fish was thick in them days. The tank diving thing was new, and let me tell you, exciting."

"So you never found anything of the Century? What was the old, white man looking for?"

"Well, he tells us we should be curious 'bout a pile of ballast stone. Now, even my Moriah has ballast stone for weight. Me knew, and Raymond knew, what we was lookin' for. Didn't see nuthin'. One night old Worely and me got rummed up. Him more than me, 'cause me was raised on cane squeezings. Well, he start gabbing away 'bout how his brother was a librarian in some sort of museum, maybe in Washington, USA." Bill swirled his bottle. "Cecilia, darling, bring another beer, please!"

The girls had finished and hung out the laundry. David squatted, brushing away mosquitoes. "What was this Worely like?"

"He was so thin he makes me look plump. Had hardly any hair, and what wisps there was, was white…but me no think he was that old. 'Cause the way he work and swum with the scuba, he had to be in good shape. But like me say, that night he couldn't handle ole Jack Iron Rum. Me 'member it well. He brings us in, and for once, comes along ashore. He was mystery man of Eastern Bay for a time. He paid us good money to never tell nobody what was up. In those days, me always answer questions with more questions. Like whats yous needs to know for? What business it of yous? We was always fishing. Think Raymond said we was guides."

"So Worely comes ashore. Raymond went to see an aunt in the clinic, so me the lone company. Now we went and bought an eighth of Jack rum at Ira Macintosh's bar. He gets buzzed after a few sips, and me starts slowly prying. Seems like his brother was older and found this story wrote down somewheres. Me never see that actual book, but that was what he was saying. Well, story was, a pirate was hung what was supposed to have died on the wreck of the Century. Guess the condemned was trying to buy some time from that court. That story says it was supposed to have gone down off Reef Island. That's how Carriacou translates — Island of Reefs. Well, that boat was headed for Barbados and gots caught in a storm, driving it farther west to here. That court couldn't be bought by a promise, so they hung him. That seaman must have been caught doing something real bad, 'cause that amount of gold ought to buy lots."

"Today, it would be a fortune," David chimed, still briskly chasing mosquitoes. Cecilia brought the next round.

"Now Billy boy, I want you to gets a good rest tonight," she said, turning for the house. "Bill, it's almost seven, please finish and come in. SP, you want to join us for a dinner of boiled fish, pigeon peas, and rice?"

"Thanks, Cecilia, but I had a late lunch."

"Well, that old guy had everything but luck," Bill continued. "We dove and towed from November 'till February, most every day except the Sabbath. That's first real money me ever make; paid for main part of this house. And set enough aside for me to quit hustling as somebody else's captain, and start building boats full time. 'Bout a year later, Raymond and me look for that wreck again on our own. We didn't find nuthin', ever." Bill tilted back his head and gulped his beer. "Yous knows, me almost forget 'bout all that 'til dose guys showed up. For years, me was hoping to stumble upon it and buy this whole damn island. But nows someone else is looking for it."

"You know Bill, what say we look again? Might be fun. I've got my dive gear and the skiff."

"SP, yous look, gives me half of what yous finds, and me still have nuthin'."

David stood and pulled Bill up as he continued, "Yeah, SP, me 'bout gone; too old for chasing dreams. Yous still gots the time. Yous gots energy and time. Me gots Cecilia, the kids, and not much free time. Yeah SP, you look for it, and me'll help."

"We'll see Bill. Might be what I need to keep me occupied until you finish my boat."

"Oh, that boat will get done SP; she'll get done. Bill gave a sort of behind-his-back wave goodbye. The screen door slammed and David threaded his way down the hill as darkness rapidly chased the sunlight.

CHAPTER THREE

Beaches are what most northerners imagine when they think of the tropics. Almost every Caribbean travel ad shows a broad expanse of blonde-white sand, so soft you sink to your ankles where it meets the ocean. A barrier line of palm trees usually edges the sand directly in front of modern, high-rise hotels, which have supposedly increased the locals' standard of living. A few streets away from the sea's edge are rickety homes for the townspeople who barely survive from tourism. The beaches on most Caribbean islands have succumbed to development. The sand, which was once the center of activity for the community, is now populated only during winter months by affluent snowbirds.

The beach on the east side of Carriacou, where David's boat was being built, hadn't progressed much since the Scottish fishermen arrived in the mid 1800s. The McQuires and MacIvers had worked with the local freed slaves to build a good subsistence industry constructing wooden sailing boats, which also served to increase shipping and fishing opportunities. Throughout the Caribbean, small enclaves of specialized tradesmen plied their talents, as had their fathers. Eastern Beach spread south from Blowing Point in the north to the Stout Estate on Hillaire Point. For centuries, this beach was a landfall for ambitious sailors who ferried cargo, only to return to their homes when their pockets were full or the boats needed repairs.

Today, the beach was a work area where the skeletons of a half-dozen boats were being built as finances and time permitted. Some boats were finished in three or four months, while the launching of others might be delayed for years, or even a decade, until sufficient funds were available to finish the project.

Just off shore was the Carenage, where the stone or iron ballast would be removed from below the cargo holds. To accomplish this, a heavy counter weight was attached to the top of the mast, or to the top spreader. The boat was winched over one side until the keel bottom had been completely rolled out of the water. This 'careening' permitted the easy completion of repairs, cleaning, caulking, and painting. Almost every busy harbor had an area determined for careening, and just as many small islets were formed from ballast piles. Near these work sites sprang a multitude of nondescript rum shops that catered to weary boat workers.

Eastern existed because sweet ground water was available to centuries of seafarers. No matter how beautiful the island, it was worthless rock without sweet water. Years of sugar cane and indigo cultivation had stripped the soil of nutrients. Now, cattle scavenged among the scrub bush, seeking shade from the tropical sun.

The village of Eastern, just beyond the beach, resisted change. Less than half of the homes had the convenience of telephones. Phones really weren't necessary for most natives, since most of those who wanted to connect were within walking distance for a chat. With the telephone came the future with the World Wide Web Internet. In contrast to the advent of modern communication technology, few rural homes had indoor bathrooms. Most families still relied on the traditional outhouse latrine. Homes were well-built of wood or concrete blocks, with open windows, usually shuttered, without glass or screens. There were many cedar-shingled houses with ornate, weathered gingerbread trim remaining from the turn of the century. Tropical elements were hard on the homes, rusting the corrugated metal roofs and quickly fading the paints. The tropical elements of rum and drugs weathered the people.

There were three stores for groceries and hardware in Eastern: a white one, a blue, and a yellow and that's how they were identified. Among the fourteen small bars, there was only one disco and that was open all night on Friday and Saturday. For chow, there was one roadside take-out restaurant that served fried fish and chicken. There were no auto mechanic shops, and the only gas station was in the main village of Hillsboro. Locals knew everyone on Carriacou, as well as, their distant relatives on other islands or continents, and they could list their ancestors. The two churches, Reformed Pentecostal and Roman Catholic, were on the shore-side of the main street, and each backed on to its own cramped cemetery of weathered headstones. Residents of Eastern came home to be buried beneath the hot sun, and close to the sweet sound of rolling surf.

About a half-mile south from the village was David's cottage. The town's center square was the hub connecting roads from Eastern to Hillsboro, the settlements at Blowing Point, Mount Pleasant, and the public dock. On his return from Bills, David decided a drive through town to check out the action might not be a bad idea. It was Thursday, and the streets were abandoned except for a few grizzled regulars, slapping dominoes at the corner drinking shops. Even on a holiday weekend, Eastern never had crowds. Crowds were reserved for boat launchings, baptisms, and burial wakes.

\\\\\\\\\

The Toyota rattled to a stop at the blue store where David bought a six-pack to finish the evening on his porch. It was almost seven-thirty as he parked and crossed the sandy yard. There was barely enough daylight remaining, but he could see two shapes walking down the road.

He stiffened as he imagined a return of Bill's intruders. Subtle laughter introduced the two daughters of Luella, his landlady. Melody, the oldest at nineteen, was holding her year-old son 'BB' (short for Bengee the Beautiful). The young mother was tall and lean, and shuffled her feet along the dirt road in furry, pink bedroom slippers. She wore a long, plain, white T-shirt as a housedress. Her hair was braided in tight rows under a Yankees ball cap; the brim pointed over her left ear. Rochelle was just barely a teenager, but early-development stretched her dark shorts and white halter-top.

David turned on the porch light to welcome the unexpected company. "Hello ladies. Out getting BB some cool night air? Can I get you something cold to drink? Water? Soda?"

"A beer, if you got it, would be nice, Mister SP," Melody replied. "This boy is getting so heavy he's hurting my back bad, you know." David opened one beer as Rochelle shook her head to decline refreshment. "So, how you been? Still liking the peace and quiet of East Bay?" Melody handed her baby to her sister, who quickly sat on the porch to play with the boy.

"I'm getting along okay, Melody. Anything in particular I can do for you? I appreciate the company. Sometimes it gets a little lonely at night. I find I can only read so much, and my TV only gets the religious station from St. Vincent." Rochelle rolled BB on his back and had him giggling as she rubbed his stomach. "So Rochelle, can't I get you something?"

"No, I'm all right. Thank you," she replied.

"We is just out for a walk and thought that you might tell us about all of the world you've seen. Doubt if Joey, my husband, and me will ever see much more than Grenada. Hell, I was stretched so big with BB by the time we had the wedding ceremony there wasn't a honeymoon! Joe's got a good future in his father's business, but I'd still like to see more like Miami and New York. You know what those places like? I've seen them on TV, but you been there, haven't you?"

"Oh yeah, I've been to almost every big city in the world." David drained the first beer and opened another. "Yeah, all the big places where the Navy's sailors can get in trouble. Anywhere can be nice if you've got enough money. Vacations usually make things look better than they are — because unless you've got bad luck, you never see the poor people. Believe me; you are lucky to have such a sweet place as here to call home."

"Yeah, sure. You is just saying that because you already been so many places and done so many things. We see all that on the tele news and now they got computers in the level-four school with the Net and everything. Ain't that right, Rochelle?" The younger sister just nodded her head. Sounding much older than her nineteen years, Melody continued, "Didn't have that when I was in school. Seems the world's wide open for everybody, 'cept us here on these little islands."

"You are the lucky ones. You know why they needed to invent something like TV and the Internet?" He sipped his beer. "Because the world out there is ugly and boring. It's so crowded with lonely people growing crazier every day. You are safe here — and believe me — safety is a rare thing in today's world. I'm sure you heard the saying: you don't know what you've had until it's lost. That's the way it is in big cities. Hell, some kids never see real grass or a cow. People have to work so many jobs just to stay even with their expenses. Everything costs so much more, even though 'they' make you believe it costs less. Can you imagine never seeing the sun because of gray clouds, except for only a few clear days a year?"

"Yeah, the grass be always greener. Me, I got my Joey and BB, so my life's pretty well settled. Now, Rochelle, this girl is a bit too smart to be happy here on this small rock for too long. Ain't that right, Rochelle?" Melody finished her beer and wiped her mouth with the back of her hand.

"I'll be happy," the younger girl sighed, picking up the baby. "I'd be happy teaching in the old school like Mr. Post. He's the one making all of the improvements in the school. Mister SP, you'd like him a lot. When I got the time he lets me work on the computer after classes end. It's amazing what you can find on the Internet. Mr. Post studied in New York and London. He got a grant for six computers the students can use, but you should see his own system."

"Sister, you'd better not be paying that much attention to a man's system or you'll end up carrying your own baby." The older girl regained her child.

Those words visibly upset Rochelle. She stood with her hands on her hips. "You shoosh. Mama told you to go slow with Joey. After all, Mama was young when she had you. Now I see how it is with you. I get to hold BB, and then give him back. I don't want a child of my own for a while. There's nothing wrong with getting married," she said looking directly at me, "but there's other things I'd like to do first."

"That's a smart approach, Rochelle," David said. "How long is Mr. Post around after school? I'd like to come by and experiment on the Internet. I've got some research to do."

Rochelle lost some of the maturity she'd just exhibited. "I'll help you Mister SP; I'd love to help you research anything. I'm getting pretty good at it and I can type about the best of anyone in my class." Her eagerness wasn't lost as she continued, "Classes finish about two-thirty and Mr. Post works for about another two hours. Sometimes he even lets me come by on Saturday if he doesn't go out hiking in the bush."

Melody was swinging BB back and forth, swaying to a lullaby only she could hear. David sensed his company was ready to depart. "I'll try to come by tomorrow and see your teacher, Rochelle. Mention it to him, please."

"Oh, you can count on that, Mister SP. Come on Mel, we got to gets going. I don't want to sleep in tomorrow."

The older sister rolled her eyes as they stepped off the porch and into the darkness. David retrieved the empty bottles, opening another for his long walk to bed.

Dive bombing houseflies are nature's most effective alarm clocks. One buzzed David's face at first light before taking an awakening seat on his stubbled jaw. After a papaya breakfast, he unloaded all of his dive gear from duffel bags stored in an overhead crawl space. The opening of the crawl space was up through the top of the closet, which meant that all of his seven clothes hangers had to be removed. The closet backed against the bath, which was the only room of the small cottage enclosed by a ceiling. The rest of the house had painted rafters and planks under the rusting corrugated tin. Although the closet was small, the ceiling portal was just big enough for him to squeeze through.

When everything was dumped in a pile on the porch, he unrolled his buoyancy vest and inflated it to check for leaks. The regulator with gauges, a compass and a small dive knife attached, was screwed onto the yellow, eighty-cubic-inch aluminum tank. It registered a full three-thousand-psi. The regulator worked perfectly and gave a nice easy breath. The trouble with diving is the basic equipment is so bulky, heavy, and cumbersome outside the water. During David's stay on Carriacou, he'd become good at breath-hold free diving. It was very simple and comfortable to use just a mask and snorkel. Once below the surface though, the scuba setup provided enough exciting memories to last a lifetime. Travels with the Navy had permitted him to experience underwater excursions in every ocean of the world, except the frigid Arctic. Diving in the southern Grenadines was some of the very best. He kept his skiff moored offshore, which forced a swim whenever he wanted a boat ride. Swimming was easier on his back than pushing it on and off the beach alone. The red, wooden, round-bottom eighteen-footer was not the ideal watercraft for scuba diving. When David had first come to Carriacou, he'd bought it from 'Loco Joe' and they'd kept it readied for each visit. Joe named the skiff 'Dolly' — and she had provided more good times than most of the other women he'd known.

With two full five-gallon gas tanks, it could motor to the north end of Grenada and then refuel for the return. Seldom did David go farther than the four miles to Petite Martinique. He had a handheld VHF marine radio in a waterproof plastic bag — in case he had problems and went adrift. However, the island governments had distaste for locals with radios in their boats for fear they'd assist the drug smugglers. Accordingly, few radios were listening for a distress call. The local coast guards were equipped with former US Navy boats to intercept and board suspicious vessels — yet they seldom monitored the radio unless they were patrolling.

David had witnessed and heard enough shipwreck stories to know the open sea was not a playground. Once, in the Indian Ocean, he was on a cruiser that picked up a small boat with two young children. They had drifted two hundred miles away from their home bay in Ceylon. The anchor line had broken as they were playing, and before they realized it, the wind, coupled with the tide, had pulled them away from home. It was lucky the day-watch spotted the small boat and hoisted it aboard. The boys and their family were safely reunited.

Just in case of an accident with the outboard, he'd stowed two gallon jugs of water, flares, a signal mirror, a few basic tools, and extra spark plugs in the covered bow area. The dive tanks were lashed to opposite sides to balance the load. Everywhere he went, he pulled a hand fishing line attached to a red feather lure. If the boat was moving, he was fishing. This morning's dive would be a mission for dinner.

The plan was to maneuver through a small passage to the outside of the reef, and do a drift dive. To carefully drift alone, he'd drop the anchor line with a small lifting bag attached. Something weighing several tons can be lifted and maneuvered easily through the water with this technique. Often the shore patrol would dive to recover evidence, or contraband thrown into the water. Instead of struggling against the weight in the aquatic environment, attaching a lift bag made it similar to a child handling a balloon. Once the bag is attached to the anchor, just enough air is blown into it from a regulator to counter the weight. Then, diver and equipment can easily drift with the current. This method increases the length of the dive, since the diver needs to expend very little energy. The boat is always above, in case of a problem — such as a shark or heavy current. If the diver finds a location to explore, enough air is deflated from the bag to plant the anchor.

As Dolly slid past the coral barrier, the story of the Century's disappearance fueled David's imagination. Shipwrecks and treasures tantalized him. Even though Bill had searched years ago and found nothing, David believed his luck might be better.

Three hundred years under the Caribbean Sea can render a wreck difficult to spot. Reading about Mel Fisher's fifteen-year search for the Atocha under the sands of Florida would make anyone think twice about instigating such a venture. The fantasy of adventure keeps hopes and dreams alive, encouraged by reasonable optimism.

Dolly moved so slow over the water that David could see fish scatter from the sound of the outboard. The vertical visibility was incredible. He could see clearly through fifty-feet to the sea floor. Residents of Eastern had enough environmental common sense not to deplete the reefs by over-fishing any single spot. Instead, the fishermen moved with each season. Early in the year, they drifted south for ocean king and dorado. During the summer, they dove the shallows for conch — and in the winter tourist season, they fished north for the plentiful barracuda and huge ocean gar known to northerners as marlin or sailfish. Some of the locals trapped fish in large cages of chicken wire. This was considered undignified in comparison to hauling in a struggling fish on a hand line. Other islands had used the trapping method to extremes, building local bank accounts while severely depleting the reef populations. Every time a trap was lost by a storm or confused landmarks, it went on killing for years until the wire finally rotted away.

Today the sea was relatively calm, with waves no bigger than two feet. David anchored and took some basic bearings with his compass so he could return to this spot if it became promising. He scribbled the directions on the small, white dive slate at the reverse side of his scuba gauges. He donned his gear quickly as Dolly rocked and lurched in the swell. Falling backward in the fashion of the sixties hero, 'Sea Hunter' Mike Nelson, he immediately relaxed and sank about forty feet. Beneath the surface, the aquamarine sea was tranquil. His anchor had disturbed a school of purple doctor fish, now weaving around a large, golden elk horn coral head. David settled to the bottom in the middle of a white sand chute, checked his gauges, and cocked his spear gun. Usually, he'd carry the four-foot gun with the two rubber bands pulled tight, just in case a grouper decided to commit suicide by permitting a profile shot. Having seen too many large, seven-foot lemon sharks in the area, he'd always wait until the end of a dive to shoot. Common sense forced him to return to the boat as soon as he speared a fish to keep the area clean of blood, a magnet for bigger trouble.

Even though there was little current, the lift bag inflated and he drifted slowly over the beautiful, living reef. Every fifty feet or so, a sand-covered valley marked the end of that coral head's mass. Reef fish are very territorial, and tend to stay where food is abundant. Some species get visually disturbed if you trespass. Bright yellow butterfly fish would travel in pairs, darting up at him to protect the particular coral they called home. Five large yellowtail snappers, the delicious racing-striped Corvettes of the reef, surrounded him with acrobatic rolls and twists, always staying barely out of range of the spear gun. Schools of silver fry, gleaming, overhead in the sunlight, camouflaged a slender, five-foot barracuda. Large purple and green parrotfish nibbled carelessly at coral, digesting and eliminating new sand as waste.

Drifting slowly westward, David imagined what would remain of a wooden ship left in the aquatic elements for a few hundred years. Among the pages of the books he'd read as a child on the farm were drawings of human skeletons with swords in hand, surrounding a pile of golden doubloons in the belly of an intact ship. This could happen as it had with the Mary Rose that sank in the cold water of England's Thames River. In tropical waters, wood-boring worms and storms made the demolition of timbers quick work. The best hope was to locate an anchor or cannon. Although both would be encrusted with coral, their shapes should still be evident if they weren't covered with sand. He guessed that the Century would have been driven on the outside of the reef in a disastrous storm, its planks splintered by the crashing waves. Except for three channels, the barrier reef was virtually impervious. It rose from an eighty-foot bottom to less than a meter from the surface. The reef was about thirty meters wide and twelve miles long. It seemed unlikely that a wooden ship could be pushed over the reef. The ballast stones and heavy iron cannon and fittings would drop where the hull split open. The anchors should be close.

During the first dive, David discovered a den of lobsters and reduced the residency by one. He returned to the surface, swapped tanks, and relaxed. After warming in the hot, morning sun, it was time to splash again. About midway into the dive, he was startled to hear an outboard overhead. Suddenly, the anchor line pulled to the surface. Holding onto the rope, he followed the anchor to discover a beautiful, young, brown-skinned woman hauling in the line. She was stunned when he reached the surface with a shout for an explanation. She reached the engine and shut it down.

"Who are you?" they both said almost simultaneously. David grabbed the oarlock, stripped off his tank, and pulled his body inside the boat. The woman hadn't moved from the rear steering seat, only staring at him with wide, brown eyes. She was definitely a woman — not at all to be confused with a girl. Her wet, gold T-shirt clung to mature breasts.

"I swam out to save this boat," she said. "I thought it broke its anchor and was drifting onto the reef. I watched it drift for at least half an hour without seeing anyone on board." As she spoke, the woman wrung water from her long, shiny black hair. "I'm so sorry!" After a pause, when David didn't respond, she continued. "I had no idea you were diving." She extended her slim arm. "I'm Feliza Dubois. I live in Mt. Pleasant. I hope this didn't upset you."

David realized it was his turn to speak — but was in such awe of this West Indian beauty that he stammered, "It's…it's okay. No problem." He hoisted his air tank into the skiff. As he unzipped his suit, he found it impossible to break his stare. Her face was exquisite: penetrating eyes, sculptured cheekbones, and an incredibly delicious mouth. When her hair dried, it would fall beyond her coffee-colored shoulders. "What did you say your name was?" he managed to ask.

"Feliza."

"Well, Feliza, why don't you start the motor and get us away from the reef."

She gave the cord a serious, practiced pull. The thirty-five roared to life and Feliza revved the motor twice before slipping into gear. The motor accelerated and Dolly banked to the right, heading for the southern passage through the reef. He watched her steer as the cool wind stuck her shirt to her obviously erect nipples. All he could do was smile at his dumb luck.

Fifteen minutes of enjoyment, watching this creature guide her way to the Mount Pleasant dock, wasn't enough. While they coasted to the dock he asked, "Are you single?"

"Why?" she replied, smiling.

"It's not often I get rescued, even if I don't need it. There ought to be a reward, like dinner or a movie."

"We both know there's no movie theater in Carriacou." Feliza tied Dolly securely with three, reverse-half-hitch knots, and hopped up onto the wooden planks. She grabbed her dive mask and fins, and stood above David like an Amazon warrior. Her sparkly, bikinied-bottom seemed to wink at him. "But we can meet again. I am single and just returned from California. And you are?" she pointed to him.

"David. David Warner. I'm staying in Eastern."

"Tourist?" She asked with a slight attitude.

"Not quite, I'm having a boat built and living here until it's finished, which will probably take a while." He stared up at her slender physique and stammered, "I'm…I'm…I'm sure it is going to take a long while."

"Then it is definite; we will see each other again. Look, I am sorry for disturbing your dive. Perhaps my imagination went haywire today, anxious for a swim or something? Shouldn't you have a red flag? I usually swim out to the reef for exercise. I'm still trying to adjust to this sleepy place from the chaos of LA. So, are you," she paused for effect, "single?"

"Absolutely," spurted from his lips. "So where can we get together?"

"My Aunt Bernadette has the Old Fort Restaurant and I'm helping her at the moment. Why don't you come by for dinner tonight at my expense for ruining your dive?"

"You didn't ruin my dive; you made my day. But I have a lobster for tonight. How about dinner at my house?" He lifted the yellow net bag and proudly displayed the five-pound lobster. It was a primeval exhibition, a sort of a 'Tarzan - Jane' thing. David was an official hunter-gatherer.

"Tell you what, let me have that little bug and I'll have it cooked for our dinner. Sound alright?" She cut his macho drama short and grabbed the bag while he just gazed at her beautiful assets. Feliza was at least a slim five-ten, with measurements meant for a Playboy centerfold. "Okay?" she repeated.

"Oh yeah, very okay. What time do you want me to come?"

She unhitched the skiff, bending over to give David the full effect of her breasts. "I'll expect you about seven for cocktails, Mr. Warner. You sure you know where the Old Fort is? Just go through the little village," she pointed, "and take the second left. There aren't any signs, but if you pass the red rum shop, you went too far." She turned and pointed at him again, shaking her finger. "Don't be late."

"I won't." She unleashed the rope and pushed Dolly's bow from the dock, facing away from him as he reversed into the bay. David watched to see if she would turn to look again and he wasn't disappointed.

The cottage's garden hose rinsed the sea salt from David and his dive gear. It was after noon — so, he prepared for the meeting with Mr. Post at school. A can of Campbell's chicken soup was lunch — and then he set an alarm for a two-hour power nap. His thoughts, as he dozed, were not of an Internet search for facts about the Century, but of the lovely, alluring Feliza.

Outside, David could hear Bill motivating Reese, and other unknown workers, to apply wooden batten strips to correctly configure the boat's ribs, and shape the hull. A lofting-board blueprint gave the dimensions and proportions of each rib. A model had been made to scale. Everything looked sweet, and Bill was expanding the model into a sleek, curved sailing machine. David's boat developed quickly. In the next days, planks should be fastened to the frame.

\\\\\\\\

The Fourth Level School in Lestaire was not an imposing structure. The yellow and brown two-story building appeared to be military barracks, except there were young West Indian teenagers in abundance. Male and females were dressed in white shirts and ties with gray skirts or trousers. No T-shirts or jeans were visible on the grassless campus. Rochelle was leaning by the front door, obviously happy to see David.

"Oh, Mister SP, I'm so glad you came. I told Mr. Post about your interest in using the Internet. He said he would be available for a consultation after meeting with a student. That should be shortly." She grabbed David's hand and led him into the building. "So what do you think of my school?"

"I think you are very fortunate to get an education in this environment. You don't have any problems here, do you?"

"Like what? Lots of kids here have problems. You have to be smart, and you have to want something to make it through level four. We call it, 'get to and get through!'" She was still squeezing his hand as they walked along the spotless corridor.

"In the United States and in lots of other places in the world, schools are violent and dangerous. In fact, they have guards and metal detectors for protection."

Rochelle stopped in front of a closed door marked COM-LAB.

"The only protection necessary is to keep the boys away. There's no violence here. If a student gets disorderly, he's out. This is the only government level-four school on the island. If you're dismissed for any reason, the only other school is in Grenada, but they don't want problem kids either. Maybe a pair of boys will scrap, but not near the school."

David lifted her hand and pointed to her. "Like I said, you're fortunate."

"Did you use a computer when you were in the Navy? I'll bet you're a whiz." She moved through a nervous pirouette. "How come you've never been married?"

"Well Rochelle…" He was accustomed to fielding this question from other guys who find him lucky for not having indulged in America's most expensive mistake: a failed marriage. He never got to his explanation. The wooden door opened and out came a short boy shaking the teacher's hand, thanking him profusely for the extra help. Mr. Post looked like he could've been a runaway from the flowering sixties in the States. He appeared to be wrinkling into his fifties, but still slim and trim. His green polo shirt showed no flab. Black, horn-rimmed glasses accented his tan and leathery face. A waxed handle bar mustache matched his neat, pony-tailed, gray hair.

The penetrating look from his blue eyes may have been caused by a partial squint.

He extended his hand. "I'm Mike Post. You are Mr. Warner. Rochelle mentioned you would like to access the World Wide Web from the school. I see no problem. Rochelle, if you would excuse us." With that, he guided David through the door and shut it in the chagrined girl's face.

"David."

"No, Mike's the name."

"No. David's my name; you don't have to refer to me as Mr. Warner. Or you can call me SP, like everyone else does on this rock."

"So, you are the Mr. SP. I've been hearing about this boat you're having built. I arrived in Carriacou under the same circumstances, believe it or not. All right, David, the formalities of 'sir' and 'mister' will remain outside that door. I find it important to give West Indian children a good schooling in manners and in proper language articulation. In here, we can call each other anything, as long as we're productive in your Net search. However, there is a cost. As this is a government service, I'll have to charge you twenty dollars an hour, USD. Would that be suitable? Of course that includes my abilities, if you need them."

"Twenty an hour is more than reasonable, and your assistance would be a definite asset. My computer literacy doesn't extend very far."

Mike sat in front of one of the five computers placed along the inside wall. Pulling off a blue cloth cover, he said, "One good thing about being the communications instructor is this room must stay sealed from the heat and humidity — thus, it's air-conditioned. However, salt air is a monster. I'm always cleaning, vacuuming the keyboards and disk drives. What are you interested in researching?"

David sat next to him and cleared his throat. "I was trained in investigative computer science by the U.S. Navy, but I'm sure science has progressed dramatically since I worked at a keyboard. Rochelle said you're interested in archeology and island history. My research will be a bit off the wall. Recently, I came across the story of the wreck of a sailing ship, the Century. I've only heard a bit. Hell, I'm going to be here a few more months; it might help pass the time."

Mike Post's expression darkened. "Pass the time and make yourself rich." He said as he stood up and walked to his desk. He pulled a pamphlet from his top desk drawer and tossed it to David. "I don't think we can continue with this arrangement. I thought you needed information for an article, or wanted to do email, not treasure hunting."

"So that's it, huh? Finished before we started?" David sighed.

"No 'huh' about it. You are definitely not using these computers or my services for a measly Andy Jackson an hour. I'd need a split where I get a percentage — and I'll write a contract. Everything must be all nice, neat, and legal before we begin. What do you say to that? You'd never have a better partner than me. I've walked almost every inch of this forlorn, parched isle, and have studied its history during my twenty-five year sabbatical from America."

"My opinion is, 'part of some is better than all of none'. I already have a friend in for a piece."

He looked at David and offered, "twenty percent of what we can keep if the Grenada government finds out. Okay?" They shook on it. "I'll draw up a basic contract and include a copy for Bill."

"Bill? How did you know it was Bill?" David was already impressed with this aging hippie.

"Because I have already researched every boat that could have sunk in the vicinity of Carriacou. Bill Steward was on the original and perhaps only search for the Century in the late 1970s and early eighties. A man named Worely came here with some private information, but his search wasn't successful."

Post opened a computer file, filling the computer screen with a picture of a three-masted schooner. "This was the Century, built in 1690 at the Copenhagen shipyard. Let's see…Betrane Volmer, who was pretty creative during that period, designed it. It was made for Stinson Brothers, which was a firm that traded all over the world. At their pinnacle, Stinson Brothers had thirty-four boats, and they supplied about a quarter of the European market with exotic spices. Their business eventually included production. They had plantations in the Banda Islands, Malaysia, Ceylon, the Caribbean, and South America."

Another series of photos switched rapidly on the screen. Most depicted ruins David recognized as local landmarks. Some had been rum distilleries with windmill towers, or indigo dye factories, and others were fortifications.

Mike continued, "I received a grant from Great Britain to purchase a digital camera to record the history of Carriacou before it is obliterated by progress." A close-up photo of a rock appeared, showing an indistinct carving. "I found this boulder five years ago during a severe drought — otherwise, surrounding foliage would've kept it concealed."

"I can't make out the carving."

"Here's a charcoal rubbing that I made." Mike unrolled a large piece of white tracing paper.

The inscription read C E N T U R Y 1699 and had a four-sided image below it. David was astounded. "Where is it?"

"Not so fast, Mr. Warner. This is a sample of what I'm bringing to this partnership of which I have only a small…," he paused, "…but appreciated twenty-percent share. What are you offering?"

David sighed and paused to contemplate his own contribution. He hadn't expected to meet someone so well versed in his query. What could gain Post's respect? "Ah…well, Mike, I think we could enlarge your share to an even split, considering all of your efforts. I am the leg man, diver, and competent researcher. Whatever you feel I should do…what would make you comfortable?"

"Do you still have friends in the Navy in Washington? That could unlock some elusive information. How about access to surplus detecting equipment? You will have to supply operating expenses. Since I'm a partner, my services are free, but my pockets are empty. Why else would I trudge through the thorns and cactus of this island if not to search for treasure and artifacts of the pirates and the original Indian inhabitants? The Lord knows I can barely survive on the stipend these locals call a salary. I've been teaching here for twenty years and have continually upgraded the curriculum. But really, a novice assistant manager at a McDonalds makes more than I — and he gets his meals free."

"So, no problems with my contributions?" David asked.

"No problems, but let's be earnest and make this happen. I'm getting too old to chase dreams for much longer. The carved rock is in Anna's Retreat, about a half mile from the beach in a rolling valley. I can only surmise the rock was too big to be moved during the island's years of sugar cane cultivation. It is huge with…" he looked through his notes, "one-hundred-eight inch circumference."

"When can we go search the area? I can get a metal detector shipped here by express," David offered.

"I've already swept the entire area with an old detecting unit that should have registered if there was something present in the ground. Nothing came up, not even a nail. Not a thing."

"What do you suggest?"

"Try whatever connections you have for top-of-the-line military surplus detectors. Since land mines are killing and maiming the third world's warring populations, there should be some new designs. I'll also give you a list of information, which has dead-ended for me. See if anyone in Washington will do you a good turn."

"Now, let me show you the rest of what I have," he proudly continued. "The Century's disappearance almost bankrupted its insurers. Lloyds of London insured it. The manifest lists eight chests of valuables and cargo with a net worth of a million pounds. It also lists the majority of the shipment as various building materials and tools. The passenger list had eight men and two women. From the names, I'd say they were related —

maybe two families. Four of the passengers had the surname of Hollenzock and the rest were Sterns. Both were old, influential, Jewish families. I can't find any reference to a description of the valuables. If these people were traveling to the Western Hemisphere to build a new life, they brought a tidy nest egg. In those days, if you had it, you carried it with you and protected it with your life. It was impossible to move wealth safely. From the various newspaper clippings I've located, the Century's disappearance didn't make much of a stir. However, the disappearance of the Hollenzocks did."

"The manifest listed the passengers as German," he continued, "and everything on board was their consignment. From Web contacts in Europe, I located a bit of history concerning Malachi Stern, who was listed first. It is amazing how far European and Jewish records go back, considering how many wars of destruction have been waged. Somehow, information survives. There are complete records of birth, death, and marriage. The research found Stern to have been a banker in the German city of Essen. He married a rabbi's daughter, Eva Hollenzock, in 1677. Ahh… they were both twenty at the wedding."

David did a quick calculation. "If it was them aboard the Century, they would have been forty-two. That's a bit old to be moving to the tropical colonies."

Mike brought up a timeline on the screen. "So they were born around 1657, after the Thirty Years' War, during a time of relative prosperity and safety. The Sterns were large landowners and merchants. The bonding between them and the Hollenzocks must have been quite an achievement for young Malachi. The Hollenzocks were the movers and shakers of Prussia — having assisted in the development of the first two banks in Venice. In reality, they had all the marbles, just as a Trump or a Rockefeller does today."

"Your research is incredible. Have you been able to discover anything about the crew of the Century and its history?" David was truly impressed. With some luck, Feliza and Mike could make his stay on Carriacou more interesting than he'd ever imagined. "How long have you been at this treasure hunting?"

"Oh, I don't know, probably got into it as dreams of wealth and success from other endeavors began to fade. Searching for treasure is one part luck, forty-nine parts research, and fifty parts energy and optimism.

The research is easy. You just have to know who to ask which questions. An example is the crew list of the Century. Who would you ask?" He turned from the computer, took off his horn rims and cleaned them.

"Obviously, I wouldn't know where to start?"

"Sure you would, at the beginning. The first source of information is the gate. Take the book of shipwrecks. Where did that author gain his information? I circumvented a lot of trial and error by contacting the author through his publishing company, say, probably ten years ago, just after the first edition had been printed. I posed as a struggling author researching his first novel, and the other writer could relate. My questions covered several shipwrecks and treasures throughout the Caribbean and Central America. Arthur Dillion, the writer, directed a huge amount of information my way."

"Back to the Century's crew," Mike pontificated. "I contacted the Lloyds Registry and found another computer buff working in the records department. I traded the genuine promise of a vacation on my boat for anything she could find pertaining to the Century's last sailing. Margaret found everything except the contents of those eight chests. For some reason the crew of a Danish ship was English. I surmise it to be that the captain, William Zane, an ex-Royal Navy man, had experience as a privateer in the West Indies. That was probably why he'd been chosen for this route. They had intended to sail to Barbados — as it was the most settled and had the least likelihood of a pirate attack. Four of the eight-man crew were also English. A Mister Allsop was the first mate and Peter Stricklind was the bosun."

"Have you learned where Dean Worely got his information for the first search?" David interjected.

"Bill said Worely's brother uncovered some information about the hanging of a pirate who had supposedly been a member of the Century's crew. If that's true, there must've been enough reason to believe it and begin the search. There were some survivors?"

"No, Bill never mentioned anything about a pirate." David replied.

"The story has a lot of holes. The carved stone lends some credence to the story that survivors were washed ashore on Carriacou before there was civilization here. All of the development on this island started about 1750. Ships watered in Eastern Bay — and the island is on some charts dating back another hundred years. But always the anchorage is shown as

Western Bay on the lee side. So that's something you might inquire about with your Washington acquaintances."

"It's three-thirty now. That makes it an hour less on the East Coast. Do you have a long distance connection through the computer?" David inquired.

"Sure do, only way to call sis back on the mainland. Help yourself." Mike brought up a telephone to the screen and handed him a head set. David dialed a number he knew by heart.

After a short series of connection beeps, David heard a familiar feminine voice. "Good afternoon, Office of the Commander of Naval Communications. Lieutenant Whistlow, how may I assist you?"

"Amy Whistlow, how are you handling the winter?" he replied. "I don't believe it! David, where are you? Are you stateside, or still on that sandy beach you call home?" In a much stricter, hushed tone, she reprimanded, "Why the hell didn't you call me sooner, you asshole?! I was worried about you! It's hard to communicate with a coconut tree!"

"Still on that sandy beach, Amy. When are you going to visit? Must be getting cold up there now. How's the family?"

"Bullshit! You're trying to change the subject." Amy admonished. "It's the first week of February. It is damn frigid. The temperature falls further than the ice age at night. Dad's still going strong, gaining momentum to be the youngest vice admiral in naval history. We all miss you. Mom was just asking about what happened to that cute guy I was dating last year. I've been wondering the same thing. What happened to him?" In a sweet, seductive voice, "I really miss the best bed warmer I've ever found for these chilly nights."

Mike Post was listening to the conversation through the system and smiling while typing notes on items needing more research. "That fellow is less stressed out since there are fewer people here to add pressure to his life. Everything is good. In a few months my sailboat will be completed. I would really like you to visit my small beach abode. I miss you more than I can say."

"Let me guess; you missed me so much you had to call after five months of nothing. Not a damn word from you. I don't think so. What do you want?" Amy switched back to the efficient business diction.

"Well, Amy, I do miss you, and yes, I need something. I was hanging at loose ends down here, reading too many paperbacks. Recently, I met some local men and have become involved in a search for a shipwreck. I know this is kind of rude to call after four months."

"Five months and sixteen days," she replied flatly.

"You're right. It's rude to call after five months and sixteen days. You know how badly I needed a break."

Amy exclaimed, "I didn't know it would also mean a break in our relationship while you rediscovered the real, non-naval David Warner! Didn't we all support your decision to retire? Dad said you cut your career too short, but he will always respect your choice. Now you are a treasure hunter. Wow! I'm impressed. So what do you need from poor, discarded Amy?"

He picked up a printed sheet from Mike. "First, what is your private email address? I'll send you a list of questions, and I'm sure with your usual efficiency, you'll be able to help. I'm also looking for some surplus top-of-the-line metal detectors for both land and water. Satellite photos of this island and the surrounding waters with the best definition would help. Now that we've reconnected, I'll be in touch regularly."

"There's only one thing I have that needs touched regularly, David." Amy laughed. "I do miss you. And for whatever it's worth, I do still love you. I'll try to help. Get the queries to me and I'll pull together all of my resources, but this is going to cost you a plane ticket and a vacation. A naval lieutenant's salary doesn't stretch very far these days. Deal?"

"Deal, Amy. Thanks for understanding."

They said their good-byes as Mike sent off the list of info. "The admiral's daughter! You sure do have some connections. I hope your vacation offer fares better than the one I told you about earlier. When Margaret arrived from London with the Lloyds particulars, my boat listed badly. She was in the hundred-kilo range." He laughed and pulled at his gray mustache, "But an offer is an offer."

"Amy's very competent and attractive. If the info is available, she'll locate it." David checked his watch and said, "Let's call it a day. It's past five and I have plans for tonight. How about we meet tomorrow, same time, and discuss it further over a few cocktails?"

Mike stuck out his hand and they shook again. "You must have read my mind. My boat is near to Mt. Pleasant Bay, not far from Rudy's

Restaurant. I'll see you there about four. One other rule: we never speak about this while others are around. Treasure lore might seem to fall upon deaf ears with the locals, but everyone loves money. You know, you could swing by to pick me up and check for email. That would save me peddling my tired ass home."

"Sure, I really have no plans for tomorrow afternoon. See you then." David headed to his truck, thinking about the agenda for this evening .

CHAPTER FOUR

David's old Toyota truck hurried through the maze of ruts and holes littering the dirt track to the Old Fort Restaurant. After a few more rattling bumps, the now not-so-clean, white pickup pulled to rest at what once had been a far outpost of the British Empire on Carriacou's southeast side. Four rusting cannons lay nestled into concrete and stone carriages on each side of the small fort. Bland, maroon paint covered what wasn't constructed of visible, raw stone. Above the open gate, carved into a keystone, was the date 1787.

Sitting on a high promontory point, extending into the reef-lined bay, this blockhouse had successfully guarded the eastern plantations. The indigo dye that had been processed nearby needed protection from the marauding Dutch and the despicable French. These four large guns could propel shots in every direction, far beyond the barrier reef. Such a bastion, so far from the homes of the defenders, must have meant either adventure or disaster for the soldiers.

A few years before, David had visited the Old Fort with a wedding party. Then, it had been an English pub with a West Indian kitchen. At that time, a cranky old Brit named Austin owned it. He had inherited the property (and all of its problems) from a seafaring uncle who had bought it at the end of the Second Great War. Austin only permitted English or Irish ballads as background music. Calypso or modern rock and roll songs were strictly forbidden. Knowing only the groom and a few people at the festivity, David had spent much of the afternoon enjoining the barkeep in conversation. Austin, then visibly in his sixties, said little except to complain about his unlucky lot of Caribbean life.

The grizzled chap stood only five-feet tall, with a full head of gray hair, and a vicious scar on his right cheek. His wife at that time, which was five or six years ago, descended from a prominent island family who boasted land wealth rather than physical beauty. His recollection of the alcohol-fogged discussion was that Austin seemed miserable. Despair enveloped him like a pitiful cloud. Over rums he told of his marriage to the young, demure, native girl whose personality had become increasingly aggressive, until she finally ruled the domain. According to Austin, he had two possible methods by which he could escape the friction of his tumultuous household. He could either buy reconciliation with his wife, Marsha, with a posh tour of Europe, or escape alone to the South Pacific. He opted for the latter, as rumor was he disappeared on a sailboat after a drunken brawl, swearing never to return.

This night, sweet, uplifting jazz chords announced a definite change. Scented, kerosene hurricane lanterns hung on the walls. Their flames flickered to the slow rotation of ancient ceiling fans, moving the cool evening air above the twelve tables. Austin's three shelves of mirrored liquor still remained. Flat, white paint surrounded naked support timbers and beams, transforming the bar into an eighteenth century tavern.

From the swinging kitchen door emerged a twenty-first century masterpiece, Feliza. She looked even more radiant than she had on the water. Her long, gorgeous, black hair ran through the triangle of a housemaid's white scarf. A tan, below-the-knee skirt hid most of Feliza's fabulous, long legs from view. A pale blouse concealed her other attributes, which had been so evident earlier. She beamed a sincere and welcoming smile at David. She ushered him into a side room, and surprised him with a tight embrace.

"I'm glad you decided to take me up on my dinner offer," she said as she released him. "I was so afraid my stupidity this afternoon had crushed my chances of getting to know you."

"Feliza, I don't think you could drive me away unless you put me on a plane out of here. You are absolutely gorgeous. There must be a long waiting list of men who want to date you."

"Actually," she paused, cocking her head to one side and laughed, "Yes, there are, but…" she paused again, and pointed her slender hand to him. He kissed it before she replied, "none as attractive as you, Mr. David Warner. Most men here can't read, don't wash, have never owned a toothbrush, and their only desire would be to get me pregnant so they could brag about their conquest to rum-soaked friends. Now that you've heard my sermon of the mount, what can I get you to drink? Everything is on me tonight, so please, no silly masculine laments."

"Sermon of the mount," David chuckled and it stretched into a lasting smile. "Feliza, you'll probably never get an argument from me. What do you recommend? You are in total control."

"Just the way I like it." She rubbed her hands together, chose bonded bourbon, and poured it on the rocks after rimming the glass with lemon peel. "Try this. I have a confession to make; I sold the lobster to that couple — so how about conch stew after a salad of local greens? I didn't think you would mind, seeing how you're an expert diver and all. You can get another bug anytime — and I'll even cook it at your place."

Half of the restaurant's tables filled while David sat and enjoyed the bourbon. This was undoubtedly the busiest nightspot on the island. The dinner was delicious, but he consumed it slowly as he observed Feliza occupying herself as both bartender and waitress. Occasionally, she would catch his eye with a smile to check that everything was alright. Only her company would have made him happier. With a sinking feeling, he realized she'd be busy until everyone had left. He could count his late nights during the last months in Carriacou on one hand. Another drink arrived as he finished the meal.

"Sorry we're so popular tonight, but it's government fortnight pay. Usually we serve four to six tables by eight and then have dinner after Auntie clears the kitchen. Locals don't come here to drink since we charge five dollars for a beer. What else can I get for you? How about some banana flan for desert?" Feliza leaned over and cleared the table.

"Coffee and conversation would be great."

She removed the dishes from the other tables and wrote the tabs even before customers requested. Just as the ice was about gone from his drink, his wish for company was answered. Bringing a tray with coffee to the bar, Feliza filled two brandy glasses. "Now, you have to be patient for conversation until my aunt finishes readying the kitchen for tomorrow. Auntie likes to make her cabbage salad at least a day before it's served. How did you like the conch stew?"

"Everything was delicious. Now, tell me about you. How long have you been on the island? I've never seen you out anywhere." David sipped his coffee and watched as Feliza took off her scarf, taking time to brush a few tangles from her hair.

She grabbed his hand and brought her brandy glass to meet his. "Here's to Carriacou and new friends. I returned from the United States about two months ago for rest and relaxation after six hectic years in California. I'll probably go back when things here get unbearably boring again."

The kitchen door swung open, and the romantic mood dissolved. Aunt Bernadette strolled to the table, carrying her dinner. She was heavy, with arms like most women's thighs, yet carried herself gracefully. From the bar, she filled a glass with brandy. "Hello, I'm Bernie. You must be the man this girl has been blabbing 'bout all day long."

She stared at David while she consumed her dinner. "Pure divine luck to have this child back home, where she belongs. She brings light to the darkness, but you know that already, or you wouldn't be here." Bernadette laughed and gulped at her brandy in good form. "You might have known my sister, Marsha. This was her place until that skinny runt Austin gave her a gloom-and-doom perspective. I'm running it until she decides to return from Florida. Luckily, my niece had some money, and we used it to wipe away all traces of that British runt. That Austin was some piece of work."

Feliza was rubbing her bare foot up the inside of David's leg. He sipped his drink and tried to conceal his arousal as Bernadette reduced the pile of food. "Girl, what you doing to this poor man? What will he think of you? Although, if I had seen him first, I'd be fighting to get to the porch swing out back."

"Whatever are you talking about, Auntie?" Feliza replied in a voice characteristic of the deep southern United States. She batted her long lashes, smiled, and replied in the same tone, "Well Auntie, if it is privacy you want, you shall have it." She grabbed her drink, pulling David onto his feet and towards the rear door.

Bernadette burped lightly, wiped her mouth and laughed. "Now you two children behave. Don't do anything I wouldn't do — and just remember, I got grown kids!"

Her laughter was overrun by the sound of a TV newscaster as they closed the heavy, planked door and were surrounded by the starry night. Feliza abruptly pulled down on David's hand. When he turned, she planted an assertive kiss, dead center. Not used to aggressive women, he froze — but quickly warmed as her tongue began to probe his lips. David's arms encircled her and pulled her snug, dropping his right hand to push slightly on her beautiful butt. He pushed their middles together. By her reactions, he knew she could feel the effect she was having on him. Everything was quiet except for their heated breathing.

He inhaled sharply as she pushed her hand between them, and began to fondle his very evident bulge. Feliza pulled her lips away and whispered, "I'm sure every girl would say this, but I'm not usually this way. I've been living like a nun since I got here and you seem like you could use a little stimulation." She squeezed and then took to stroking. "Maybe I should stop?"

Coughing to clear his throat, David replied, "Be careful of where you want this to end — otherwise you might just over stimulate."

"I know exactly where I want this to lead." Feliza pushed him back onto the swing and sat across his lap, positioning herself so she could easily pull down his zipper and unleash his point of pleasure. "It's time to ask that important question." She breathed heavily as she licked his ear. "Do you have protection? Are you a Boy Scout? Prepared?"

"In my wallet." David moved, but her hand was already at his back pocket. After finding the condom, she brought the packet to her teeth and ripped it open, never pausing her tantalizing strokes. While he was fitted, he explored under the long skirt to discover no panties, just smooth skin. David wondered if this was planned.

She moaned and bit his shoulder as he touched her wetness. He probed with his finger while Feliza rotated her hips. Finally, she moved slightly and as they were joined, they both groaned. "Fuck me slowly, Mr. David Warner," she whispered, "You'll never know how much I need this."

"Me too," was all David could reply before she began to really grind. This was no lovey-dovey encounter, just pure sex. And it wasn't the mechanical version either. After three virtually continuous sessions, they parted with a seething 'see you soon' kiss.

David barely pulled into his parking area and straggled into the house before his eyelids closed. He awoke to the late morning light with a grin planted on his face. Feliza's scent and taste still unmistakable. He brought a pot of coffee to the boat builders. Bill and three men were using stainless steel screws to secure the planking to the ribs. While they mixed their coffee to the correct shade of light brown, David inspected the fastenings.

Bill followed, waiting for a response. "So, everything okay, Mr. SP?

Me following yous instructions to predrill each screw hole, and then making a countersink so we can putty over screw heads, like you want."

David walked on, leaving Bill in a quandary.

"Yous all okie-dokie, boss? Yous just walking like yous on air or something. Never see you sleep so sound. That boy made us the first batch of coffee this morn and he say yous sleeping on de couch just smiling with your arms crossed like you hugging something. Maybe time yous find something real, warm en soft to hug up for a while."

Without turning, David replied, "Maybe I already have? Everything looks good. Drive the screws slowly so the Phillips heads don't get torn up. Okay? If you don't need anything from town, I'm going out diving."

"Everything is cool here, SP. We gots enough fasteners to build this and the next one. Planking is going on smooth. Reese is starting to pound caulk between the boards. So, you gonna look for that pot of gold? Take a look round Indigo Bay. Years ago, me hear one guy saying he found a big anchor that could hold his boat in a big swell. We was drinking rum, and me asks him about how big it was. He say that it would stay where it was, 'cause nobody could pull it up. Something put that on me mind yesterday."

"Indigo Bay is inside the reef. How would an anchor from the Century end up inside, if the storm drove it onto the outside of the reef? Strange." David mused. "Thanks Bill — I'll take a look. Do you remember the man's name?"

"That was Sonny, Sonny James." Bill answered. "He used to fish here, but think he moved to Brooklyn in past years. He told me 'bout this maybe ten, fifteen years ago. Then me was rummed up, and it didn't cross me as belonging to the wreck we had looked for. Anyhow, me wasn't diving no more by then, 'specially after Raymond died. There'll probably be someone around there that can tell you where Sonny kept his boat."

"Good, Bill. I'll head directly there and have a look. Keep thinking about the wreck. I'm putting some effort into discovering the entire story. I'll keep you posted, but — and this is a big but — don't repeat anything I tell you. Don't mention a thing, even to Cecilia. From there it would be all over the island. I think there are a few others around here who know of the wreck story too — and I'll bet they'd be interested in finding it first."

Bill looked at David curiously and said very seriously, in a whisper, "Me know how to keep me mouth shut. Me also know why yous grinning.

Don't you trust a sweet thing either, not with this real private information. Watch out, young man."

After loading his dive gear, David headed for the southeast part of the reef. The sea inside the coral barrier was usually calm, but today the surface was like glass. Without the white line of the reef breaking, the blues of the sky and sea merged. The skiff planed without problems, and the ride only took twenty minutes.

Indigo Bay got its name from the indigo dye factory that produced the main cash crop in Carriacou's early days. A stone levy, that centuries before must have led to a dock, still remained. In the bush, far behind a small cluster of fisherman's homes, lay the extensive ruins of the plantation. Two small canoes were anchored off the beach with landlines attached to nearby palms. David anchored Dolly and swam ashore. If he could find an old timer whose wits hadn't been rummed out, it would save some time.

He followed a path through the dense bush. The foliage cleared as an odor announced a pigsty. Four large, white pigs with long floppy ears lulled in wet, sandy shade. None moved beyond a switch of their tails. As there was little moisture, the swine looked clean and behaved like lazy dogs. Beyond the pigpen sat a small house sided in cedar shake and trimmed with recently painted, ornate, gingerbread trim. It had maybe three rooms — yet from the noise, it sounded as if there were a crowd of people inside. The path led around the outhouse to the front entry. As he turned the corner, he encountered an assembly of about ten, small, preschool children. All the children wore the same faded-yellow T-shirts with a Seventh Day Adventist Church School logo. Two matrons held either end of a clothesline, teaching the children to jump rope. David coughed to be noticed.

"Yes, can I help you?" the older of the two women asked. She was a very slight woman with almost white hair.

"Well, yes. I'm sorry to interrupt, but I'd like to meet someone who remembers Sonny James. I'm told he was a fisherman from this village."

The slighter woman shielded her eyes from the sun to get a better view of David's face. She asked, "What you want with Arthur? That's his Christian name, Arthur James. I'm his sister, Ursula, and this is Daisy. This is our school," she said proudly, "to care for the younger children so both parents can work. You know how things are these days. People don't have enough money for what they want."

"Or they wanting too much," sister Daisy continued in a very delicate voice. The two women dropped the rope, permitting the children to chase each other in raucous play, while their instructors enjoyed a conversation with the stranger.

"Oh, it's nothing much. My name is Warner. I'm having a boat built in Eastern. The boat builder told me Sonny — or rather Arthur — used to talk about having his fishing boat tied to a really big anchor. I thought perhaps I could buy it from his relatives. That is, if Arthur isn't coming back?"

"Oh, Arthur won't be back, not to fish anyway. He got himself diabetes real bad. What a shame! But I don't know much about the anchor you're looking for. Arthur always kept his boat right off what's left of the stone jetty, to the south, behind the small point where our family lived. It should be almost directly behind this place. What did you say your name was?" She cupped her hand to her ear.

He raised his voice to be heard over the noise from the children. "Warner, David Warner. Bill Steward is building a sailboat for me."

"Ah, Billy Steward, our daddy fished with his daddy years ago." Ursula looked at her friend Daisy and sighed, "Seems as if everything was years ago." She paused and shushed the children. "We have to give these kids another hour of religion — so, if you will excuse us. But look out there, just inside the point."

David returned to Dolly and slowly motored to the darker water that denoted sea grass, where conch thrived. He hoped that the grass had always been here and was not a recent change in the marine environment. If the bottom had originally been sand, then the anchor might be covered over with growth. However, iron rusting underwater usually kills surrounding vegetation. For an hour he wore his dive mask — and kept sticking his head in the water from the dinghy. He ran four searches, both north to south and east to west, without success. Donning a tank, he stuck the dive flag in the oarlock and went down the anchor line. The water was crystal clear — and according to the dive computer, only about twenty-feet deep. Instead of just a depth gauge, the small computer told depth, how long it was safe to stay submerged, and how slowly to come up.

Adjusting his compass, David headed east into deeper water. Luckily, he had brought a net bag and was able to grab some mature conch for appetizers later. If this action with Feliza continued, he would need all the protein he could find. Swimming along the grassy bottom, Feliza occupied his thoughts. What a lucky discovery he'd made on Carriacou.

After a half-hour swim, David was only in thirty-five feet, and the sea grass was fading to barren sand. In the final few feet of grass, a coral-encrusted circle caught his eye. It was about a foot-and-a-half in diameter, the ring of an old anchor. He sat on the bottom, and took off a fin to brush away the sand. A little effort revealed a massive, eight-foot-long anchor. Surfacing, David took three compass bearings and wrote them on a dive slate so that he could easily return to the site. Things were looking better and better.

His thoughts were split between Feliza and the anchor during the slow boat ride back to Eastern Bay. Returning to the mooring, David found the boys still busy on Summer Breeze.

"Bill, I located what we'd talked about, but there is nothing to prove it comes from the wreck. Since it's close to the indigo factory dock, it could be from one of the trading ships that carried the dye to Europe. All I've found is an anchor. It's something, but it doesn't point directly, or indirectly, anywhere." David handed two conchs to him for his family.

Bill looked at him and said, "Damn straight, it points to de boat we'se looking for. Now, if yous was an experienced sea captain who wants remain a captain of a good ship, why anchor a big boat dere, when in closer there was a dock to tie alongside? Those days was no different than these. If there was a boat on the dock, then the other boat would have to wait. Not there, but on the leeward side, 'case a blow come up. Wasn't like this was busy Barbados, or St. Thomas; there wasn't many ships calling on this rock. Those trading ships off- loaded goods they carried from Europe in the protection of Western Bay. When the dye was packaged up to load, they come over here, get in, and get out soon as possible. Me know 'cause that's the way it still being done."

"Bill, it is a possibility, but until we find some positive proof, we'll be chasing everything, everywhere. Thanks for remembering this."

"Me know that it seem strange the wreck's anchor is inside the reef, but a huge wave could carry it over. Not real likely, but could happen. No old wood around it? We both seen the ocean do some unexpected shows of strength. Right SP?" Bill was happily shuffling his bare feet. "Nows maybe yous search inside of the bay, huh?"

"No, nothing but the anchor and it's pointing to the reef. We can't jump to any conclusions. I'm going to do some more research first." David checked the day's progress and showered, hoping to catch Mike Post before he left school.

\\\\\\\\

The computer monitor held Mike's attention while David quietly entered the classroom.

"I know you're there so don't try to play any surprise games. You forget, David, I must observe forty or more students, seven hours a day, five days a week." Without moving his eyes from the screen, he pulled his ponytail and said, "There are two more eyes under this. That's why I don't cut it. Anything new and exciting to report?"

David's thoughts immediately returned to Feliza, but she wasn't Mike's business. He'd learned from experience that pretty women, and the envy of those without, can jeopardize business arrangements and friendships. He quickly filled Mike in on the other events.

"Yes, that does sound promising, but you're correct. Until we find something that positively identifies the wreck, we're still searching. Couple that anchor with the carving on the boulder behind the indigo factory, it starts to get interesting. Oh, by the way, we haven't received anything from your contact in Washington."

"It will come; Amy is very dedicated."

"Dedicated? It didn't sound like dedication over the phone last night to me. It sounded like affection to the degree of affliction. Look, I'm almost finished here — so why don't you give me a ride to my home where we can share a few cold brews? That way, you'll know where I live and we can formulate our strategy."

David's thoughts drifted again to his mystery woman. He decided calling her could wait. All that about 'absence and the heart' has been time proven. Besides, Feliza had the upper hand, and he could contact her tomorrow. "Sure, Mike, since we're partners now, we ought to get to know each other."

He paused and laughed. "That is, if you ever get to really know anything other than what people want you to learn? Well mate, twist my arm after I've tipped a few, and I'll tell you anything," he paused again, "but not everything. Hah!"

On the drive through Mt. Pleasant, David bought a pair of sixes — and in a matter of minutes opened two to sip as they drove. He was directed to take a shore-side left. After a few jolts and a couple of clatters, the truck pulled in front of a nicely painted sign that read: 'MIKE POST'S OUTPOST — If you are not invited — stay away!' Mike stepped out of the pickup and unlocked the chain gate.

"Really trying to entice visitors, I see." The driveway made a sharp turn to Mike's homestead. David laughed. "You are really something."

"First thing I learned was never spend twice for what you already bought once." Mike rested the package of beers on the hood as he opened another. His house was different because it had begun its existence as his boat. "Yes, that's the girl that planted me here on this beautiful isle. I bought her after dropping out of the business community in the States. You know, I was a charter member of the young and upwardly mobile, soon to be deeper in debt with greater addictions' club." He gulped from the bottle and wiped his mouth. "Yeah, come on in. In another half an hour the mosquitoes will be on us. This lot is kind of low and after last month's rains, the little buzzers are being pesky. Better roll up your truck's windows."

He led the way to a screened entry. His boat, a sloop, had been hauled on shore about two hundred meters and buried in the earth to its waterline. It was an ultimate statement of a sailor who was truly landlocked. Mike held the door as David entered the patio. Beyond, after three steps, was a curved entry door cut amidships, between two ribs. The hatch opened upwards on a double pulley mechanism mounted above to the end of the mast's boom. They each took nicely upholstered seats cut from old rum barrels.

"You're probably thinking you've gotten yourself involved with a demented old man who resides in a true houseboat. Really, it's one of the sanest things I've ever done. Please sit, and a bit later I'll give you the grand, two-minute tour." Mike lit an oil lamp suspended from a porch rafter. He opened another beer. "It isn't often I get company."

"With a sign like that and the chain, I can see why."

"Oh, that's to insure privacy. If the locals here like you, they can disturb you at any hour they feel is reasonable. As I'm considered to be one of the 'haves' among a multitude of 'have nots', they were always over here, chatting, borrowing, or nosing around. Finally, I painted the sign and decided it wouldn't do any good if they couldn't read. So, I started teaching them." He laughed heartily, "Besides, I had to do something to keep all those sweet young things away from ruining my good reputation."

The inside of the patio had shelves filled with plants, antique bottles, and pieces of encrusted iron, including a few cannon balls. In one corner was a small pile of rocks sitting on a bigger rock. Mike caught David's glance.

"Ah, that's an Indian grist mill — or mortar — for pounding cassava or grain — if they were lucky enough to have it. I found all of these artifacts on Carriacou. The Indians must have had an idyllic life before the curse of the Europeans befell them. I found all of it here when I dug this hole for my boat. About a hundred yards to the west, there's a natural well in the cleft of some boulders that I'll show you sometime. It's been used since before Columbus. That's why I chose to live at this location. It is timeless."

"Yes, it is very nice."

"You seeing something that I don't? Very nice! Well, enough of the false sentiments!" Mike's mood took a mean swing. "Hell, I don't need to be told I'm living okay. I know I'm scrimping, and have to scratch for everything." He slammed his beer onto a wooden cable spool that was his patio table. "Well, I got fed up with false sentiments and gracious comments when I worked in New York, selling advertising. All advertising does is tell you to use, to discard, and to buy more. After a few good solid commissions, my conscience wasn't into the game of success anymore. I bought this wooden fifty-footer and renamed her 'OUTPOST'. Unfortunately, I didn't really save enough to live in the style to which I was accustomed. Nobody ever realizes how much money it takes just to cruise around and be lazy."

"Maybe I can learn something from your experience — as I'm about to begin a similar venture."

"Stop with the patronizing remarks! You can only see the error of a middle-aged man's ways," Mike said and ushered David into the boat. He switched on the lights to reveal a beautiful interior. "Outpost was just starting to rot. Hell, I bought her after seven years in the water and sailed her for another ten before realizing that I'd either have to replace the bottom, or lose the boat. I stayed on Carriacou for two years because it was the least expensive, least repulsive place. I had just enough cash remaining to buy this lot. Other than some labor, and the hire of a big tractor truck, the transformation from salty dog to landlubber was easy. And I didn't waste a thing."

A nice galley was preceded by a good-sized salon with a dining table. Beyond the galley was a spacious stern cabin. Screened ports provided a fresh breeze. Mike's neatness surprised David. Usually bachelors, who aren't expecting visitors, tend to not keep a place tidy. Amy had once mentioned that most bachelors have an order unto themselves. The bow revealed the head and shower alongside another large berth.

"I just dug the hole for the keel and another for the septic. She catches water from the patio roof, the decks, and the rear shed, which you haven't seen yet. With a wind genny and back up diesel genset, I've still got cold beer and pressure water." Mike opened his cold-box door and placed the remainder of the beer inside, removing two that were much colder. He directed David to the built-in couches on either side of the salon's table. Mike walked over to what had been the navigation station across from the galley and turned on some classical music, quite low. "Yes, all the comforts of home."

"This is very nice. You've got a good set-up." David's gaze spanned the shelves of treasure-hunting books and artifacts that bordered the cabin. "Have you ever been successful in finding any treasure?"

"Yes…I'm here. That's a treasure unto itself." Mike imitated a staunch British accent. "Hell, matey, I didn't even care about looking seriously when I had the money to do it. Seems that when you have money, you don't have time, and when you have time, you don't have money." He opened a small cabinet behind the couch, where David was sitting, and removed a coffee can to dump the contents on the table. He picked through the pile and selected a few coins.

Holding one, he explained, "This is a silver Spanish Cob dollar from 1715. I found it metal detecting along the dock in Western Bay. This one is a Dutch guilder, and these are early English shillings. In the old days, seamen would accumulate various monies visiting different countries. When they beached a boat in heavy surf, or were intoxicated, all types of money fell out of their pockets. What about you? Have you ever searched for treasure before?"

"Obviously not." David shifted his posture, rummaging through the rest of the can's contents. "Perhaps I can use some of the same skills that helped me locate some lunk who stole a payroll."

Mike cut him off, "Sounds like the opening line of a job application. But are you hungry or desperate? I think not. Treasure hunting is passion taken to obsession — and it's an art form. Today, we could almost call it a science. But you have to want to find it." He pulled three books from the shelf and retrieved a plastic Ziploc bag from a drawer. "Promise to keep these nice and dry, always in this bag, and you can take these with you. This one has some info on the Century. These two are mostly history books pertaining to the Grenadines. I've tried to pinpoint the hurricane that put the Century to her grave, but there seems to be none recorded for that year. However, it could have been overlooked."

He relaxed and finished his beer. Checking David's, Mike brought two more from the cold-box. "You are a quiet one, Mr. Warner. What's your story? The abridged version only, if you please."

"I'm not much of a talker, especially about myself. It comes from being in the service. I went in at seventeen as an insecure farm boy out to see what was beyond the mailbox at the end of our driveway. My father taught me there was more to be learned from listening than from spouting off. I watched the other swabbies getting into fights from making their views and opinions public. When the time came, if asked, I had an answer, but that's about as far as it went. Once I got into the Shore Patrol, I became even more tight-lipped. We were not well liked by the enlistees." David paused to guzzle the remainder of his bottle and belch. Mike watched him intently. "A few years ago, I started feeling left behind from the rest of the human experience. The farm had controlled my adolescence, and the Navy had directed me as they saw fit. It seemed I'd never had a chance to be myself." David tilted the bottle again to discover only drips.

"Hold on, I think we have another round." Mike was beginning to slur his words.

"As I was saying," David took another beer from his host, "I feel that I've never been in control of my own fate. If I would've stayed with the Navy, I knew my life would be prescribed, and my future dictated. I'd marry the admiral's daughter, do another ten years duty at least, and then I'd retire to private consulting work, but still on a government agency's payroll. Now, if I have a boat, I'm in total control. It is only me, David Warner, against the elements. Yah-hoo!" David laughed and toasted Mike.

"Yeah," Mike interjected, "against the wind, sea, and peril of the rocks. Except now you have a little time to play around with treasure hunting."

David told Mike what had befallen Bill. "What happened may have been coincidental. Bill searched with Worely. Others may think he knows more, especially if they are willing to strong arm him. So we should watch our backs and always remember to check if someone is watching. Trouble is, while I'm diving the reef, my boat can be seen from almost anywhere on the hillside."

"We can't be paranoid. That was a word dedicated to the late sixties." Mike toasted his brown bottle to the air. "We are now well over the famed millennium. Paranoia does not belong. 'Big Brother' has been around long enough to get his pension, and I know him well." Mike burped, sat the beer down, and began to clean his glasses. "Are you going to dive again tomorrow?"

"Well yes, I'm definitely pumped up by finding the anchor, but I don't think there's any way in hell this anchor belongs to the Century. That close to shore? No, the ship would have splintered on the broad reef. The anchor would be one of the first things to sink. Nevertheless, I'm going to drift through that area tomorrow."

"Give your Navy honey a call if she doesn't check in, alright? Give her the weekend, and a couple of days to sort out the info. The list that I emailed was extensive, but I did include sources where she could begin her research. We don't want to irritate her, do we?" Mike rested his bearded chin on his hands. "I usually have Sunday free to snorkel search — and my old frame could use some exercise. However, I already made plans for tomorrow before we met yesterday. Next week I don't have Computer Club. It meets every other Sunday afternoon — so the students and their benefactor can try to gain a semblance of a life beyond the classroom. Then I could help with the actual search."

"Part of this mystery is the lack of info on the storm," Mike continued. "By 1699, there was reasonably good record-keeping. The British had Drake and Hawkins wreaking havoc on the Spanish settlements since 1570. There has to be a mention of a hurricane of the strength that could lift a three-masted schooner over thirty yards of reef."

"Could have been a freak storm that accelerated in this vicinity and then ran out over the sea to the west. One place, almost uninhabited, gets hit hard. Who's going to tell about it if they were lucky enough to live through it?" David surmised. "You're right; the storm or rather, the wreck's cause is the story. Zane and the crew, you say, were well accomplished. Unless it was pitch black and storming, how could they have hit such a visible reef?"

"Especially when they were supposed to disembark passengers and cargo at Barbados, which they would've had to pass about a hundred miles east of here. I think the only solution is Mother Nature's fury. An incredibly violent storm, the Century is blown far off course, and all persons vanish. Except some of the crew are discovered alive, and hung at the gallows. Facts may not substantiate that. Barbados was settled in 1627 and should have a record of every storm. There was one recorded hurricane, about a month earlier. The Century should still have been in Europe." Mike chatted as he grabbed the last two beers from the cold-box. "So, they were shipwrecked and picked up by pirates? That's a possibility, but they would definitely know where the wreck of the Century lies. Why not go back and salvage, as they couldn't have been rescued very far away? I'll bet they made it to the beach just beyond the wreck."

"Probably," David answered. "If they had salvaged the mysteriously valuable strong boxes, then why were they still robbing ships, risking being hung?"

"Greed," Mike returned. "Same as us. Never changes. If we find this, we'll probably search for more."

"Whoa there. You maybe, but not me. I'm off to sail the Caribbean with no definite direction known."

"That's what I said when I dropped out, but here I am," Mike spread his arms and slowly turned, "about as landlocked as a sailor can get. Carriacou is a wonderfully slow, beautifully boring existence. You should keep an open mind about making a bit of this paradise your home base. Hell, do what I do: subscribe to the book and CD of the month club. Those with a couple of magazines, which are at least two weeks old by the time they arrive, and you can almost get a handle on how crazy the mainstream world really is. To that, I could no longer adapt."

"Well, I like this small island — but I believe occasionally I'd need more stimulation," David said as he tried to raise himself from the comfortable, padded-canvas bench.

"What type of stimulation are you in need of that you cannot discover on this beautiful island? I'll admit that female stimulation is mostly native, but these women are very capable and pliable. Try one, you might just like it. It isn't like they require a license, or even a courtship. These women are true hedonists. You work hard all day in the garden, and I'll bet TV isn't the most satisfying escape. Get yourself a maid — and I do mean get her." He lit a small, foul-smelling cigarette and inhaled deeply. "It's not what you think, not ganja. Contrary to my teaching contract, I have been known to infrequently partake of the local, home-grown herbalists' remedy for a sore head or lack of appetite." He pointed the cigarette towards David. "These are made from cloves, supposedly non-addictive smokes. I quit those cancer sticks years ago, yet still occasionally crave warm smoke, especially when I'm imbibing. But, back to what we were talking about — stimulation and sex is available on the Internet. Movies, pen pals, research, novels…and if that isn't enough, get a satellite dish and really stay in touch with the issues facing this nutty world."

He rose as Mike threw his bottle into the trash bin. "I've got to get going. This is the most I've... imbibed...in quite a while."

Mike groaned as he pulled himself out from behind the table. "See there? I've stimulated your vocabulary already." He clasped his arm over David's shoulder as they entered the patio. "My advice to cut the unstimulating boredom is to get a local honey sweet on you. Believe me; I wasn't kidding about being hounded by the local women... and the girls." Mike grinned. "Don't get more than one though, or you won't have enough energy to get out there and dive."

"Okay, okay, Professor Post. Do you want to warn me about STD's and contraception?" He shook Mike's hand as he leaned on the side of the truck. "Well, Mike, now I know where you live..."

"Call first. Always call first. Never know what I might be doing."

"I didn't realize that you had a phone here. What's the number?"

"I don't have a phone at this humble abode, only at the school. But call or stop by after classes, and we'll make some plans for searching."

Nodding, David started the truck as he thought of following Mike's advice for stimulation. He wasn't thinking of the Net, or a satellite dish.

After five or six beers, his thoughts came from his loins, and were centered on Feliza.

\\\\\\\\

David was shocked to see the lights were on in his cottage. As he started to park, he saw that the front door he'd deliberately shut was wide open. Instead of stopping, he drove on a hundred yards and pulled off the road. Since Bill's encounter with the cigarette and chewing gum pair, his main defense was a two-foot-long piece of thick, steel construction rod beneath his truck seat. It could be considered a deadly weapon by the local constabulary, but it could also be explained as a part for his boat, or his truck's jack handle. The rod's surface was crisscrossed with raised webbing, which would leave a tell-tale welt on its victim.

Expecting to find his place dark, empty, and ransacked, he did a quick surveillance along the outside perimeter and quietly peered in the living room window. Everything was in the same condition as when he left. He entered through the back door, quietly passing through the kitchen to the dark bedroom. There was no one, or any disarray visible until he turned on the bedside lamp.

There was a sizable lump in the middle of his queen-size bed. Feminine clothes were neatly arranged on the room's only chair. As he pulled down the light cotton blanket, a shock of hair suddenly turned to look up at him.

"Feliza! You gave me quite a start," David gasped. "You're quite a nice surprise, but what are you doing here?"

She stretched and looked at her watch, "It's eleven at night — and you are supposed to be a policeman. Why would you ask such a stupid question, Mr. Warner?"

"Feliza, call me David."

"I'll call you David, or anything else you want me to, as soon as you put down that length of pipe."

He realized he'd been in a Mark McGuire stance, holding the steel rod as if ready to hit number seventy. "Oh, sure," he agreed as he sat on the edge of the bed and stashed the bar underneath. "Now, what are you doing here?"

"Well, David," she pulled herself up towards the bamboo headboard and made it evident that nothing concealed her beautiful features, "If I have to tell you what possibilities exist between two consenting adults, then I guess I came to the wrong man's house. Maybe you want me to leave?"

"No, absolutely not," He coughed to clear a slightly nervous throat, "I can't imagine a better surprise, but with Billy Steward getting roughed up a bit on his boat the other night, I wasn't sure what to expect when I saw a light on."

"So, all the hard core criminals of Carriacou leave the lights on to commit burglaries?" She reached out and grabbed David's thigh where his shorts ended, pushing her slender hand up along his leg. "There's only one thing this lonely girl wants to steal from you, David." She found her goal, and gave his pride and joy a slight pull.

"I don't know what to say — except that if I had come home accompanied by another friend, this could have been risky."

Feliza searched his eyes with as lustful a look as he'd ever seen and breathlessly said, "Do you need a road map, or do I need to make an appointment? What we had last night was good. I'd already checked you out before dinner and knew that you had to either be horny, or ready to join the monastery. I called cousins and friends to find out about the handsome, white American living in Eastern. It wasn't too hard." She swayed again, "Not as hard as this. Now kiss me."

David obeyed, loosened his clothes, and crawled under the sheet. She continued, "When I meet a man with some style, who intrigues me like you do, and they seem to be free — not connected to any local women — then I set my sights." Feliza pointed to David's heart and at the same time squeezed him with her other hand, "If I don't get you one way, I'll get you the other. Am I so bad? I learned a long time ago not to let opportunities slip by because of perhaps," accented with another squeeze, "being shy."

"I promise I'll never describe you to anyone as being shy, Feliza." He stroked her hair and pulled her chin up to savor a long, wet, noisy kiss.

She pulled him to the center of the bed and sat up on top of him, in control again. "We finished early tonight...ahh," she had found the spot to couple them and began the timeless motion. "I am so bad...but damn! This is so good. Ahh!" Now riding the waves of sensual friction, "I don't have to work tomorrow," she panted, "I thought we could spend the day together."

CHAPTER FIVE

"Get out of my chair, you dumb oaf. You know that's where I always park my butt to watch good old Jimmy Kimmel. So move your arse. Now!" The short man shouted to the larger one while waving his right arm. His left was carrying two glasses of golden rum on ice. "Here you go, Tony. Don't say I never did nuthin' for you. Aye, matey, but you can't have my seat. My back's bad, you know. Take your grog now, like a good soldier."

The big man put his weight to his calves, collapsed the footrest, and rolled out of the white vinyl convertible chair. He leaned to his right side as he rose, farted loudly, and threw up his middle finger to his mouthy associate, Palmer. Tony lay on the floor and stretched out to his full, six and a half feet with clasped arms over his head as he twisted and stretched his brawny physique.

Palmer slid his wiry five-three frame into the chair and grabbed the TV's remote control. The room was sparse with only a table and two wooden chairs beside the TV. Their beds were against the other wall of the room. A hanging light with a bamboo shade reflected a puzzle of shadows on the peaked ceiling. The pale-yellow walls were bare, except for a large watercolor of a queen triggerfish between the beds. A tiny kitchen backed on an equally small bath. Tony hunkered into a crossed-leg yoga position and then grabbed his glass of rum while maintaining perfect posture.

After minutes of channel surfing, Palmer grabbed his reading glasses and checked the weekly TV listings in the local newspaper. "You can never believe this schedule, Tony. They always say, 'movie to be announced,' but there is seldom a full-length one." He gulped some rum and wiped his mouth with his ever-present handkerchief. "It's always some stupid shit, like four segments of the Jeffersons. Nig TV! No, that's not what we come to nig paradise to do." He gulped more rum and rattled the cubes. "No Jeffersons, if you please." He clicked to another, "No cricket that was played four days ago. It is the world's most boring game, and they save it for repeats at night." Another click and international news appeared. "Yep, the lap of luxury, that's where we're at. This is the only decent rental on this forlorn isle. However, it does have its own satellite dish, and we can watch almost the entire eastern coast from the balconies."

"Now we can appreciate the world's humor." Palmer paused on the news channel. "How many U.S. postal workers or high school students went amiss today with automatic weapons, huh? You know, Tony, I think you're getting less and less sociable the longer we wait for Tunaman. You never seem to be in a good mood, chum. He'll be here soon enough, though, and then we'll be out of this claptrap shack, and onto the luxury of the yacht. Tunaman's no fool. He don't spend a cent on us if he ain't here to indulge his own flabby ass. But hey, for once we are in the lap of luxury. These is the premier digs on this rock," Palmer said sarcastically. He waved both arms as he looked from the sliding glass doors on one end of the square room to the stainless steel countertop of the kitchen on the other. "Imagine that, will ya, after this deed, we can each have our own yacht with a satellite dish to get every damn channel being pumped into outer space." Palmer clicked the remote a few more times and then settled on a rerun of MASH. "Okay with you, Tony?"

Tony shrugged as he sipped his drink. Palmer rose and brought the bottle of rum to the chair to refill his drink. "You ready?"

Tony just shook his head.

From the floor, the shorter man grabbed a stream of cords and expertly wove them into a loop. "Been here over two weeks and I'm about ready to do something. Maybe we ought to go out on a sortie again tonight. A good reconnaissance mission, maybe over to that swabby's house. What you say, my friend?" He belted more rum and wiped his lips. He never watched his hands as they rhythmically moved the cord strands over and under. "We need to know as much as we can before Tunaman gets here with the big boat. He always wants to know every little, teeny-weenie detail before he does something." He gulped again. "Or rather, know everything until you and me go do it. You think he's ever done any wet work? I thought he might have done that guy over in Palau that time we got jammed up waiting for the stuff last year. Thinking back, that guy might just have had a heart attack looking at Tunaman with that shaved head of his, 'cause I don't really remember hearing a shot. Really I don't. What you think? It's always you and me at the dirty end of things, matey. The dirtiest ends we always gots to clean up, and leave it neat and quiet."

Tony shrugged again, put his glass down, pointed at the door, and shook his head to indicate that he wasn't going out. He pointed to the nearest bed and then to himself.

"So, no desire to prowl around in the bush tonight, listening to all the native girls get stupped by their fathers and brothers? Har!" Palmer laughed, coughed, and reached into his pocket for a cigarette. He lit and inhaled deeply. "You know, Tony, of all the places we ever been, Carriacou has to be the sleepiest corner I've ever seen. I love the big cities, like Tokyo, Bangkok, L.A., and New York, where something's always happening. This is like being dead and not knowing it. Thirteen-channel Sat TV for entertainment, boiled roots stewed with everything, rot-gut rum for sustenance, and just maybe throw in a fucking banana. All that, and with no ladies of the evening to relieve some of the pressure."

Tony moved his right hand up and down, pointing towards Palmer who recognized the gesture and replied with a single finger. The big man laughed hoarsely, almost gagging. Both men were in their late forties, with toned physiques. Tony's long hair was graying. He sat in the lotus position, while his thumbs traced circles on the first two fingers of his huge hands.

A tattoo of an eagle silhouette riding the number "107' encircled his wrist. It was an identification bracelet. He had well-contoured arms. His muscles didn't bulge — but instead rippled every time he reached for his melting drink.

"You'd think Tunaman could have told us a bit more about this assignment. Here we sit with four thumbs up our arses, waiting to hear about his graciousness's purpose and goal. All we know is that the old boat builder knew something about a shipwreck and his only possible consort is the recently retired swabby, the guy he's building a boat for. That old nig didn't tell us word-one. You put him to the test. Yes you did, Tony. If he'd have known, he'd have damn well spit it out when you was standing on his back. Har! Your big foot almost squashed the old nig like a cockroach." Palmer stubbed out the short butt, resting it in a bowl that overflowed with the like. He quickly lit another, and inhaled as if it were his last breath. His dark, wavy hair surrounded a pair of tortoise-shell reading glasses like a helmet. A tank top and cut-off sweat pants revealed his arms and legs had been scarred from numerous burns. "So what do you think, mate? Are we to just sit here on such a fine night and wait again for another dawn to come?"

"Damn, I wish you weren't mute! But I say that twice a day, don't I? And wish it more than that, you can be sure. Remember there used to be posters that said 'loose tongues lose ships'? Well, Tony, your tongue's out there loose on some ship! Har, har!"

The big man rose and smacked Palmer on the back of his head with a flat palm as an answer and headed for the toilet.

"Yes, Tony, these is exclusive digs on this rock. Perhaps one of the few rentals with an indoor shitter. The locals fertilize the bushes. I'd love to see one of these big mamas squatting, doing their business. Most are so big they can barely get out of a chair, let alone not soil themselves. Yes, we are swaddled in opulence."

The big man returned, wiping his hands, and swatted his cohort on the back of his head again, intending this as a good night. He straightened the rumpled sheets and crawled on the small single bed beneath the front window.

"You know, Tony, you snore like a frigging bull elephant. When you lost your tongue, they ought to have carved out those damn sinuses, adenoids, and tonsils. Then, maybe I could get a peaceful night's sleep." Palmer tipped the bottle to capture the last drops of rum. "Yes, there was a time when we both slept well. Jesus K. Christ, that was a long time back. Australia, Indonesia, Southeast Asia…they all seem like a century ago. But here we is, lovely friggin' Carriacou. The tourist pamphlet says it means 'Island of Reefs' in some god forsaken, long-forgotten Indian language. I say it means island of creeps. Yes it does, Tony; this place gives me the bejeebers."

"We being of the few with pale skin, we stick out like foxes in a hen house. It's only safe for us to reconnoiter late at night with face paint. These people who live here must not have any imaginations; otherwise, how could they not want to be somewhere else?" A blunt snore from Tony signaled the end of the conversation. "I must say that you are one lucky fellow. Yes you are, Tony, to be able to sleep deeply after all we've been through." Palmer swirled his last portion of diluted rum and gulped. "Yes, Tony, you are a lucky one. I'm always listening for footsteps coming from the shadows. Once we gets squared up, again, I might even go back for one of those puffed- up bastards who did us so much damage. You sleep well, my friend, while I try to relax."

\\\\\\\\

David slept with Feliza in his arms. Suddenly, his fantasy of retirement had become reality. He was on a tropical island with a beautiful woman in his bed. Everything that had occurred the past few days was exciting. Why him? He couldn't shake that thought. Not the type of guy who thinks negatively, but he was a realist. From between his ears came 'why ask why.'

Since he'd moved permanently to the tropics, morning had become his favorite piece of the day. It used to be the absolute pits, waiting until lunch, sitting behind a gray desk in a pressed khaki uniform. Here, the temperature rises quickly — and if the breeze dies it can get damn uncomfortable and unproductive. The morning is always cool around the first pink light. The usual morning ritual begins with coffee and exercise, but that morning he indulged in his very favorite activity. His touch startled Feliza momentarily — but after a short gasp she moved back against him, opened her eyes, and smiled over her shoulder. Coffee came later.

"Well, that's one thing we don't have in common," she murmured. "I am definitely not a morning person. I've always liked to rest after such a strenuous night. And today is my day off. Auntie probably wonders where I am. She always expects me to be on the pew beside her in church." She hugged him again. Her beauty was dramatic in the soft sunlight. Dark curls dangled long past her elbows and shielded her eyes.

"I don't want to break your heart, but I'd hoped to go do a few dives today."

"Now I understand why you are alone. You're too stupid to realize a good thing when it's right in your bed." Feliza kept her face pointed to the sunrise through the window.

David countered, "Let me finish. I'd like nothing better than for you to join me. But there's absolutely no rush."

"Smart guy." She rolled onto his lap, threw her arms around his neck, and began to lick his ear. "Let's go back to sleep and be lazy today."

He was a smart guy; at least that's how he'd always thought of himself. They snuggled into the late morning — and then he made omelets to replenish their energy. It was almost noon before Dolly was loaded with diving equipment.

"At least with you along today, I don't have to worry about my boat disappearing."

"Oh, so that's why you're permitting me to tag along, to be your boat keeper? Hey, I'm trained in scuba. Don't you have an extra setup for me? I thought we were buddies." She punched his shoulder, "Dive buddies?" She looked ready to dive wearing a small, sparkling white bikini she had taken from her shoulder bag. "I really don't need to work on my tan, or hadn't you noticed."

David remembered Bill's warning not to tell anyone, especially a woman, about the search — as David crawled into the storage space and retrieved the other BC, regulator, and mask. "Fins may be a problem, Feliza. All I have are size nines and you have such slender, beautiful legs." He said, running his hand across her thighs.

"If you'd have mentioned diving, I would've brought my fins and mask. You don't know much about island girls, do you?" She pushed his hand away and tried on one of the yellow swim fins.

"But I'm sure you're going to teach me. I promise to be an avid pupil," David said, smiling.

"Well as unladylike as it sounds, we island babes have bigger-than-usual feet. Comes from walking barefoot for centuries, cutting cane, and carrying lots of heavy babies. Second, I swim every day. I could probably out swim you, with or without fins," she boasted while pulling the fin off. It was too big, but this time he responded to his better judgment and said nothing.

"Do you have a pair of athletic socks? I think that'd make these fit," she asked.

They loaded a small cooler with frozen water bottles from David's sparsely-laden fridge. "You really are a bachelor," Feliza quipped. "Not enough here to keep you alive for more than a day. How do you get by alone? You need a woman to take care of you. And I could be just that woman."

"Are you applying for a position to be filled?" he asked.

"I think by now I've been filled in almost every position," she laughed. "But really, you ought to have more than beer, soda, white bread, and cheese for staples."

From the cabinet above the sink David pulled out soy sauce, hot green oriental mustard, a bag of crackers, and a bottle of Chardonnay.

"I am corrected." She sat at the table and read the wine label. "Maybe you're more resourceful than I'd thought. With some luck, we can have a first-rate sashimi lunch out on little Sandy Island." She stood, reached her arms around his neck, and kissed him passionately.

"I'm sure I was wrong about your resourcefulness."

\\\\\\\\

They headed to the east, through the reef's central passage. The sun blazed as David explained to a beautiful, nodding, but inattentive head, where and how they would drift dive to hunt a suitable fish for dinner. He thought there was almost no chance of finding anything of the wreck, since Bill had searched the entire outside perimeter of the reef at least three times. What problems could Feliza hold for their hunt? If David saw something, he'd steer her away from the area. If she saw something, he'd downplay it as a natural rock formation. That is unless they came across cannons, anchors, or gold coins. Besides, they were only doing one dive. David didn't like to break oaths or not abide warnings, but women — specifically beautiful, lusty ones — have a way of overruling common sense. The Evinrude outboard droned out any chance of further conversation without yelling.

"Hey," Feliza pinched David's attention. "You seem like you are a million miles away. I hope you aren't feeling guilty about an old girlfriend or something." She successfully tickled his ribs. "You're wearing a stern face like you just got caught doing something naughty." She held his chin in her delicate hand. "Are you thinking naughty things, present or past?"

"No Feliza, I was only thinking how my luck has changed lately." He pecked her on the cheek. "Let's dive here." David slowed the motor and shifted into neutral as she readied the anchor.

They settled into the water and held on to the anchor rope like an elevator as they dropped through a shimmering, blue prism, down sixty feet of cool saltwater. The outside of the reef was a dramatic mix of older, dead, gray coral overgrown by new, much more colorful, vibrant varieties. Fish of all sizes, shapes, and colors darted everywhere. Descending slow enough to equalize their ears, Feliza squeezed David's hand, and pointed to a beautiful spotted eagle ray that danced a few circles before vanishing. As they reached the anchor, it was his turn to point out a harmless, six-foot nurse shark sleeping under a coral ledge. He'd expected a startled reaction from his companion, but it didn't seem to affect her as she helped him fill the lift bag.

Once the bag was full of air and the anchor slightly buoyant, they drifted quickly, watching the bottom about fifteen feet below. The current of the tide was stronger than it had been during his previous dives. It pulled them back through the cut and into the inner reef.

David knew the wreckage could be under the sand, three-hundred years' worth of living coral, or hidden by coral fragments that had been broken and piled by countless hurricanes. Using a sophisticated metal detector would be the best search tool, but equipment like that would attract too much attention on this basic island. Of course, if mounds of sand and coral buried the valuables, any recovery methods would be very conspicuous. What would it take; a crane on a barge or explosives? Neither option was very discreet. Perhaps that's why some treasures remained lost. With these questions in mind, he searched visually for a gouge in the reef where a big, heavy ship might have plowed into the coral wall. A notch from a boat's bow can remain evident for centuries. At least that's what he'd read.

The area inside the reef was usually shallow, except where the middle passage, a canyon about twenty feet deeper, was cut by timeless tides and currents like the one they were riding. David had logged a lot of dives over the years, and knew eighty feet was a dangerous depth. A diver must always consider the bends, or decompression sickness. The bends happen when a diver stays down too deep for too long — or surfaces from the deep too fast. He hadn't even thought to locate the nearest decompression chamber. They floated at sixty feet and coasted above the sandy area. They passed a few more lost, native anchors resting in the deep water before Feliza got his attention.

In the distance, almost at the sapphire edge of visibility, was a singular coral head about twenty yards in diameter. By pointing at her eyes and then at the mass, David's dive partner made it clear she wanted to explore. Kicking with the current, they maneuvered closer until they were above it. At first glance, it looked like an ordinary rock structure — but at the south end he could discern some shapes that didn't look all that natural. Two were circles that took on a different color tone than the rest of the mound. As underwater depth increases, less light can penetrate — so the color schemes change. The color red is the first to change into a muddled brown. Green is hard to distinguish, but this looked like green, the green of old brass portholes.

Feliza tugged at him, wanting to go deeper to explore. She knew enough to pull the exhaust cord on the lift bag and dropped the anchor directly on the mound. It was still early in the dive and because they were drifting, they still had almost twenty-five hundred pounds of air in their tanks. David checked her air pressure gauge, then his dive computer, and had to give the thumbs up, knowing they could remain at this depth only ten minutes longer. The area just to the west, where the current would carry them, was shallow. They could swim at thirty feet for the remainder of the dive. She turned and her white-socked ankles gave strong kicks towards the bottom. He could only follow her dark buns separated by the sparkling, white bikini.

The mound was adorned with several very mature coral heads probably a few hundred years old. A mound like this one might be composed of a couple zillion, minute, coral skeletons fused together by Mother Nature's concrete glue.

The pile's circumference made for a good swim. Its edge, bordered by sand, did not touch the steep canyon walls. The mound was elevated from the bottom, perhaps two to three feet, and covered with living, soft, waving corals. The round shapes, which had attracted Feliza, were on a slight incline. She unsuccessfully attempted to pry one loose. They hadn't brought a traditional dive knife. The current tried to sweep them off the coral surface, making her efforts doubly futile. Feliza swam off and returned with a hard, palm-sized rock. After a few solid hits, the object popped free.

Because any underwater activity consumes air quicker than does just drifting with the current, David monitored their dive time and tried to memorize the location with compass bearings as he searched the coral head's perimeter. At the east side, where the mound met the sand, an overhang appeared. The space under the ledge was only about a foot above the sandy bottom. David pulled himself down, wary not to disturb a moray eel, and waited for his vision to compensate for the lack of light inside the crevice. From a gap in its roof he saw dinner. It was a big claw, almost four inches long, obviously attached to a creature whose body was obscured.

No, it wasn't a lobster, as the warmer Caribbean variety is clawless. Instead, it was a delectable crab, and just the perfect thing to use to distract his dive buddy from further explorations.

He retrieved a wire lasso from his BC pocket and skillfully snared the claw. Then the fun began. The crab had lots of legs and natural strength to resist his efforts. The crab's body became visible as David's eyesight began to penetrate the natural camouflage. Out of a crack came the stone-like back shell, as big as a dinner plate. Everything is magnified underwater, but this was a big crab — and it knew it was fighting for its life. Smart divers always wear thick gloves for times like these. Luckily, for once, he was one of those smart guys. It was a typical judo move. His nylon orange hand moved the crab backward in the direction it was also pushing. A lunge, a grab, and a pull were all it took to capture the fine specimen.

David's net bag was a nightmare to open one handed. Distracted, the crab shot away to return under the ledge. It took a quick kick to catch him again before he found a protective lair. It was then David noticed the foundation of the crab's castle. This mound could be a ballast pile that had accumulated sand and coral on top of wooden beam-ends.

Damn, this had to be boat wreckage!

Well, the crab was the real prize of today. Now to get last night's prize and swim to a shallower, safer depth, and away from the mound.

He had tried to convince himself those weren't portholes Feliza was retrieving. Feliza had both rings and was waiting at the anchor like a seasoned diver. Her skills were impressive. He showed her the crab, and tied their combined goodies to the anchor. Once they started drifting again, their air gauges illuminated only half an hour of air remained.

It took a few minutes to slowly drift up from the sandy, barren grade to a grassy, much safer, thirty feet. The current diminished as it funneled west, depositing them in a quiet, white, sandy pool. Dolly had been towing well, and she provided a good shadow. Feliza came toward him, removed their regulators, and managed a kiss without touching facemasks. Her eyes locked his. She pointed up and David signaled they had another ten minutes. The rings took their attention. Each was heavier than expected. His dive buddy must have been straining. He used the point of the spear gun to scratch the corrosion, revealing bright brass or bronze.

After they completed a safe, shallow interval to reduce the nitrogen from their bodies, Dolly was welcomed. Even though the Caribbean waters usually stay above eighty degrees Fahrenheit, total immersion below a body's 98.6 becomes chilling. The breeze at the surface did nothing to warm them.

"Where did you become such a good diver?" David asked as he stowed the tanks. "You're definitely the best trained woman I've ever dove with."

"You know, David, I just can't figure you out." Feliza had coiled on Dolly's rear seat, enjoying the sun as she brushed her abundant hair. "You tell me you were in the naval police. Boy, you dumb or what?" She spouted a local patois accent. "I barhn here. Me a wata woman. Wata all 'round, meson. Wata all 'round." She laughed unrestrained. "So, what you tink? Me a woman, must make only Johnny cakes and coocoo? Cook de good crab back for you tonight, white mon."

Back in easier-to-understand English, she continued, "I fished with my father since he had no sons. I was the oldest and lived for Saturdays when we'd leave before dawn to haul up his fish traps. Scuba was available, as was everything else — and I do mean everything. That was after I started to sprout my femininity." She rolled on to her back and loosened her bikini top. "Wouldn't you agree I sprouted?" Just like Perseus, David knew that if he didn't look away, the perfect brown orbs would mesmerize him, and something would turn hard as stone.

He quickly attended to raising the anchor — which was quite a chore now that its weight was combined with the artifacts. His posture turned to the bow, away from his companion. "I don't even have to look. If they are going to clone someone for future generations, you're first nominated." After a few grunts the anchor and chain, combined with the newly found pieces, were piled on Dolly's small covered bow.

"Careful now with what I found. Anyway, whether you'll look or not, a German diver thought I had what it takes, so he took some of it to take me diving. From then on, I was searching for my father's lost traps." Feliza came forward to inspect her find. "I think they are old portholes. What do you think?"

"Could be anything. Let's get to Sandy Island and clean them up. Maybe there will be a forging number, or a factory name on them." He thought identification would be unlikely, but something definitely was buried beneath that coral head. It was probably the reason the head grew in the sandy location. Changing the subject, he held up his prize, "So, what do you think of my crab?"

"Not bad for a tourist." She placed her head on David's shoulder and whispered, "I really like you. I mean I really, really like you, even if you are a tourist." She bit his ear gently and scampered to Dolly's stern, starting the motor with one pull. As it went into gear, David dropped from the bow to the middle seat looking astern — so he could enjoy the view of his windswept, topless pilot.

Sandy Island is a popular local retreat, only accessible by boat. It's a small sand bar with a few coconut palms about a half-mile off of the Hillsboro shore and has been the backdrop for numerous TV commercials. Dolly rocked back and forth in the calm, afternoon sea. Ashore on the sand, shade was at a premium. A cloudless sky guaranteed glaring, unobstructed sunshine until dusk. Their dinner dangled, submerged from an oarlock, while lunch surrounded Feliza's discoveries. A flat screwdriver from the toolbox opted as her best available scraper.

"You could be scratching something very valuable. Maybe you ought to wait until we get some acid to remove the crust," David cautioned. It was no use; she was intent on discerning the rings' purpose. The wine did a good job of washing the sea's salt — and it brought the yawns. Soon they were dozing, leaning against each other under a palm tree.

That night, David discovered his dive buddy's talents included cooking. The crab dinner was accompanied with seasoned rice and boiled plantains. "Mom had three daughters…" Feliza decided to tell her life story after showering. "Dad wanted a son, but mom had trouble with my little sister Julie. Took her strength having that last baby; mom sort of faded away in the next few years. Just wore away to almost nothing." She stood at the sink counter with her back to him, shaving some carrots for the rice. David poured more wine and handed her a glass.

"So I became mom, son, and sis. Then my sister Kari took over. I got lucky and got one of those few-and-far between scholarships. Lucky, huh?

How lucky can you be to get assistance because you lost your mom? But I did it, and so did Kari and Julie."

"Is your father still on the island?"

"Nope, he's dead too. My second sister is in Brooklyn with a dentist husband and three children. Julie is now at Howard University in her last semester. Me, I went on to be, let's see, what did I become?" Her voice trailed off.

Common sense told David to let the comment pass. Whatever either had done before was inconsequential. These moments were precious like ice in the tropics: you know it's eventually going to melt, so be ready to enjoy the cold, ice water. Here, David was Walter Mitty, watching this incredible creature he had met three days ago gracefully move into his living space. They seemed like sudden friends, definitely not a product of the desperation samba routine. Hell, they hadn't made contact through a personals ad. He couldn't care less about what Feliza had been before — and readily accepted what she was now: just very, very nice.

"So, Mr. Warner, what about you? I know you are a retired, ex-navy guy; what else do you have to say?" She pushed a carrot stick into his wineglass. "Do you still have any family back in the States?"

For the second time in as many days, David recited his resume in a hundred words or less. Been there, done that, but anyone else can wear the traditional, accompanying T-shirt. They ate, cuddled, and slid between the sheets. The day's exertions, accented by a few glasses of wine, and some more exertion, quickly brought a deep sleep. When David awoke at dawn, Feliza was gone. It was one hell of a good moment not to be pressured to compose a gracious goodbye. His grin spread to a smile. He couldn't let this piece of tropical ice melt away just yet.

Bill and the boys got coffee later than usual that morning, because the last few freeboard planks were hard to fit. Everyone moved a little slower on the first day of the workweek. Reese was sluggishly dragging a huge block plane along the sides of Summer Breeze.

David's job was to keep the construction machine moving until his boat was finished. Watching each piece come together was an absolute delight. Everybody in the tropics suffers from 'the first and midweek', 'the day before and the day after midweek', and the 'last day of the work week' blues. It's not a prime place to do business. Only severe discipline lets hard work flourish in such a beautiful setting. The work ethic doesn't come to the local island people like it does to those almost-always-in-debt, semi-fast laners. As he was once told by an old time islander, 'You gotta work work, so work don't work you'. Survival on Carriacou was easy. All someone needed was a bellyful of rice and fish — which were always close at hand. If you had two sets of clothes, one to wear while the other is washed, you were rich. And you were really lucky if your roof didn't leak.

Bill followed David to the beach where his Moriah swayed at anchor. Her white hull was streaked with rust from the deteriorating fasteners. "Yesterday was a good day. I found something on the bottom, at the middle of the center passage yesterday. You ever dive through that cut?"

"Oh sure, me dive that cut lots of times and never see much. Most always, me was on the outside. Never looked inside the reef 'cause the old man just plain figured no wreck could make it over. Cut was checked, but me never see a thing. So, what yous find?" Bill asked.

David had to fight back the excitement in his voice as he relayed the events of the dive. "In the center of the cut, about a couple-hundred yards inside the reef, is a coral mound, smack in the middle of the sand valley. While grabbing a crab, I saw board ends sticking out from under the rocks. You'd have to be looking straight under the ledge to see it. Coral covers almost everything. I think the ballast pile is right there with lots of coral growing on top of it."

"Dat sounds good, SP, but who was yous diving with? If dey knows we'll lose it sure as sheet! Me told you not to take anyone else. Yous a lucky guy to go out for just two days and find two things. But if yous too lucky, might lose the whole thing. So, you had womanitis. Dat womanitis sure can confuse good judgment. But don't have much to lose." Bill swirled his cup to mix the grounds with the last few gulps of sweet, tan liquid.

"Hey, she didn't see the wood under the ledge bottom…but she did find metal rings that resemble portholes. Besides, I don't think it interested her that much!"

"Paah! Yous really got the womanitis bad, SP. Not interested? Yous must be sick. That woman yous playing with, is playing you. No offense, SP, that's what they all do, my Cecilia included. Give you everything you seem to want, as they's having just as good of time giving it. But bam, bam, bam! They's always get what they want. It's the same, all the ways, all the times. Me tell you, women rule!"

"But..." David tried to edge a word of defense; the lecture continued.

"The one you frol-lickin with is skilled. Me think that girl was born with a natural talent for driving men crazy."

"So you know Feliza?

"Course me knows her. She me good friend Raymond's eldest." Bill explained. "Been gone to the States for years, and can see it ain't damage her goods much. She's a Dubois. Like Raymond, she was born to the water, but maybe also born to tragedy. Her mama died slow, putting that whole house in gloom. Me gots to say she matured quick, and weren't much she couldn't do. That girl worked hard as anyone to help the family survive. After Raymond wash up on the shoreline, she just folded."

"A lot of that she told me," David said. "Bill, she's quite a woman. But I hope we're just having fun, and she's not really after me for my money." David held his arms open, laughed, and posed. "Maybe it could be otherwise, but I like to think it's my good looks."

"Okay, Mr. SP, maybe she interested in only you and a good time, but don't never tell her a thing. Woman is bad luck on energies. Yous knows that."

"She's quite a good diver. You say you aren't in shape to do it anymore. Mr. Post isn't able to do much more than snorkel. I think we can use another diver who can work during weekdays." He heard himself pleading his case to have the tan beauty as a coworker. "I'll see what Mr. Post says this afternoon."

"Yous ain't anxious to go back out there? Mon, if me had seen it, been back there first light. See, laziness is first symptom yous got womanitis real bad. Not only is you not thinking straight, your little head is only thinking 'bout keeping itself straight." Bill pushed him and laughed. "Mr. SP, just chiding you. Hell, if me could dive with that fine thing, me would — no 'ands' or 'ifs' and some nice butt 'bout it. But don't let her knows too much. Listen to me; woman can be a pipeline a lot of ways. Hey, you talk to the teacher and see what he thinks. Me gots to get these fools mo-ti-vated."

Bill shouted as they turned away from the shoreline. "Get up! Yous luckless wonders — and let's get this yacht ready to float!"

David rattled his pickup to the closest hardware store to get acid — and returned to clean the artifacts while refilling yesterday's dive tanks. Feliza's finds were actually an inner and outer flange, fused together by saltwater oxidation. Each set was a full twelve inches in diameter, including a two-inch wide, flat washer-type flange. This made the opening just less than eight inches. Each flange had six holes for the bolts and a hinge that opened the port. Luckily, both flanged circles fit inside a plastic five-gallon bucket. He let the two flanges boil in green sludge for about an hour. They remained a dull brown after a fresh water rinsing.

A close inspection revealed no identifying marks. Both were virtually identical. Perhaps Mike Post could discern more with his trained eye and a magnifying glass. If Feliza returned wanting her goodies, at least one would be available. After showing Bill the cleaned articles, he concurred to take them to the teacher. David's route included a lunch stop just outside of Hillsboro at a small bayside bar and grille, the Excellsieur Restaurant. Maybe Bill was right. Could be womanitis made this a lazy first day of the week. More research on the subject of womanitis would be necessary.

"So nice to see you." Excellsieur hugged David tightly. The petite owner and cook barely stood five feet. He could easily see over her head to read the menu on the wall. "Where you been? You was coming here three times a week. Nows I ain't see you in what, two weeks maybe? Someone else steal my customer?"

Lunch talk included all the new mothers and babies in the village, a couple of illnesses, and one departed. Not much was happening on Carriacou. The fish and vegetable broth with egg dumplings was satisfying — and the sharp homemade ginger beer cured his thirst.

"Have you been serving many tourists this time of year?" He remembered to inquire after being asked about Bill's condition.

"No, a few Germans last week. I thought dey was stayin' around Western Bay at some guesthouse, but dey might have been up around Mt. Pleasant. Me, I don't pay attention to much other than food orders. Yeah, dey came for three days. I think they all liked the lambi. Why, you lookin' for a stray?"

"No way, just thought that the two acquaintances I recommended to you might have stumbled in. They were two guys. One is tall and big, and the other is short and small. I think they were American, and both in their late forties. Told them you had the best eats at the most reasonable prices on this rock."

"What you tell 'dem?" the little woman wrinkled her nose and let loose on him. "Yeah! Dose two was in here. Right! Dey's both white, but the big guy is gray with lots of hair — and the other short, thin one did all the talkin. Yeah, dey was here almost two weeks ago. Came in and ordered a pizza. Well, I guess dey was used to another type of pizza that I don't make, 'because dey sure didn't like mine. Dey ate it, of course, but the short one complained and suggested I ought to do dis and add dat. I mentioned dat he could buy my place and do it himself. He said dat he'd think about it. The big one with the mustache, he just ate and not a peep. Never looked up. But dey haven't been back. Maybe dey making dere own pizza at home. I hope so, anyway!"

"Well at least I'm thinking about you. Trying to send you business." David gave her a good squeeze.

"Take care now, SP. Come round sooner next time."

It was a short hot walk to his Toyota. Before he reached its relief, he could feel the accumulated afternoon heat of the asphalt burning his feet through the soles of his sandals. Opening the driver's side door, David noticed a five dollar EC bill resting in the gutter near the front wheel. There was no one close as he stooped to retrieve it from the curbside puddle.

The bank note hadn't absorbed any of the oily mess on which it floated. As he looked at the green image of Queen Elizabeth, a man with dreadlocks approached from the shaded outside corner of Excellsieur's restaurant.

"Hey, mon, waat chu find is mine."

David covered the currency in his hand. "What did I find of yours?"

"Yeah, mon, see chu pick money, right dere. If it dere, is mine. Dis my yard."

The West Indian was in his twenties — and it appeared that those years hadn't been easy or educational. The Rastafarian hairstyle of dreadlocks tucked under a knit cap bearing the Ethiopian colors, red, yellow, and green, made him seem taller. With the hair in a bag tilted towards one shoulder, he seemed like a Dr. Seuss character. A wide pair of Wayfarers style glasses hid his eyes.

The usual strategy in this type of confrontation was to ignore and hope the beggar, which was the best description for this man, would leave. He appeared to have no trade and was a typical pseudo-Rasta parasite. As he neared, the strong odor of marijuana barely overpowered his need of a body-cleansing shower. David reopened his door, but the beggar stepped up and blocked him.

"Hey, white mon, chu deef. Said, waat chu got is mine." He bared his teeth to reveal a dull, stained overbite. Large beads of sweat glistened on his pockmarked face.

David turned to the man dressed in a 'Lion of Judah' t-shirt and cut-off jeans that drooped to reveal lime green boxer shorts and said, "Tell you what, my friend. You tell me what it is I have in my hand and you can have it. Otherwise, according to my rules, finders keepers."

Five EC dollars isn't even two bucks U.S. It wasn't worth enough to argue over, but this guy's 'gimmee or I'll take it' attitude irritated David. With no wind, the sun was baking, adding to the tenseness of the moment.

The black man put his hands in his side pockets. "Dis no game, mudda skunt. Me ain't playin wid chu. Me no fren. Got dat, white mon? Anyting dat here is mine. Dis my yard. Got dat? Now give waat chu gots, or be a sorrier mudda. Chu don't wanna to be bloodin up de street."

"Your attitude toward tourists needs some work, bud," David suggested. Then, smiling, he continued, "I'm the wrong guy to try this begging stuff on. Go sleep it off, or you're about to be embarrassed here, on the street."

"Whitey," the beggar pulled out a small carpet knife with a four-inch curved blade, "me no foolin. Now, 'stead of waat yous gots in chour hand, now me wants all chu gots."

"Excuse me, did I miss something?" David returned coolly, "Are you supposed to be a tough guy? Because all I see is a wannabe, punk-ass Rasta! Now go home, boy, before you get what you're really looking for — trouble!"

Emphasis was on the "boy' and it brought results.

"Oh, white mon, me nobody boy," the beggar shouted as he lunged. As the small wooden-handled knife came up, David slammed the truck's door shut and pushed his assailant in the same direction. The beggar hadn't expected any resistance, and was painfully surprised as the door closed on his wrist. The knife fell as the man cried and grabbed his wrist.

"Chu, chu, damn chu. Now me goin to de police. Chu break my hand en chu are gonna pay, white mon." Just then, Excellsieur smacked the attacker with a large cast iron skillet square on the back, pushing him to his knees in the dirt of the parking lot.

"Bitch, me gonna fix chu whitey-lovin ass. Den me..." was all he uttered before Excelsior smacked him again. This time he was flattened.

"Sorry dis happened outside my place. I should have had his black ass run off, but I was bein' kind, lettin' him sleep under the building if he cleaned up around the outside. He ain't from here, but from Canouan. I 'tinks he gots the crack devil in him. His name is Gaston, or least dat's what he told me." She headed into her shop to call the police. After picking up the knife, David knelt on the beggar's shoulders and pried off the sunglasses with the curved blade. He laid the knife's point at the corner of the reddish-streaked eyeball.

"Now, it seems like you got a real problem, because this lady is the sister of a police constable. If you had been even slightly polite, you would have had an extra five dollars. But instead you had to run your mouth full of racism and hate. What's wrong with you? You know what, boy?" David took the knife, pushed back the knit cap, slid the blade behind two of the locks, and sliced. The blade wasn't sharp, but it did saw away a piece of matted hair. "I know who you are. If you ever think about doing anything to this lady or to any other tourist and I hear about it, I'll cut you so clean you'll look like an eight ball. Got that, boy?" David pushed the five-dollar note in the beggar's ear. "Do I make myself understood?"

With David on his shoulders, it was difficult for him to nod — but he did convey a semblance of understanding. Two officers arrived, and a half-hour later, amid the dreadlocks' rants, their statements were compiled. The man was led to the lock-up. Over the years, David had placed a few naval personnel in island holding cells. They were appreciative when they were finally transferred to a navy brig. Jail in the Caribbean is what it used to be: uncomfortable time, not well spent. The cells are hot and overcrowded with bad sanitation. There's no TV and few books other than the Bible. Offenders from other islands are considered outcasts, and lucky to survive the penalty for intruding on another inmates' territory.

Even with all of the excitement, it was only two-thirty. It would be another hour before Mike was free for a conference. It seemed Bill's assailants were on Carriacou — but must have been keeping close to home. David tried to look into every car that passed, and visited the only two car-rental agencies without any further success. The only full-time realtor had never seen them.

\\\\\\\\\

"Mike, hope your day was better than mine." David recounted his afternoon as Mike organized his desktop — swiveling back and forth on a modern, well-padded, office chair. The pony-tailed teacher started to hum the Mamas and Papas 'Monday, Monday'. David's account of yesterday's discovery piqued Mike's attention and brought a change of the accompaniment to 'Somewhere Over the Rainbow'. David opened his shoulder bag to reveal the porthole.

"You found this where?" Mike queried. "You were alone?" Again, David related Sunday's activities, in more detail, including Feliza. Mike sat and listened while he studied the brass flange under a large magnifying glass.

"Too long ago to be able to get a drawing of the Century. I have a layout, but it doesn't reference any portholes. They were common from 1650, combined with the use of deck prisms, especially in the captain's or owner's cabin." He twirled the heavy, brown circle on his right wrist. "This has no uniquely identifying marks. It could have come from our boat, but who knows? Who the hell is 'Feliza', and why haven't I met her? You sure are tight-lipped." Mike slapped him on the shoulder and said seriously, "So, this Feliza knows there's a wreck?"

David began his explanation again while Mike reconnected to the Internet. Among the email messages was a note from Amy saying she was working on getting the info — but not to expect anything until Wednesday.

"So, why aren't you out there diving instead of here shooting the breeze with an exhausted teacher? If I wasn't so decrepit, I'd drag you back out there right now, give you a flashlight, and make you dive into the night!" He turned off the computer and, rubbing his hands together, said, "Our fortune may be out there and it's up to you to get it." Mike patted him on the back in an 'atta-boy' gesture. "Now, those eight strong boxes should have been really heavy, constructed of metal, filled with heavier wealth, and shouldn't be far from the ballast. But, if they broke up, they'll be buried in the sand, spread like grain sown in the breeze. Then it won't be easy work. How well do you know this Feliza? I mean, you didn't do a D and B on me, or ask for a resume and a police record. What do you think about her? Any weirdness, possible crack head?"

David realized their short relationship could merely be two adults enjoying a wild weekend. Nevertheless, Feliza was a very competent, very attractive diver. "I think we can trust her," he maintained.

"I hope so." was Mike's emphatic response.

CHAPTER SIX

The Caribbean's turquoise plain stretched west from the barely visible brown streaks of Eastern Bay's outer reef, to the glistening white sand shore. It was one of those rare breezeless days in the Grenadines that brought stifling heat before nine in the morning. The sea's surface looked flat, only broken by small patches of ripples belying the undercurrents. Dolly lulled at slack anchor while David readied his diving equipment. Feliza had not made a cameo appearance, or called last evening. Today it was a solo show.

The dive computer registered a maximum depth of 83 feet during Sunday's dive. That gave a safe working bottom time of twenty-two minutes. Never wanting to push to the danger limit, David set his watch alarm to buzz at fifteen minutes. With decompression stops at twenty and ten feet, he figured the dive should be well within the safety limits. What good would it be to find the treasure, and have to spend it from a wheel chair after being severely bent? Fifteen to twenty minutes wasn't much time to penetrate a three-hundred-year-old rock pile. The only tools he had were a three-foot pry bar and an old, short-handled sledgehammer.

Not knowing the mound's exact location, David tried to see it from the surface. His anchor was about two-hundred yards to the east. A net sack filled with the heavy tools, an extra dive weight belt, and the lift bag slid down the anchor rope. He inflated the lift bag, but since it was slack tide, he had to swim Dolly and the tools to the site. Every shape appeared distinct in the crystal water and he quickly found the overhang with the plank ends. The old wood was lying a foot deep under rocks. A separate piece of large, dead brain coral had bonded with the mound to create the overhang. He strapped on the extra weight belt before removing his fins to work easier, kneeling on the sandy bottom. The fins were stored in the net sack to keep them from floating away.

Using a stone as a fulcrum, David pried up with the bar. After moving the pry point four times, the big piece of brain coral started to budge slightly. He positioned the bar at a crevice on the mound side and pushed down with all his strength. The ledge broke away, overturning on to the sand.

Underneath, were layers of rocks about twice the size of large loaves of bread. A metal detector would have helped determine where to concentrate his efforts. He peeled five layers away to get a view of the planks and take a sample of the wood. Since he was far offshore, the bottom was pure sand, without mud. The activity only slightly clouded the visibility. Small sea creatures scattered at the invasion. Fire coral stung his wrist after he rubbed against a mustard-colored glob on a ballast stone.

He focused on avoiding a couple of painful little guys that reside in the sea floor. Bristle worms are the dangerous, undersea versions of stinging centipedes, and had to be feared as much as the sharp teeth of small spotted moray eels. Varieties of small, brittle starfish crawled from the disturbance, and into the new pile he was creating. Then it dawned on him: he might be covering something rather than uncovering. If the coins were scattered over the sand, he was making the job twice as hard. Pulling more rocks to uncover the wood, he saw something white, the side of a teacup with the delicate handle attached. The dive computer permitted ten more minutes.

During every dive, David's mind divided. One part concentrated on the bottom time, air consumption, and not getting bit, cut, or pinned doing something stupid. His imagination controlled the other part, turning every dive into an old Sea Hunt episode. He was focused, searching for a glint of gold, or an unusual shape among the stones, while also keeping an eye out for prowling predators. At eighty feet in this reef canyon, the big boys — tiger, lemon, and bull sharks — cruised. The smaller, dangerous black tips and sand species were also in the shallows. All sought a meal and most returned to the deep, cooler, dark-blue water outside the reef. This canyon was one of their routes. Usually, underwater activity keeps them away, or just out of sight. A few four-foot barracudas hovered nearby. Although they appear vicious because of their toothy snarl, 'cudas seldom attack. However, the presence of these predators accented the adventure.

While on Navy duty, he'd done exotic, shallow reef dives, deep dark wall dives, and various wreck dives. Most were very rigidly administered by a dive master — so, little of the sea environment was damaged and no artifacts were removed. Here, David was tearing the bottom apart. He couldn't deny that the term 'treasure hunting' was definitely more romantic than the true catalyst — 'greed'.

David pulled away a dozen more rocks and saw about a square foot of the planks. The wood was soggy and broke easily under the strain of the bar. The pieces went in the bag with the teacup. His watch alarm signaled to start wrapping it up while the air gauge read only fifteen hundred pounds, a half tank. Although brief, the exhilaration consumed the compressed air rapidly at that depth. He pulled at a few more stones and revealed another piece of white ceramic — half of a dinner plate. Knowing the encouragement of a new discovery could endanger his bottom time, he put on his fins. The extra weights, hammer, and pry bar were left neatly hidden under the first piece of brain coral.

The activity created a prime feeding station for sleek yellow tail snappers, large-eyed red squirrel fish, and cautious groupers. Slowly ascending the anchor line with two prizes, he looked down and knew anyone overhead would easily be able to recognize that the ocean floor had undergone a slight excavation. He had to resolve this problem. Also, a metal detector might help from moving the entire mound, bit by bit — but non-metallic things like the porcelain cup and plate, and gems wouldn't register. No — on second thought, he realized he'd be pulling the mound apart literally stone-by-stone, then sweep — and perhaps sift — the encircling sand.

The air pressure gauge read a thousand pounds at a depth of fifty feet, after maxing at eighty-four. The proper rate of ascent is one foot per second, but David went even slower as he reconsidered the logistics of this project. An additional tank would have to be tied onto the anchor line at forty feet, in the event an error in judgment occurred. This would be a necessity, coupled with marking twenty-foot intervals on the anchor line with knotted loops. Then divers could attach themselves and the extra tank with a D-ring. That would keep fingers from cramping during periods with strong currents. At least one other diver was required

A three-person team would allow one member to stay in the boat as a further safety precaution. Yeah, a lot of aspects of this operation needed refinement.

After two, ten-minute rest stops, dreaming about what was below, David crawled back onto Dolly. The computer said a minimum two-hour surface interval was recommended before descending to eighty feet again. He examined the two ceramic pieces under a makeshift tarp rigged from an old, striped windsurfer sail stretched from the prow to over the middle seat. This made the hotbox slightly cooler. Several notes concerning compass bearings, and about improved safety precautions, were scrawled on a plastic dive slate. He dozed, deliriously dreaming of Feliza splashing around naked in the surf.

Almost three hours had passed before he awoke to the swell from a motorboat rocking Dolly's hull. It was well past one in the afternoon when David strapped on the second tank. The computer signified he had almost completed his off-gassing. He had nineteen minutes to explore — so the digital watch was set to buzz at fourteen. Again, the salt water was invigorating as it trickled past the neck of his wet suit. He descended straight to the mound, wasting no time and returned to moving more stones from the same area. He consumed a thousand pounds of air in seven minutes to reveal the edge of a large, heavy, iron ring under a coral crust. More glass and ceramic pottery shards were collected in the net bag.

Moving another fourteen stones to the sand revealed that the ring was attached to the shank of an anchor equal in size to the one he'd found off Indigo Bay. A compass bearing determined the anchor was resting east to west. A sparkle of glass appeared to the left of the ring. His glove swept away the sand from the object, revealing a palm-sized bottle. It was delicate, yet intact after years of resting among the stones. He picked it up and placed it under his shorty wet suit's elastic leg. The alarm buzzed. The second dive had to end.

With two short dives, David had removed about a four-by-four area down to the wooden base, which was probably a lower deck. He'd found one anchor, seventeen pottery pieces, and the bottle. It was enough to keep him interested. By three o'clock, on his return to Eastern, the day was scorching. Bill was sending the workers home after a productive day.

The tanks began to fill as the garden hose rinsed off salt. David opened the first beers in the security of his kitchen before showing Bill the day's finds.

"Bill, how about coming over to the teacher's for a discussion and to examine these items?" David asked. Bill kept fingering the items. "Mike's got one of those mounted magnifying lenses for working on small things, like watches."

"Never know what might be written on these pieces that'll provide clues. The brass portholes didn't have anything stamped on them," David excitedly rattled on. "What do you think about the anchor resting among the pile of stones? Why do you think it's there — could that be the bow section?"

Bill pulled on his beer. "Say SP, where yous keeps your anchor? It's up in the bow, right? Yous gots a spare hook? Where it? Lying on the bottom of the boat somewhere just waitin' for when yous needs it, right?" He drank and belched.

The pieces were spread on the table with the small bottle in the center. Bill examined each and continued to speak. "Ahh, that anchor could be a spare for hard weather, or if the main one get stuck and couldn't be hauled up. Shit mon, every boat gots to have lots of ground tackle. Was few docks then, and no motors. If yous gots stuck, crew boat would have to lift the anchor, row it a ways out, set it good, and then pull the ship out to it with the windlass. That anchor was 'bout the best thing they had, next to compass and sails." He held the small, clear glass bottle to the sunlight.

"If it's my boat, the spare anchor would be lashed in the bow so it could be raised fast and easy if needed," David offered.

"Me no know. Should been right on the deck, but me don't think they wanna be moving it from below. Could break loose in a big sea. No, probably lashed to the bow gunwale. They'd raise it with a block and tackle from the boom. Most likely it was in the bow, no farther back. Yous say it was laying with the ring to the east? That make me think her bow ought to be pointing east. But that makes her leaving not coming. Must be storm done it. Seems they'd want the flukes' weight hanging over de bow, just like now. Me would. That way the ring and shank could rest on the deck. Oh, yeah, like in dem old pirate movies, the flukes are over the side and the ring is pointing to the helm. Yeah, dat's the way it got pointing east. Yeah."

Bill straightened and cracked his back. "Like to come with you tonight, but have to make it later in the week. This little bottle's really something; can't say me ever seen one like it. Real sweet. Try and set up a meeting for Thursday. Me buy beer, and let's go to eats somewhere. Make me feel like we big time 'ontapenors' or whatever they is we gonna be. Yous knows, big shots. Me being partners with two white guys and all." He laughed deeply, "Shit! We might get rich from this thing any old ways, huh, SP?"

"Yeah, we just might, Bill. So, you think it was a spare anchor? When it's completely uncovered, I'll measure it against the one in Indigo Bay. We'll have to do a lot of work to move that entire pile at least twice. That anchor will have to be lifted to get at the area underneath. It's settled into the shifting ballast." David agreed.

"How thick yous say that pile was? How many rows of rock deep?" Bill asked.

"It appears to be four or five layers thick."

"That 'bout right for a loaded ship, say hundred-plus feet. Me no know how big this boat was 'posed to be, but the old Moriah has three rows in the center and two fore and aft. So five and six is 'bout right. One thing SP, yous gots to think 'bout them two guys is watching for you. Theys get to see your launch in the same place every day, then theys gonna knows yous on it." He held up his brown bottle to toast. "Another good day all 'round. Gots some good work outs of them boys, even in the heat today. They was thinking 'bouts quitting and going home to the woman after our noon meal. So me tells them how it is so hot that loving would taste bad. Hah, hah." He laughed raucously, happy to have made a joke, and then gulped from the fresh beer handed to him. "So me tells 'em if they work another three hours, they'd have money to spends towards a fan. Then that woman be cool to touch, and not so cranky when theys gets to it. Hah, hah!"

Bill examined each ceramic fragment closely, cocking his head to each side as if it provided a better view.

"Find anything of value among my litter?"

"Ain't no litter here, meson. If that's the Century, all this is gonna be worth something. Yous see, them people crazy for old-time trash. But me thinking there's a lot of stuff like this on the beach south of here. Just south of Hillaire Point. Me always thought that was trash, but nows might be from part of the boat." He drained the second bottle and rose, pushing away from the table. "Now, got to go. Cecilia has some social thing at the school tonight and me stay home to watch the girls. Cecilia figger tomcats be getting the scent soon enough. But me, thinks me really protecting the boys. 'Cause yous knows that female gets smart way front of the boy. Shit!

They leads them little fellows 'round by the pecker. Talk of such, what's wid yous en dat girl? Yous better keep tending that fire. It ain't gonna go out, but someone else might throw another log that make it flame brighter than yous ole log doing. Hah! Hah!"

"I'm just minding my own business. You know how it is Bill — chase it and you lose it. Let her find me, and she'll work harder to figure out why I'm not chasing her. But I'll let her win."

"Whether yous lets her or not, that woman can't lose." Bill replied. "Me sees her in town one Saturday, late, at the market. She looks like she's gots her own cocos, walking like she dripping a trail of sweet mango. Nah, that woman cannot lose."

\\\\\\\\\

David called Mike's school number from the phone outside the post office to ascertain if a visit was possible. A sweet, juicy mango filled his thoughts as he drove to the Outpost. He dropped Bill at Top Hill's Low Road Shoppe, where he picked up another six Caribs. The chain was down at Mike's driveway and he took his truck to the hitching rail. Mike came through the door, exuberant, and holding two open beers.

"Here's to the conquering Mr. Warner. You are a lucky devil. What did you find?"

"Whoa, cowboy, let's put these beers in the cooler and I'll tell you everything." David stopped him. "First, there are a lot of details that we have to work out. Bill couldn't make it tonight, but let's set up for a meeting Thursday. That could include Feliza — if she shows her pretty face before then."

"Okay with me. Whatever you say. Where's what you found today?" Mike inquired, slightly impatient.

"Whoa, whoa, whoa! Let me go through everything on my mind and what else needs to be done. You can keep the pieces I've found to examine at your leisure, Teach." David recounted all of the safety items and necessary equipment, some of which would have to be purchased stateside. Mike listed everything in a notebook. "We'll need a couple top-flight metal detectors and a good underwater camera. Do you know anything about laying out a pseudo-archaeological excavation?"

Mike never looked up from his monitor. "I can access the Internet from school whenever Cable and Wireless' service is up. Never forget where you are. The modem speed has nothing to do with speed of access, as the lines can only go so fast. Due to the antiquated system, I can make calls, but can receive only email. There are some sites for metal detecting equipment and treasure hunters. Let's see," he noted, "I'll try www.treasure.com. The underwater camera should be your choice. Your admirer in Washington will have to send it. You'll never find one here."

As they brainstormed, Mike continued to write a growing list of items and procedures. "We need to make a couple decisions concerning the archaeology. I've always thought about finding something like this, but now that it's here, it's almost frightening. Obviously we're breaking Grenadian law by violating a shipwreck, not to mention damaging an underwater reef. How should we approach this endeavor? Are we naturalists or realists? If we go to the government, we can forget ever going back to that site in the next five years. The elected island demigods will have a bacchanal about two white Americans stealing local heritage. Bill will hang with us. Personally, I say we continue very discretely and bring little or no attention to the site or to us. The latter part is going to be the most difficult."

David toyed with the small bottle, listening to Mike's opinions.

"The way I see it, we've got four enemies: one of our group saying or doing something indiscreet, the government stumbling upon us, Bill's supposed attackers, and other locals." He turned and pointed his finger for emphasis. "Never forget for a moment that this is a very small, dull island. Locals will notice anything out of the norm. However, most of the population is numb above the shoulders. How can the surface boat be in a different place each day, so that we don't give it away?"

"That would be difficult," David answered, "not impossible. We can rent or borrow other boats. Each time we can move the anchorage slightly. Even better, a third person like you or Bill can drop us, go fishing, and return for a timed pickup. That makes me shiver though, not having Dolly above in case of an accident — or if a predator takes interest. If there's a current, we can drift with it as we decompress. I guess on every dive from now on, I'll take an extra tank and a power head."

"Power head?" Mike asked.

"It's a screw-on adapter that fits at the threaded end of my spear. A waxed, waterproof, 44 caliber cartridge fits inside a stainless tube that slides when you take out a safety pin. All you have to do is hit your attacker with the spear. The shell case slides back and explodes against the firing pin. Blows a big hole — a big, big hole." David put both thumbs and forefingers together to demonstrate.

"I can imagine. Where does somebody get such a contraption? I've never heard of one before."

"The one I have was made in a ship's machine shop. You can buy them through commercial dive catalogs. They come in shotgun grades, 38 and 44 caliber versions. The big problem is, when you blow a hole in one shark, the others get excited into a feeding frenzy. Seen it happen once in the Seychelles. Not a pretty sight."

"I can imagine. Sounds dangerous." Mike surmised.

"There is a safety pin, a split cotter key, which you must physically remove. There has to be enough warning to arm the head. Once armed, all you need to do is hit the target without the spear ricocheting. After the explosion, the spear shaft comes back faster than when it left the rubber slings of the gun. Of course, it can go right through you." David warned.

"Okay. Got you. Just be careful. We've all got to be careful we don't get spanked, imprisoned, or deported by the government — or even more screwed by thieves. Previous investigations, like when the carved boulder was discovered, demonstrated that there's virtually no way of claiming a particular site on or offshore in the Grenadines. It's the-finders-versus-the-government-keepers. Can't blame them though, the economy is so depressed because our stateside motherland took away the islands' exclusive, European banana market. They could use the extra funds for schools, hospitals, and social programs. Ahem, however, we both know the politicos would just steal it for themselves and waste it. I feel if somebody's going to waste it, it may as well be us!" Mike raised his right hand for a high-five as he rose to get more beer.

"So, everything is agreed between us, and I think Bill will concur; another diver and a few simple ruses, with the emphasis on safety, are necessary." David said. "You'll get on the Net tomorrow and seek out product reports concerning underwater detectors if Amy can't come through with a Navy unit. I'll set up the drop lines and extra tanks with regulators so we have an out if we ever get into a dangerous situation. You find where the closest, operable decompression chamber is being operated by the best techs. There should be one in Trinidad, definitely in Caracas, but maybe there's also one here in Grenada."

David handed the small bottle to Mike who placed it under the lens. He neatly arranged the pottery fragments by size and color. The biggest piece was the half dinner plate. Mike identified a reddish-brown piece as the top of an ink well.

After inspecting and measuring the bottle with calipers, Mike rose and removed two books from his bookshelf. "This bottle probably held a woman's perfume. Delicate and round makes it feminine. Men's scent bottles had sharp corners." He turned the bottle to reveal a rough area inside a small indentation. "This is the pontil, which wasn't ground away in this tiny kick up. It's all that remains of the rod of glass from which it was blown. As it is rough, I'd say this bottle was produced very early, perhaps before the 1600s. Northern Europe, where the Century's passengers originated, had an area specializing in glass blowing for ages. In fact, it's still famous for producing glass objects d'art. That means this could be our boat. But a collector could have carried it on a later boat; or it was refilled, a sentimental heirloom. Could be the same with the portholes? They could have been removed from an unseaworthy vessel, and refitted to a new hull."

"Then," David interjected, "unless we find a nameplate that says 'Century,' we'll never know?"

"Let's say the gold coins from the chests might take some of the doubt out of it." Mike answered. "We might find a bottle with a dated seal, an engraved ceramic, or a design on a cup or plate. There's no list in the manifest of personal effects of the passengers."

"Even if we find distinctive jewelry, it still can't attribute origin. We might get lucky with a sword hilt, a musket, or a pistol ornament, which shows ownership. This bottle is a good sign, but the ceramic pieces point to British glazing — which was supposedly the best in the world at that time. Elitists would've always had the best — or maybe they stopped at London to supply for the Atlantic crossing. These could have also belonged to another boat stocked in London. It'll come. More pieces of the puzzle will paint an increasingly better portrait of the buried vessel." Mike slapped him on the arm and laughed. "Damn, some of those sparkling coins could do the best painting."

David opened another beer as Mike asked, "How often do you think it's safe to dive?"

"No more than two dives a day, at least two hours apart. If I splash at eight in the morning, I can be off the water by noon. I've been thinking we should organize a rotating schedule to make it seem random. Say I dive tomorrow late in the day, at two and four; there will still be plenty of light. Then there'll be no diving until Saturday. You take me out just after dawn, and we're back in before nine. On Sunday, Bill can take me out later — say noon. Then we won't be diving again until Wednesday, and then Thursday, Sunday, and Tuesday."

David looked at his watch. "What do you think about including Feliza as my dive buddy? Perhaps I ought to talk to her about splashing tomorrow? Might be too late to call her where she works by the time I get home?"

"I'm all for safety, but let's face it: none of us knows the others very well." Mike replied. "You know Bill probably the best of all. He knows her, and you know her…intimately," he chuckled. "What I'm saying is we're all strangers to each other with the common denominator of greed. That could add up to disaster, but what are the options? Say you found it alone, shipped in some naval associates, shipped out the loot; that's a better scenario. In this imperfect-world situation, we've got to watch each other, trust, and pray. Pray: a-y, not e-y. I think it will all work out."

He looked around the interior of his boat home and waved his hands quickly, ending with a loud clap. "Yes, you are correct; I'm risking all of this." Mike shook his nearly empty beer and sternly said, "Mr. Warner, you seem old and wise enough to be able to discern if this woman is credible." Relaxing, he quipped, "Credible and edible."

"Alright, I'm off. On my way back to my homestead, I'll call her. Who knows, if I'm lucky, she'll be there when I get home. Man, time flies! It's after nine. Maybe she…" David thought of what he was about to say. "With or without help, I'll dive again tomorrow. As unnoticeable as a boat all alone can be, I really don't think the locals will take much interest. People are always feeding their families from diving inside the reef. But being in one of three cuts, other boats are going to be passing. I think we can chance it."

They shook hands and David gathered his wits to make the bumpy ride to Eastern over the irregular roads. Mike, a master of organization, found enough energy to begin charting the bottom, noting where each item originated with a short description.

The drawing held David's attention through two yawns and three comments. He couldn't think of anything that hadn't been mentioned, asked, or answered. He had to decide what tactic to use to contact Feliza. He could drive the distance to the restaurant. No — he'd locate a phone and call first. The problem was that in Carriacou, public phones were scarce. Phone lines weren't strung along every road. The nearest phone would be either in Hillsboro, or at Eastern's post office.

\\\\\\\\\

Arriving at the row of four phone booths in Hillsboro, he dialed information, and waited twenty-three rings before a lady provided the number of the Old Fort Restaurant.

"Hello. Who this?" It wasn't Feliza. "Who's this?" was David's reply.

"This is Bernadette at the Old Fort. We closing up now, so you'll have to come tomorrow."

"Yes, Bernadette, this is David Warner. I met you the other night. I'm a new friend of Feliza's. Is she still around?"

"You are 'bout lucky. We was just getting into a car to go home. It was a slow night. What did you do to this girl, Mr. Warner? She all listless and slow-eyed. If you is going to tire her out so, I'm gonna have to regulate these dates so it don't affect her work schedule."

David could hear her talking away from the phone, mentioning it was for Feliza.

"Hello, what has Auntie been telling you, David? How are you? Did you miss me? I know that's why you are calling. Admit it, you miss me and can't live without me." Feliza teased.

Feliza's voice brought a good shiver, maybe goose bumps, or another type of lump. He did miss her.

"So what are you doing now?" he asked. "How about another dive tomorrow?"

"Standing here talking to you, what else?"

He was quickly rebuffed for not beginning with the necessary pleasantries. "Yes, yes, yes, I miss you. You are the best and prettiest dive partner I've ever had." David ensured. "I'll pick you up and we'll stop and have breakfast in town. Then we head out for a couple leisurely dives. I promise to make it worth your while." She'd soon learn how much it could be worth. "Wait, don't hang up. I don't know where you live?"

"Tell you what," she answered, "how about I meet you at the Hillsboro Café after eight? Tomorrow fresh produce comes from Grenada. I'll have to help Auntie buy — and she can arrange return transport. Then I'm all yours for the day, but I'll need to be back at the restaurant no later than four-thirty with some bounce still left in my step."

"I don't see a problem, Feliza; if you're sure it won't inconvenience your aunt. We'll make a nice easy day of it." He agreed. "Get a good night's sleep, and I will meet you at the Hillsboro Cafe. If you get there first, order me coffee. Miss you. See you in the morning."

After replacing the phone, he realized that he still didn't know where his secretive courtesan lived. Tomorrow afternoon, he'd make it a point to take her to her home. Hopefully tomorrow would erase some of her mysteries and fill in some blanks. His concern was how she would accept the knowledge of the wreck site. During the ride home, he tried to design a diplomatic approach to the island beauty.

A weather system moving south from the East Coast of the United States sucked all the wind to a storm hanging just north of Antigua. The wind blew less than ten miles an hour for three days, erasing any chance of waves. Placid seas made excellent diving conditions — while ashore was blazing hot from sunrise to sunset.

Despite the heat, an easy sleep enveloped David after the day's exertions.

Everything proceeds at a slower pace throughout the Caribbean — and the pace is considerably slower in the early morning hours. A scarcity of fresh water and indoor bathroom facilities provide few wake-up showers to wash away the drowsiness from the locals. The blast from the air horn of the inter-island freighter delivering fresh produce from Grenada was Wednesday's alarm clock.

The old, red-and-white steel freighter delivered necessary goods each week. Grenada's lush elevations and higher rainfall make it the breadbasket of the Grenadines. Bananas, citrus, various root starches, eggs, poultry, and local vegetables are delivered along with bundled lumber, bagged cement, and steel for construction. Mail, current newspapers and periodicals were safely stored in the pilothouse. Ladies in their second-best dresses (the best saved for Sunday church service) and bright head wraps crowded the dock, awaiting personal parcels. This was a centuries old tradition along the string of island ports.

Most of the produce would be sold during the following days inside the local market. Being at the dock early was the only way to obtain fresh vegetables without paying an extra handling price. Truckers spooned broth from white plastic containers as they lingered near to their vehicles. They awaited the appearance of the freighter's crane operator — who also sipped a tea while chatting with the slow-starting ferry crew. All of today's cargo would be off-loaded by noon. Then, in the heated afternoon, the return cargo would be slowly loaded. Heavy, mooing cows were swung over the steel gunwales and secured to the deck. Their first-and-only sea journey would deliver them to Grenadian butchers. Cardboard boxes of belongings accompanied the few passengers who would ride the three sunset hours south to St. Georges harbor.

The cafe where is a center of activity during the early hours. Most locals consumed a breakfast of cornmeal porridge with tea or leftovers from last evening's dinner. Tea might be real, East Indian Ceylon tea — or, it might be sweetened cocoa. Those who left home hungry gathered at the Hillsboro Cafe for saltfish cakes with coconut or fried bakes. Some of the secretaries, dressed in uniforms of their particular office, purchased cheese and bread to carry out. It was a West Indian standard to take time from the employer to eat on the job.

The restaurant was bright with unshuttered windows facing the street. The decor of white walls, and white tables with chairs on a black-and-white-checkered vinyl tile floor welcomed the patrons. Curtains or tablecloths were too delicate for the clientele. Rows of pastries racked on aluminum trays disappeared fast. Eggs sizzled on the cook's griddle. The coffee urn gurgled out cupfuls, and the toaster erupted for the benefit of the few tourists. A regular, stateside breakfast is rare throughout the Caribbean. Eggs were consumed hard-boiled or on sandwiches and bacon was almost nonexistent.

An orderly line among those waiting for service was also not essential. Everything depended on eye contact. The harried counter girl refused to look at another customer until the present order had been completed. Relationships didn't matter unless they came by prearrangement. Shouting didn't make the service move any faster — yet most burly young men tried that tactic. Fifteen minutes after David had found a good seat where he could sip his coffee, the counter slowly cleared, giving the cook and waitress time to regain composure before the lunch rush began in three hours.

His attention was distracted from a slightly sticky cinnamon bun as he watched Feliza saunter down the street. She wore a purple-print sari, which reached only to the middle of her excellently shaped thighs. Her arms strained, grabbing nearly a dozen sagging, black plastic bags. His gentlemanly qualities provoked an assist, but before he could rise from the chair, Feliza had swung her purchases into the side door of a parked, blue transport van. Bernadette, in a bright orange dress with matching scarf, waddled from the Market Board toward the same van. David noticed the pleasant exchanges between the two women as Bernadette squeezed her hand and kissed her cheek. The older woman was still rattling directions and pointing her finger, as Feliza slid the van's side door shut.

The beauty caught his eye through the open window and blew a kiss. Thirty-nine isn't old unless you're sixteen. David's age seemed to drop to that of a teenager as that kiss struck home and made his insides queasy. It was too soon to register this as love. Instead he interpreted it as a mixture of lust and respect.

During the Navy years, he'd been fortunate to meet women from all parts of the world, but had never met such a complete wonder as Feliza. He beheld her beauty as she gathered the edges of her wrapped skirt and smoothly ran across the street, beaming a smile meant only for him.

He tried to rise as she entered, but she rushed and pinned him to the chair with a hug. Feliza nuzzled his neck and bit his ear to the bewilderment of the other customers and staff. "I missed you so much," she breathed just above a whisper.

"Me too," David stammered.

"Me too, what?" she returned, laughing. "Tell me you missed me," she said for the benefit of the onlookers. "You are not getting out of here without exclaiming your affection for little ole me."

By then, his face was burning red from embarrassment. Not being one to proclaim anything, let alone display devotion in front of strangers, he hesitated and whispered, "I hope someday to be able to tell you how much I have missed being with you. Unfortunately, you're with a shy guy."

With her arms still cradling David's neck, Feliza winked at the counter girl.

"Rona Mitchell, does he look like he's shy?" The girl pursed her lips, fighting a smile, and shook her head no as Feliza continued, "That's what they all say to get out of sharing their feelings. You know, Rona, now in the new millennium, men are supposed to be changing for the better. We females are supposed to get more compliments from our men — since they are to be better in touch with their emotions. But this guy," she bent and kissed his cheek, "he just wants to feed his ego — and then maybe throw me a scrap," Feliza said to everyone's visible enjoyment.

"So, how are you? Please, don't get upset at my little bit of fun," she said as she took the chair opposite David and moved it closer to his side of the table. She spoke seriously, "I really did miss you, too much. I feel like a school girl out on her second date after becoming infatuated on the first." Feliza squeezed his hand for emphasis. She bent closer and sniffed him. "I thought you might be wearing one of those ultra-attracting colognes, pheromones, to put me under your spell, but all I can smell is sweat. Good sweat. Look at me; I'm all giggly and babbling on. Rona, can I get a cheese sandwich, a fish broth, and a glass of water, please? Thanks. Now darling, you shall have my complete attention until four in the afternoon."

"So, how are you David?" she asked again.

Nervously, he coughed and cleared his throat. "I'm a lot better now that you're here." He kissed her hand and then moved his lips to her cheek. "Where does a slim woman put all of that food?" Quietly, he said, "I've seen every inch of you and there's nothing extra."

"Fast metabolism and a lot of activity keeps me slim." She smiled. "You know, David, we've known each other for about a week. Is this to be considered a whirlwind romance? Well, to keep up this whirlwind pace you are setting; I've got to get nourishment." Just then her breakfast was delivered. He looked at the bowl of fish broth and saw a barracuda snout glaring out of the oily soup. His stomach couldn't handle much before noon — so he was forced to look away as Feliza noisily sucked the fish head clean, draining the bowl quickly. His coffee was refilled at the counter as he purchased the necessities for an easy lunch.

Their drive to Eastern began like teens headed to a picnic. Feliza sat close, draping her arm across his shoulders. It seemed like a good time to discuss why we were diving again today. "You're not interested in those things you found Sunday?" David asked.

"Oh, yeah," she replied dreamily. The sun streamed directly into the windshield, projecting a warm, yellowish light. "Did you get a chance to clean them at all?"

"Ah, no. Looks like they were parts to a porthole. I really don't know how to approach this," he paused.

"No, I won't marry you." Feliza giggled, "Not yet anyway."

"Hey," he exclaimed. "Are you interested in a little bit of an adventure close to home?"

"Is this a recruitment pitch for the Navy?" she laughed.

"Wait a minute. My reason for diving Sunday was to look for evidence of a shipwreck. You found the portholes, and I think I located the wreck." The interior of the truck cab was quiet. Feliza turned the radio off, shifted her position to lean against the passenger door, and stared at him.

David explained, "Before we met, I had just gotten involved with two other guys in searching for shipwrecks. Sounded like a fun thing to do while my boat is being built."

"The Century, you're looking for the Century," Feliza muttered with conviction.

He could have lied, but why? It would be transparent and would snuff out any possibility of trust. "Yes, the Century." His answer hung in the air. Several seconds passed. Feliza turned to look out the side window as they passed through the shade of a long row of tall mahogany trees.

"Why do you think you found it? My portholes?" she asked.

The explanation of getting the crab and seeing the beam-ends began to anger her. "You couldn't tell me on Sunday? Why? You had to ask the other boys if it was acceptable to bring in your girlfriend?"

He slowed the truck and turned to his passenger, beaming, "My girlfriend? That sounds nice." He leaned to kiss her, which was successful after some slight resistance. "Hey, you can join the group if you want to. There are definite risks. The diving is deep and it'll be tedious. It'll be hard and time consuming, but it won't become work. I figure it'll take maybe five days, ten more dives to clear the pile. Never know what's gonna turn up. The government could put the whammy on us. And others might be interested enough to cause problems. What do you know about the Century?"

"I know my poppa looked for it. He never saw one piece of anything that looked like a wrecked boat. Now you are diving with me and you find something. Make me a believer!"

"You'll see. Nothing precious has been found, but I just started yesterday. So are you a risk taker; a holder of an E-ticket, or just intelligent, beautiful, young, and sexy?" He teased.

She slid across the seat, thigh against thigh. Her arm returned around his neck as she kissed his ear, whispering, "Let's go for it. At the least it'll allow us more time together." She finished the kiss and said, "Even split, though. Who else is in on this?"

David mentioned Bill and Mike. Feliza obviously knew Bill and agreed to his judgment. Pulling into his driveway he surmised, "This'll cut down on hanky-panky time, especially if you work nights."

"Oh, I think we'll fit in some affectionate moments between dives. You better get in gear and make Dolly more comfortable, or it's back to the monastery for you, buddy boy." As David turned off the ignition she poked her finger in his side for emphasis. "Comprende, amigo?" She laughed again and scampered out of the truck.

There are a lot of near perfect days in the Caribbean. This was one of them. Not much was said as they prepared Dolly. Gear and necessities were placed in the front section. Plenty of water, frozen in plastic jugs, filled the cooler. It's amazing how diving dehydrates you while you're completely immersed in water. For more shade they brought another tarp, opaque white, and propped it with a bamboo post for better ventilation. This all materialized from Feliza's inventiveness. Two blue foam swim mats were arranged in the center of the skiff for cushy reclining. That was David's plan; if he could keep his dive partner comfortable and excited by finding goodies every day, he knew she'd be satisfied and content.

Proceeding slowly to the site, David detailed what they'd be doing, and what to look out for. With five tanks aboard, one tank would stay hooked onto the anchor line at forty feet. He'd made loops every ten feet to the surface. Knives were buckled to their calves. The spear gun with the power head attached came along just in case. Feliza already knew how to use one.

They enjoyed excellent vertical visibility as the anchor dropped on the sand exactly next to the mound. Equalization was easy, and descent took a minute. David had set the bottom-time alarms and warned Feliza not to wander off. She hovered over the area he'd already worked, wide-eyed at the view of the old timbers. He'd already begun moving ballast stones and enlarging the hole when she grabbed one herself. Although able to move it while obviously straining, it was easier for her to work and lift with his help. At every level, they stopped to rest and check for artifacts. Five stones later, she pointed to something in the pile and slowly bent to retrieve it. His advice had been to cautiously examine the surroundings of anything that became visible. That way, they wouldn't miss something else slightly obscured nearby, or have to confront a disturbed underwater creature. David reasoned that if wood ran beneath the entire mound, it would act like a floor — keeping objects they missed from getting lost.

After several delicate pulls and a pry with the bar, a gray rod appeared from between the rocks. Before rising, Feliza pried another small object from the bottom layer and tucked it into her suit top. At ten minutes, the hole had almost doubled through their combined efforts. Mike had suggested they excavate in one direction, cutting across the mound. Feliza reached into a slight gap between four of the stones. David couldn't see what she was after, but he could see her eyes beaming inside her mask. After prying and tugging she turned to show a fine gold chain, intact in a loop. It was the first real treasure. That also went into her breast bank.

They spent the last few minutes prying the top layer of coral loose — so during their second dive they could just move the underlying rocks. Feliza swam ten feet above the mound, gazing down at it while she slowly rose to meet David on the anchor line. Her incredibly beautiful eyes beamed when she removed the chain from her top. The chain was almost a foot in diameter with quarter inch links. While they hung at thirty feet, she fondled every link — and there were many. His mind whirled at what they'd find when they got a metal detector. Then he remembered today was the day he had planned to call Amy. She'd love to hear about all of this. Well, maybe not everything.

Splashing to the surface after fifteen minutes of feeling like big fish bait dangling on the anchor line, Feliza exclaimed, "Yah-hoo!" Due to the dive-gear, she grabbed him awkwardly and hugged. "You really did find a wreck. I really did find a wreck. We really have a wreck. Yah-hoo, ya-ya-yahoo!" She released her tank into his hands like a pro and swung her shapely legs into the boat.

They both examined the finds. The gray rod blackened as the air hit it. Holding it on the wooden cap rail, David tapped it with the broad back of his dive knife. The encrustation shattered in a myriad of quickly disappearing pieces — revealing a short, three-inch silver handle. The cross brace had a slot where the steel blade had fit before disintegrating through time. It was a pattern of ropes coiled about the thin stock. The other piece she'd retrieved was indiscernible — but could have been a coin. It would need delicate restoration.

Feliza propped the tarp high letting in a refreshing breeze from the east. She dropped her hair and brushed it out. Before straightening she unclasped her top, draped the gleaming chain around her dark shoulders, and threw her head back like a tribal queen — and in a sultry voice said, "What do you say, partner, is this me, or is this me?! I love this; I love you for this." Then she reached for a kiss.

"Hopefully there's a lot more where this came from. If you can swing it, I'll get Mike and Bill to meet you on Sunday. We can exchange info, and look at all the trinkets." David replied.

She fondled the chain. "I'm there, whenever, wherever Mr. Warner. You are quite a guy — and you have just acquired a second shadow. We are going to stick close together. And I mean close. This is the most exciting thing I've ever done," she paused, "and that says a lot."

"It's understood; you cannot mention anything about this to anyone. Nobody. Not Bernadette, your sisters, or cousin Ernie." David pressed.

She laughed, "I don't have a cousin Ernie, but I understand. Nobody will know anything. I can imagine what problems could come from this. Believe me, I know. Now, come over here." She pointed to her side. "I know it's hot, but let's rest together and," she giggled, trying to tickle him, "have some afternoon delight."

During the second dive everything went well. After moving another two rows of rocks, a pile of seven, fused together, small-diameter cannon balls protruded from the bottom. In the final minutes, David used the bar to move a larger-than-usual stone. Feliza whisked the remaining sand and uncovered the nose of a small, five-foot bronze cannon. He pointed at his watch, and then up. She shook her head and pointed to the cannon. He grabbed her wrist and they swam up the anchor line.

She watched him intently, pouting as they slowly surfaced. "I can't believe we left that cannon down there," she shouted as soon as her regulator was out of her mouth.

"Wait a minute, don't get upset. There's still tomorrow, or the next day. We've got to decide what to do with this stuff. It'll be pretty difficult to deny what's going on if we show up on the beach with a brass swivel gun. Besides, we don't have a lift bag big enough. It'll have to be a night time beaching with help from the boys."

"I know you're right, but that cannon's so cool. I can't wait to see it all. How are you planning to retrieve it?" Feliza asked as she stowed the gear. David hauled the anchor, and she started the boat.

Doing his best Bogart imitation, "Well sweetheart, here's what we're gonna do. That cannon will be harnessed to something that can float it — like the lift bag I use on the anchor, only bigger. It shouldn't take much, because it probably only weighs, maybe two hundred pounds. The real effort will be to get it into the boat. Probably have to float it all the way in. Once on the beach, it'll be damn heavy. That will be a very straining dead lift. That's why we need the boys. Now, let's go back and shower — then I'll take you home."

"Are you in a hurry to get rid of me, Mr. Warner?" The transmission clicked as she shifted into forward and gave it some throttle. She turned and smiled, "My watch says it's only two. I think we can squeeze in another power nap."

CHAPTER SEVEN

The ride to the Old Fort was quiet. They were tired. Feliza was quiet, lost in thought. His own thoughts were about luck. Things were going good, but he tried to think what could go wrong. Then he realized everything could …unless they were very careful.

Slightly sunburned from the excursion, his thoughts bounced to why the small wing windows had been discontinued from truck doors. It certainly reduced ventilation. The floor vents only transferred the road's heat and dust into the cab. The radio droned local calypso intermixed with current stateside hip-hop and rap.

Feliza requested David drop her directly at work rather than her house — so she wouldn't have to locate another transport later. Bernadette was already there with the car, cooking that evening's specials. His dive buddy didn't require much assistance to enhance her looks, but her small, yellow duffel bag contained soaps, creams, powders, scents and lacy unmentionables — which she displayed to obtain his attention as he parked.

"David, come get me tonight, please?" Feliza quietly asked. "I'd like to stay with you. Something strange is happening. Me, tough woman, miss you, tough guy, too, too much. Really, I do. It'll make everything easier to go out again tomorrow."

"No complaints from me. What time will you be finished?" he agreed.

"It's Wednesday, a slow night, so come before nine." She kissed him as he nodded agreement and then bolted from the truck.

Turning, she blew another kiss. "It's exactly four. Thank you, David. See you tonight."

If David hadn't backed the pickup out of the parking lot, they would have chatted and kissed for another half-hour. His route took him to the Cable and Wireless office. With notebook in hand, he dialed Amy in Washington. Local communications had evolved a lot in the last few years on Carriacou, but long-distance calls could not be made from an average home or business. Sitting at an almost-private booth with the assistance of the AT&T international operator, he punched twenty-one digits. After passing through a couple of correct extensions, he heard a familiar voice —

only fourteen hundred miles away.

"Lieutenant Whistlow, how may I help you?"

"Let's see, I can think of about a dozen ways," he stated a bit too quick.

"David, I've been expecting your call since this morning." Amy laughed lightly, "I could spank you for being so inconsiderate."

"How have I been inconsiderate? You said to call today. I know you religiously work until five. It should be three-thirty where you are. I apologize if I should have called earlier, but I just came in from diving."

"You should apologize for treating me so poorly. I thought we had a great relationship — and yet you deserted me," Amy chided.

"Come on Amy, you know you always have an open invitation to visit. You could have written or called."

"David, you're an ass. I did call. Remember? I'm certain I wrote you a letter each week for the first month. All were received without a reply — not even post cards, not even with a simple phone call. Now out of the blue, you need info and ring up little Amy. Really?!"

The line carried a heavy silence.

"Amy you're exactly right. I am an ass, but this reprimand is costing two USD a minute." He couldn't discern if she was sulking or grinning on the other end.

"You sound like a little boy with his hand caught in the cookie jar. You know I'll always help — even if you don't care about me." She laughed. "I emailed all the info I could scan. Seems like you're on to something. The ship, the Century, is real enough — and according to Lloyds, a fortune in insurance was paid when it was lost. But the really incredible thing is there were at least two survivors. I cross referenced the list of crew and passengers you supplied through about three dozen European historical data banks," she cleared her throat for emphasis. "Few others could've gotten access to — such data or even realized — it existed. Europe has lost a lot of info due to constant conflicts and wars. However, they seem more interested in logging every remaining bit into computers, so it doesn't disappear forever. Britain had a wealth of info, as did the Netherlands. The two men I discovered were listed as pirates captured in 1701 and hung the following year. However, it doesn't say much about an inquiry. It seems that they were tried collectively with two ships' rosters. Their names, nationalities, and a curious reference to the Century, were listed at the time of their punishment. I have the names of the officers of the tribunal. Doesn't that just amaze you? It really amazes me."

"Yes it does — and you always will amaze me, Amy dear. You didn't see any treasure maps with a big 'X' — did you? Things have been very interesting here. I don't want to talk about it on this phone. How secure is email?" David questioned.

"Not very, but someone has to be purposely watching to notice anything. Do you think you're being observed?" She inquired fretfully. "This isn't dangerous, is it?"

"Not yet," he replied. "If we do find something significant, there will be problems. Always is around big money. Maybe you shouldn't visit until it's over. I'd hate to see you get involved in a mess since you're a commissioned naval officer from a prestigious Navy family."

"Wait a minute, Mr. David Warner; you pick my brain, pique my interest and then say stay?" she admonished. "No way, Jose! I'm making plans to visit in three weeks and stay for two. That way I can get a super tan and look simply scrumptious for the Academy's graduation at the end of April. Think of me all tanned, wearing my whites. Doesn't it make you want to reenlist?"

"Makes me want to do something, but it certainly isn't exactly building any desire to hang out around Annapolis." David checked himself before he began chewing on his toenails. "Unless you and I were alone. That's the problem about a visit in three weeks. I'm doing a lot of diving, and I can see it's bound to increase. We wouldn't have much quality time together. Really, I leave every morning after checking in with the men building my boat, sorting out minor problems, and then I dive all day. Listen, Amy, I did find something. Oh, while I'm thinking about it, add a simple dependable underwater camera to the list and some of those small flotation bags."

"Yes, David, really? Don't try to change the subject. Who is she? You want to take her picture?" Amy quipped. "I can tell when you start using this quality time bull. Don't you think I can occupy myself — or do I have to be with the macho diver every minute? Let me remind you, I am also an excellent sport diver and can always help. If you want more research, I'll compromise, but you better send me a plane ticket. Remember a deal is a deal — or you'll be walking with a serious limp. You'll get the camera and satellite photos when you meet me at the airport in Grenada."

"Amy, thanks for reconsidering. That's a fair compromise. Come the last week of March. That way, you can have a radiant tan and a great story to entice the graduating cadets. In a few weeks my boat will have its mast and rigging. It should be in the water. By the time you show up, we ought to be finished salvaging and I'll be able to take a break. I promise. I'll send the ticket this week."

There was utter stillness on the telephone. "Alright David, but if you call and delay, or stand me up, I swear you will pay dearly. David?"

He coughed, "Yes?"

"I still love you." She cooed.

"Thanks Amy, that sounds good," he hesitated.

"David, say it. Don't you love me anymore?" Amy imitated an adolescent whine.

In his best attempt to copy a president and commander-in-chief, he responded, "Of course Amy, we just might define it differently. I will always care about you, but at this moment, we are worlds apart. I'm still finding out who I am."

"Cut the crap," Amy blasted. "Worlds apart, huh? Well if this world doesn't meet your world the Monday of the last week of March, you will never get these legs apart again. Do I make myself clear? You have weeks to locate whatever it is that will return the old David Warner charm. At least say you miss me?"

"Amy, you are constantly in my thoughts. Look, I'm sorry. It has been a long, hectic day, and it's only half over. This retirement is a lot more strenuous than I imagined. We will have a great time. Got to go — or the old phone credit card is going to get a hernia."

After a few more endearments, David headed for the Outpost. Unannounced, he knew today's finds would guarantee a warm welcome. The divers had hurried past Bill and the crew when they unloaded on the beach — as Feliza didn't want to take the time for proper introductions. He'd hear about it tomorrow morning and see all the goodies in the evening. He beeped his horn since Mike had the chain across his entrance. He appeared after a wait and chatted without dropping the barrier. Finally, he seemed convinced David had something important, but still wasn't interested in company.

Mike seemed irritated, which wasn't out of character — but considering the team would hopefully progress from partners to friends — it was unreasonable. He offered little hospitality and no drinks. He claimed he had a guest, who must've been out of sight in the aft bedroom. He made it obvious the present was definitely not a good time. They would stick to the meeting the following night. Feeling slightly put off, David never pulled out the day's finds. He began to wonder why half of the people on Carriacou made it a point to be mysterious. The wreck waited hundreds of years, so another day shouldn't matter.

Another phone call saved him a late-night ride when Feliza said she'd make her own way. If he was sleeping when she arrived, which he was, she promised to wake him gently, which she did.

\\\\\\\\\

It's an understatement to describe the rush hour in Annapolis, as hectic. Leaving the small port town for the Washington Beltway is a tedious journey. The six-lane highway gets so congested that no one can rush. Traffic barely crawls.

Midweek February meant the sun exited at five-thirty. Airborne pollution reflected the sunset into a collection of purple and rose half-tones that blended into the grays of a sporadic light rain. There were no visible early evening stars. The moon would hint a luminous glow, if anyone cared to look. A squat, dark blue, four-door sedan inched toward its escape from the congestion.

Amy turned from the car window's dismal view. "Father, David's not being uncooperative. He is in transition. I mean, you couldn't just retire, could you? It would take some time to adjust to having an entire day for your own ends," Amy lobbied. "Well, he's discovering what to do with the second part of his life." She slid across the rear seat and hugged her father's arm. "You always said he was like the son you never had."

"Yes, Amy, yes, but I thought he was going to be a son-in-law. Everybody has to find him or herself today. When did they get lost? Hell, the service keeps you from disappearing, makes you part of a country. David had a great future with you and the Navy, but no — he wanted to do a

Hemingway stint on some Caribbean island and abandon everybody." Vice Admiral Charles Whistlow looked out the side window as a light drizzle began.

In his mid-fifties, Charles Whistlow was still trim and conditioned. His realm as Chief of Naval Communications at the Academy permitted plenty of time for the gym. He was barely computer literate, and had minimal knowledge about the modern communications that had succeeded the Morse code and signal flags. His square jaw and graying crew cut could usually be viewed at the head of a table surrounded by ranked tech types — who were building, refining, and accelerating the best, most complex, utterly secretive com systems in the world. From spy satellites to trained dolphins, Commander Whistlow stayed out of the loop, except in crisis situations. "Now, Davy boy wants some U.S. naval resources to do what — treasure hunt? This is the part I don't quite understand. He drops out of the Navy as soon as he's eligible for a paltry monthly pension. Drops you like yesterday's newspapers and..."

"Dad, he did not drop me! I thought riding home and having dinner with you might soften your perspective. We'd discussed his trip to the Caribbean and the sailboat. Somehow, David's got a connection with that little, backward island... what's its name? Carriacou, I think. He'd been there before. I liked him because he was an individual. But he couldn't be entirely comfortable any longer in situations crowded with too many nameless faces." Slightly huffed at her father's bluntness, Amy turned to view the monotonous, slowly passing roadside.

"And now, he wants all the assets of the US Navy put at his disposal. He expects you to perform at his beck and call. I thought my daughter would have more sense." Her father cut the sentence short. David had been one of his favorites among Amy's many suitors. He had provided good company and security on various international fact-finding missions. A good golf game coupled with adequate poker skills had accented his future 'in-law' status. Anyone else would have pumped such connections for promotions or favors.

Still squeezing his right arm and snuggling closer, Amy continued to lobby. "Well, Dad, David just wants to get some info and a couple of sophisticated, hand-held metal detectors. The Navy will have a field test of its latest equipment. I've already sent the satellite photos he requested and some other stuff. It's not a big deal, Dad. David is flying me there in a month for a reunion. Who knows, maybe I can work my feminine charm — woo him back stateside, and into private work."

Amy had few of her father's features, other than his temperament. Overly confident and assertive at five foot seven, she was slim and well-proportioned. Unmarried at twenty-eight, she continually turned heads in the Academy's hallways. Her strawberry-blond hair was cut stylishly short to highlight her radiant, green eyes. Of her three siblings, she was the only one who had enlisted in the service. Two older sisters followed her mother's path as pampered, suburban housewives — and her younger brother Joe was a budding minor league baseball player.

As a child, Amy had always been an organizer, keeping everyone on schedule, paying attention to the details. Computer-sophisticated by her twelfth birthday, neither the classroom nor the gym presented any problem at the Naval Academy. She continued at the academy as a research-instructor for the communications division. Most of her life, her father had been away at sea doing equipment trials. Three years ago, he had accepted a transfer to figurehead the communication division. Daily contact with him had created surprisingly few chafing moments such as this.

She and David had met when he studied advanced computer training within her department. She'd taught a three-day seminar on locating information systems and caches. The Shore Patrol sent him to enhance their present referencing system. Incapable of the complex task, David returned to his tutor, Amy, for help. Working together spawned playing together. Again, she was practically begging permission from Daddy to retry the same 'working together' tactic to regain David's attention.

"Yes, Amy, I'll help, but only along product test perimeters. If something happens, no mud gets on our shoes. Understood?" he emphasized. "Prepare proper test contracts for two metal detectors. Supposedly, Seal Team Four has used them, and the detectors can be calibrated to discern the metal in a computer chip underwater. Everything goes out super quiet. I'm betting that his search is in the waters of another sovereign country. If David gets into a squeeze and our satellite photos and info are discovered, it could make for an international scene." He thought for a moment. "Send him some UW radio equipment so he can communicate with the surface. We always need that stuff field tested." He nudged Amy who was now smiling.

"Thanks, Dad. I'll have everything coordinated and sent tomorrow. If anything else comes up, I'll let you know." She rested her head on his shoulder as the driver finally approached their exit.

\\\\\\\\\\

"So what you think, mate? That swabby's diving on something out there? What's it been now, huh, three days in a row? I say he's on that wreck."

Tony overflowed a hammock that was strung between a hook on the wall and a support post for the upper sun porch. He laid motionless watching the last rays of light recede from the eastern horizon. The two men had enjoyed a bottle of rum with several juicy limes during their day of binocular spying from the balcony. Palmer sat in a chair with the back tilted against the wall; his short legs were wedged against the railing.

"Look, Tony, the old nig building his boat must've told him something. Damn, I wish Tunaman would get here with the yacht. We got to do more reconnaissance — you and me, mate — before Tunaman shows up. If we don't have the facts when he gets here, shit, he'll be a raving lunatic again. And you well know that shaved-headed prick loves to bitch and moan."

Palmer cut another small lime and squeezed it into his rum glass. Then, he smoothly measured two teaspoons of brown sugar into the liquor. Practiced stirring caused a continual clanging as the spoon rattled against the side of the tumbler. After a sip, he continued, "Not tonight. We're a bit in the bag, aren't we, for a mission tonight. Tomorrow night, rain or shine, we're going to investigate him. For his sake, I hope he has other plans. Never really did like swabbies, did we, Tony?"

The bigger man reclined, dressed only in white Fruit of the Looms. He hadn't responded as much as a twitch to his friend's monologue. Tony didn't care what they did, as long they did it organized and sober. Only once had he and Palmer been forced into a confrontation unprepared, and more than slightly intoxicated. They'd lived through it — barely. That was a lesson that guided their lives: if they were to continue working in the international shadow world, and excel through greed and enterprise, they'd have to remain continually on guard.

This island offered a rare moment of relaxation. As long as they didn't create an uproar too soon, they could relax in anonymity. Basically, their business was to live unnoticed while carrying out Tunaman's projects. He owed Tunaman, big time, a debt that might never be repaid in full. What else did he have to do? Hanging with trustworthy comrades and running little adventures in far-off, out-of-the-way places hadn't been a bad life. But it couldn't go on forever. Tony turned carefully in the hammock to lie on his side facing the sky's colors as they retreated over the hill.

Maybe this could be the last little adventure. 'Little adventures' was what Tunaman liked to call his projects. Go here, meet so-and-so, and get this. If there's any resistance — you know what to do. There would always be resistance, and Tunaman would stay in the shadows until another mess was finished. They had enough money, but they continued the little adventures for the excitement's sake.

After meeting Palmer during a Vietnam tour in the late sixties, they'd become mercenaries with excursions into Laos and Cambodia. On the last covert mission for God and country, they'd been misinformed. The pack train from the North wasn't carrying SAM rockets, but kilos of opium. Realizing a potentially profitable diversion from their present occupation, the duo defied their government superiors and a Thai warlord. It was the latter who taught the lesson about preparedness.

Palmer and Tony had carefully taken the captured opium by boat to Bangkok, where a buyer could be discreetly located. They had hidden everything with no other helpers, or witnesses. After patrolling the bush for six weeks, relaxation with young oriental women beckoned. The Thai warlord had located the two Americans while they were enjoying a drunken weekend with several local girls. Two white soldiers — one tall, the other small — were easily noticed loitering on the streets.

They had made their first mistake by believing the pack train was opium grown in Laos. However, it wasn't Laotian. Instead, it belonged to a powerful, unrelenting Thai warlord who would not permit such an insulting theft. The sale of the raw drug could purchase more armament — which could further increase the warlord's area of control.

The two teenage whores put barbiturates in Palmer's and Tony's beers. When they awoke, each man was tied across the back of a donkey heading back into the mountains. Not one word was spoken among any of their captors during the four-day trek. Finally, the trail arrived at an old monastery on a ridge above the jungle. Surrounded by crumbling walls, the warlord, Li Mal, sat in a large, wooden chair in the center of the stone-paved courtyard, enumerating his loss and remorse in passable English. The chieftain explained he had worked on a French ocean freighter as a cook's helper. Young, ambitious, and intelligent, he learned several languages while visiting various ports around the world. He regaled that at eighteen, he'd met an Arab in Algeria. The Arab could trade opium from Li Mal's village to the French for weapons and gold. After two deliveries, the Thai no longer needed the Arab middleman. Now at thirty-two, a ripe old age for a drug dealer and a highland warlord, he would not permit a robbery by two young American soldiers.

Palmer and Tony bargained the stolen opium's location could be traded for their safety, but there was also the accounting of the men and the donkeys they'd killed. After all, this was business. During a week of imprisonment, they realized they'd been forgotten. The two Americans vowed to remain silent. If they died, the opium would be lost forever. Although the huge stone building was almost in ruins, their separate cells were impenetrable. Commotion from outside wafted in through the only air vent — which was the size of a shoebox. Another load of the drug had successfully arrived from the North, further reducing the prisoners' value. Now their pain could provide amusement and a lesson to those who might ponder crossing the chieftain. Tony hadn't said a word to his interrogators. In full view of Li Mal and his people, Tony was tied to a chair in the courtyard. With a pair of pliers, his tongue was pulled and sliced. Palmer had been caught smoking a cigarette he got from a guard. Li Mal felt it was fitting that his first punishment should be burns — hundreds of burns — inflicted by a glowing cigarette.

Each day, they grew weaker and more morbid. Tony had the stub of his tongue cauterized with a soldier's red-hot bayonet, but Palmer's blisters festered. The torture was extended each evening for entertainment. Everyone loved demeaning the GI Joes. Li Mal brought them from their cell for a fourth consecutive night of slow torture. The big white man was tied into the chair again and had bone needles driven under the nails of both big toes. Through his pained gaze, Tony thought he discerned another white man sitting beside the warlord, seeming to enjoy the spectacle. Palmer, almost unconscious, was hauled in, stretched by his hands and feet between two ancient stone pillars. The warlord laughed that he was doing a good deed by making the small man taller.

Li Mal's white associate walked into the torture arena and inspected the victims. After looking each directly in their eyes, the burly young man took the warlord's ear and they sat whispering. While the conversation continued, a wave from the warlord halted the torture.

Tony, his chin resting on his chest, was exhausted from the excruciating ordeal. His head bounced up as he heard soft words clearly, in his native language.

"You are a lucky son-of-a-bitch today. I've just bought your mangy ass, and your mangled friend, from little Attila. You belong to me until you repay the debt with interest." The young white man dictated. "If you anger me or don't abide by my orders, your death throes will make this look like a birthday party. If you understand, nod your head." The voice moved away and suddenly the needles and the bindings were removed. Tony collapsed from the chair, only to be dumped with his hands still tied into a cart drawn by a water buffalo. Face down, he hoped the other immobile parcel in the cart was Palmer. A fitful hour passed as he awaited his escape. The wagon finally began to roll down the trail into the jungle. Almost a half-day later, the wooden wheels stopped creaking.

Tony was rolled over and his bonds were cut. Two large, oriental men carried him to a stream, where a young woman bathed and treated his wounds. His tongue would be gone forever, but at twenty, he healed quickly. The trio left Thailand within two days' time. The memory never faded. Palmer was rehabilitated in Australia with salt-water baths and skin grafts. Although their bodies healed, their hatred blossomed into a total disregard for any authority, except their savior. Their savior was Thomas J. Briscoll Jr., nicknamed 'Tunaman' because Thomas J. Briscoll Sr. owned Briscoll's Canned Tuna. A series of inane TV ads with a big tuna sitting in an underwater school, learning different casserole recipes had made Briscoll's Tuna famous. Thomas J. — never Tommy — would inherit his seven-digit trust fund at twenty-one and set out to make his own larger fortune, not by fishing or with drugs, but with antiquities.

After a prep school visit to Sotheby's before he became a teen, Thomas J. realized a small sculpture could buy a Lear Jet — and dogs hadn't been trained to sniff for artifacts. The Euro-American judicial system played easier if you stole the mementos of a long-gone culture, rather than robbing banks where the payoff was considerably less. During school vacations, Thomas J. became an expert at buying antiquities low and selling high. Parents of classmates became his clientele.

Li Mal had accumulated several miniature statues from paramilitary forays against other warlords and chieftains. The Asian's international savvy and connections put the collection on the black market. Tunaman was receptive and able to respond personally. Who could be trusted to carry a sum of gold sovereigns to the Highlands of Indochina? The first security guards had been vicious Korean thugs, but they couldn't be trusted unless their loved ones were held hostage.

Tony and Palmer proved their loyalty again and again — thus restoring their leader's faith in man's undying greed. In those early days, Palmer continually talked of revenge against Li Mal, but as their quality of life enhanced, the pain of the memories ebbed. Strong bonds grew between the three. The two ex-soldiers never wavered from their profession — continually honing their skills while awaiting their next little adventure.

After enjoying and recuperating from soirees, they returned to Bangkok and retrieved the opium. Through his channels, the load of two-hundred-sixty-four pounds of blackish-red tar was packaged inside ten fish destined for a family cannery in Seattle, Washington. People who bought ancient art often dabbled in other illegal sources of income. That was their only instance of drug smuggling. The opium money bought a custom, thirty-meter motor yacht — which became their home when they were working or relaxing in the Western Hemisphere. From South America, valuable Incan trinkets were easy to collect and held Tunaman's attention during the years.

"Hey, you big, dumb ox! I'm talking to you and what do you do? You turn your damn back to me!" Palmer bellowed. "Tony, tomorrow, no sauce — and we'll survey this Navy dude's place. I tell you, I think he found something. Tony, you listening to me? Hell, I might as well be shouting to this wall as I try to get your old, gray ass to respond." Palmer staggered and leaned on the railing while relieving his bladder to the treetops below. He grabbed the side of the hammock and gave a strong push.

"Har, har, matey, I'm going to get some shuteye and you ought to do the same. We'll need the rest for tomorrow. Not as young as we used to be, you know," he chided.

\\\\\\\\

Somehow, Feliza made her way to David's cottage. Dozing, he never heard her transport — and she never mentioned how she got there. Both exhausted, they slept deeply until the alarm erupted at the ungodly hour of five. He calmed her with the lure of the bronze cannon and the potential of what else they might find. Some soothing attention applied to her tired muscles got them to Dolly before six. The explanation about varying their dive times and days had no opposition. At that early hour of the morning, the sea looked and felt incredible. It was cool, the surface like glass. Dolly pushed along at a quiet half-throttle as his dive buddy reclined on the middle seat, not even bothering to coat herself with the usual, massive quantity of sunscreen. Again, they dropped into the sea exactly on the mark. Early morning dives are usually incredibly tranquil. Fish are just waking up and slow to react. A pair of bright blue-and-yellow French angelfish swam up close, as if to say, 'It's too early for work'. Feliza began to brush sand away from the wood they had uncovered with yesterday's labor. David saw her movements quicken as she placed several objects in her yellow net bag.

Independently, he began to clear the area surrounding the anchor. It appeared the anchor was resting at a level of two ballast stones above the small cannon. This might indicate that the cargo hold had shifted as the boat sank. His shoulders and arms ached from moving a hundred-plus rocks during the past days. Every now and then, he'd get a shove from his dive partner — as the movements dumped more sand on to her almost-clean wood floor. In the first twenty minutes, he had uncovered the entire anchor. The shank was definitely crossing their cannon. They'd have to wait for bigger lift bags to move this obstacle.

On the surface, Feliza carefully examined each piece she'd placed into the bag, asking again and again what he thought the corroded chunks might be. Too bad — most appeared to be fasteners from the rotting hull. She'd found some blocks from wood pulleys, two more small perfume bottles, and a handful of lead balls, either for muskets or fishing weights.

Her best find was a flattened, brass funnel that may have been the captain's megaphone to shout orders to the crew. To protect the fragile items from heavy scuba tanks and careless feet, and prying eyes, they stored each item in a five-gallon plastic bucket that was capped and placed in Dolly's bow.

"Not a bad dive. What do you think, David?" she asked as they reclined, spooning, under the tarp. "How old is this ship supposed to be? Everything seems pretty new." She turned her head and kissed his cheek. "Hey, where'd you put the necklace?"

"Not to worry. It's in a safe place."

"I was thinking I'd like to wear it the next time," she coughed, "rather, the first time, you take me to the Abacus Hotel for a night out — a real date."

"We'll have to discuss that with our other partners."

"You know, David. It was you and I that found this site. Here we are, risking our lives to pull it apart and these other men, your supposed friends, are going to take a share of our labors. Somehow I can't figure their participation in this thing." Feliza pushed herself up on her elbows. "My father and Bill searched in the beginning, but we found it." She extended her arm to show various scratches mingled with bruises, "And it's only the two of us taking the punishment. Where does this teacher fit into all of this? Don't misunderstand me. I'm not really complaining, but this is more work than fun. I'm a strong woman, but not a dumb one. I just don't want to be working for someone else's profit."

He expected this issue sooner or later. "The other two will have specific roles in this. I'm not sure what yet, but Bill will help with the salvage when he gets my boat floating. Then, the carpenters ought to be able to construct the interior after the mechanics set the diesel engine. That should be finished by the end of next week. According to Bill, the mast is waiting and the engine, transmission, shaft and prop are all on island." His hands wandered to her brown shoulders and began to knead and rub. "I thought we ought to take a break for the next two days — until Sunday when all four of us can work out here. I don't know about you, but I'm getting tired."

"Oh, that feels so good, don't stop." She straightened so that he could relax her tight muscles. She continued in patois. "Yous boss man, me only little black slave girl that does her chores. No problem."

"We'll need everybody, early on Sunday, to move that anchor." David said. "The cannon might be the first piece that could identify the wreck. It'll take some jerry rigging, but it can be floated away from the pile. The way it looks now, I may have to double or triple my estimate of ten days. The pile is a lot bigger than I thought. Seems like it's tilting to the north, since the hull would be lying on one side. Where we started, the rock pile was five stones high, but at the end of the anchor flukes, it's seven thick."

"What do you want to do on this dive?" Feliza asked. "It looks to be about another ten feet, at least, to cut across the pile to the next sand patch. We're not finding a lot of remnants of cargo. We can't keep going under that anchor."

"You've got to figure, as the boat broke up, the majority of the cargo floated away. My knowledge of old ships doesn't go much further than Moby Dick or Horatio Hornblower books," David continued. "Can't really say what we should expect to find. That's up to Mike; he's the amateur archaeologist among the group. Tonight, I'll ask him to reference other wreck sites and what they've found. Let's continue in the same direction, but we'll have to make our path narrower to avoid the anchor sliding. When we get closer, don't place yourself where it can pin you down if it happens to slip."

Feliza looked up and turned to him, "Let's lie here. I'll place myself where you can pin me down, boss man." She laughed and licked the salt from the stubble on his chin.

The second dive offered a welcome respite from the rising temperature. It was after eight when they reached the bottom. Since Feliza had meticulously cleaned the wooden bottom, they piled this dive's stones on it. After about twenty stones were moved, David saw something bright white among the next row. Feliza was occupied carefully retrieving something large from the right side of their burrow.

Prying gently with the bar, David dislodged a stone to reveal the remains of a wooden box that had collapsed upon its contents from the weight of the stones. Its square, brass top had been protecting the white-clay pipe that had attracted his attention. Swirling the sand away, he revealed three more white-clay, foot-long pipes. After removing two more top stones, three other pipes of various styles appeared with a glob of metal that had fused in the salty environment. Turning to get the bag, he found his co-worker still trying to pull a cylinder from under the pile. Together, he pushed the pile up with the bar as she shook the object back and forth. With a sharp pull, Feliza retrieved a large, intact, clay cylinder. Their bottom time was almost maxxed.

Each dive produced more artifacts. Soon they'd each have a bag. Everything was clipped onto the anchor chain as they decompressed. For safety, they disassembled the power head and replaced it with a spear point before surfacing.

The diving was exciting, but certainly hard work. Lots of hours spent in Navy gymnasiums had conditioned David's appendages — but working underwater where carbon dioxide and nitrogen were new factors, caused cramps and aches in unexpected muscles. Feliza was also feeling the strain, but she remained silent and poised. She accepted the return as worth the effort. Part of his return was having her company every night. Each visit brought more feminine articles to the closet and bathroom. Even if this wreck offered nothing more of value, David considered Feliza's mark on his new life to be a fair treasure.

Underwater, the exhausted air from the regulator created constant noise. About the only other sound was the clicking of the stones as Feliza and David flipped another on top of the new pile. It wasn't until they had swum up to thirty feet that an outboard could be heard above. David cocked his head to see a small boat near Dolly. Feliza signaled to go up. He indicated they had to wait, especially since this was their second dive and they had been down for the entire twenty-two minutes. The arrival of company had to happen, that's why they carefully stashed everything incriminating before each dive. This dive's finds were resting fifty-feet below, but their visitors seemed to be cautiously approaching thirty-feet above on the starboard side. David waited ten more minutes, checked Feliza's remaining air, and indicated she should stay under while he surfaced.

Splashing loudly to warn of his approach, David found two Eastern fishermen sitting calmly in their small canoe. The boat belonged to Old Joe Simmons. Pete Liburd was throwing a weighted hand line. "Mr. SP, how tings? Yous been divin' dis place for a while now. What chu gots?" Joe smiled with a mouth almost vacant of teeth.

Placing the spear gun over Dolly's side, David disengaged from his BC and followed. What excuse could he invent to explain without attracting more attention? If he said he'd seen a big lobster, it could potentially attract other divers. "Well Joe, Sunday I got a big crab here, but did something stupid." He took a swallow of ice water from their jug and offered it to Joe and his friend. "I must have snapped the band on my good dive watch." Pointing to the inexpensive plastic digital, "It didn't cost a lot, but you know… has sentimental value."

Pete splashed some of the cold water around his neck. "Yass sir, mama ocean swallow up a lot de tings, mon." He was probably twenty or thirty years younger than Joe, but the Caribbean had weathered them almost identically. "Yeah, mon."

David's attractive dive partner, breaking the surface, interrupted him. Not saying a word, she took off her tank and climbed into the boat, pulling her gear behind. As she grabbed a towel and wrapped it to conceal her scanty two-piece, both fishermen stared wide-eyed. Finally prepared for an island exchange, she said, "Hello fellows, catching anything? Pass me that water, will you please?"

Joe spat and reached into his pocket for an unfiltered cigarette as Pete handed over the water jug. "Not much bitin' today, sweetie." He turned to David, "Sorry to botta you, SP. Tot yous was on de lonesome outs here, buts me sees dat you done caught da best ting." The two fishermen laughed, pushed off and slowly motored away, continually turning with hope of catching another glimpse of Feliza's curves.

The excuse seemed plausible, but the locals would have rum shop gossip tonight. It wasn't important where they'd been diving. What would stick with them was the attractive, native girl diver. They might associate Feliza with her father, but maybe not. They rested and organized their equipment until the fishermen had moved a good distance and then began pulling the anchor.

Bill met them on the shore and assisted unloading Dolly. The large towel still shielded Feliza as they rinsed everything. Bill whispered, "Sides her, what you got good today?"

"Oh, let's not talk about it now. Everything's in that bucket. If it's alright with you, I'll take you straight from here this afternoon to meet the teacher."

"OK with me, SP." Bill whispered again, "She coming 'long with us tonight?" He pointed as Feliza entered David's cottage. David continued to rinse with the garden hose.

"No, Feliza has to work. She'll chat with all of us about the project on Sunday. How's everything coming with Summer Breeze? Sorry I didn't make coffee this morning."

"No problem, SP. Reese did." Bill answered. "The diesel soon ought to arrive with a cherry picker crane. That prop shaft is ten feet. Got that drilled and placed already with the stuffing box and cutlass bearing. Once the Yanmar engine arrives, we'll set the stringer mounts, and bolt it up by Saturday. Poly tanks be fastened on each side 'fore and aft'. Carpenters should be able to conceal everything. Me knows that you wanna gets at the motor easy like — so me gonna design a little room that opens on both sides. The ladder from the deck hatch will come down right front the engine room. Your cabin will be aft."

Every so often, Bill would turn his head, trying to catch a view of Feliza through a window. "Mast be set with the same crane tomorrow. See, all clicking together."

David's new roomie could be heard singing above the sound of the shower.

"Yes sir, SP; you right in getting that girl to help. Just seeing her brightens everything 'round here. Hell, me gots to corral the workers and keep them out of sight of her — or they be slipping rest of the day on their slobber. Yeah mon, that's some piece of woman yous gots."

"I know, Bill, I know, but what about this afternoon?"

"Oh, me wait here for you and when the meeting's finish, me sleep on Moriah. Mon, all this action, and that young woman gots me heart pumping. Now Cecilia's getting better treatment than she's had for years. She's thinking me found some of that vee-agger stuff, good for the wood." He laughed loudly and looked at his watch. "Truck driver ought to be here 'fore noon, sose me gots to get back to pushing the men." He chuckled, "Yous probably wanna gets back to pushing, too."

David walked in to find a freshly scrubbed-and-scented Feliza sleeping soundly on the bed. Sitting at the table, he rinsed the seawater from his throat with a soda. He was certain his partner was down for a long nap. Not wishing to disturb her, he snoozed on the daybed. When he awoke four hours later, she had again vanished. The note on the table said she'd return later that night.

At three, David phoned Mike to confirm he was in the proper mood for their meeting.

The crane truck had arrived. The polished, new diesel engine already sat regally amidst the wooden ribs of the sailboat. It would produce only fifteen more horsepower than Dolly's outboard, but it should push Summer Breeze when the wind couldn't. From a ladder, Bill directed the men inside the hull coupling the shaft.

"Hey Bill, did you see my buddy leave today?" David inquired. "I can't figure out how she gets back to Mount Pleasant. She arrives quietly at night and then disappears."

"Nah, Boss, me no see. Nah, me was watching this motor slide right in there. Me thought yous was doing the same." He slapped David on the shoulder. "Yous must a been awful tired to let that girl outta yous sight. There been a few buses by. Everybody's interested in how this boat coming. The village's already expecting a good launch party. Yous been to a few other launches."

"Yes, I have," David replied, remembering foggy, drunken outcomes. "Do I have to make an appointment with the parish priest to bless her?"

"Where you think you is? Hell, if there ain't someone dying, then Priest Paul probably in his garden. He ain't got many souls to save when it ain't Sunday service. Been to too many of his long-winded sermons 'bout all this island's evils. Think he says de same thing over and over. Rum, dice, other men's women… straight to Hell we'se going, so he says. Nah, let Priest Paul know we'se christening the boat two weeks from Sunday. Everybody in the town will bring food if you supply booze," he laughed. "Coo-coo and stewed fish, ummm, rice en pigeon peas, maybe you splurge for a young piggy, and we roasts it over coals. Now that yous connected," he nudged David in the stomach, "to Mt. Pleasant, those fellas might want to visit the festivities. Get big old Bernadette over here, shaking her bumsy. You know her and me had a thing when we was kids. Cecilia had the luck of hooking me. Hah! Yeah, her bait was tight skirts — and the piece of land on Top Hill. Bernadette lived in those shacks where she's still at over in that dry, airless valley next side of Prospect."

"You mean they're living worse than my cottage?" David asked.

"Well, me ain't gonna say worse, 'cause it what she used to. Maybe they got inside water, but me no know. Place was her pap's, and he long gone. Bernie worked up in the hospital's kitchen 'til she took government retirement. When her sister left, she took over that bar. Me knows better than to drink over there. Cecilia won't even let me take her to the Fort for dinner. These island women never forget that jealousy stuff. But maybe Bernie's getting along better these days."

"Where exactly is her house?"

"Why, yous ain't been there yet?" Bill seemed shocked.

"I told you, Feliza comes and goes like the wind. I've never seen her anywhere, only at the restaurant." David lamented.

Bill took the time to explain all the roads and turn-offs that led to his friend Raymond's family property. Although Carriacou was a small island, there were many roads David had never traveled. According to Bill, Feliza lived less than a half-mile from Eastern, midway to the restaurant in Mt. Pleasant, on a severely rutted road carved into a steep hillside.

"Yeah boss, me suppose Dubois been up on that barren slope since 'fore the British took this place from French, way back when. Their daddy raised cotton and goats. The mama taught all of them to sew, weave, and knit. If yous wanted something made, a shoulder bag or a sweater, that's first place yous go. But all that ended when ships start bringing more stuff in de early sixties. Raymond was first fisherman in the bunch. When he drown, it signaled he was gonna be the last. Rest is still up there tying goats to trees. Tell you what SP, me can show you the road to their place on our way to the teacher's."

Before heading home, the boat builders carefully wrapped the exposed engine tightly in plastic. Bill freshened at the hose, sipped a beer, and rattled on about the oddities of the Dubois and Mt. Pleasant. The grass is never greener between small island communities, only competitive. Bill had risen to relative prominence by sailing trade goods from all the communities to other islands and better markets.

As they drove, he pointed to a rusty hip roof on a weathered, brown wood house. It protruded from the steep hillside held high by cement and stone pillars. The house looked like it had survived from the thirties or forties. It was sided with cedar shingles and wore what had once been ornate, white gingerbread trim on the eves and windows.

Although in need of paint and repair, the small cottage — probably only three rooms — nobly faced north from its perch, surrounded by a light tan hillside of dry, rutted pastures. Each window was shuttered and the doors were closed, thanks to the new advent of crime. Five or ten years earlier, the split front door would've never been shut, let alone locked. On tiny Carriacou — even in Mt. Pleasant with a population of maybe two hundred, crime prevailed — and usually went unpunished.

"That's where yous girly friend raised and probably still lives. Time was as many youngans up there as chickens. Bernie had a few, Raymond had three, and Marsha might had a couple 'fore she hooked up with that Brit guy."

David slowed the truck to hopefully see Feliza. There wasn't much that denoted comfort. Years of trampling had left the earth surrounding the house parched and sterile of vegetation. A large stone cistern sat behind the house — yet there were two blue, plastic barrels under the downspouts of rusty gutters. Behind the main building were two smaller structures of the same design, probably a kitchen and an outhouse. A thin goat ranged farther up the hillside, followed by its two kids. There was no car parked on the flat spot beneath the stone steps, where the deeply rutted driveway ended. The restaurant would be open soon — so both women were probably busy at the Old Fort.

After seeing where Feliza lived, she became more of a puzzle. Her beauty, composure, and talents did not befit the residence in view, or the sleepy rural Caribbean neighborhood. Carriacou was a great place to grow up — after adolescence it was a better place to be from — but far away from. Beautiful as islands go, it was a difficult place to prosper. If she had made it to the States, why had she returned? By her own admission, her sisters had done well for themselves in America.

The tropical ice wasn't melting yet, but had just lost some of its clarity.

CHAPTER EIGHT

Bill didn't say much after purchasing a half crate of beers. They rattled out of Mt. Pleasant, past the ruins of the indigo plantation, and along the cliffs to the Outpost. Bill's eyes widened when he saw the landed boat that was Mike's home.

"Me who builds she," Bill said reverently. "Was in eighty-tree for a guy from Petite Martinique. Them boys was just learning how to builds boats over there. They had me build this one and watched every step like four frigate birds. But they don't have a lick of wood on that rock. Not like we'se gots here. So, for years they used this one bringing sweet timber up from Guyana. Let me member now, they called her some almost religious sounding word — Magdalena. Yeah, that was it, Magdalena. Now me know who this schoolteacher is. Shit, he used to be bumming all 'round Eastern, long hair tied with a red bandana."

As if that was an introduction, Mike appeared from the inside and beckoned. David retrieved the two plastic buckets loaded with sea floor artifacts from the pickup's bed. There was still a bit of daylight, but a crescent of the new moon hung just above the beach palms.

"Bill, meet Mike Post." They moved into the screened patio. "Mike, I forgot to bring some newspapers to place what we found on; it'll be a bitch to clean up without them."

He withdrew into the interior and returned with an inch stack of Grenada national newsprint. "First, gentlemen, before we get our hands dirty, I propose that we get some of the legal aspects out of the way." Mike handed each a form contract agreeing whatever found would be divided into four equal shares.

The one-sheet contract contained five sections: Partnership, Salvage, Expenses, Sales, and Silence. For anyone else to become a full-share partner, they'd have to vote on them. If the government got a share, the partners' shares would be equal after their slice. Receipts had to accompany all expenses — and it suggested that each throw three hundred E.C. dollars into an account for expenses such as gasoline, boat maintenance, dive gear repairs, and long-distance phone calls. Just shy of four hundred and fifty

U.S. — twelve hundred E.C. — not much to begin a business. Every article to be sold had to have the sale price reviewed by the partners before any transaction was completed. There would be a receipt of all sales. Although none were attorneys, and no one knew any other group member well, the agreement would bind as well as anything else. They'd have to rely on that fateful word: trust.

Bill looked at David quizzically. "What yous think, SP?"

Mike straightened from peeking into one opened bucket. "This is a simple, basic contract. Hopefully we're friends, but this ties up a lot of loose ends. The nondisclosure part at the end means if one of us tells any outsider about this salvage effort in order for them to better the rest, then that partner's share is forfeited. It is pretty simple and up front. I just took it from one of my Law At Home programs, and added this and that to make it pertinent to us."

One of those things he added was the title, Contract for Salvage Within the Waters of Carriacou. Although this was definitely illegal, the contract made the fly-by-night operation sound official. David took the time to explain all of the consequences to Bill.

"Listen fellows," Bill began, "me knows this not gonna be easy. But if that wreck's really out there, let's do what necessary to get its treasure. Hell, none of us is spring chickens. We'se each had offers we either passed over or fouled up. So here we'se is, sitting round this picnic bench. Me is the eldest, but I'll strain everything if it will give me girls a better start on life."

Mike interjected, "There's one more thing. When we hit it — if we hit it — we can't all go out buying new cars and boats. The government will catch on and neighbors will be envious and questioning. So...we go slowly."

"Slow's all rights with me," Bill said in his best English without the usual island rhythm. He was on his best behavior trying to cast a proper impression to Mike. He reached into his pocket and unrolled three, one-hundred E.C. dollar notes. "When you need more, let me knows."

"Same here," David added, pitching his dues and Feliza's.

"Next problem is the contents of those two buckets. We are getting a lot of bits and pieces that might provide a clue to which boat we've found." Mike took one bucket of corroded metal and dumped it on the folded newspaper.

"To me," David said, "most of this stuff looks like fasteners, bolts and such."

"I don't think bolts were around at the end of the sixteen hundreds. I'll have to check," the teacher chimed as he inspected each piece, never losing track of the conversation. "I'll get some more plastic buckets, soak some in acid, and buy a battery trickle charger to do reverse electrolysis. The good stuff we'll keep, and the trash goes back to the sea."

The second bucket of glass and pottery chards held Bill's attention. He spoke holding the neck of a black glass bottle, "Lord, think how many of these bottles me broke as a kid. What would a whole one be worth?" he asked Mike.

"From catalogs of auctions, a bottle can bring as little as ten U.S. to thousands, if it is unique." Pointing to the two perfume bottles, "Those are sort of rare and definitely old, maybe fifty each, maybe more. We'll group together a bunch, as many as we find, and cut a deal for the auction. The price will climb on everything if we positively identify the wreck — but also if we're legally permitted to do the salvage. It'll probably work to our benefit not to have a legal salvage permit, because then we would have to give half away to the government. Then of course, there would also be high income taxes."

Mike measured the ceramic cylinder bottle that Feliza had found. It was fourteen inches high by three-and-a-half wide. Its reddish-brown glaze bore an inscription of a lion's head. "This is an old German water bottle. The ship's water barrels could be easily contaminated. Water from an island town could be deadly. Travelers carried personal water in ceramic bottles such as this one. Notice the name 'Nassau' neatly inscribed under the bottler's symbol, the lion. That's a town in southern Germany. It's no different than the Perrier bottled water we drink today. You should find a lot of these. For that many passengers, there should've been a couple hundred at least."

"Yous knows how many people was on the Century?" Bill asked.

"Sure do. I can tell you their names. In fact," Mike turned to David, "from your friend's information, we now know there were at least two definite survivors from the crew. Hey, your female friend in Washington really produced some incredible information. Did you call her? As you can see," he handed him a printed copy, "she's definitely coming for a visit."

"Speaking of which," David said, "Feliza can meet with you on

Sunday if we're all going to make a dive. That way you guys will know firsthand what we're talking about, and you'll be able to offer suggestions. She wants to meet you — and she'll need a contract. I've thought about it considerably. I truly think she's good for the project and shouldn't bring any problems."

"Yeah," Mike quipped, "I'll bet you thought long and hard." Bill laughed, hiccupped, and asked where the beer was.

Mike pointed and continued, "Your friend also says the equipment will be delivered no later than next Monday to the Chargé d'Affaires Grenada, a Mr. Lucas Shremshock. David, you'll have to go down there, sign for it, and transport it up here. I suggest you arrange discreet transportation, both on Grenada and a ferry."

"Wait," Bill mentioned, "me'll get Allister Hope's motor boat if this stuff ain't gonna be too big. Be three hours each way to St. Georges, maybe sooner if it real flat. Me gots lots of cousins down there that have cars and trucks. They knows me always get things for boats shipped in there."

"OK. Sounds good to me," David replied. "I'll call Monday to certify everything was delivered. You make the arrangements for Tuesday or Wednesday. Those metal detectors should make a big difference. I'm afraid I might be covering up treasure with the ballast rocks. Seems a hardship to have to move them twice. After two dives, we are beat."

"Yeah mon, me sees yous coming in, dragging both tails. If yous wants to, could use some of those stone for ballast on Summer Breeze. Something to think 'bout. Let them sit in the sun for 'while to kill the smell. The rest, me could stack right on the beach and sell them. Good river stone hard to come by on a dry island. Lead too expensive. Lots of guys have been mixing concrete, but sooner or later yous should remove it if yous gots a leak. Didn't yous ever see old Frenchie's pile of rocks over at south tip of Western Bay?"

"That's a very good idea, Bill, as long as it doesn't draw attention and it saves me some money while we are at it."

"Hey, wait a minute," Mike interrupted, "You have to buy those stones from the group." He saw two pairs of eyes stare from over their beers. "Just kidding, it would be great to recycle the stones. Give them new life on sea in the next millennium. But it seems it'll take a hell of a lot of work."

"Yous moving them now, right?" Bill reasoned, "Yous move them into a bucket or a net and puts on a small lift bag. We'se pull it easy to the surface and then drag them to the shallow with Moriah. Shit, me can get the construction crew to help by saying you found an old dump. See, every island port once had a ballast island made from dumped stones. Ships came 'in ballast'. That meant the ships came in with just stones for ballast, but empty of cargo. They'd dump the extra stone ballast before loading. If they dropped off cargo and didn't pick up much, then they gets necessary ballast from the pile. So, we just tell 'em it's junk. They help, as it is part of building the boat. They's knows."

Mike returned with more beers. "Sounds good to me," he said. "Tell us everything about the site again so we can think about it over the next few days."

Starting with the crab and finishing with the clay water bottle, David concluded they'd already moved almost a hundred stones. The anchor, Bill thought, could be brought in for a mooring. The report of the cannon thrilled his comrades. Having set the stage, David pulled the corroded disks that could possibly be coins from his shirt pocket.

The three little circles resulted in 'oohs' and 'aahs'.

Now that he had them primed, he withdrew the necklace and placed it onto the picnic table. Everything seemed to go silent. The gold shimmered, bathed in yellow from the bug light. Without a word, Mike shined a flashlight and stared at it.

Bill fondled it between his fingers, but didn't pick it up. "Yup, that's treasure; treasure damn straight." His scruffy, bearded face unfolded into a huge grin, a smile, and then a laugh. He slapped David on the shoulder and gave the high five. He giggled, "All those years me dream 'bout this, somehow me never think it would mount to something. Something like this!" He laughed again, a long, wholesome belly laugh.

"Wait a minute," Mike resembled Sherlock Holmes as he inspected the chain with a large, hand-held magnifying glass. Handing me the lens, he said, "Here, look, it says 'made in Taiwan'."

As David stooped slightly to look, he laughed just as heartedly and slapped the other shoulder. "Mr. Warner, you have found something of worth. I figure by weight alone," he dangled the necklace from his finger, "three ounces. That's mucho dollars, then add its styling, and that it's an antique, which brings its value up to at least several grand. So boys," he hesitated and raised his bottle for a toast, "and girls, we have made our investment back already."

Glasses clinked. David was thinking Feliza would love to keep the chain, but hopefully they'd all have a few from which to choose.

Mike unfolded copies of the email Amy had sent. "Well, it seems your friend knows what she's doing research-wise — and took time from her busy schedule. The man who first searched for the wreck was a Captain Burkeston, sent from the NVOC to locate the wreck in 1700. His schooner, the Mermaid, searched through the Grenadines and around Barbados without finding any wreckage or survivors. The family of the Hollenzocks and the insurers commissioned his voyage. Now Bill, the man you met in 1979 was Dean Worely, a petroleum geologist, who had worked for Shell Oil." Mike paused and read on. "According to their company records, Worely made a bundle from a percentage of oil field finds in Trinidad and Venezuela. He retired as a relatively young man at thirty-eight in 1972, with at least a couple million, plus stock options. He was one of the glory boys of the Rockefeller group in South American oil exploration. Says here, he's still living in St. Petersburg, Florida. Once a year, he teaches a seminar on oil bearing geologic structures at St. Pete's University."

Mike turned to another page. "I'll give you each a copy of everything, if you want them, but it's for our eyes only. I repeat; this stuff should be kept safely away from prying eyes."

"No, that's all right," Bill said. "If me wanna, me can read SP's after work someday."

"I'll take a copy and give it to Feliza to examine. It would be good to think everything over and chat a bit Sunday at my place before we go out to dive," David remarked. "Let's plan on getting on the water early. Then we can have a late lunch at my place," David paused, "after we move a hundred or so stones."

"I've got to bicycle over," Mike began, "unless you want to pick me up." David shook his head. He hoped to spend the prior night with Feliza. "Didn't think so."

"Well, to get on with this," Mike shuffled through more pages, "Worely's brother was a curator at the Smithsonian in Washington, DC. He's one year younger and retired in 1990. Guess where he lives? St. Pete. Must be one happy family where one brother researches and the other searches."

Mike rambled on, "According to what Amy dug up at the Smithsonian, seems brother Frank's specialty was the American revolutionary period. I'd guess he turned up some valuable evidence of the Century's wreck site among historical articles. Amy got into that section of the museum's database and scored a hit — because I was able to give her the names of the Century's crew and passengers. Seems she came across a reference to First Mate Allsop in a registry of pirates compiled …by…come on, now guess who compiled the list…you got it! Frank Worely, for a display and pamphlet published in 1967. She's enclosed the article, but it's pretty dry reading. However, Frank uses Allsop as an example of a good seaman who turned to piracy."

David got the last round of beers. They'd been chatting for nearly four hours. As it was almost ten, he hoped Feliza would be at his cottage. Their plans said she'd make her own way. Bill's head was slumped to his chest, breathing deeply in the midst of a good nap.

"Last, but certainly not least," Mike said as he grabbed the beer, "Amy cross-referenced those names again with the Dutch and British Naval records. She used the Common Market Historical Society to run it again, and came up with just about what I had on the Sterns and Hollenzocks. But here's the kicker, Mr. Warner, your darling friend, Amy What's-Her-Name, found the records of the piracy case against Allsop and Bosun Mate Peter Stricklind. Let's see, it names the trio of judges — and gives the charges against all twenty odd defendants. Allsop and Stricklind were captured by the HMS Defiance in New York Harbor among the crew of — are you ready for this? Captain William Kidd as he tried to surrender in July 1700. They were on a boat named, ahh, Antonio. Seems it was a sloop accused of pillaging several Portuguese and French merchant ships in the southern Caribbean. The Crown's reward for the rebellious privateer's capture was one thousand pounds and the captain kept the sloop Antonio to be sold at his discretion. Whatever Kidd's ships had done while off the East Coast of Africa must have been very bad — because it was shortly before the Spanish War of Succession in 1701. Most men, criminals or not, were conscripted into the navy to fight against Spain, but not Kidd, or the two survivors of the Century."

David looked at the old-fashioned brass table clock behind slumbering

Bill. It was late, and he could feel every bit of the long day.

Mike caught his eye. "Yeah, the clock's ticking. One more bit of interest though; Allsop and Stricklind were not tried by the usual tribunal. Only one judge, a Joshua Bergerman, heard their case. It was he who sentenced them to the gallows. My guess is he did that because these men were supposed to have already died. Guess Bergerman didn't want to make the deal. Anyway, on March 12th, 1702, they were hung — which was almost a year after Kidd's bones began to bleach."

"Seems a long time to keep them in prison back then, if they were captured in 1700," David observed. "When did the Century sink?" He reread the first page of Amy's message. "September, 1699. They survive the crash on the reef, or the storm, and are floating or beached, but picked up by a pirate ship in need of good sailors. They join, plunder, and perhaps die; or, they stay marooned and definitely die. They are shipwrecked for how long, two months or longer? Say even four, if they are beached. They pirate for an ill-fated six months, and are captured in 1700, a little less than a year after the Century sinks. There's no chance the boat they were captured with was the Century?"

"Hardly, it was reported to be a seventy-eight foot sloop of Spanish island design," Mike read. "No, if these two guys were shipwrecked, captured, forced to become pirates, and then captured by the Brits, they had a phenomenal run of extremely bad luck. However, they may have reasoned that the best avenue by which to receive a pardon was by surrendering to enlist with a warring navy." Mike began organizing a stack of papers to carry as David picked up the empty beer bottles and rousted Bill.

"I think I'll contact Amy again and ask her to check any more references to Judge Bergerman, the tribunal, HMS Defiance, and Captain Sheerson. If one of these men got the info on the wreck's location from the two remaining crew, they should have some fantastically wealthy heirs today. That result could be the end of our story. Those years were the heyday of piracy on the high seas. During the first two decades of the seventeen hundreds, Gentleman Stede Bonnet, Calico Jack Rackman, and Blackbeard met violent ends."

"So, the two Century sailors were in prison with the famous Captain Kidd. If he couldn't save himself with the amount of treasure he had amassed in the Indian Ocean, they must've had little hope in buying their freedom. I'd always heard Kidd was innocent and was hung due to trumped-up evidence to get at his gold. Supposedly, he was executed because he killed a mutinous sailor by hitting him in the head with a wooden bucket. He had been commissioned to sail as a privateer against the French, and to suppress any piracy they encountered. The issue was muddied." Mike sighed.

"Come on, Billy Boy." David grabbed him by the arm and led him to the truck.

"Mike, all this loot is yours to examine. I've already made a list, but I need the buckets back."

"Dump the remaining pieces on the newspaper and I'll sort it out tomorrow. Partners, see you early, like sixish, on Sunday morning?"

David pulled the truck door closed, "Let's make it sevenish, but be ready to go." Waving, he pulled out of the driveway. Bill was already asleep.

\\\\\\\\

Daytime temperatures in the southern Grenadines almost always hit the nineties, before dipping slightly to the eighties by sundown. The crescent moon became more visible as the sun set. Hard-packed, dry, dusty earth still radiated heat in the early evening. It was the dry season — so only scrub bush remained slightly green. Grass, not shaded or watered, had become brittle, golden straw after being deprived of moisture for more than a month. Wild tamarind and thorny bushes thrived in Carriacou's climate of eleven months of drought and one month of flood.

Scrawny cows showing ribs dragged almost empty udders. Dogs were emaciated and cats nonexistent due to the constant heat. Occasionally a pungent smell, mixed with a swarm of green flies, signified another animal had succumbed to thirst. Red as the clay they wandered on, scorpions and centipedes, fed from these carcasses. They were the only dangerous creatures on the island, other than man.

That evening, two stalkers scaled through an array of trails under a scant canopy of scrub bush. The taller man wore dark green pants and a like-colored, long sleeve shirt, buttoned at the neck and cuffs. A dark bandanna covered the top of his head, concealing shoulder-length gray hair from snagging on a thorny bush. For his size he was agile and quiet, intensely concentrating on every step. His gaze first scanned the immediate vista for anyone who might witness his movements. Then, he would watch the trail ahead, so as not to step on anything that might make a sound and attract attention. Years of similar activities had honed these skills to precise traits.

The shorter man was wearing the same style of shirt and pants, but in dark brown, especially darker where perspiration dampened the material. His hair was tucked into a brown pilot's skullcap. Their outfits were not meant to camouflage in the bush, but instead to disguise their identities as mechanics or tradesmen, which might possibly go unnoticed in this area.

It would have made no difference if they had been of African heritage instead of white continentals — because everybody knew who belonged in the neighborhood and who didn't. The best strategy was to stay out of sight. Both wore thin, black leather gloves, and carried a small, black canvas shoulder bag. They moved quickly through the brush, careful and vigilant.

The route from their residence on the hillside above Eastern took them through a labyrinth of old sugar plantation roads, which switched back and forth across the slope. They had hiked and mapped this area a few times during the previous weeks, placing empty Coke cans at intersections to mark turns. A narrow goat path led to the lower pastures of a small cattle farm named, Panderosa. Wiping sweat from their faces, the two waited silently at the hedgerow boundary of the dry field until they were certain they could cross the expanse without being observed.

Once the crossing was completed, the last row of the dozen or so houses furthest inland from Eastern Beach appeared. Three more, equally dusty cross streets separated them from the row of homes closest to the shoreline. They slowed their pace so no sleeping yard dog or guard rooster would awaken to give loud notice. The two men became detached observers of the island's home life. They noticed dinner dishes were rinsed in the outside tubs where families also bathed.

As they made their way along the shadowy roadside, radios, and occasionally televisions, could be heard from within the shabby, clapboard homes. It was seven-thirty and their destination of the beachfront cottage was probably another half an hour of quiet stealth away.

The acrid smell of smoldering garbage denoted someone had emptied a trash bin. Two girls carrying a baby walked two feet away as the two men hunkered, motionless, hidden among dried pigeon pea bushes edging the dirt road. The two men waited for the shadows from the row of trees bordering the beach to lengthen. They slipped through the withered stalks of last season's corn and bolted to the side of the small house.

The cottage wasn't locked. They entered confidently. Small flashlights from their bags provided just enough illumination through red plastic lens. They were alone and comfortable in the belief that they would hear the approach of any vehicle.

They propped open the back door so they could silently exit if necessary. If the occupant returned, they planned to escape quickly and safely, which translated to 'no confrontation'. After drinking his fill of water from the sink faucet and wiping his face, the bigger man immediately began to search the kitchen cabinets, shaking and feeling the shelved foodstuffs. He silently tapped the table in search of a hidden compartment before checking the underside and the accompanying chairs.

The smaller man searched the bedroom, without disturbing much, and found even less of value or interest. He methodically went through every book on the shelf and the small desk. Lifting the mattress, he checked for cuts along the seams where papers or valuables could be slipped. The painted wood floors were tested for loose boards, which might conceal a hiding place. A book on shipwrecks rested with two other books in a plastic bag. With slight satisfaction, he turned his attention to the closet and checked every pocket of the few hanging garments — and shook each of the neatly arranged shoes.

The other man was inspecting the toilet tank and the medicine cabinet in the bathroom when a lamp in the living area switched on — as if it were a surprise party, surprising the wrong people. The small man tucked silently into the closet and held the door shut by the knob. In the quiet of the dark bathroom, the other waited.

They smelled her before she was visible, floral perfume. Surely it wasn't the swabby. The woman was singing softly to herself the Tracy Chapman song, 'Fast Car'. The man in the closet could hear packages drop onto the table — then water running in the kitchen as the fridge door opened and closed. He silently scolded himself for not checking if the renter had a maid, girlfriend, or whore. The thought brought a smile since he knew one of the local lasses would gladly be all three. Either the search had been competent, not drawing attention by items misplaced, or she wasn't familiar with the house. He smiled to himself; again thinking she probably only got a good look at the ceiling. He quietly removed a small, strange-looking pistol from his pack.

Unknowingly, the woman walked to the closet to get a long T-shirt to sleep in — at least until her friend returned. The closet dweller was sweating profusely as he listened to her feet pad across the planks in his direction. Reliving times in an unventilated jungle prison cell, every nerve perked to listen. Fears from his past amplified his apprehension.

Feliza grabbed and turned the knob to pull, but the pine door pushed open violently, its edge thumping her in the middle of the forehead and nose. Shocked, she screamed and grasped her head with both of her hands. Feeling the wetness, she screamed at the discovery of blood on her beautiful face. Without ever seeing what had pushed the door open, she was silenced by a pair of strong hands. She heard a 'phfft', and then felt a sting. That was all Feliza would remember.

The slight crescent moon had passed the sky's midpoint by nine. A man was slowly picking his way through the rugged spiny bush. He was of Afro-Amerindian descent, and had better opportunities than outcomes. At seventeen, a cruise ship line had hired him as kitchen help and transported him to Miami. That had been the best time of his life — hanging with new friends from the world over and always having more than enough to eat. He'd bought nice clothes and went to South Beach discos when he had a night off before starting another cruise. Partying with the ever-present 'white dancing dust' deluded him into believing the good days would last forever — that he had truly risen above the others of his island village. One all-night party, which almost caused him to miss the ship, coupled with written reports of unruly disobedient mornings, ended his short career. The company wasted no time returning him home to the St. Vincent Grenadines.

His bank account and his possessions disappeared. His weight dropped by a dozen kilos after he had acquired a habit of sniffing the white powder. An uncle, who worked transporting the product among the local islands, fed his habit. Uncle Chaka smuggled coke to upscale brothers in the French islands in an overpowered Scarab speedboat. Nephew Gaston lost his job providing sixteen-gauge shotgun security after two kilos inexplicably became four ounces lighter.

Run off by his family, Gaston left Cananoun to plunder Carriacou. Although addicted, his basic reasoning was still good. The best houses would have the best stealables. He'd been sleeping on a folded-cardboard, refrigerator-packing box in the bush. Sheltered by a large mango tree, he watched a group of apartments. The slim West Indian removed a folded packet from the pocket of his shirt. He anxiously stared into the darkness for movement. The small glassine envelope opened to accept his thin, red-striped cocktail straw. Gaston had learned this sorting trick from a Jamaican bus boy on the cruise ship. The small straw's end was packed with the crystal stimulant. Rather than inhale it through the straw, it was turned with the loaded end inserted into his already large nostrils. Placing the straw as far up as possible, the index finger capped the exposed end. Once he began inhaling, the finger was removed, and the tiny amount of drug soared into his tortured blood vessels and nerves.

Eyes watering, Gaston inhaled sharply several times as he rose from the cardboard mat. He reasoned everything should belong to him — until he sold it to buy more incentive. It didn't matter if the unlucky person was white or black, home or absent. He was going to take enough tonight from the apartments to carry him to Grenada. There, he could find more targets, much easier targets with bigger payoffs. Stripping to only green, nylon boxer shorts, he grabbed the thick-bladed cutlass. His left hand felt for the patch of missing hair — and then felt the bruise on his forearm. The white asshole had caused him pain. Next time their paths crossed, he'd see to it he'd be the victor.

Barefooted, the dark man virtually disappeared among the shadows, only to reappear against the side of the pink, two-story building. The Abacus Hotel Apartments were the only attempt at condos on Carriacou. Four buildings with four units each surrounded a minuscule pool that should have been labeled a hot tub.

Local planners complained that the boxy, pink buildings looked grotesque on the hillside when viewed from the sea. The German developer had an expensive, private conference with the local government rep and then continued to build as he intended. Nowhere else on the island offered the convenience of a laundry and maid service. Unknown to Gaston, this season was slower than normal. Tenants only occupied half of the units. Shutters covered the other eight apartments to reduce sun damage. Each had steel bars across windows and doors in case it stormed before the Europeans returned in August. Cursing, the frustrated burglar tried an entirely closed building before he tripped and stumbled down concrete steps to an unbarred door.

The cutlass blade encountered only a latch and the door opened without alarms. Not bothering to close it, he headed directly to the refrigerator, guzzled three beers, and left the empties on the sink counter. Two slices of bread with a slab of cheese were consumed followed by a chilled mango. He grabbed a handful of candy from a bowl on the table and filled a garbage bag with more beers, fruit, and bread. The thief searched for items that could be converted to cash. The German owner trusted no one — so the television and VCR were bolted to a black, metal stand cast into the concrete floor. A Sony Discman and a stack of discs, followed by two wristwatches, joined the foodstuffs.

On the bookcase, he found two cartons of cigarettes, and another bowl of candy with five packs of chewing gum. In the closet, he found a pair of Nikes almost his size. The rear of the closet held two gray, plastic toolboxes. One was filled with electronic gadgets. Removing the top plastic tray revealed two pistols in holsters. Gaston almost orgasmed as he instantly envisioned himself an outlaw, a two-gun robber. Now nothing and no one was safe. He quickly popped open the other gray box to discover two mini radios and a stash of money from various countries. Still kneeling over the booty, he waved the stack of bills in the air.

Suddenly, the West Indian man was wrenched to his feet by his raised hand. The money fluttered into the open closet. The upward movement didn't stop until the black man squealed from the pain of his dislocated shoulder. As he was turned, a hand slid professionally under his neck, and grabbed the stubbled chin to stuff a rag into his bawling mouth. An unseen face whispered against his ear. "Boy, you picked the wrong supermarket tonight — and I'll wager you'll never have the opportunity to choose another." The black man struggled to reach the cutlass, but his head was pulled sharply. A snap, signifying his end, was followed by the click of the lights coming on.

"What a night, eh, Tony!" Palmer growled. "What a night! We get caught like rats, and scurry home to discover another rat is at our cheese! Jesus K. Christ! What's this quiet island coming to, a frigging crime wave in Sleepy Hollow? Look at this specimen of local intellect, barefoot with a cutlass."

Sniffing the air, "Let's not forget unkempt and unbathed. Frigging imbecile was taking all of my fags, your sweets, and shoes." The two men changed into casual clothes, walking nonchalantly around the body. "What do you think, Tony, shark bait? We could steal a truck and send him off the cliff? It's almost eleven; the world of Carriacou is asleep. This is Thursday night. It is very quiet, except for a couple of folks we know sitting about, wondering what happened. Har, har, har!"

The big man pointed to the balcony and gave an indication to throw the body over the railing. "Yeah, you being funny or what? You want to smell this poor, colored prick rotting like those cows we stumbled upon tonight? Tell you what, Tony, let's take him to the quarry and toss him like he had an accident." The smaller man fingered his mustache and chuckled, "You know, he did have an accident. He met us. After our bit of misadventure, he paid the price for violating our space."

Continuing after gulping a beer from the bag, "Speaking of violating, that bitch back at the swabbie's is the first wench I've seen here who could command a hundred US a night. Wonder how he got to be banging her? If we'd had more time, I'd have liked to inspect the merchandise better. How about you my friend?"

Tony shrugged and fitted his left thumb and index finger into a circle, stroking his right index finger through it. "Yeah, we could have taken a piece, but then she'd have to disappear. We wouldn't want to arouse suspicion, would we?"

The speechless man pointed to the dead thief on the bedroom floor. "Oh, no, this bugger won't point to us." He splashed some rum into the motionless dreadlocks. "No, this motherless son was out drinking, and fell into a ravine at the quarry. Can't see anybody, but bad luck being blamed for his misfortune. Is spaghetti okay for dinner? I don't know about you, but these little missions work up my appetite. We'll eat and then work off the calories dragging this bum to his final resting place." Palmer flipped a coin. "Heads says you carry him first. Har! Heads it is!"

The big man laid a dark-green blanket on the floor to wrap the intruder for transport. Everything was replaced from the thief's bag as Palmer prepared dinner.

\\\\\\\\

Listening to a radio reverend preach about the soon-to-arrive Antichrist made the cool ride a little quicker than usual. The sermon was transmitted from St. Louis, Missouri to save pious island listeners from temptation and to loosen their purse strings. If the villain wasn't already among them attempting to pit the super powers against each other, he soon would be. A slight Midwestern drawl listed a multitude of worldly conflicts. Africa, Europe, Asia, South America, and the States simmered in a kettle of evil broth. That bubbling broth was green from dollars spent invigorating the disciples of the devil. However, by making a three-digit contribution, the entire world could be a better place. The minions of Satan could only be fought with an army of crisp Ben Franklins.

Bill finally awoke with the last bounce, as David hit the rut outside his cottage. Without a word, Bill straggled to his dinghy.

Everything from the meeting was collected — and out of habit, David locked the truck. The cottage screen door was shut, but the main door hung open. He switched on the bright, overhead light and placed Mike's information on the kitchen table next to Feliza's purse. Trying not to awaken her, he slipped quietly out the rear door and relieved the evening's drinks. Like they say, beer is only rented.

At the garden hose, David took off his shoes and freshened a bit. The moon had disappeared from the night sky. A far-off-rumble from a truck was the only disturbance to the gentle lapping at the shore. The village of Eastern had turned in for the night, and he was about to join.

He gently closed the doors and switched off the light before heading to bed. In the room his feet shuffled slowly along a practiced route, but they stumbled at the foot of the bed. Feliza must have brought a bag.

Reaching, he touched soft, fragrant hair that felt somewhat sticky. As his pulse quickened, he felt for hers and found it. The culprit might still be present, or outside knowing David would return.

He moved Feliza's legs from blocking the closet and shifted the upper panel concealing the small storage space. His fingers trembled as he stretched his hand between the walls just beyond the storage hatch. He located a lump wrapped in an oily rag between the rafters. Definitely illegal, his Walther pistol had been reasoned as worth the risk. Handguns were rare among island businesses and homeowners — and as a continental he couldn't even hope to obtain a license. But this island had been intended only as a stopover before beginning to sail Summer Breeze into the next phase of his life. His rationale for the risk was the fear of drug smugglers. It seemed better to have a gun, even with the possible problems, and hopefully not need it, than to need it and not have it.

David found his flashlight next to the bed, scanned the room, locked the doors, and pulled the slatted shutters on the three bedroom windows. Although they'd still be visible as silhouettes, a shot or intrusion would be difficult. This situation was unexpected, but his security had been lax. Now, a beautiful woman was paying for it.

Cringing at the first sight of Feliza's bloody face, David grabbed a wash cloth from the bathroom. Her supple form relaxed in an almost fetal position between the end of the bed and the closet. She lay on her side and it appeared David's opening of the closet door had pushed her legs. He glanced at his watch and found it was Friday morning by ten minutes. Dabbing Feliza's face cautiously, he saw that the majority of the injury was a lump on her forehead, but it looked worse because of a slight cut. She was knocked out still clothed, and nothing in the bedroom seemed out of place. Perhaps his imagination of an intruder was exaggerated; he reasoned that maybe she had fainted.

After David cleaned most of the blood, he rinsed the wet cloth and folded it to fit her forehead. His whisper into her ear brought a slight movement. Gently, he inserted one arm under her neck, and the other supported her hips to get her on to the bed. She might have a concussion, but he knew this woman was healthy and definitely strong. First aid training dictated a visit to a doctor, which meant a jarring, uncomfortable ride to the clinic. The clinic might have a sleeping nurse on duty, but certainly no doctor would arrive until morning. Only midwives made house calls. Feliza moved her legs, slightly twisting her toes into the bed sheet. David filled a bath towel with some ice and returned to the bedside. As the cold cloth rested on her face, she regained consciousness with a jump start. Her arms flailed at him as she screamed. The beautiful brown eyes went wild.

David's arms encircled her as she squirmed, fighting desperately. "Feliza, it's me, David, take it easy. Lie down; you're safe. I won't let anything happen to you. Promise." He squeezed her, and she seemed to comprehend. Her surge of energy drained and she sank to the bed. "What happened?"

"Oh David," She tenderly felt the swelling cut on her nose and forehead. "I don't remember."

He brought a glass of cool water and two strong, codeine aspirins. "I must have got here a little before ten. The night at the restaurant was very slow and Auntie decided to close at nine. I got here and…" she took the wet cloth, wiped her eyes and around her lips. David rinsed it again and returned to sit next to her. "Wow, does my head ache. I vaguely recall coming in. The front door was unlocked, but closed. I put some leftovers in your cold box and came in here to change clothes. Next thing was a couple minutes ago when you found me. Oh, David," she grabbed his hand in hers and clasped it to her chest. "I really don't remember. Did I faint? I feel like I'm coming awake after an operation. Really groggy, like I was drugged."

"Feliza, the strong aspirins I gave you should make you groggy, but they don't work that quick. Don't think about it now. Relax and try to sleep. We'll talk it over in the morning and inspect the place. Nothing seems missing." David unbuttoned her white blouse and helped her remove her clothes. He extinguished the light, took the other side of the bed, and cuddled her on his arm. She kissed his cheek before dropping off. His thoughts raced from Bill's accident a week ago to the Rasta confrontation in town. Could this have something to do with the wreck?

Noise from the boat builders awakened David slightly before eight. He lay there watching shadows dance across the closed shutters. The shipbuilders must have realized his cottage was locked for the first time, and been polite not to wake him for coffee.

Feliza rested with her head sideways to him on a slightly bloodied pillow. She must have moved during the night and opened the cut on her nose. The lump on her forehead had swelled to the size of a silver dollar and was solid purple. As he lifted the sheet to slide his legs off the bed, she reached out to stop the movements. Her soft, slender hand slid from his thigh to the warm pocket he was leaving, stretched, and drew back into a comfortable, much-needed rest.

David's quick inspection of the four rooms discovered nothing missing or out of place. Mentioning the incident to Bill could wait until Feliza explained what she remembered.

Everybody was busy getting the diesel tanks installed by the time the mechanic finished aligning the engine. Bill was in the heart of the wooden hull, directing every detail. Catching Bill's eye, David left the percolator with tins of milk and sugar. It seemed very important to be bed-side when his island girlfriend awoke. He pulled the sheet back over her shoulders.

CHAPTER NINE

David awoke slumped at his cottage's white enameled kitchen table and recalled his reason for having come to Carriacou in the first place to have a boat constructed. During the last two weeks, his life had gone askew. Suddenly, he had three partners he hardly knew; one was his new girlfriend who could make even a blind man drool. The problem was simple: protect their lives and the wreck site from these intruders while preventing the government from interfering with the recovery if they found treasure. This had to be done, if possible, without using his pistol for defense. In the small village of Eastern, the echo of a shot would attract too much attention.

Feliza would stay with him and only be at risk while working. Billy could stay in the company of the construction crew or with David. His family and Feliza's aunt would have to be warned of strangers with some plausible excuse to keep them quiet. Mike's place was isolated, yet easily accessible from the beach or through the bush. He'd have to think of something. Perhaps get someone to stay with him until this was finished. But how long would it take to finish this adventure?

There was no way David could ask Amy to send weapons. His Walther pistol with a full box of bullets, a spear gun, and a couple of flare pistols were all he had to protect this operation. He certainly didn't want to have to use them. The equipment Amy had already sent would be delivered by Tuesday. Because of last night's incident, they'd have to be as secretive as possible getting the shipment from Grenada. They had to assume they were being observed. There wasn't much they could do to disguise the wreck site. The search would have to accelerate as much as safely permitted.

David's coffee cup had been empty for a while, as he stared at the curtained window. Feliza stirred in the other room, resting with her face in her hands. "How are you doing, sweetheart?" David asked.

She pulled herself up to a sitting position, bolstered by two pillows. With a fingertip she outlined the bruises on her cheeks and forehead and winced as she identified the point of impact. Her nose had a thin, red cut along its ridge. The blow had swollen her cheeks, and slightly blackened the area below her eyes.

"Not too good at the moment, David. What happened?" She recited what she had told him the previous night. "The front door was closed, not locked. I let myself in, put some food in the fridge, came to hang my restaurant clothes in the closet, and that's all I remember." She rattled as he handed her a damp washcloth.

"It appears there was someone in the closet. It's difficult to determine whether or not he had expected you. I found you unconscious. Someone searched this place. It's probably about the wreck. I'm sorry I got you involved in this." David leaned over and kissed the side of her neck. Feliza cocked her head and raised her beautiful eyes.

"Lie down here with me, David." She moved slightly away from the center of the bed and poked his side with a sharp finger. "Are you sure you didn't get your rocks off last night smacking me around, playing cat burglar?"

"What?"

"You know, some sort of sexual fantasy, your very private thing."

"Are you serious?"

"Just asking. I didn't see your truck, but you could have parked it around back."

"Feliza, I can't believe this. Do you actually think I was hiding in the closet waiting for you? This really offends me."

"Look, we don't know each other very well. We are obviously compatible, but come on; there could be some skeletons in both our closets. I find it hard to believe whoever it was is after you, or could even know about the wreck we found."

David got up out of bed in a huff. "You better re-think this Feliza. I'm not a weirdo. I can get my rocks off just fine the regular way. But we need to focus more on our safety, as do Billy and Mike Post. Whoever these people are, they are here about the wreck. Billy has already suffered a bruising for info concerning the search he did with your father. Last night they weren't expecting to be interrupted without first hearing the truck. I believe someone was in the closet because the toes of my extra three pairs of shoes are squashed as if someone stood on them. There's a little red clay, but I might have carried that into the closet. By the way, how did you get here without the intruders noticing? You come and go so mysteriously." He said standing at the foot of the bed.

"Mysteriously — I suppose I'm a suspect. David do you have more aspirin? My head is throbbing. How in the Hell am I mysterious? Didn't you ever see my bike, you fucking, deviant detective?" She flung the wet washcloth, as he handed her two Tylenol. "I pull it into the hedge. Sometimes a last customer is coming this way and I beg a ride and then take a bus in the morning. You are some observant policeman, David Warner."

"Feliza, I just wondered. No different than you asking if I'm a violent pervert. If your head is still aching, maybe I should take you to the clinic."

"Oh, I'll be all right. My bell just got rung, that's all. The clinic would ask a lot of questions concerning abuse. That's a big thing here at the moment. Women's groups and the police are trying to stop wife beating. I don't think we want to be interviewed. Do you?"

"You mean the authorities would actually think I beat you, even if you said I didn't?"

"West Indian women are supposed to be docile and stand by their man, or take a beating. Hell, I'd suppose more than half of the children in these islands are conceived while the women have sex in fear. Some people are conditioned to have a beating as foreplay. Does that excite you, deviant detective?" Feliza moved onto her side and pulled up her legs. "With this type of injury, I'm certain if I walk into the clinic with or without you, it will be more than the usual twenty questions. Anyway, lie down with me and comfort my aching body. Only comfort, no hanky panky. Come on; give me a little companionship, if you please." A nap soon enveloped them.

Revived, Feliza showered while David told Billy what had happened.

"So what yous wanna do?" Bill asked.

"Well, we've got to be aware we're being watched. Be careful and tell the wife and kids the same. Maybe tell them there's supposed to be a pervert thief on the island. Keep the doors locked at night. If you want to quit, okay, but it might already be too late. If this burglar has seen us, they may suspect we are after the wreck together. Mike is the only one who may still not be known. I don't think they have a car. I'll be watching to see if my truck is followed, but these guys will probably stay out of sight. They must walk or boat to these little escapades. Regardless they seem to know what they're doing."

"What they doing is gonna end them up in a fish trap, and we'se gonna fry and party with what we catch off them bastards!"

Billy was right. When their payback came, it wouldn't be nice. The locals chat about fish-trap justice. Criminals, especially rapists or thieves from other islands who harass and steal, often disappear. Relatives mention they were lost at sea, but often they are hacked with a cutlass and placed alive, into a big wire-mesh cage that's then lowered into the sea. After a few days, the fish have picked the bones clean. The trapped fish that do the cleaning are fried and a party ensues. If someone molests a child, chances are they are helped to hang themselves in the forest. Island justice is swift — and definitely not nice.

"Just be careful, in everything you do. Try not to be anywhere alone and keep out of the rum shops. When this is over, you'll be able to own a string of ten shops on every island. All we got to do is stay alert and get this done."

Bill took a bus to Top Hill as David watched the polished, dark-green Land Rover with 'POLICE' in big white letters on the door bounce along the beach road. Officer Richmond was his usual starched self, mopping his forehead with a bright-white handkerchief as he stepped out of the truck.

"Mr. Warner, how are you today, sir," he asked.

"Officer Richmond, what brings you by? It isn't often you come visit Eastern Beach. I'm sure your duties as immigration officer keep you very busy at the port. It must be nice to come here for a swim. Can I get you some refreshment?"

"A little cool water would be nice. Cool, not cold, if you please. I've read lately one should never drink anything less than air temperature or your entire nervous system can go out of kilter." They turned and walked to David's front door. He didn't want Richmond to enter after what Feliza had said about her bruises perhaps causing a grand inquisition — yet he couldn't see any choice. "Sir, I'm not here for a beach outing." Richmond's voice lost any tone of familiarity.

Feliza appeared at the doorway with her bruise concealed by a towel wrapped around her wet hair. The cut on her nose and the rings under her eyes were obscured through the shaded screen of the door as she passed two glasses of water without opening it fully. "Officer Richmond, how nice of you to come by and visit."

"Miss Dubois, how nice to see you. I certainly hope your Aunt is well and in good spirits. I'm very sorry to interrupt your afternoon."

"Oh Lionel, the only thing you're interrupting is me drying off after a day of house cleaning for Mr. Warner. I'm getting prepared to go to my second job at the restaurant."

"Miss Dubois, somehow I can't imagine a woman with your style and beauty being a house keeper." The policeman was now openly leering at Feliza's body, shielded only by two bath towels.

Feliza cocked her hip and replied haughtily, "Well, Lionel, can you imagine such a stylish woman starving? I work out of necessity, and do whatever it takes to care for my aunt and myself. The restaurant isn't as profitable as it was when Aunt Marsha was here. Everything is so expensive these days, but I'm sure that's evident to you."

"There are many things evident, Miss Dubois," he looked at her squarely and lowered his voice, "I won't intrude, Mr. Warner, but you may want to discuss this matter privately. This island has a coconut telegraph expert for spreading rumors."

They walked to the beach. "Mr. Warner, I must say you must be paying well for a woman like Miss Dubois to scrub your bathroom." Officer Richmond grinned and almost slipped into the island dialect. "I hope that's not all she's scrubbing, but let me address my present concern."

He opened a large, brown envelope and handed a photograph of the fellow who accosted David in town over the five dollars. It was obvious this Rasta wasn't going to move from the pictured position, crumpled and bleeding among boulders.

"That's the man who caused the disturbance in the parking lot of Excellsieur's restaurant. What happened?" David asked.

"His body was discovered at the quarry early this morning by some men loading building stone. It appears the young man was intoxicated — and unfortunately met his demise by stumbling into the ravine. His name was Gaston Benedict. He had been released from custody after two days detention. Hillsboro really doesn't have the facilities to hold such unsavory characters very long. It is an expense to feed and guard. It seemed once justice had been served he was to be sent back to St. Vincent, but the airline was fully booked. Unfortunately, we had no extra officers to accompany the fellow on the ferry. We put him on the boat, but as the photo depicts, it seems he returned. Did he attempt to take revenge on you, Mr. Warner, for what might be construed as racial conflict?"

"Wait a minute Officer, racial conflict? That man attacked me. Excellsieur was a witness. After he was taken into custody, I never saw him again. What are you implying?"

"I'm not implying anything, only following a natural series of events and contacting all those who had interaction with the deceased. Although it appears the man fell, of course, it's possible he could have been pushed."

"Are you insinuating?" David interrupted.

"I am not insinuating anything, Mr. Warner. You had an altercation and it is possible the young man returned for revenge. But if you say you never saw him after Monday, then so be it, until other information becomes available."

"Other information?" This dialogue was making his stomach queasy. The last thing he needed at that moment was to draw extra attention from the constabulary.

"You see, Mr. Warner, the young man fell about forty feet, breaking his neck. Although there were severe lacerations to the body caused by the sharp rocks, there was little blood. The body may have been dealt a blow elsewhere, and dumped to seem as an accident. The local clinic did a quick blood toxicology this morning and found both alcohol and cocaine. A street person of this nature operates a large portion of the waking hours with those drugs in their system. It also follows that if an individual wanted to, let's say ready himself for an opponent, he would ingest the same substances."

"Well, well, well," David coughed. "From what you are telling me, I'm a suspect. If you want to search my transport or my accommodations, please do."

"Mr. Warner, your personal record is impeccable. But you must appreciate my position. There hasn't been a questionable fatality such as this in three years. The last one was a woman drowning after her husband discovered a love triangle. Obviously, I must check every possible detail. I'm sure you understand." He extended his hand to shake and headed to his car. From the vehicle he said, "Ah, Mr. Warner, if you have any arrangements to travel from Carriacou, please notify me. Thank you for your cooperation in this matter."

David leaned on a rough palm trunk, watching the dust trail as the Rover clamored among the ruts. It seemed he was now a suspect in a murder investigation. What could happen next? He excused the issue by telling Feliza the police wanted his opinion on an accidental death, which wasn't far from the truth. Her headache had lessened and with a bit of proper make-up, she looked as ravishing as ever. He transported her to the restaurant, promising to return at ten. Next stop was to inform Mike of the recent events.

\\\\\\\\\

The Caribbean Sea was transforming to its nightly shades of darker blues as David's truck jostled along the beach lane. Rain a few weeks before had produced tender roadside foliage, attracting every grazing creature. Twice, David had to get out from behind the steering wheel and prod sizable cows off the dirt track. The rains also spawned swirling mosquitoes that feasted on any unprotected skin. His 'shoo bossy' routine was accompanied with a jiggling dance to keep the biting pests at safe buzzing distance. It had occurred to him these cattle could be a roadblock intended to waylay him — so his prodding was done with his favorite three-foot length of construction steel — which he usually kept in the truck bed as a jack lever. He wandered on various roads until he was fairly certain he wasn't being followed.

The road to Mike's was one of the most isolated on the island. No headlights followed David's slow progress. He was breaking Mike's personal rule; this day had been too hectic to announce his visit. Although it was Friday night, he expected the pony-tailed teacher to be at home. 'Thank God it's Friday' didn't apply on Carriacou, as Saturday was work again as usual for at least a half day. The rum shops would lighten local pockets after the produce market, and builders' supply equipped them for a busy Sunday. Although the Caribbean seems slow, it's really busy at a leisurely pace. A lot of work gets done — yet, few jobs are ever finished.

The chain gate was locked. He used the horn to announce his

presence and started walking toward the grounded boat. The interior door was closed, but David could see the deck hatches were open for ventilation. One light glowed through the brass ports of the aft cabin. His knock on the latched patio door went unanswered for long minutes. If his antagonists knew about Mike being a partner to the search, he might've met the same fate than Feliza, or worse.

Although the small, screened area was dark, David could see Mike's bicycle inside. If he had gotten transport, he probably wouldn't have left the lights on. David boomed his name several times and finally got a response.

"Coming! This had better be urgent to disturb my Friday night." The yellow porch light illuminated his thin, tanned body — attired only in blue satin boxer shorts.

"David, David, David," Mike said in a coaxing tone as if he were speaking to one of his troublesome students. "What am I going to do with you? I've asked you to always call me at school before you visit. Believe it or not, I live in this remote place for privacy." His tone increased to irritable, "Capital P-R-I-V-A-C-Y, just like the sign reads. Understand, my friend, no call, no visit!"

He slowly walked down the steps. He picked up a pack of clove cigarettes and lit one. His gray hair was untied and dangled unkempt below his shoulders. Mike made no effort to unlatch the screen door and let in his visitor. "Look, David, I get up early and pedal my ass to school five mornings a week to get there before seven-thirty. Then in the heat of the late afternoon, I again traverse these glorified donkey cart paths. To make my money, I force myself into educational surroundings that are antiquated at best, and coexist with those of drastically less intellect. But in the evening, my time is my own, and I make my own schedule." Back to the cajoling tone, "Now tell me, David, what does your stateside thinking mind consider so important it cannot wait for our meeting scheduled the day after tomorrow?"

Mike took a deep draw from the cigarette and exhaled in David's direction. "I'd open the door, but then you might think you're welcome."

"Mike, you are virtually unreachable, except at school. Sorry to intrude, but there's been another suspicious incident. Feliza interrupted someone in my house last night and was knocked unconscious. She never saw who or what hit her."

Genuinely concerned he asked, "Is she all right?"

"Yeah, seems so. Hell of a lump on her head, a few scrapes, and bruises, but she's at work now."

Mike walked up and then unlatched the screen door. Before David could enter, Mike exited.

"I'll be frank with you," Mike said. "You are not the only continental who has an amorous relation with a local woman. Just the same as the last time you barged in, I've got company. Private company presently enjoying an intimate evening, I'm certain you can respect that. Now I don't want to abandon that very private and amorous company for very long, or they might lose interest. I certainly don't want this conversation overheard and broadcast throughout the neighborhood. Let's walk to your truck. Was your place torn apart?"

"No, nothing was noticeably out of place, but I can tell someone was in my closet, probably waiting for me to arrive. So I'm here to warn you. It seems logical that whoever it was who hit Bill was also in my house. They may or may not know about your involvement. But it is wise to be careful."

"You're certain nobody followed you out here?" He took his final drag and flipped the cigarette into darkness. The clove smoke seemed to repel the mosquitoes.

"No one followed this time, but I can't say for certain about previous trips. My intuition is the intruders don't have transport — because that would make them too conspicuous. They are probably sneaking around on foot. If we are being watched at Eastern Bay, they'll know of your association Sunday."

"Uh-huh. Hmmm," Mike rubbed his bearded jaw. "If these people are outsiders, they'll have to ask someone about my identity. Maybe we can get a line on them by asking some of the locals about inquisitive continentals. Perhaps we should start a reverse investigation."

"I've already asked the immigration officer, bartenders, and shop keepers. I got a half-assed description, but they must be staying indoors during the day. No one has seen them out, even shopping for food."

He swatted his thighs. "Look, now's not the time or place to discuss strategy."

"Oh, yeah," David mentioned as he open the truck's door. "There was a Rasta killed last night. He was a coke addict who caused me a problem in town. The police came by and questioned me about it."

"Murder or accident?" he asked.

"Could be either. Might be just a coincidence. All of this could be coincidental, but all of it is attracting unwanted attention." He started the truck. "Do you still have a VHF marine radio on board the Outpost?"

"Yes, but I don't have it wired to the converter. Why?"

"Hook it up and try to call me on channel sixty-eight, Sunday before you leave here. That might be the best method of communicating if you get yourself in a situation. Then I wouldn't be interrupting your nocturnal activities."

"Thanks for coming by. I'll keep a look-out for unsavory characters lurking around, but if I don't go give some attention where it is now overdue, I'll have myself in enough of a situation."

\\\\\\\\

David affectionately doctored Feliza with breakfast and a late lunch in bed on Saturday. She rested her pretty, but slightly aching head. Summer Breeze progressed — with the mechanics, tanks, basic plumbing, and electrical finished. The decking was almost completed, but the mast still had to be stepped to the keel before it would be floated. The crane operator hadn't appeared during the last two days — which was quite common. He had been paid for placing the engine — so he probably wouldn't return until the next workweek started. Reese had suitably smoothed the bottom before applying several coats of sealers and protective paints. In a few weeks, the boat would be christened, blessed, and pushed into the Caribbean by locals who would party on the beach until the rum bottles were emptied. David hoped he and his three new friends and himself would be healthy enough to enjoy the festivities, and not in jail.

They readied the dive equipment for the following day's excursion. The compressor jammed air into all eight tanks. It would be the first time the four would be working together. Bill and Mike hadn't seen the wreck. David wasn't certain if either was capable of diving to the eighty-foot depth. It wasn't necessary for them to work underwater, moving the ballast stones, but each needed to see the initial layout of the ship's stones to offer insights.

Bill's duties would be to keep the topside crew moving the stones up to the Moriah. Bill found four good-sized pieces of heavy netting and strung the edge with a line to make a drawstring. Each net was stuffed into an old pillowcase to make handling easier. Removal of the entire pile would be a tremendous amount of work, necessitating many trips to the shore. The Century had been over a hundred feet long and the size of the ballast pile could reveal, to a very experienced boatman, how heavily it had been loaded with cargo.

They cleared a space on the beach to pile the ballast for cleaning before placing them in the belly of Summer Breeze. It was common for ballast stones to be passed from boat to boat, but these would be traveling again after centuries of rest. If they were lucky, maybe they could move two-hundred stones a day. At eighty feet hard labor could suck a tank dry in twenty minutes. Another tank would be necessary to fill the lift bags — and yet another to breathe off while making safety stops before surfacing. The boats would have to be anchored on the pile, permitting the bags to rise — but just distant enough so if stones dropped, they wouldn't bombard the divers.

Bill provided more anchor line for Dolly — which would float it away from the Moriah and make the safety stops more gradual. While Feliza and he rested and off-gassed, the Moriah would tow the two loads to the beach. As long as they had the nets cinched tight, with the lift bag tied close to the load, they could float into shallow water. Then, local boys would carry them to shore, brush each with diluted acid, and stack according to size. It was a project that would take several days and a lot could go wrong. But the least of David's worries were underwater.

The hand held marine VHF radio crackled at six in the morning to Feliza's awakening dismay. Teacher Mike called to announce his leaving. Coffee was prepared as Bill took David's truck to roust that day's labor force with the promise of good money and cold beer when finished. David's roomie was cheery as the mirror reflected the bruise had receded enough and would no longer require makeup. The cut on her nose had almost healed.

"Mr. Warner," Feliza wrapped her arms about his waist and pulled tight against his back as he stood at the kitchen sink rinsing a few cups. He could feel hard points on her soft curves. "It looks as though you won't have to associate with the Wicked Witch of the West anymore." Her hair was brushed and pulled back. "Thanks for being such a good nurse." She returned his kiss with the embrace of a healthy woman.

He poured two cups and the couple toasted, "Here's to a quick recovery. No headache?" he asked.

"Clear as a bell. It felt like a hangover, but I think it was more from the stress of the incident than the bump. I guarantee that if my path crosses the person who startled me; they'll have a much worse pain in an appropriate location." She led David to the front porch where they could watch the ocean with islands in the distance. "This incident has made me remember how crazy the world is beyond this horizon. That insanity is slowly creeping here. Imagine, I could have ended as the Rasta creep Lionel had mentioned."

"Let's not think about either. Just be extremely careful." In the distance, the morning sun glistened off the dry road as a lone cyclist approached with ponytail flying. "That's the fourth member, Mike Post," David laughed. "Just be extremely careful."

Leaning on the weathered wooden porch railing, the Caribbean Sunday morning echoed nothing except quiet tranquility. David's lovely cohort snuggled close as Mike approached. "Let's get it straight from the very beginning," she tugged at David's very private spot with a quick unstoppable response, "with whom I'm aligned. It will save a lot of time and unpleasant conversation." As the teacher parked his bike, David was pulled into a very sudden, but definitive embrace.

"Aha, now do you understand why I have the chain across my gate?" Mike extended his hand to Feliza, but she didn't break her hold around Dave's waist. Faltering, but still smiling he announced, "Hello, I'm Mike Post, and you must be Feliza, woman-diver extraordinaire. Both of my associates in this venture spoke highly about you at our initial meeting the other night. I'm sorry that you weren't available. I can tell they didn't exaggerate."

She reached for her cup and replied in the local accent. "Mr. Post, you not yet see me dive. Save dem opinions. Coffee? David, you want de next?" She retreated to the kitchen and returned with three cups, sugar, canned milk, and two oranges quartered on the cottage's cutting board. Mike stared at the bay as he packed a pipe and lit it.

"This is a great place you have. The hull over there on the shore must be your vessel. When I first visited Eastern, they were simultaneously building five boats along here. Everyone was busy either building or sailing these crafts." He rattled his cup as he stirred sugar into the tan mix. Feliza sat on the porch at Dave's side, in a sort of Caribbean-Norman-Rockwell pose.

"Feliza, you were born here?" Mike posed.

"Uh-huh," was her rhythmic reply. Feliza was purposely aloof.

"So, what's on today's agenda?" Mike addressed Dave. "Are we raising the stones as planned?"

"We'll get started when Bill returns with the crew. Feliza, do me a favor and make another pot for them while I show Mike around." She rose quickly and professionally cleared the cups, almost curtsying as she left.

"Got up on the wrong side of the bed today?" Mike asked, "I haven't gotten that cold of a reception in years. You are a lucky guy. What she lost in pleasant personality, she gained in beauty."

"Seems she's a bit worried about strangers these days after the incidents I've mentioned. We really don't know each other at all."

"With her attitude, we never will."

"I think that's her tactic." He slapped Mike on the shoulder as they walked to the netting and dive tanks ready to be loaded on Bill's boat. Dolly had five tanks stacked across her middle. Another tank had only one regulator — and two more were completely set up with regulators and buoyancy vests. Reels of line were coiled and attached to the anchor.

"Everything seems prepared. I'm not sure how much use I'll be as a diver. I haven't been very far below the surface in years."

Dave handed him a small, red pill he pushed out of a plastic package. "Take this. It's a decongestant, so you can clear your ears while going down. Whatever you do, don't say anything in front of the crew. Bill's told them we are clearing an old ballast dump. So, no 'oohs' or 'aahs' until we're alone." The pick-up truck rolled along the main street of Eastern with a bed full of loud men.

"Mike, you and I will dive first. If everything is comfortable for you, I'll start filling a net while you float around checking out the anchor and the cannon. If you don't feel up to it or if you've had enough, just come over and I'll put you on the anchor line. Whatever you do, stop at twenty feet for about five minutes."

"How will I know that? I don't have a diver's waterproof watch. I think it would be safer if you tagged along with me." He sounded worried.

"Sure, nothing to it. Just fall in the water and pull yourself down the anchor. Go slow. Make sure to pop your ears. If your ears don't clear easily, please don't force it. I'll bring you up if you need help, but that will cut my precious bottom time. There'll be a flag on the anchor rope at the correct depth for a safety stop. Just count slowly to three hundred. No problem?"

"No real problems, except for those my vivid imagination creates. I'll do okay, but keep an eye on me." Mike retrieved fins and a mask with a snorkel attached from a towel roll strapped on his bike.

The Toyota rattled to the beach. Its load jumped out even before Bill parked. Three of the men were builders who needed the extra day's pay, but four were schoolboys who would stay on the beach to unload the nets. "What you think? Ought to be enough men to make a hard job E-Z. Reese, that lazy boy, ain't nowhere to be found. But they's plenty. Tell you what, me no need to dive today. Much better me stay on top." Bill told each what to do, when, and where to do it. He preached — so few details were left to chance. His Moriah would join after the skiff was anchored at the site. Feliza appeared, hiding behind large sunglasses, a wide-brimmed straw hat, and an over-sized shirt. She handed Bill the coffeepot tray, and joined Mike aboard Dolly.

David handed her a pair of binoculars. "These are for the person top side to watch the shore and approaching boats. This is serious business."

Feliza hugged his arm tightly, "I know, I know."

Dolly putted slowly as she was a bit over her weight limit. There was no need to hurry. Today they were supposed to be a group pleasure diving. After anchoring, David put up a dive flag and tied an extra tank to the line as Mike donned his equipment. The teacher dropped over the side with an ungraceful splash. He began his descent — getting the feel of the regulator and clearing his mask.

"Be careful," David said, tilting the brim of his companion's hat and kissing her barely visible cheek.

"You too. I don't like Mike. There's something about how he looks at me. Watch out for him down there. I don't think you'll have as much problem with him as I will. Promise me we'll drop him off after this dive. I don't want to sit here and have him leering." She kissed David again as he nodded agreement. "Good luck! Hey, Mr. Warner, it'll be my turn to show my nurse appreciation when we're finished today, if that's alright with you?"

"Absolutely. Keep an eye open." David bit his regulator as he rolled into the water, holding the spear gun and power head. He grabbed two weighted pillowcases from his favorite dive buddy and started making bubbles. Mike clutched the anchor line about thirty-feet below the surface eagerly watching David's approach. He returned a thumbs-up and signaled his ears were all right.

There was no current and the visibility was excellent. David pointed to the hole they'd penetrated into the pile. When they swam to the excavation, the cloth cases were emptied and the nets were weighted by the stones to keep them from floating away.

With a swish of Dave's gloved hand both the cannon butt and the wood planks appeared to Mike's excited eyes. Dave pointed to the anchor ring and visible fluke — and then spread out one net with a stone in each corner to hold it stable. Keeping close track on the time, he loaded twenty, good-sized stones in ten minutes — having used up a thousand pounds of air.

David signaled to Mike, pointing to his watch and then up, but Mike motioned for David to join him. He was furiously brushing sand away from a clump of rusted steel. After he freed the narrow, three-foot long clump, Dave motioned for him to take it to the surface. Mike had been on the bottom for sixteen minutes, and Dave still had more rocks to move.

Twenty-two minutes isn't long, especially when you're distracted, but he did get a total of thirty-four stones in the net by the time the wrist alarm buzzed. The lift bags filled and their loads of stones followed as he rose. A boat motor could be heard, but he wasn't certain if it was the Moriah or another visitor. The lift bags splashed to the surface.

At the tank with the regulator clipped to the anchor line, Mike was hanging, intently scrutinizing what he'd found. David took a cord from his vest pocket and tied the clump to the safety tank. Pointing up, he signaled to listen, indicating that there was another boat arriving. Placing his fingers to his eyes, he shook his head — meaning, others shouldn't see anything coming out of the water except rocks.

Mike waited out his time making certain to suffer no ill effects. Feliza held David's tank as he pulled his weight into Dolly.

Everyone relaxed as Bill appeared and dropped anchor precisely on the spot. With a bit of help, Mike climbed aboard — wearing a toothy smile, and wiping his bedraggled hair from his face. "Yes sir, you two have found an old wreck." He reached out to pat shoulders. "It's cause for a good celebration. Not here and now, but soon. What do you think the clump is I found?"

David put a finger to his lips, meaning quiet. "Mike, I think we'll save this discussion. How about you help Bill and those guys while Feliza and I get ready to splash?" Feliza pull-started the motor and David pulled the slack anchor line as she angled to the white sailboat. "Take these glasses with you and keep a look out without being too obvious to Bill's men."

"Sure thing, skipper. Now I have seen the dream; just point and direct me to useful duty." Dolly nudged the larger boat and Mike boarded.

"He's all yours now, Bill." Making a suitable excuse, "The teacher says he wants to get into shape on his days off. So, work the sweat out of him." Everyone laughed. Feliza stalled the engine and Dolly drifted back into her proper position. They pulled the tarp and rested.

The day was long as they pushed three more dives, netting almost two hundred stones. It was considerably easier with the net than the basic straining method they had used to move the others into the sand. The pile had shrunk considerably. Bill hoisted the loads when they were well out of the way — in case some came clattering back to the sea floor.

They pulled the pair of nets with the windless until the boat was almost bow-down under the combined weight. Moriah's anchor line was left floating with a buoy and the nets were pushed to shore. Each time they returned in less than an hour with empty nets, ready for a refill. Mike strained with the crew to haul the nets as close to shore as possible — so the boys could get them ashore. Bill constantly glorified their labors by sermonizing about the rebirth of a boatyard to build island sloops. He promised to save the wood-working art from extinction by the modern fiberglass versions.

Their dives had not stopped to collect any artifacts unless corrosion had welded iron to the rocks. What they found was visible on the planking. More bottles, pottery, and clumps of iron objects rusted beyond recognition lay waiting. No gold appeared, and it would have been hard to contain the jubilation if it had.

On her second dive, Feliza found another clump of black disks that resembled coins. She interrupted David's methodical movements of pry, lift, carry and drop, to point out that snappers were swarming overhead taking lunch from the disturbance. The last dive of the day could only be fifteen safe minutes. Feliza wanted to gather the small artifacts in the goody bags to examine later. Everything they'd already found had been taken to Mike's house. David had never seen any woman work so hard and comfortably above or below the surface. Feliza continually earned his admiration and respect.

Her wavy hair ballooned in all directions from the strap holding her mask. The continuous stream of bubbles intertwined and gushed to the surface as though a vent had opened from the local underwater volcano. Feliza rocked gracefully on one foot as she lifted and placed. They'd removed their fins, standing normally on the bottom — careful not to step on a three-hundred-year-old spike from the decaying timbers. Her arms revealed slim, strong biceps that could carry or squeeze and her shapely butt was only evident as she bent to lift another stone. Her suit bottom strained as much as her arms.

They'd been under the tarp more than the required hour, sweating and dozing through another surface interval. It had been quiet until another outboard signaled company. Mike had the field glasses, but was unloading stones ashore. The small craft passed outside the reef about two-hundred yards from them. The dark green or black boat looked familiar, but was too distant to describe.

Feliza dropped heavily into the water. David scanned the horizon, checking for nonexistent company before he rejoined her. Occasionally, a big grouper would dart from a coral head on the side of the undersea valley and capture an unwary yellow-tailed snapper. As they literally pushed through the fish, the size of their excavation was gratifying.

David's job of moving rocks continued monotonously. It took only a minute to stretch out the thick, blue-green net by pinning the corners. The procedure was to pry as many loose as possible from the pile, ten or fifteen — and then lift, rotate his body, and drop the load. All had to be completed without crushing a foot or pinching a finger in the process. David was tired and could feel his legs about to cramp. This routine permitted him to watch his dive partner indulge in an underwater version of Supermarket Sweep. Wearing her fins, Feliza pumped along fanning sand, snatching what appeared. Occasionally the feeding fish would totally obscure her. She tied her first bag to the anchor and started to fill another.

The fish-feeding frenzy attracted more attention. Two big, six-foot lemon sharks cruised through the marine free-for-all. The divers' bottom time was almost exhausted as David pulled the cinch line on the nets tight, tied them to the surface rope, and filled the lift bags. He really didn't want to stay down much longer. Feliza seemed oblivious to the two gray intruders. Seconds after a medium-sized, twenty-pound black grouper snagged a smaller yellow-tail, the jaws of one of the marauding sharks chomped the grouper. With an audible snap, the grouper's midsection disappeared in a gulp. The bloody head and tail dropped, but didn't hit the bottom before the other member of the gray team scooped a snack. Both sharks were now in full action — arching their backs and making unpredictable lunges. One of these two hundred-pound gray torpedoes wouldn't have to bite to kill. They could crush ribs with a forward thrust and leave you, swallowing seawater after spitting out the regulator,.

The power head was within reach, but Feliza wasn't. David could see her fins pumping, but the top of the rock shielded her body. One lemon shark darted near her. Another shark passed too close and its skin gritted against David's bare calf. The power head would put too much blood into the water. At this depth, it could only be used as the last defense. The grouper's sacrifice attracted four more sharks. Finally, David grabbed Feliza's leg and got her open-eyed attention. She had been digging at something and motioned for him to wait one more minute.

Another smaller, four-foot black tip shark swam directly above Feliza's shoulders. With a smile, she grabbed the bag, pointed, and gave the thumbs up as she finally directed her gaze to the underwater wild kingdom. The small, black tip shark kept circling as they slowly ascended up the line. Feliza tied the last bag to a catch ring on her vest and grabbed David's hand, squeezing hard. At forty feet the black tip was diving straight at them — first from below, then from above. On one move from the left, the dangerous beast got so close that David prodded him with the power head shaft. They settled into what seemed to be an extremely long, ten-minute safety stop at twenty-five feet while he checked her air gauge. Feliza was below the safe five-hundred-pound limit. She began to breathe from the hanging spare tank.

Feliza's legs coiled around the anchor rope, her arms around David's legs. He showed her he'd removed the safety pin to activate the power head. Minutes seemed slower because every few seconds he looked at the dive computer. Sharks near the surface on a necessary safety stop are a true nightmare — but he would rather fight it out with the demons of the deep than be painfully crippled for life from decompression sickness.

With only four more minutes until they regained the safety of Dolly, another shark joined the first black tip. The predators seemed to be swimming in smaller, concentric circles. The divers had one bullet, a forty-four magnum. David's dive buddy felt like a second skin as her head was now on his shoulder, watching exactly what he saw. They rotated on the rope like chickens roasting on a spit for these predators.

One shark came closer, with jaws pulled back, teeth bared. At nine minutes, one came directly for their legs. David used the side of the spear shaft to thump it away. Unfortunately, it swerved with pumps of its tail fin and instantly returned. David motioned for Feliza to loosen her vest. He did the same. As the shark neared, David swung his vest at it. The grey-suited guy was aggravated and tried to bite the tank. David pushed his wild-eyed dive buddy up into their small boat and she shed her gear.

In one fluid motion she kicked up and over the side into its relative safety. Still sucking the remaining five-hundred pounds of air, David watched the two gray culprits approach. Feliza grabbed her tank and pulled it over the side of the boat as one shark broke thesurface. As it descended within five feet of David's extended arm, he struck him full force with the spear, detonating the cartridge.

Instead of the anticipated noise and action, everything slowed. After a pop and a burst of green bubbles, the shark just stopped and started to sink. Because the shot hit it head-on, the blast penetrated, but didn't exit, producing very little blood. There was enough blood to enthuse the other shark that darted from beyond the edge of horizontal visibility to shred the dead one. The next split second seemed to last forever. There was no defense available except for prayer if another crazed intruder appeared. David watched the deep aquamarine below and saw one shark consume its Sunday dinner in three gulps. Totally engrossed in the drama he hadn't realized his almost-empty tank had floated him to the surface.

"Are you mad? Get the fuck in this boat David," Feliza screamed as she grabbed his hair and pulled. "Enough of this high-fucking-adventure shit for one day. Damn it, I want to live to be too old for this!" He threw the spear gun to her, held the vest by the regulator hose and rocketed into her arms. "You are a crazy man. Those sharks could have killed us, and you want to float to watch the show." She kissed him. "David, I love you, but never, never, never worry me like this again."

He slipped out of the wet suit, looking around to notice if Bill and the boys had been witnesses, but they were just returning for the last load. "Thanks for the vote of confidence. It's just a few more details we'll have to take into consideration before we go down again." David shuddered and laughed maniacally. He felt drunk from the adrenaline — stretching out on the seat with his chest heaving.

"No more sharks! Eels, big fish, monster crab I can handle, but no more three-ring circuses with the big gray boys." She peeled off her shirt and suit top, revealing her two luscious-brown orbs. "See these buddy? Another situation like that," she moved very close to his face, "and no more nuzzling." David was about to take a lick as she turned to get the goody bag. "Close your eyes, darling."

When she tapped him, his eyes opened to see two sparkling gold coins resting atop each breast. "What do you think? Would my tits sag too much if I hung a coin from each pierced nipple?" She twirled the prominent brown points and uttered a schoolgirl giggle.

They laughed and dropped out of sight under the tarp. "These were all I could find. They are dated 1688," she said.

David pulled her down and kissed her passionately. "Feliza, you are quite a woman."

"And you are a crazy man, but that turns me on. Hey, does it seem like there's a lot of water in the boat? Our escape must have thrown in more than usual," She speculated. They were sloshing in water above the floorboards. "Let's continue this back at the ranch, partner. I'll bail while you get the anchor."

"Aye, aye." David mounted the small deck and started pulling. He groaned, pulling the extra tank, Mike's trophy, and then the anchor with Feliza's other bag.

"You sound like an old man, David. I'm not making much headway bailing. You'd better start the motor and get Dolly into the beach. Maybe our last leap sprung something loose."

The motor growled to life. "David, I think there were other sharks out here today. David, look here!"

A foot astern of where the small foredeck started on the portside water line, were four, quarter-inch, round holes copied by four larger exits on the port. "Feliza bring the bucket and sit back here. We'll try to keep the bow up. Seems we were very lucky today."

"I'd say so. Doesn't look like shark teeth! They're what I'd imagine bullet holes would look like. If we'd have been snoozing under the tarp when Dolly was shot, they wouldn't have missed us."

"Yeah, I think that's what the sharp shooter had hoped. Had to be from a passing boat; maybe that dark green one. I didn't hear any other." David frowned at how serious this had become, but the four coins on the seat elevated his greedy spirits ever so slightly. "The shots were for us otherwise they'd have aimed for the air or gas tanks, and blown Dolly apart. This could be considered a warning."

"Consider me warned!" Feliza said earnestly bailing water, keeping at a steady, 'too high' level.

"We can't report this, too many questions to answer. Bill will have something to put in the holes until I can get the boards replaced."

"Is that what you'd say about me?" she quipped, nervously biting her lower lip.

"What?" They were nearing the beach and he cut the throttle and turned to her.

"Put something in the holes until you can replace me!" She threw her arms around him and started to sob. "I don't care how much money is out there, it's not worth dying over. We'll never live to spend it! I'd rather be alive and poor, working in the restaurant for the rest of a long life."

CHAPTER TEN

By late afternoon, everything was stifling under a cloudless, breezeless sky. Fishing birds were slowly returning to their nests from offshore feeding grounds. The big, frigate birds circled and sometimes plunged downward two-hundred feet to grab something from the surface of the water. Their prehistoric pterodactyl shapes chased the smaller white, long-tailed tropicbirds until they noisily relinquished their beak full of small fish. Glossy, brown-feathered, red-footed boobie birds bathed and squawked on the transparent sea. Waves created a hardly perceptible sound as they washed the white sand beach. Skinny brown island dogs lay motionless in the little shade under the sea grapes that grew just beyond the fringe of coconut palms. It would be less than a half-hour before the blazing globe would cross beyond Top Hill to commence another warm evening on Eastern Bay.

Two of those tall, untrimmed coconut palms formed the boundary posts of a relatively neat pile of mottled ballast stones. This was Bill's section of beach, now cordoned off by a five-row, highly stacked stone wall. Summer Breeze had been undisturbed the entire Sunday — and had provided only limited shade for the teenagers who had carried, cleaned, and stacked the round, gray, European river stones. Each dark boy was drenched in sweat and hoped his efforts would secure him a future role among Bill's shipwright crew. The older men, who worked for Bill as carpenters, taunted their younger counterparts while everyone drank chilled, sweating, green Heinekens. As the afternoon heat flared, everyone waded into the sea, except Feliza and David.

They didn't need any more of the sea at the moment. Feliza was sleeping — or at least trying to, on cool, white sheets. Sleep was the best reprieve from the exertion and tension of the previous few harrowing hours. David sipped a beer and watched Bill stimulate his workers into good spirits — thereby guaranteeing tomorrow would be another productive day. Mike sat cross-legged in the water, chatting with past students who had helped move stones. Neither Mike nor Bill had been told what was found — or what had happened during the roller coaster final hour. No one would know until the crew dispersed to their homes.

Everything resonated danger and insanity. Movements amid the few shadows, a creak during the windless hours, or a brilliant reflection of the searing sun on an ocean ripple pushed the alert button. During the preceding two days, the divers' situation had started to stew, finally reaching its boiling point.

"One thing certain, dis ain't termites," Bill pointed. "But me fix it quick tomorrow with dowel rods and epoxy glue. So, you think someone shot at you from a boat?"

"Very remarkable shot, I'd say," Mike added.

"More than remarkable, extremely well trained and equipped. Looks like an M-16 with an arrester to keep it quiet. Shooting from a moving boat to a rocking boat, this pattern is almost unfeasible. A dark-hulled outboard passed about one to one-thirty, a good ways outside the reef. Couldn't make it out, but it seemed there were two people in straw hats," David answered. "The rifle had to have been silenced; otherwise, on a windless day like today, a high-powered bang would have carried a long way. This was done by a professional."

"Hit man, in Carriacou? After we?" Bill questioned.

"Not necessarily a hit man, like in the gangster movies, but maybe. A good guess is it was the same guys who worked you over, searched your boat, tagged Feliza, and searched my house. Now Dolly's shot and it could have easily been us. By professional, I mean trained — probably in the armed service, maybe Special Forces. That's not a long shot, a couple of hundred yards. Probably traced the initial bursts on the water and led it right to the bow. Getting the rifle is no big deal — and with the right connections any weapon can be silenced for a price."

"So, what now?" was Mike's sullen reply. "We've got a pile of rocks, a cannon, and an anchor. Where's that piece I found today?"

"Everything is at the house, but it can't stay there long. It's a flip of a coin if your place is still safe." David led the way across the beach road to his cottage.

He placed his handkerchief, holding the newly found coins on the white metal tabletop. Both of the men gasped and sank back into the kitchen chairs, each fondling a golden disk.

"These are Spanish ten-escudos; and they're in extremely good condition, considering they've been under water three hundred years." Mike continued, "They are gold tens like the silver Reales are known as eights. These were used throughout the West Indies and most of the civilized world. Even though the Spanish Armada was defeated in 1588, Spain's coins were used everywhere. They were smelted at Potosi, Bolivia from about 1600." He smiled and looked at his fellow treasure hunters.

"The least these are worth is five thousand - but probably more."

"All them?" Bill pondered.

"Each."

"Sheet. And yous expect there's thousands of these close by? Sheet!" Bill muttered.

"Shit is right!" Feliza stood leaning in the doorway, looking as exhausted as David felt. "Did you tell these two topsiders how we almost met our end? Five thousand each, huh?" She picked one from the table. "I'll take my share now."

"Absolutely," Mike smiled. "I know a reputable coin dealer in Florida who can get us top dollar with only a few questions answered."

"Are you reputable?" Feliza moved behind David and dangled her arms over his shoulders. "After today, this is the only man I trust. You take care of yours, and I'll take care of mine." She slipped her coin into her swimsuit bra.

"So, guys, what are we going to do about these intruders?" David posed the serious question. "With guns like they have, we aren't safe anywhere. They could pop us off right here, now, by the light of the kitchen bulb." He did believe it — and couldn't fathom a reason other than good old-fashioned greed. "So, Feliza, you still want out?"

"I'll reserve judgment until after one more dive. If the guys in gray suits intrude again, or if another bullet goes whizzing by, then I'm definitely history. David, are you driving me to work? If not, I'd better get a taxi."

"I'll give you a ride and then take all of this to Mike's for safer keeping. Bill, I'll drop you off last so we can arrange everything for Tuesday's trip to Grenada with Allister."

Feliza disappeared to the sound of the shower as David said, "Maybe Wednesday we can move another load of stones. I think that should about finish it."

"Yeah, the Century was traveling light on ballast. She musta had a good load of cargo. Those stones ain't much for a boat her size. That makes 'bout between two and three tons. Me figures you and sweetie moved near a ton today. Yous asses ought to be dragging off to sleep. She still gonna work?" Bill twirled a coin on the metal tabletop. "Gonna work after a payday like this; Lord, that's a damn good woman."

The day's labor wasn't finished until everything had been unloaded at the Outpost. Finally at Mike's after a round-about route, they planted a wooden footlocker into the soft, sandy earth. Filled with plunder minus a few objects to study, it was covered and topped with spiny cactus. That spent the last bit of energy any of them could marshal on that Sabbath day of rest.

\\\\\\\\\

Allister Hope was a sturdy man with almost silver hair. A little taller than David, his presence was marked by starched and pressed khakis held together by a web belt with a well-polished brass anchor buckle. The pants ended in a neat, sewn, cuff just above bare feet. His business was boats — and he had a fleet consisting of two decked sailboats and two diesel-powered, inter-island motor sailers, which distributed goods from Trinidad or Barbados to the smaller out islands.

He also had three locally constructed cigarette-type speedboats for carrying tourists to isolated beaches. Purposefully he had enough children to captain each vessel. Hope's private boat was a Florida-built fiberglass Formula — powered by two supercharged six-cylinder diesels. It was at least thirty feet in length, pearl white, and would probably cruise a solid thirty miles an hour in any sea — almost fifty on a calm day without using the turbos. On the side of every vessel he owned was his logo, 'All things can be done with Hope'.

Bill and Allister chatted in private — and then both approached where David sat dozing in the truck. "So, you want the fast Grenada shuttle Tuesday morning?" Hope had the shining clear eyes of a much younger man. He pulled at his salt-and-pepper mustache.

"Not just quick, but also quiet," Dave replied. "We clearing customs, or not?"

"Yes, everything is legal, but private. You do this often and have contacts to handle the custom papers?"

"Yes, but everything is always on the up-and-up. That's how I keep those connections. I'm not saying anything about what you're bringing in; I'm only saying what I'm bringing in."

"Sure, Mr. Hope. Bill and I need to get down to St. George's and pick up the papers at the Embassy. Then I guess we'd clear customs at the airport. What we need is transport back to Carriacou directly to Eastern. I'd like to get back here in the early evening, just after dark."

"You sure everything is on the up-and-up and I'll personally bring you through that reef at midnight if Bill says so." The two men grinned and hugged. "You know, Bill helped buy me the second diesel boat by captaining the first one so competently. Yes sir, Mr. SP, if Bill says you're okay, you're okay with me." The gentleman extended a firm grip.

"How early you want to go, Mr. Hope?"

"That's up to you. To get there at eight we should leave at first light, no later than five-thirty. So be at the boat at five. You hear me, Bill? No over sleeping or excuses about how the woman wouldn't let you out the bed." Hope laughed and jabbed a smiling, but unusually quiet Bill in the ribs. "How is Cecilia these days?"

"Still pretty, ruling the roost with them young girls 'bout to drive her crazy. Is she who wanna keep trying for a boy, Hell, me'd a quit after the first one. So now we'se got grand kids."

"Hush. Children are a true gift of the Creator. My sons from my first wife, God bless her soul, are now in their forties. I've got great grandchildren, you know. It'll be one of the family helping in St. George's. Do you need dependable ground transport — because it can be easily arranged? It's a long way from St. Georges to the Embassy." "I'll put everything in your hands, Mr. Hope. I just want to be back here Tuesday night."

The next day was definitely a Monday. Feliza and David ached where they never knew they had muscles. After a fitful sleep, he gave her a good oil massage and reaped the rewards of his kindness.

"Let's go out again today," Feliza startled him as she came from the bath.

"You sure?"

She rotated the gold coin in the early light, catching a sparkle. "If there are more of these out there, I want them. The underwater jungle has probably calmed down from yesterday's feasting."

"I don't know. There are a few tanks already filled. Bill's going to repair Dolly today. We'd have to find another boat. Probably should wait though — because Wednesday we'll have metal detectors and can do a much more thorough job."

Still glistening from the baby oil, Feliza slithered under the sheet. "I think we can start a much more thorough job right here, right now. She grabbed him. "This entire plan is wacky if you think about it. You and I are doing the ass-busting labor and almost getting eaten by sharks or murdered by snipers. Mike and Bill are reaping the rewards."

"They moved as much as either of us and they each had valuable information. I know Bill can be trusted and Mike seems like a straight arrow." David winced as Feliza tightened her grip. "Can't change the split now. Soon we'll need all of the bodies to get this finished. The 'mother lode' won't be easy to sell. That's where Mr. Post comes in."

"I'm not sure that I trust him. You ever see the way he leers at me?"

"That's normal. You are a very attractive woman. Mike is lost in the sixties. You know, he's just a pony-tailed hippie looking for some free love."

"He wouldn't get any of this love — even if he could afford to pay for it." She released her grip. "Yesterday really turned me on, after that shark and the gold. You saved us. I've never had anyone risk anything for me. It was a new feeling and it made me hot. But the bullets kind of took the air out of that balloon. Let me see if I can blow that balloon up again." Her head disappeared beneath the sheet.

Before eleven they dove with a quickly repaired Dolly. It was taken for granted they were being watched. Perhaps the snipers thought they missed completely — or, the divers had nerves of steel. It was simply greed. Feliza successfully lobbied to continue — so they took out the nets and filled them in preparation of Wednesday's return. They found another two gold coins and nothing else of serious danger appeared. With the possibility of finding two coins a day, there would be no stopping.

\\\\\\\\

Feliza had the night off and stayed over the following day to watch the dive site from David's porch. Bill was ready before a hint of light appeared on the horizon and their trip to Grenada went easily — as the sea was low with the current and tide pushing at the stern. That's how Hope described it.

"Be ready on the way back for Kicking Jenny. We was lucky coming down, but probably the tide will be running against us and we'll have the wind in our face. It's always nasty there, next to Diamond Rock, when the current fights the tide. Makes that edge of water almost try to stand up. I can get us through no sweat, but it might be a bit damp."

Hope looked official in a khaki work suit. His big, brown feet bottomed with pink soles steadied him as he stood square-shouldered behind the high windscreen. That glass blocked any forceful air. Bill and David were enveloped in extremely padded chairs — which made the ride almost relaxing.

Raymondo met them before eight at the Lagoon dock in St. George's. He was Hope's second son by his second wife. Built solid like his father, Raymondo was a handsome, younger version of Hope with an off-set look that never quite made direct eye contact. The transport vehicle was a well-used Land Rover truck, which David suspected still had its original shock absorbers.

The U.S. Embassy in Grenada embodied America. It was painted pistachio green, and the ground area had been comprehensibly paved inside the guarded, chain-link fence. All the necessary flags waved in a slight breeze.

"Mr. Warner, I was given instructions you are to wait until the Charge` d'Affairs, Mr. Shremshock, has a free moment. He wants to deal with this personally." The young, female marine sergeant spoke decisively as if this were her only reason for living. That decisiveness had a southern drawl. "According to his schedule, that will be around nine-thirty."

"So, that gives us about an hour to get acquainted." David looked closely at the nametag on her left breast. "Officer Reynolds, could you show us where the coffee and donuts are hidden?"

Minutes later, Shremshock appeared. He was a short, burly, middle-aged man with a neat, graying beard that hid a weak chin line. He padded, flatfooted, without a trace of poise. As a representative of their country, he'd probably been chosen for his brains or connections rather than his image. His pudgy hands were stuck into the front stomach pockets of a pale-blue guayabera shirt. He could've been a New Orleans chef. He extended his hand for a limp, docile grip.

"Mr. Warner, pleased to meet you," Shremshock also spoke with some southern U.S. flair. "Come into my private office, please."

David followed, leaving Raymondo sitting with the sergeant. They passed through a spacious office, dominated by a huge, polished mahogany desk aligned by an arrangement of three, red leather chairs. They proceeded into a windowless kitchenette. Shremshock pointed to a built-in cafe table. David sat as Shremshock operated a noisy cappuccino machine. When finished, the Chargé turned the radio to a calypso station and cranked up the volume. He put a finger to his lips and indicated silence as they sipped.

Shremshock leaned close. "They listen to everything. I've tried to get the State Department to budget a monthly debugging, but they feel that we aren't doing anything of interest to anyone — so why bother. Why bother? I told those that would listen," he sipped, "and they were few, that this compound is part of the USA. But Grenada, at the end of the Caribbean chain, isn't very important to the powers that be these days. Back in the day, Ray-Gun Reagan had a different emphasis." He blew on the coffee and looked David in the eye. "So, what's happening I should know about?"

"Ah, Mr. Shremshock, I really don't think anything is happening." At that, Shremshock shed his decorum.

"Stuff it, Mister David Warner, if that is really your name. A load of Navy Seal equipment lands here with a diplomatic ticket and I'm to disperse it without any knowledge of the why's and wherefores. I really don't think so. Admiral Whistlow, chief of Navy communications, sends a package to a supposed retired naval police officer. Give me a break. I want to know the nature of your mission, or exercise, or whatever you want to call it. But I need to know so I can shield the heat if something goes wrong." In a much sweeter tone, he continued, "Surely you can understand, can't you? I don't want any, I repeat: I don't want any ripples on my quiet little pond. I don't want to be stuck here much longer. Get my message, Mister Warner? My career is still moving slightly upward without a blemish and I want to keep it that way."

"Mr. Shremshock, I think you are reading more into this than is really there."

"Oh, am I? I suppose that you are just buddy-buddy with the Admiral and he just sent you some toys to play with during your retirement!" His tone had risen above the hushed whisper. He unfolded a copy of the equipment manifest.

David could tell the burly man had read one-too-many spy novels. But this was a treasure story. "Actually, I am a very personal friend of the admiral and might become his son-in-law someday. This equipment is for metal detecting — and I'm getting a small addition to my meager Navy pension to test it in these waters."

The Chargé leaned so close that David could smell garlic, probably from last night's dinner, on his beard. "Metal detectors — so they think there might be terrorists attempting a plane hijacking?"

"No sir, these are for detecting underwater, as is the underwater communication equipment." He pointed to the list. "I'm having a sailboat built on Carriacou that should be finished in the next month.

Presently, I'm suffering a combination of being light on funds with a surplus of time on my hands." David couldn't believe how easy it was to exaggerate this lie.

"What exact type of metal are you detecting for in the sovereign nation of Grenada?"

"Well sir, if you must know," David leaned forward and unfolded the lie directly into his ear. "Word is the Ruskies left a stash of Kalashnikov rifles buried on a beach. Since the Soviet breakup, information has become a bidding war. I'm sure you heard of the Colombians buying a submarine from the USSR to transport cocaine. Imagine a thousand AK-47's in the hands of that type. That's what I hope to prevent." He swirled the cappuccino and whispered, "It was brilliant of you to see through the cover."

Shremshock's pudgy arms pushed against the tabletop until his back straightened. He poured two more coffees. With the fifth or sixth cup of the morning David's bladder was about to burst as his nervous system rippled.

The Chargé proceeded excitedly. "A thousand rifles stashed since the supposed insurrection? That's enough for another revolt. Aha, I knew it! The jungle drums on Mt. St. Catherine and all the never-ending communist manifesto trash." He grabbed his bearded chin as if to milk it. "Is there danger? I mean, am I, or rather, is this compound, in danger?"

The lie had spiraled almost out of control. "Actually sir, no one is in any danger. The informant gave vague positions, for a fee. I'm here to discern if that info was correct or just a ploy to get funds. To my knowledge, no one else knows of this. That's the way the U.S. government wants it. I am really retired — so that keeps Washington's hands virtually clean. Of course, you won't say anything?"

Shremshock looked at him, "Of course, my good man, Warner; who could I tell?" That sentence dripped out slowly as the Chargé pondered his most self-beneficial position. "But also, I expect to be liaison to any discoveries, and want it channeled through this office with my name beside yours on the bottom line."

"Well, sir," David rose and extended his hand, "you can count on that." Leaving, he realized what a hole he had dug for himself. If something happened, he couldn't turn to his new bearded friend for help. However, Shremshock did seem to be a man whose attention could possibly be obtained by Ben Franklin — and a gold escudo might get a handstand out of the fat man.

Customs at the airport was slow — and wanted to know why the Chargé hadn't come for it himself. Of course he was a very busy man — and David explained he was just his gofer, demeaning himself as much as possible. Each container was about four-by-four-by-two high with four handles, banded by two straps crimped with the USN stamp. The two fiberglass crates fit as though they were made for the exact space behind the two rows of seats in the Formula. Hope used a blue tarp to conceal his cargo.

The stretch of water in the area of the notorious underwater volcano was delightfully flat. Once the turbos kicked in, nothing could be heard over the roar as the boat cut a vivid path though the soft water. The captain pushed the inboards above three-thousand rpm to successfully impress the passengers. They cruised at about forty miles an hour, with plenty of throttle remaining, and arrived just before dusk. The crates went from the dock on Grenada to the truck bed in Eastern in less than two hours. Feliza was at the cottage to help unload. David let Bill take his truck home as he wasn't going anywhere, except to bed.

Beginning with a dinner of conch chowder and flaky biscuits, Feliza demonstrated her domestic capabilities. The meager cottage was spotless and reorganized to accommodate more of her girlie things. As David washed away the day's salt spray, he noticed the shower curtain rod held an assortment of small bits of alluring lingerie waiting to dry. The inside of the wall cabinet revealed more feminine items — such as scents and shades — all of which David happily welcomed. He noticed either a towel or a sheet now obscured the view from every window. The unexpected sight of Feliza's appetizing, pantied behind blocked the cooking range from his view. A frilled, pink cotton apron protected her front gems.

"Looks like you've moved in," David said as his arms encircled her waist. "I like having you close at hand." He nibbled on her earring. She reached back and patted his most vulnerable area.

"Is it good having me close only because you don't have to use your hand?" Feliza giggled like a schoolgirl. "I just thought why pack, carry, and unpack every day going to Auntie's and the restaurant? If you don't mind, I'll just leave all of my necessities here and that will keep Auntie out of any trouble we might attract."

David kept pulling at her ringed ear with his teeth.

"I thought you would be too tired to fool around. That's why I made conch chowder for an aphrodisiac." She turned and planted one of her now familiar wet kisses on his lips and whispered, "Guess my allure, or my perfume, isn't wearing off yet." The embrace strengthened to an affirmative.

Feliza ladled bowls and they sat in David's small kitchen. "David, I've been thinking."

"Uh, oh."

"No, you left me here alone all day and my mind just started to wonder, Mr. Warner." She grasped his hand across the table, "I feel so alive. The adventure, the adrenaline, never have I been involved in anything so exciting. Just think, if I hadn't seen your dinghy floating away, our paths might not have crossed. I just want to keep it going. You know, keep the pressure on so we can share the excitement of every moment — but only between you and I."

"I don't see any problem — except, forget about anyone finding out about this and the site becoming famous like the Atocha find. Fisher needed the notoriety to continue funding his long search. Our situation is just the opposite. We have to keep this very secret — even if we find the main load of coins." David continued to consume the soup as he squeezed her hand in the affirmative.

She shook his grasp and sat back in her chair. "That's not all I want to keep secret between us. The last two coins we found, I think ought to be ours and ours alone." He put the spoon down and looked at her. "David, we are doing all of the hard, very dangerous stuff. A few coins outside the split ought to be generous compensation for the health risks."

"Whoa there, Feliza." He rested the spoon and leaned back on the chair. "This is how it always begins in those mystery crime novels that spells a falling out among partners."

She grabbed two cold beers from the fridge and rubbed one between his shoulder blades as she returned to the table. "Falling out? Partners? Pardon me, but I feel that I'm getting fucked better by them than by you! Do you realize how much danger we're in? Not them, but you and I? If those spooks had hit their mark, Mike and Bill would still have our shares to spend."

"Spooks?"

"Yeah, you know, spooks, like in those secret agent books. I thought you said they must've been professionals," Feliza gulped her beer. "Whatever, whoever they are, they are threatening us, not the others! I feel it's just not fair!"

Something, just a small something, had hit a nerve. He hadn't heard the 'spooks' ever mentioned in the Caribbean — or for that matter outside of a service operation, a movie, or a spy thriller. "You must be reading a lot of undercover novels."

"Whatever, spooks, spies, snipers — their bullets all go whizzing by, unless they hit their target. And we are that target Mr. Warner, not our two out-of-sight, not-nearly-so-hard-working partners!" Feliza drained her beer and started moving dishes from the table before either had finished.

"What's wrong girl?" He grabbed her wrist and she shook it loose.

"What's wrong? What's wrong? You want to risk our lives for the profit of two men we hardly know. And then you question my use of words!" She dumped the dishes loudly into the sink.

"Sweetheart, I wasn't finished with dinner. The conch soup was excellent and starting to take effect." He sipped his beer, watching her harried, erratic movements.

"David, don't you get it, any of it? I'm scared." She sat on his lap. "All day I was alone with my thoughts and fears." Her long index finger traced the line of his jaw. "I just waited for your return. Never have I been so tormented. A real, deep-sea treasure hunt and a real threat to my life are a bit too much to handle. David, don't worry about what I say, or how I say it; just settle me down with the therapy I need." Feliza's strong feminine arms encased his willing body and they enjoined with gentle urgings.

\\\\\\\\\

The next morning, Bill was busy stepping Summer Breeze's mast in place with the assistance of the no-longer-errant crane operator. Feliza and David quietly unpacked and examined everything Amy had sent. Amy… he couldn't forget her.

The clock was ticking — and more sooner than later this feminine duo was going to meet. David explained everything to Feliza as their relationship progressed, including his distant, dormant, stateside relationship.

The new dive masks were an evolution of the self-contained Mark V helmet. Each set of headgear contained wireless transmitters and receivers — making audible communication between divers, and to the surface, clear and easy. The upper-left quadrant of the mask had a semi-transparent screen that displayed info such as depth, allowable dive time, and air pressure — with timed decompression stops, flashing red if necessary. Feliza balked at wearing a rubber-cap helmet, but quickened to the adjustment once she realized they could chat underwater. The regulator, coms, and detector plugged into a small plastic box worn on their weight belts.

"So, since we have no one to hear us, it can be our own 900 sex line, huh?" She still looked ravishing with the black rubber hood hiding her voluminous hair — as she stared ET-like from behind the lens.

He removed his and responded, "Not quite. Talking's distracting and it eats up air — so we'll keep it to a minimum. If we get into another situation, remember not to scream or shout — as it might damage my ears. Take a look at these metal detectors." The two he'd unpacked were only stainless rods, a meter long with plastic handles. Placing the gold coin on the floor, he felt the handle vibrate as the rod swept across it. He plugged Feliza's detector into the plastic box for the mask system she was still wearing.

She emitted a muffled 'wow' from beneath the mask. The small screen showed a bar of gold and whined loudly when he brought the rod within six inches of it. "Someone in Washington must really like you to trust you with this equipment. Aha! That's it. This is to bring the relationship back to life. Sleeping beauty awakens, but not to a kiss; instead she provides the means to afford the fairy castle! So, what does that make me, the silly pumpkin that doesn't fit the slipper anymore once we divide our find? Or am I the mean stepsister who imprisons the fair prince?"

Feliza removed her mask and took his hand. "No matter what else we find, David, I don't want to lose you."

"Not to worry. Amy Whistlow is a career officer in the United States Navy. She's over our relationship — yet, we remain the best of friends. Honestly, her father wanted me to marry her, but I wanted other things. Feliza, you've become very important to me in these last few weeks. I wouldn't trade what we have for anything."

"Sure, sure. I suppose Officer Amy knows all about me and you staining the sheets? Huh, Mr. Warner? Did you tell her every little thing about us before you begged for this stuff?" Feliza prodded him in the stomach with the metal-detecting rod. "If you think you're going to drop me once you've milked all of my usefulness, I'll show you right now where this thing will be detecting next! I think I'll call this my magic wand and make it disappear inside you." She proceeded to jab his belly.

"Hey, that's a delicate apparatus, be careful."

"You had better be careful, buster, or this dumb little island waif is going to plant her magic wand where the sun don't shine! Us little island girls have feelings too, like jealousy and revenge. I take the matter of keeping my man seriously."

David swallowed hard as another avalanche of evasion began.

"Nothing to worry about. Amy, Washington, the Navy, and the States are in my past. Feliza, you are my present and future. Take that to heart." He pulled her close and squeezed out another one of those kisses in a strong embrace.

As the embrace broke, she continued "If you are shitting this little island girl, I'll give you something sharp and painful to take to your own heart. My feelings are nothing to be toyed with. You read that loud and clear?"

"Loud and clear." He could hear the beginnings of the snow breaking loose at the mountaintops — which would produce an avalanche of dramatic proportions.

\\\\\\\\

"So, SP, how's all the new equipment?" Bill asked, looking over his shoulder while he helped pull Reese to the masthead to start the rigging.

"About as good as this mast going into place makes me feel. Seems like we're close to floating Summer Breeze."

"Yeah, SP. Just so hope we all live to see that day." Bill tied off the rope leaving Reese swinging forty feet up in the boson chair and walked away from the workers remaining on the deck. "Now Reese, boy, you had better follow me instructions to the letter — or you will sit up there all night 'til the 'morrow and get it right then. Take these stay wires and attach turnbuckles to the mast collar. That boy's not near so dumb or lazy as he makes out to be. Once you've got him where you can watch him, then he'll do some work. Yeah, boat's getting close to finish."

Bill caught sight of Feliza hauling an air tank over to Dolly. "Going at it again? You either the bravest, greediest, or dumbest. After Sunday, me thought that girl would have enough. Bless her energetic soul. Me thinkin' last night, well, yous really don't need me anymores. Guess yous never really did, 'cept to get you rolling with some old man's tales of younger days. But now, me'd rather sit close to home to enjoy them days with grandchiles. Kinda take my share. Then you can tear up that partnership paper."

"Bill, you are the most important person of the four. Without you, I'd have never heard of the Century. Hate to see you pull out before we hit the big load. It has to be out there; otherwise our competitors wouldn't be taking it so seriously. Now everyone needs to stick together. There can't be many of them, or we'd have seen them somewhere on this small island. There's four of us, and we..."

"Don't mean to cut you short SP, but they only three of yous now. Me was laying with the missus last night, listening to her heavy breathing, and decided that me had enough of this adventure sheet. Hell, looks at me with gray hair turning white. Muscles soon to go flabby. What me gots now is better than anything that yous is gonna drag out of that sea. It ain't fear," Bill ran his forearm across his mouth, "Nah, ain't fear, but it is the certainty of things changing."

"Changing?" David questioned.

"Well, sure as we sit here, things have already changed on this little bit of rock. All our talk of what we'se gonna do if and when the gold's found. Well, that change is what me don't want. Me wants me house to stay same, the girls to struggle with their men, and succeed in theirs lifes. Sure that gold could help them some, but me think not for better. And me think that having more now would confuse life. Could make it harder. Sheet, me should have thought this all out first, but everything was rolling so fast. Honest, SP, me never thought that yous find a damn thing out there."

"Bill, it is your choice to dissolve your part of the partnership, but I truly could use your help. There's a lot more boat work necessary — and to say the least, you're one of the very few souls I can trust on Carriacou."

"Well, months ago me took on this load of boat work," pointing to the nearly completed Summer Breeze. "Now me wanna do another for that bald guy. That might be it. Sure, there won't be enough to take Cecilia on no trips, but this is what me do and me think me gots to stick to that. Me no know."

"All right, but as far as it goes, Bill, I'll consider our friendship a great treasure. You'll have to keep watch anyway in case the bad guys don't realize you're not a partner any longer."

"That's what me figures, too. Backing out now might cost me two ways, but like me said, me woman and the chiles are enough. What me do, me can keep on doin' 'til two feet in the grave. So," Bill extended his hand, "shake on this share. Rest that comes after belongs to yous three crazies."

Feliza appeared again with another full scuba tank. "How's Dolly coming, David? There are two more tanks filling and we ought to be ready to go. Why the long face?"

He explained to her the conversation with Bill and her spirits seemed elated.

She clapped her hands. "These island people are so dumb and easily scared. Hell, Billy didn't get shot at, only a bit roughed up and that was weeks ago. Now he wants to throw in his cards and hide. Okay by me, give him his coin and let's go find some more." With that, she pulled David close for a kiss. "That's for all the good luck we've had so far, and for today's bit of luck having one less share to cut."

As David carried all the remaining necessities to Dolly, he realized that he trusted Bill more than his other two partners and was sorry to see him leave. Bill Steward had taken him at face value years ago and made him welcome in Eastern. Mike had a slick, big-city edge to him. It was evident to him they were all being used as a last chance for Mike to grab the brass ring from the old merry-go-round. Feliza was a basket full of questions, but the only thing David could answer was she wanted more, more, and more. Soon, conflict would arise between those two. Perhaps it was time for him to throw in the wet towel, have his boat christened, sail off into the sunrise, and let these two build their own partnership. He knew Mike would love a chance to crawl on top of Feliza, but she'd only permit that if she were dead.

They pushed off and Feliza kept her wary, binoculared eyes scanning for other boats. The sea had a bit of a chop — so they took time meandering before setting anchor just east of the site. The hook caught in about twenty feet of water. Just beyond their stern the sea bottom dropped off quickly into the cut of the channel. David reasoned they wouldn't be bringing up any more ballast. With the detectors, the job of locating unseen treasure would be made easy. If the gold was there, they would find it.

The first job was getting Feliza's hooded mask to seal around her hair. The equipment was designed for crew cut Navy divers, not copious curls. After a series of gagging attempts, the flooding was finally stopped by tightening the straps to their fullest. Finally, David heard the beginning of what was probably the longest, one-sided underwater conversation ever.

"Hey, you okay?" Feliza asked to his thumbs-up response. "Coms check, buddy."

"Feliza, I can hear you. Let's cut the chatter to a minimum. You search the area where we moved the stones, and I'll check the remaining pile. Go slow and don't scream out if you find something. Please remember always check the area where you find something again. Just because you've found one thing doesn't mean it's the only thing buried there."

"Okay, boss, I'll try my best," she gleamed up at him, "but to give the girl a telephone, and then not let her use it is sheer torture." David watched her shapely legs pump off as she started singing, 'I'm Feeling Hot, Hot, Hot' over and over. Usually when he was diving he let his mind wander and listen to the sounds of the exhaust air bubbling upwards. Maybe other divers sing or recite poetry in their heads. Feliza's rendition was an alluring accompaniment. Every so often, he'd hear the tempo increase, as she must've gotten a hit on the detector.

Each detector had a discriminator he'd set to block out worthless metals as steel, iron, brass or bronze. If this discrimination hadn't been precise, the fasteners of the planking would have kept them busy digging the entire dive. Instead, he had only a few hits resulting in more clumps of silver coins. He realized any valuable artifacts or jewels, unless they were mounted in precious metals, would never be found without some sort of air dredge.

The cargo of gold coins was lost and had to be here. One more of the sparkling specie turned up under the ballast — and then two more before his air ran low. Today, they weren't disturbing the bottom very much. The fish remained calm and the sharks stayed out of sight. He grabbed his dive buddy and saw radiance in her brown eyes. As they decompressed, listening to more of 'Hot, Hot, Hot,' he calculated the haul from this dive alone had paid for Summer Breeze.

"So Boss, you find anything worth talking about?" Feliza couldn't resist.

"Not much to mention, darling. How about you?" Her head went up and down, acknowledging the detector had worked. After they pulled everything into the skiff, she dumped her bag out to reveal six more gold coins, several clumps of silver, and a few jeweled rings. "Wow! You hit the jack pot," David exclaimed. Feliza just leaned back and tried on the ring. "Must be because the area was already cleared. Guess we'll have to move the remaining ballast." He poured out his pieces and then put everything in another bag to hang on the anchor during the next dive — to keep away from any floating intruders. As he crawled under the shade tarp, she was still admiring the ring.

"David, the ring fits like it was made for me. Look at it; you haven't even taken the time to admire my find. Look, it has two emeralds and four small, pink diamonds. It fits so well. Maybe we could use it for a wedding ring?"

"Ahem," he cleared his throat and spat over the side. "So you want to get married now? I thought you'd just throw me away after we brought up our treasure."

"David," she crooked her finger. "I'd never let you go; after all, we're partners — and it's definitely our treasure."

The second dive proved to be quieter as Feliza chose not to sing. David swung the rod in a slow semicircle, crawling on his knees across the site. This gave him time to consider — maybe he would marry Feliza. No, that could and probably would get him seriously injured by Amy. Feliza, with that wild look, would soon tire of his conservative old self and find other, more suitable, upscale beaus. Yet, that might be years down a very satisfying road.

This search hadn't been initiated to hurt anyone. Now it seemed only Mike stood a chance of being a total winner. Bill had withdrawn — trying to cover his bets and get out while everyone was still safe. Feliza could've just been jerking David along to get what she wanted. Nonetheless, it was a finely trained and experienced jerk. Amy was now being used by their friendship to get necessary tools so he and Feliza could get rich and sail away to a better life — leaving Amy with a bitter life. No way could he rationalize not telling her about Feliza without hurting her. However, the sooner he told her, the less impact it should have. If she arrived, David considered with a frown, and expected to share a bed, it could be crowded.

Just then his mask lit up with a line of gold, high on the right lens, and everything started to vibrate. He swept away a little sand with the back of his hand and saw a big piece of brilliantly worked gold. His breathing halted while he slowly brushed away the remaining sand. The oval was about six inches long, embossed with curling shapes, and had a slimmer handle of the same length. He realized it was a lady's hand mirror. The glass was still in place, but the seawater had dissolved its reflective silver backing. It was heavy and probably solid gold. He placed it inside his zippered dive suit and continued to search.

Feliza was also having success. Occasionally he could hear a faint exclamation and see sand flying around her. The yellow tail snappers were back in numbers feeding from their efforts. At twenty-two minutes into the dive, he alerted Feliza to ready for ascent, but she was scraping something out of the sand and motioned for him to join her.

The computers read twenty-eight minutes at the beginning of the dive, and David hated to push it to the limit. Feliza was pulling and waving sand as he swam over. He could see it was something big and had to be made of a precious metal to register on her magic wand. He hovered over her as she delicately retrieved a long, slim dagger from the sand. The entire foot-long knife appeared to be solid gold. From its heaviness, David guessed it weighed about two pounds. She looked up at him and contentedly smiled, while putting it in her net bag. Feliza swept the area again like a professional to make sure she hadn't missed another hit.

They ascended slowly, admiring the dagger. It had similar swirls to the mirror, and at the ball at the top of the grip were three stones. Gold couldn't keep a sharp edge, so this must have been something ceremonial. Feliza's eyes beamed, estimating the value of the find. David knew this was going to present a further problem of dividing with Mike. He decided to keep quiet about the mirror. This could somewhat compensate. A deal is a deal, and if Mike could squeeze good money for these items, he'd have served his purpose.

As an enforcement officer, David realized a lot of misdeeds are discovered by the perps trying to sell their wares. If he had to chase through a series of antiquities dealers to find one who wouldn't report them, or rip them off, they'd probably end up in prison. No, let Mike earn his keep and be the shield for their efforts. After all, part of some money spent in freedom is better than trying to spend all of it from behind bars. Feliza had gold fever and would never understand. And where did she get 'spooks' from? Why did it bother him? Maybe on the next dive he'd ask her to sing again so he wouldn't think so much.

CHAPTER ELEVEN

At precisely three twenty-five in the afternoon, Officer Richmond took position in the shade of a towering mango tree behind Mike Post's houseboat. The slim West Indian removed his cap — retrieving a handkerchief to wipe his shaved head and wave away mosquitoes. Lionel Richmond watched anybody and everybody as often as he had opportunity. For him, spying on people was more enjoyable than wasting time reading paperback novels, and certainly more interesting than watching television. As a successful voyeur, he realized no one knew what was seen until he used the information to upgrade himself through blackmail. On three previous occasions, Mr. Post had been observed unnoticed from this same spot. It never ceased to amaze the immigration officer how stupidly these supposedly intelligent persons behaved. Mike Post was an exceptionally good and apparently dedicated teacher — yet he'd developed a tutoring program that taught more than the local curriculum permitted.

The young officer stepped behind the tree trunk as he heard the rattling approach of a bicycle. The teacher had returned slightly earlier than usual. He parked and cable locked the bike — which meant he was probably not leaving. From inside the house came music — the type Americans called 'big band' or 'swing' style. It was what Mr. Post had listened to on the other three occasions. The volume dropped to accommodate a conversation with someone who had entered almost unnoticed. Richmond moved closer to the open windows of the master bedroom in the aft cabin.

The overhead fan made a 'loop, loop, loop' sound in the background of the conversation. "Oh, my! You did look nice in class today." Mike Post murmured to his visitor between kisses. "Thinking about this afternoon made it almost impossible to concentrate on anything else. Especially when I knew that you were wearing my special gift." He kissed her again.

The visitor was almost in a swoon from the attention. "But if my mommy or my sisters see these panties, I'll never be able to explain how I got them. They sure don't sell this type on Carriacou."

"Don't worry about that — now that you've worn them for a day, you can leave them here." Mike Post was visibly leering at the young girl. "Pull up your dress slowly and let me see them. I knew you would look especially good in the pink satin." The girl turned her blushing face and lay down on the bed, reaching behind her to pull at the hem of her gray pleated skirt. Temptingly slow, she revealed a shiny thong laced between her solid, brown bottom. Mike began to nuzzle her legs as he moved to undo her skirt and blouse.

"I think I'm the luckiest girl in school to have you teach me all about life. I know none of the other girls my age have ever had sex with a partner."

"Hey, you're not telling anyone about us, are you?" Mike sat up and removed his satin boxer shorts while continuing to fondle his almost naked conquest. "You know our deal and how much trouble I could get into — not to mention it would seriously foul up your chances for getting a scholarship to go on to another school. This is a private session concerning young women's health studies. I'll give you pleasure and continue to teach you everything so you can protect yourself and your future. That way you won't have an unwanted child like your sister. It is always the woman who must take the precautions. Remember, with my help, you can go to a college in the United States for free. Once you know how to make good, passionate love, doors will open and the world will be yours."

"Are you taking the BCP's that I got for you in Grenada?" The gray haired teacher continued.

"Yes, every morning I make sure I take one — but again I have to hide all this from my family. If mommy knew I was getting sexed she'd scream murder."

"The birth control pills are a backup, and will always be free at Planned Parenthood clinics. You are not just getting 'sexed,' you are being loved in the broadest sense of the word. Now, roll over and try to put in the diaphragm like I showed you. That, and always making your partner wear a condom, will protect you from dreaded diseases."

"Mr. Post, you take precautions, why do I have to do all of this?" she asked.

"Well," his hand began to stroke her firm left breast as she lay on her back. "If you do it correctly, you can live healthy and have only the children you want with whom you choose. Inserting a diaphragm and the condom can be part of sex play. Believe me; don't hide anything from your partner." He lifted her hair and kissed her neck as she busied herself with a tube of jelly.

Officer Richmond was visibly aroused, listening to the exchange from inside the room. He waited patiently until the conversation lapsed into sweet moans. It was now four-fifteen. He took off his hat and mopped his head again. His past hidden surveillances had uncovered infidelity only among consenting adults. This had enabled him intimacy with women who would never have listened to his first word. Lawyers, businessmen, and politicians with younger mistresses who couldn't afford an outcry, silently acquiesced to the incriminating photos and his extortion that might last forever. Officer Richmond had become a very popular man with the ladies.

He had once taken action against a man involved in a tryst. It had been the manager of one of the two local banking institutions. Richmond had wanted a new vehicle to serve as his own, but there wasn't enough money in the local budget to purchase another Land Rover. He had once read the advice: 'When you need money, go to the bank'. He did exactly that. After watching a prominent manager for a month, it was evident a regular beating of his wife accompanied the manager's drinking session every Friday night. Rather than make an issue of it, Lionel asked the bank to contribute a four-wheel drive under the guise of community-business relations. The banker wasn't spending his own hush money and quickly agreed. He still got drunk and beat his wife — and the immigration officer occasionally viewed the basic family relations and drove away in the new vehicle.

Mike Post had nothing Lionel wanted. However, an older white man taking advantage of a young island girl was inherently wrong. The girl was his aunt's youngest daughter and this slightly complicated things. During the prior observations he had only seen this girl, but he knew there must have been a long list of teenage victims during Post's tenure at the school. Officer Richmond saw no reason to upset these lives. The issue of the underage girls went against basic morality and it was time to end Post's after-school sex lectures once and for all.

Lionel realized, if any of these supposedly smart people had taken time to feed a watchdog, he wouldn't have been able to easily infiltrate their privacy. It took a few minutes to lift the inside gate latch with his penknife. From his belt, he produced a small metal baton that telescoped to two feet. With that and his pistol in hand, he approached the rear bedroom. Pushing aside the door did not disturb the engagement of the occupants. The pupil was astride her teacher with her back displayed. With a sure movement, Officer Richmond swung the baton, hitting the bare insole of the educator and causing a shocking scream of pain. The girl was flung off by the sudden jump from ecstasy to painful reality.

"What the hell?" Mike Post screamed.

The baton connected with a shin dangled over the lower edge of the bed. "Holy hell, what are you doing?" Again the baton fell, this time slapping a shoulder blade. Post fell back onto the rumpled bed with his arms extended in protection — and both were slapped again. The young girl had curled between the bed and the wall — grasping at the sheet edge to cover her nakedness. "You must be crazy, Richmond, to burst into my house!"

The baton didn't fall again, but was delicately thrust between the white thighs of the naked man — resting on his genitals. "So, Mr. Michael Post, you feel I am crazy, but it is certainly not me who is caught having sex with a teenage student. Rochelle, how old are you now, seventeen or eighteen? Rochelle, this is serious business that involves you and your teacher. Your mother will probably save the government a trial."

"You not gonna tell mommy are you? You right; she'll kill us both. Please, Lionel..." Rochelle hadn't looked up and attempted to shield herself from what was transpiring on the bed beside her. "Please, Lionel, I'll do anything so mommy doesn't find out."

"What about that Mr. Post? What is this young West Indian Island girl able to do? You taught her all the intimate knowledge. With what does she have to bargain? What do you have for bargaining?" Lionel raised the baton again, which brought a quick cringe from the sprawling teacher. "What do you have I might want, Mr. Post? What could possibly be worth saving your white ass from the public outrage that will definitely follow exposure?"

"I have some money. Not a lot, but I can make payments. You have my promise. I'll never do anything like this again. I'll leave Carriacou and disappear — if you'll give me that chance."

The officer brought the pistol into better view. "Is that promise similar to getting this young lady into a stateside college? No, Mr. Post, your shallow promises fail to penetrate my callused ears. Save them for your vulnerable pupils." Richmond racked a shell into the chamber. "Yes, Mr. Post, give me money, and anything else you think might barter adequately for your continued breathing."

"Officer Richmond, Lionel, you don't think you could get away with shooting me and the girl. I'm an American Cit..."

Just then the negotiations were shattered as the pistol spat a bullet out the open window and filled the room with the acrid smell of gunpowder. "Mr. Post, please stop that inane rhetoric about your rights and privileges. I have no interest in harming my cousin. You hear me Rochelle?"

The girl never turned from facing the wall, but shook her head in quiet agreement.

"Rochelle, baby, I want you to stand up. Mr. Post, if you move even slightly, I'll consider it a further attempt to resist arrest and respond accordingly. Rochelle, drop the sheet and come over here." The girl staggered forward to within an arm's reach of her uniformed relative. "How long have you been having sex with this man?" Lionel reached out with the baton and rubbed the girl's nipples, which immediately became erect.

"Me and Mr. Post have been doing this since last September when school started."

"Baby girl, hasn't he taught you anything?" He reached down with the baton and skewered the tiny pink panty. "My, my.... Rochelle, it is 'Mr. Post and I'. Never forget proper grammar," he said as he brought the shiny item to his nose. "Rochelle, come closer."

Keeping a stern eye on the reclining man, Lionel reached between the girl's legs. "Rochelle, you are very excited. I expect you to continue these studies in the future at my convenience. From now on all this activity will be kept in the family." He took her hand and put it gently on his crotch. "I'll be gracious and continue to attend to your education without mention of this traumatic incident to your mother, my dear aunt, as long as you prove a worthy pupil. Do I make myself understood?"

The girl brazenly squeezed and kissed his cheek. "You will always be my favorite cousin," she breathed.

"Get dressed and go directly home. Forget this. I mean absolutely forget any of this ever happened." He pushed the metal baton into its case on his belt and put the panties into his pocket. Rochelle hastily dressed, brushed her hair in the mirror, grabbed her books, and left without another word.

"Now that she has successfully negotiated, it is time for you and I to come to some sort of viable arrangement." Richmond looked down at the prone, cowering example of a lecher. "Money isn't everything, but I can be bought. This breach of the teacher's ethics is a serious offense. Even with good legal assistance, Mr. Post, consider yourself in ruin and probably behind bars with a bigger black man fancying your backside for the rest of your natural, unhappy life. Since they don't permit distribution of condoms in the men's incarceration building, you might as well consider it a death sentence."

Mike Post lay there with red welts rising on his shoulder and leg. His face was ashen to almost the shade of his hair. "I don't make much as a teacher, as you well know, but I have some saved. This is definitely a rainy day. Could I buy your silence and friendship for five thousand?"

"Sir, is that in U.S. or E.C.?" was the curt reply.

"U.S. dollars — I have it in a bank account and it will take me only a few days to get it. Look around," he swung his unhurt left arm to encompass his small domain, "Anything you want is yours."

"Mr. Post, if you don't mind my saying, you don't exactly live a life of luxury. Actually, I think I'd be better bringing you to trial. The publicity of catching a man of your demeanor could possibly make me a senatorial candidate."

The officer instructed the teacher to clothe under a watchful eye and then installed handcuffs. "I can pay you more for your discretion, Lionel, just not right now," Post bargained.

"How soon?"

"I don't know. Maybe in two or three months. I have some investments maturing. All I have to do is cash them."

"Are the investments here or elsewhere?"

"To secure the funds, I'd have to go to Florida," Post hesitated, as he knew this wasn't what the officer wanted to hear. Quickly he added, "But you could go with me. I wouldn't run away from so gracious a favor. Lionel, I have to work at something — and a story like this means definite devastation."

"Yes, definite ruin. You should have thought of that." The officer began to look around the small home. Drawers were opened and papers shuffled as he searched, but everything was neatly replaced. The kitchen refrigerator yielded two beers. As the young black man attempted to cool his face with tap water, a black rock fell out of a dishtowel that had been folded on the counter top. He wiped his head and dipped to his knees to retrieve the stone from the floor. However, it had shattered into three round disks.

"Aha, what were you saving these for?" Richmond felt each black, slightly greasy disk between his fingers.

"Those are just some curious stones I found on the beach last weekend. Look around, I have lots of other island curiosities." Mike Post tried to shift in his seat, but the cuffs and the bruises made movement painful. "Take them all, Lionel, I'll do anything in my power to compensate your gracious discretion."

"Well, well, well, that sounds distinctly interesting, almost as interesting as these coins." Richmond wiped a disk on a green scrub pad that was lying in the sink. "If I may believe my eyes, these are very old Spanish coins. More than likely, they were retrieved from salt water. How did they find their way to your kitchen counter?"

Mike swallowed hard. He knew that to lie now, after a hesitation, could mean disaster. "I found them metal detecting along the beach at Mt. Pleasant two weekends ago. That's why I have to go to Florida. There I can get a reasonable price, and pay you my ransom."

"Mt. Pleasant...are these three all you found?"

"No, I found a few more things already shipped to a dealer. Perhaps I will find more. I believe someone must have wrecked a small boat, dumping out some valuables."

"Aha." Lionel Richmond sighed as he inspected the slightly cleaner coins under a light.

"You found these when you were alone?"

"Well, yes and no..." Post stammered.

Richmond lifted the automatic pistol from the counter. "Please don't embarrass yourself with a shallow half-truth. It could be dangerous to your health."

"I was with some other continentals when we made the discovery."

The officer leveled the pistol at Post's forehead. "Who were they?"

"Visitors that wanted to try their equip..." another shot went through the window and cut the sentence short. A wet spot formed in the front of Mike's shorts and drained to the floor. "Richmond, don't fly off....It was

David Warner." As he mentioned the name, he realized his position had just worsened. But by breaking their oath, he was cursed either way.

"Really, Mr. Post, I'm the immigration officer." He prodded the teacher's cheek with the warm pistol barrel. "I would know if there had been anyone who looked familiar enough to make your banter reasonable. So, Mr. David Warner is actually securing artifacts. You are, shall we say, marketing valuable, if not priceless artifacts of the sovereign nation of Grenada, Mr. Warner — and," he prodded the cheek again; "I'll wager that Ms. Dubois is also in the pact. It is amazing how you white people tend to gravitate toward one another when there's money involved. And it is evident, at least to me, that Feliza Dubois involves herself with whoever has money."

Mike shook his head in silent embarrassed agreement. Now every door of opportunity he had hoped would provide an easier future for him slammed shut. "It's about time I visit the lovely couple. I'm sure you will join me in a drive, won't you Mr. Post?"

\\\\\\\\\

Feliza sat at the glossy porcelain table, wrapped in a bulky white terry cloth robe with Miami Hilton stitched above two crossed polo sticks on the pocket. Her wet hair was tucked into a white towel turban. She was intently studying the dagger she had found. It was a magnificent example of craftsmanship. The center of the eight-inch, well-polished blade was raised and inscribed with intricate script. The handle appeared to be made of two crisscrossed quarter-inch rods of gold that began at the ornate, sculptured guard. The three junctions where those rods intersected trapped an astounding blood-red ruby flanked by two smaller sapphires. At the end of the handle was a small globe with a half-moon crescent.

Feliza cradled the knife in her left palm slowly rolling the handle a quarter turn at a time. Its beauty, or the presumed six-digit invisible price tag, demanded a hypnotic stare. She kept rotating the dagger, her mind transfixed with hidden thoughts.

David was mixing two strong rum and tonics as he heard a truck approaching. "Better hide that," he said as she jumped to adjust the wooden window louvers for a view. He took the gold knife into the bedroom and swiftly put it in the crawl space above the closet unknown even to Feliza. His fingers brushed the oiled cloth wrap of the Walther pistol that lay above the golden mirror handle he'd already secreted away with the coins. Grabbing the pistol for protection was a thought that quickly vanished. He accused himself for exaggerating every unnatural sound and attempting to create a scenario equaling Hitchcock's suspense.

"It's all right. We can relax. It's only Officer Richmond, again," Feliza said as David returned to the kitchen. "God, don't let that twerp see anything — or he'll want an even share at the very least. What can he want at this hour? It's almost nine."

The truck slowed to a stop. They heard two doors slam in succession, followed by a serious knock at the door. As David opened it, he saw Mike's sad face pushed against the mesh screen. Behind him stood an agitated Richmond.

"What do you want? It's getting a bit late for visitors. We were about to go to bed." The uniformed officer pushed a haggard Mike through the doorway — and then David noticed Mike's hands were cuffed behind him. He drew a deep breath, expecting the worst. Then he saw the pistol.

"If you don't mind! What are you doing here? You've no right to barge into my home, day or night, Richmond! I don't give a damn how many government badges you wear."

The young West Indian officer waved his nine-millimeter handgun and directed everyone to sit at the table. "That's exactly correct; I have no right." He waved his pistol and said, "However, I do have this very influential Glock 17. That's the badge that attracts the most attention — and it is a very good invitation. Unfortunately, I must use it, as it seems you forgot to invite me, Mr. Warner. You obviously invited your two associates, Mr. Post and Ms. Dubois."

Attempting to sit staunchly under the pale glow of the kitchen's ceiling light, David's mind suddenly shifted from near exhaustion to terror. Guns being waved in the air always have that effect. Big drops of sweat were beading on the immigration officer's shaved head and seeping down his face. Mike sat rigid in quiet submission. Feliza looked alarmed, yet for once, kept her mouth shut.

"Mike Post, what happened? Were you in an accident? What is the meaning of this intrusion? No more riddles, Richmond." David asked with as much firmness as he could possibly muster.

"Riddles? Riddles! You think I have riddles!" He laughed heartily. "Mr. Post has very little to say," Mike cringed as the pistol prodded his shoulder. "Isn't that correct, Mr. Teacher? I don't expect you, Mr. Warner, to waste my time with riddles either. Mr. Post has informed me of your search."

Mike's eyes met David's for an instant, before they fell to the table. David's tried not to reveal anything to their antagonist. The room remained grossly quiet. Then Richmond continued. "Yes, I know all about your treasure hunt. You see, I happened upon Mr. Post while he was probing another treasure." He placed the cold barrel against Mike's cheek. "Isn't that what you were doing, Mr. Teacher? Weren't you probing when I interrupted?"

Mike tried to look away, but the pistol controlled the movement of his face. "Lionel, I think there's some confusion..." David said calmly.

The dark, slender hand cocked the hammer back with a significant click. Unruffled, he continued, "I was very sincere about not permitting any more riddles. Please don't tempt my fleeting patience. Mr. Post, tell them of your activities earlier this afternoon when I encountered you."

Mike swallowed hard and finally spoke. "Officer Richmond caught me having sex with one of my students."

"Yes, it was a young girl. This forty-seven-year-old man, a virtual pillar of the educational system, was fornicating with a teenager."

Feliza suddenly stretched across the table and slapped Mike in the face. "I knew you were a pervert," she spurted. Then she turned to Richmond. "What does that have to do with us? We are consenting adults. You can't think David and I are mixed up with this…this slime ball."

Officer Richmond turned the fourth chair and straddled it, using the back as a brace for his weapon. "Yes, yes, yes. Ms. Dubois, during your supposed educational sabbatical in America, several inquiries were made concerning you. Yes, you seem to have made some money while consenting. Yes, consenting to prostitution with other American slime balls."

Feliza rose; her face infused with a deepening color. "You son of a bitch, calling me a whore!" She fanned the air, furiously attempting to slap him. He pivoted the pistol towards her.

"Sit down and I might forget the ignorance of your false indignation.

Mr. Post can see you for what you are, which is slightly better than his own falsely esteemed character. Mr. Warner is saying nothing in your defense. The poor ignorant American has sampled your experienced charms and confused them for true, local passion. I, on the other hand, have not inspected your talents... yet."

"You go to hell, you asshole. You ever touch me and it will be your sorriest day." Feliza drew the robe tighter around her body and sat back in a dignified huff.

David watched the young man and wondered if he would really shoot. He held several important government positions for the island. How much would he risk? Mike was slightly shaking his head as if reading David's mind. With the pistol racked, it could go off either purposely or accidentally, possibly wounding someone. As almost the ultimate, unquestionable police power on Carriacou, there would be little or no charges levied against the pistol-wielding official if he did shoot one of them.

"Actually, my dear threesome, this is definitely your sorriest day. You see, Mr. Post has exposed part of your treasure, and I want the remainder."

"Or what?" David asked.

"So, you no longer choose to refute me? Mr. Warner, I'm certain during your shore patrol days you must have conducted an interview with a difficult subject — just as I am doing at this precise moment. However, as a member of The United States Armed Forces, you were forced to perform within certain guidelines with regard to prisoner's rights. Here, to the contrary, I can act virtually independent without much recourse. Consider this perspective: you three were involved in a crime against my country and, as outsiders, with the exception of Ms. Dubois, you were deported and coincidentally disappeared en route to an unknown destination. If inquiries were made, they would be directed to my office. Of course, since I would relinquish all the pertinent facts pertaining to your departure without any impediment, where is my implication? Also, at this very moment, I'm having a prayer session with one of my young female cousins, troubled by a relationship."

Richmond paused for everything to sink in and then continued. "Now the methodology of your demise, should you be uncooperative, has been more than adequately outlined. Who wants to begin?" Flashing a full, gloating smile, he tossed the three black coins on to the white, metal tabletop. Their clattering resonance sliced through the small room. "Mr. Post wants to buy his freedom with these. Doesn't seem like a good price for the pardon of a man literally caught with his pants down. However, he says you have more. I take it the other coins must be here."

"Look, David, Feliza, I told him I'd already sent what we found to Florida to be sold, but he refuses to believe me. You try to convince him," Mike said unevenly, almost out of breath.

"So, you are giving away clues about your original interrogation, Mr. Post. You should know better than to talk out of turn. Rules of parliamentary procedure and all that, my good chap." Richmond unexpectedly backhanded him in the throat with the pistol, leaving Mike choking. "I think I should have left you at that rotting hulk you call a home. This is not open for debate, nor will there be a lengthy time limit."

The officer looked at his watch. "Oh, I'm so sorry, time is up." He ripped the towel from Feliza's head and ceremoniously wrapped it around the pistol. Holding their intent stares, he put the towel covered pistol against Mike's upper shoulder and fired. The sound was muffled, but the pure force of the impact knocked Mike backward in the chair. Everything hit the floor, a crash ending with a loud agonizing moan. Feliza screamed, and bolted toward the bedroom while David sat frozen, gulping for a breath.

Richmond deliberately pointed the towel to the ceiling, and with a voice much calmer than the situation, he ordered, "Ms. Dubois, unless you return to your seat, empty handed, this instant, Mr. Warner will fall victim to a similar fate as Mr. Post." The sound of vomiting echoed from the bathroom.

"I'll be there in a minute — just don't shoot David," was the retching reply. David hoped she wouldn't try anything foolish. As he watched, a crimson stream welled out from under Mike. He appeared unconscious from the wound. The area of the shot wasn't life threatening unless from the blood loss. His two co-prisoners hadn't been acquaintances, let alone good friends, long enough to try a silly heroic effort ending in becoming worm food.

"OK, Lionel, what do you want?" David asked. "Do you mind if I attend to Mike?"

"Ms. Dubois, come here, immediately!" Feliza entered the room with wide, wet eyes and a hand towel. "Do you have anything I might construe as a weapon, Ms. Dubois? Open that robe and let me make sure."

Feliza glanced at David and then slowly opened the robe, displaying only bare skin. "Ah ha, I can see how your attributes could bring a more-than-adequate livelihood. Please return to your seat and relax, Ms. Dubois. With that body, you definitely have the best chance for longevity. And you Mr. Warner — I think we will let Mr. Post lie in peace for the moment, as your earnest cooperation during this investigation will dictate his well-being. Hopefully, your statements will not conflict with those he previously gave. Since he can't give you any innuendoes," Richmond looked down and snickered, "or meaningful nods, I think this inquisition will now continue. Where are the other pieces of treasure you found?"

David thought it was a pretty good bet Mike had said little more than to basically incriminate them. At that moment, it seemed the official wasn't interested in any specific amount, because this had gone far over the line of rationality. Whatever they gave him would mean their doom, because it could never be enough to equal his fear of being discovered. "Listen carefully, Lionel, we found several clumps of these silver coins accidentally while I was getting old ballast stones for my boat. Mike realized what they were and supposedly had contacts in Florida who would clean and sell them for us. I think, in total, we've found twenty-three silver coins. Those three turned up last Sunday. Mike thought we'd get around fifteen thousand for our share, but that was for only half. The rest went to the Florida middleman for his efforts," David spewed. "There are probably more under the remaining old ballast, but it will take time to get them. Mike is the only person who knows the contact, so please, let's try to keep him alive."

"Fifteen thousand for twenty-three ancient Spanish coins seems low." Richmond was pondering the reply.

"No. As I said, the person in Florida gets half as commission for cleaning and selling them with no questions asked. For a little effort on a few dives, we each get five grand. Not a fortune, but it was a windfall, until now."

"Until now!" Richmond echoed. He wiped his head and neck with the towel he'd used to quiet the shot. "What can I do with you? Fifteen thousand from the broker is arriving when?"

"Only Mike knew," David answered.

"We trusted him," Feliza quietly chimed.

"With what do you offer to pay your fine?" Richmond leered.

"What do you want from us?" David searched Richmond eyes and didn't like what he saw.

"I want enough money to be able to take off this uniform once and for all and wear a dapper, light cotton suit to conduct my future businesses. Do you have access to that amount?"

"I'm not sure. How much do you need to let us go?" David questioned. "Perhaps I could scrape up an additional ten thousand — which makes about twenty-five combined."

"Twenty-five thousand American dollars to keep three people breathing? That would be a bargain at triple the amount. I don't think that will suffice. I believe a quarter-million U.S. could perhaps provide a defense fund and pay your fines." Richmond was serious.

Feliza slumped at the table. "What is our second course of action, Lionel? We don't have that kind of money combined," she asked without raising her head.

"Ms. Dubois, I think you and I can work out something satisfactory. However, these white men are another story. I cannot understand what could have attracted such a beautiful woman to such a weak specimen of man." Richmond looked directly at David while he delivered his black supremacy speech. "You see, Ms. Dubois, the black man has been saddled with the labors and promises of the whites for over three centuries. We, as a group, have watched and learned. We are now ready to return the reins of power to the rightful masters. The three-hundred years of torment have not been wasted — because our numbers are now huge, well-fed, and educated. Through the electoral process, we will take control of the world without a struggle. Once the white man is subjugated, a woman such as you could rule as a queen."

Without moving, Feliza returned, "Lionel, you have forgotten one main point about power. It is dictated by money. Whether the right, left, good, bad, white, yellow, or black rule, he who holds the bank also pulls the strings."

"Aha! Miss Dubois, you have acquired the Americanized 'power from the pocket' credo, but that won't last as people of color are now ready in every possible location to readjust those purse strings. The white entrepreneur is so weak and lazy; he permits faceless assistants, via computers, to learn his intimate finances without expectingeventual recourse. Change is only a matter of time. The clock is ticking."

David stayed quiet while listening to the racial discourse. It was obvious Richmond had stifled a hatred for the 'invading' mainlander, so he could rise above and exert a certain power over his own community. He had been waiting for a chance to escape. The exit sign had appeared when he'd found the three coins.

Feliza spoke again. "Isn't it funny how you're ready to abandon our island for a fixed sum that can buy what you deem as necessary luxuries? Then what? Lionel, let us go, and we'll split evenly with you. With some luck, the monies that return from Florida will be more than expected. If we are able to locate more coins, then we'll all make out better. Mike can be hospitalized as an assault victim and very little will change. You still keep your office, I can still wait tables, and David will sail away. We are all better with a nice nest egg. If you kill us, you get little more than those coins you already hold. Sooner or later it will all catch up with you."

"Isn't it amazing how those already caught worry about their not-so-gracious opponent getting entrapped? Ms. Dubois, as I matured in England, my lessons taught me there are few real opportunities in life for a black man born to poverty, especially a Caribbean islander. If not sired from an important vendor family, then one must work and survive while waiting for, as they say, our ship to come in. Well, my daring duo, reduced from a trio, my ship is at the dock and I am ready to depart. If I let you go, the equation would not return to the original combinations. If I had not discovered your intentions of locating treasure, then my opportunity wouldn't be viable at this moment. If I compromise and lower my pistol, I will lose my momentary power base and probably my life. It is up to you and Mr. Warner to sweeten the ransom."

"Lionel," Feliza finally raised her head, revealing tearful red eyes. "I don't want to die, but there's not much left to buy our freedom. Something has to be done soon or Mike's life is going to drain away and he will be on your conscience."

Richmond solidly kicked the unconscious man. "Mr. Post is the epitome of an American. He has brought knowledge to the island for a corruptive price." He kicked him again, and the blow lifted Mike's torso like a rolled rug. "I hate him and all that his permeating, sadistic culture stands for." The black officer was sweating profusely; his eyes were staring beyond the kitchen as if he knew he had gone too far for any adequate return to normalcy. "You love to love Americans, don't you Ms. Dubois? Or do you just love money?" He spat onto Mike's motionless body. "I love to hate them. Their culture of greed has made me sad and almost forever unhappy. They commercialize and ingrain what you should work for. Work to buy happiness. Happiness is a tricky word. Happiness dampens dreams, yet it's intended to expand an invisible monster economy. That farce ended this afternoon."

"OK, Lionel," David said slowly in resignation. "I guess you might as well shoot us all and get it over with. We don't have enough money — so we're at an impasse."

"Not quite, Mr. Warner. In good American economic sense, I have, what I think is called, covered my bets. Now, Ms. Dubois, put on something suitable for travel. You see, she is the bet that needs to be covered."

"Where are you taking us, Richmond?" David asked. "I think I'm going to just sit here. If you want to shoot me, then okay. But it will be here, leaving a mess to implicate you."

"Ah, yes. I forgot you were a detective. However, Mr. Warner, exactly who would be investigating your murder and disappearance?" Richmond's neck veins bulged. "I am the examiner on this island, and I will find the lowlife scum who committed this combination of murder and burglary…" Lionel's eyes grew larger with emphasis. He leaned forward and glanced at Feliza, "and rape. And as unpredictable as it seems, that lowlife scum will most assuredly resist arrest and meet a sudden, tragic end. Investigation closed."

His lips curled to reveal a tongue awash in a large mouth, shouting dramatic orders. Damp perspiration soaked through his uniform shirt. David again attempted appeasement. "Lionel, please sit and have a drink. Let's look at this situation calmly — and we will be able to plot a better course of action and profit for you. If you shoot us now, what do you gain except those three coins?"

"Diminishing returns," he retorted, hardly audible. "The law of diminishing returns. I shoot you now, and finish it. I accept my loss, but then I diminish the complications of letting you survive. You know the American movie mode where the hunted has his chance to kill the hunter, yet doesn't take it. My mistake was haste. I should have watched you — and it would have been so easy to choose a truly vulnerable moment. Damn my impetuousness." The young man inhaled deeply and held it for several seconds, as if it would help him better cope with the situation.

"Listen, Lionel, we know what we've done is wrong and we're willing to give you everything plus our silence. I guarantee we will leave. I know I will leave as soon as my boat's finished, or before, if that's what you want. Hell, you can have the boat. Mike will definitely leave as soon as he's able, which would be tomorrow."

Feliza added, "This is my home, Lionel. But I promise I'll leave for a while and you can spend the twenty-five thousand or more in peace and quiet. Please, Lionel, listen to reason. We know you've won, so we won't argue. Just don't complicate things for yourself. You are on the edge of the freedom you have worked for."

David liked Feliza's tactic. "She's right, Richmond. If you shoot us, certainly there will be questions asked — persistent questions that will haunt you. The three of us will take our losses and start over elsewhere. You can live well with that amount. Start businesses and with your position, you can't fail."

Never altering his vacant stare, Richmond seemed not to have heard a word. "Did you misunderstand my command to dress, Ms. Dubois?" He leveled his gun at David's head and shouted, "We are leaving. Woman, put on something suitable. Now!"

Feliza quickly appeared from the bedroom in a T-shirt and shorts. Her eyes welled with tears. "Lionel, I don't want to die, certainly not because of money." She shuddered and burst into tears, slumping onto the kitchen table. "We can pay you. Just give us a little time."

"Ms. Dubois, I guarantee you will be the last to die." He threw two sets of handcuffs onto the table. The clatter startled her to jump back into her chair. "Lock one arm each in the bracelets and around a leg of the table. Be quiet while I search the cottage to determine your truthfulness. If I find more coins, you will be dealt with severely. As a sincere warning, tell me where the others are. Pray, don't let me waste my time. Time is extremely precious to everyone in this room."

Richmond poked into every cabinet and drawer throughout the kitchen. David doubted he would notice the trap door in the ceiling of the unlit closet. All the valuables that hadn't been buried in the trunk at Mike's were concealed in the cottage's crawl space attic. The pistol was close inside the ceiling door with the golden dagger just beyond.

Feliza exchanged anxious glances, and David nodded, indicating they should remain quiet. It was evident they were in deep and that nothing would buy time except the combined, overwhelming force of pure greed. The gold dagger had to be worth twice the asked ransom, but Mike's puddling blood signaled its insignificance in the face of the penalty facing Richmond if they continued to breathe.

After several minutes of rustling noises from the other rooms, the officer appeared from the bedroom.

"I didn't find anything," he said softly.

"We don't have anything to find, Lionel," Feliza grunted.

"But that doesn't mean you are not lying, Ms. Dubois. You found enough wealth worth better concealment than Mr. Post's efforts. I think by the time the sun rises, I will know with certainty of your veracity." He handed her the key to the handcuffs. She unlocked them from the table and then she relocked their hands in front of them. "One of you get on each side and raise Mr. Post. I suspect he'll come out of shock any moment."

There appeared to be no avenue of escape. The immigration officer was wavering under the stress, but never took his eyes off David. There were few people awake at that time of night. Even if they screamed and were shot, it would be more than minutes if someone responded. It was a definite no-win situation. They knelt to get their third partner off the floor. Feliza took the towel lying on the table and stuffed it under his shirt to absorb the blood.

"Where are we going, Richmond?" David asked.

"Do not question me! Just get this bundle of waste to my Rover. My program revolves on equality. I swear if you make an effort to call attention, I will shoot this lovely lady in the back of her lovely head, undoubtedly damaging her beautiful face. I guarantee the report of my pistol will equal your efforts for attention to your problem. Then I will shoot you. My Glock will give all the signals necessary to attract your desired commotion. However, you will be very dead, and undoubtedly not notice, or be able to use the help you so dearly want when it comes."

Richmond had submerged into total insanity. What began as a

blackmail scheme became a reign of unrestrained terror. David decided that at some point before they entered Richmond's four-wheel drive, he would have to make an attempt to kill him. David wished for a chance to get to his Walther.

Everything felt too bizarre; David was contemplating killing a man in self-defense because the man had stumbled upon their treasure. A treasure they would probably never spend would cause their demise. Even more ridiculous, combined and unrehearsed, they had stuck to their greed, coveting the treasure in the face of a maniac. David believed it was entirely his fault. He had pulled the information about the wreck of the Century from Bill. And now Bill was safe because he was the least affected by greed. Efforts to organize the search had drawn Mike to disaster. Sheer bad luck of retrieving his small boat would cost Feliza dearly. This was entirely his fault — and if he didn't do something within the next minutes, they would surely perish.

A frightened Feliza staggered and steadied unconscious Mike as best she could between herself and the table's edge. His weight made the table slide across the floor until it wedged against the wall. The screeching metal sound brought a wild look to Richmond, who began erratically waving the pistol.

David bent and placed Mike's weight on his shoulder. A sizable puddle of Mike's blood might be the only clue to their disappearance. Rising, he could feel the warm life's fluid soaking though his shirt. Feliza's gulping sobs could be heard above his heavy breathing.

Richmond took his position behind Feliza with his pistol against her head. He held both doors open while David walked through and then shut the doors tightly. The moon was bright enough that David could easily see his footing. His mind raced to reach a solution. Once on the sandy road, David noted only a few lights appeared throughout the village of Eastern. Silence enveloped everything.

They shuffled to the truck, where Richmond opened the rear door and shoved Feliza into the back seat. He then opened the tailgate. Mustering all of his strength and agility, David used the metal gate as a fulcrum and sprung Mike off of his shoulder and into the truck's bed. As Richmond moved to close it, David laced his fingers and swung both arms, luckily connecting with the officer's jaw. The blow staggered the young black man backward a couple of steps. Dazed, he crumpled to his knees. At the noise, Feliza dove for the floor of the vehicle.

Lionel tried to regain his balance, placed one arm on the ground to steady, and swung the pistol in David's direction with a clumsy motion. All it took was a little skip to close the distance, and David kicked a fifty-yard field goal. Richmond's arm flew violently upward and collided with the underside of the Rover's tailgate. The pistol didn't fire, but the night was punctured with an audible snap of his elbow. A sharp exhaust of breath exited the official with a long, loud cough as David gave his right side one more good kick. The usually dapper immigration agent sprawled backward in the dust.

The immigration officer tried to shift his rapidly inhaling frame to grab the Glock with the other arm. David's body was rocking with emotion. The pistol had been thrown under the truck and out of easy reach for either of them. David leaned to see Feliza cowering in the darkness. His hands rapidly groped around Mike's body throughout the truck's dark bed, searching for anything of weight he could use to finish Richmond and end the ordeal. Behind the mounted spare he discovered a small jack. The West Indian stretched to reach the gun while David's palm fit nicely around the small hydraulic jack. It could deal a nasty, if not final blow.

David raised the jack with both arms. Richmond made no attempt to escape, only to regain the weapon. Without a twinge of guilt, and while his conscience hid behind the nearest palm, David was going to end it. He knew this would begin a new series of troubles, but at least he'd still be alive to deal with them. But then David felt a sharp stinging on his back. Everything dissolved into a numb darkness.

CHAPTER TWELVE

So little do we see before us in the world, and so much reason we have to depend cheerfully upon the great Maker of the world, that He does not leave his creatures so absolutely destitute, but in the worst circumstances they have something to be thankful for, and sometimes are nearer deliverance than they imagine, nay, are even brought to their deliverance by means by which they seem to be brought to their destruction.

Robinson Crusoe 1670

Usually more time is wasted during a life than one realizes. Whatever the price, precious seconds can't be bought when the grim reaper calls. It was exactly like the cliché, 'He never saw what hit him'. David was truly in the dark. A truck might have smacked him downtown anywhere, at any moment. Then came the realization, he wasn't in the hereafter. He was breathing — his chest expanding. As if a blown fuse had been replaced, his mind suddenly began to reel. But his vision couldn't penetrate the surrounding darkness. His dry tongue pushed between even dryer, cracked lips.

He calmed himself from overwhelming panic. Next he tried his old terrestrial body. Surprisingly, toes squirmed, calves flexed and fingers curled. His back sensed sweat and stuck to a cushion, perhaps made of vinyl. For some inane reason he laughed out loud for merely remembering vinyl existed. He could discern a faint vibration beyond his immediate environment.

So the ears also worked! If he concentrated and strained, he could smell a sweet, fruity, maybe orange scent.

As his foggy memory cleared, a beautiful woman came into focus. She perhaps needed protection. Two men also appeared: both probably in need of medical attention, or an undertaker. Where were they? David could remember the conflict. Had he connected with the cruel blow of the truck jack? Rapid deep breaths brought calm.

A fetal curl permitted his fingers to check for cuts and punctures. None were found. The search determined he was naked. A decision to rise for a better survey of his surroundings seemed reasonable. If this was in fact the afterlife, he estimated, he may have already spent a century here, and might have a few more centuries yet to search the opaque perimeter. With fingers clenched to the cushion, he timidly extended a leg, stretched, and finally touched a cold, smooth surface. There was a top and a bottom; his conditioned mind suggested he was in a box. Questions remained. Was it a coffin? Where was he now — and was there an escape?

It was hard to imagine a completely darkened, totally quiet, climate-controlled room anywhere in the Caribbean, where he had been in his last waking memory. There was no breeze, but closer to the floor the scent of oranges emerged. Richmond would have put him in a wood box without ventilation. By now, that would have been unbearable or deadly. He couldn't feature anywhere in Carriacou as comfortable, quiet, and clean as where he was now. His faith in religion began to mend.

Intense paranoia overtook his initial sense of claustrophobia. Again his fingers traced almost every square centimeter of the floor and walls. Finally, without relief, he found another set of multiple gaps, or rather slits from where fresh air emanated. He had surveyed his smooth, seamless cavity and could relax in what he believed to be air conditioning.

David remembered a joke about the engineer who had been sent to Hell by mistake, and built a cool ventilating system. Seems when God found out what had happened he wanted the engineer back — but the devil refused. Then God threatened to sue, but there are no lawyers in heaven. Had that engineer been David's benefactor? He savored the cool air. As his perceptions cleared, his pulse rate decreased. Naked, he lay awaiting judgment in some sort of pod while a flood of memories of a half-spent life washed through him.

Perhaps he dozed. Neither awake nor asleep, he explored a timeline of his memories. This odyssey began during 'lually mogumbo,' the dark of the moon. All the characters of the past few weeks cluttered his thoughts. Other than Feliza and Richmond, there wasn't a person who knew his whereabouts. If able, Richmond would probably be shoveling sand on top of this crypt. Feliza offered a slim hope.

Breath after breath diluted his headache to a manageable pain — and some unfathomable time later, it finally disappeared. A clearer head pieced together the evening of terror. How could he possibly prepare an offense or a defense for whatever might come next? Richmond, with a broken arm, might be the least terrifying opponent. As that thought dwelled, David moved back to the vinyl couch and relaxed. His body could exist without food for several days at least. He was thirsty, but because the temperature felt comfortable, his need for water wasn't a pressing issue. Just then, after a clicking sound, his darkness became the brightest light. His eyes weren't open, but the beaming light penetrated through his eyelids. Disorientation lingered for a split second, until his unconscious reaction to open his eyes at the sound, brought immediate blindness. His arms flailed as he lost balance and fell.

Gloved hands grabbed his arms as he was pulled, tossed, and pushed on to a cool, damp surface. He was awash in a perception of the sea, and immediately sensed heat and humidity. His arms, with which he wanted desperately to shield his watering eyes, were grabbed and manacled behind his back with a plastic zip-tie. Another push against a wall, his shoulder sensed a doorway. He stumbled down two steps, tripped and rolled along until he jolted against a something round, maybe a pole. Loud, booming voices accented the bedlam.

David pulled himself into a taut ball — arms cradling his head as he waited for a blow. Finally an unfamiliar voice called out his name. "Mr. David Warner, do come to attention, puleese." He didn't move an inch. "Puleese, Mr. Warner, sit up and enjoy the moment. I'm sure you thought your car had crashed."

The voice had a lispy, British resonance, but it was so loud it sounded distorted. Gloves grabbed David and shook. "You can hear can't you, or did that blighter immigration officer crack your head worse than we think? Puleese nod if you cannot otherwise respond. I've had you confined in a quarantine room on my yacht after finding you unconscious on the beach during my early morning stroll."

David coughed and rasped, "Who... are... you?"

"Thomas J. Briscoll, at your service. It was Jr., but my dear father was gracious enough to pass over last year."

"How do you know my name — and why am I here?" David uttered.

"Well, full of questions aren't you lad? You are definitely a typical American, without a word of gratitude for someone saving your life. In a minute, you'll ask for the bill. Mr. Warner, you had identification in the pocket of your shorts. Mr. Palmer, throw the man his clothes. I've taken the liberty to have the items laundered as they gave off a certain aroma of fear — if you know what I mean. My man, Palmer, has military medical training and took care of your trauma."

David realized the clothes had been thrown from another direction than the voice, but nothing indicated the position. He was grabbed and his hands freed. "Mr. Warner, there is no need to struggle. The hand wraps were installed only to dissuade you from hurting yourself or jumping blindly into the sea."

He managed to get the shorts on, zippered and buttoned. Still almost blinded by the bright light, he considered it important to cover his nudity. The voice laughed in derision as David twisted on the floor and then staggered to stand. As his pupils rapidly adjusted to the light, he could determine a large silhouette looming close.

"Am I correct to assume you have absolutely no recollection of how you were saved?"

David nodded.

"I, Thomas J. Briscoll, am your guardian angel. My associates are also your guards. And believe it or not, in this eventuality, you are also a guard of sorts."

"I must be missing something. You saved me during the confrontation with Officer Richmond when I had the upper hand? Where are the others?" David asked.

"Ahh yes, Mr. Warner. May I call you David?"

"Let's stick to the impersonal, mister."

"Oh, Palmer, I do believe we have offended this gentleman — and that is the last thing I ever intended," Briscoll joked.

David rubbed his eyes back into focus, as soon as his arms had been released. The speaker was a big man, standing directly in front of a mirrored bar in a room of sterile white. The man was at least six-three and bulky. He wore white shorts with a loose, collarless shirt. It was like something from a hospital orderly, but in pink. He was totally bald and seemed to command the completely white room with two incredibly radiant blue eyes. Only one eye moved. He remembered the man who wanted Bill to build a boat.

"We certainly don't want you offended," Briscoll continued. "After all, I believe my action prevented the young, misconstrued Grenadian official from causing you bodily harm. Or it could have had a worse outcome, permitting you to deal him a true, conscious blow, which would have shortened his life by many years. I still haven't heard a dribble of gratitude. You could thank me. This is the second time I've asked."

"Thank you, Mr. Briscoll. Thanks for everything. But I'd like an explanation of events and the location where you found me. Forgive me if I seem a bit disoriented, but that chamber seemed to be either Purgatory or a prison. What happened to Officer Richmond and Ms. Dubois?" David inquired.

"Ahh! Again being the American, always wanting to ascertain the facts and only the facts. Our dear immigration officer was also brought here, as was the heroine of your adventure. If I may say so, Ms. Dubois is quite ravishing. However, as you can quickly ascertain, they are not here in this room. Here, by the way, is grand salon of the motor yacht L'Attrapis, which is my home and office, while away from home. Needless to say, I'm away from my delightful, permanent habitation much too often, thus the necessity for the comfort of this vessel. I hope to help you enjoy its relaxing features during your stay."

"Whoa! Unless there's something else, I can't see why you should imprison me on board your boat!" David demanded. With a quick swivel, he saw two other men at each corner of the room near the exits.

"Imprison is such a harsh term among…" Briscoll's voice dropped an octave as if waiting for the roll of a snare drum, "partners. Yes, I think saving your life is worth a partnership in your very illegal salvage operation. Officer Richmond also consented to forgive and forget for an equal share. Ms. Feliza Dubois was gracious enough to give us an accounting. I should mention that her conversation was separate from Richmond's. Yes, she accounted your total find of gold and silver items."

David took a swallow of a clear liquid, rattling the ice cubes, and refilled the glass from a crystal decanter. The bald man filled another glass and pointed. The taller of the two men at the rear came forward and brought the glass to him.

"Drink up, Mr. Warner. Accept us as equal partners. You really don't want to debate the issue further. My associates have been keeping track of your curious activities for weeks. Mr. Post was a surprise, as was the retreat of Mr. Steward. My associates told of their first encounter with your shipbuilder — and it was obvious the man had no stomach for such exertion or risk. Probably connected with his ancestral lineage. Another water?"

David relinquished the glass for a refill, and sank to the floor, assuming a cross-legged position.

"I do think there is something to be said for ancestry," his captor continued. "Sir, my business is antiquities. Keep that very clear. I said antiquities, not antiques. Various items of by-gone epoch civilizations are extremely valued by an elitist group with money. My clientele has money to buy any priceless 'objects of art,' simply for beauty, and of course, as a hedge against inflation. There is so much money out there for these collections. Spielberg's Indiana Jones cannot rival my expeditions to acquire such curiosities. During my career, I have acquired credibility. The main enemy of this type of endeavor is the preponderance of fakes that permeate the market. Never once has one of my items been other than genuine. Every item I purvey is always exactly as described. As you can see," he spread his arms in a reverent manner, "my operating costs are high. My expeditions have visited the far corners of the globe. My associates, Misters Palmer and Mullen, provide certain technical expertise useful to obtain the desired items without suffering unnecessary personal harm or injury."

"If you listened closely, you noticed I said 'unnecessary'. Look at these men, Mr. Warner. At first glance, they seem almost normal — everyday men seeking a reasonable wage in today's marketplace. Mr. Palmer, raise your sleeve."

The diminutive man at the left of the doorway slowly raised the sleeve of his dark shirt to reveal a severely scarred arm.

"Mr. Mullen, please say 'ahh'," Briscoll drooled on. The beefy gray-haired man Auntie Lois had described as a 'beach boy type,' opened his mouth wide to reveal no tongue. "As you can see, these men have suffered incredible personal losses working to accomplish our ends. Nothing will deter their zealous efforts once a course of action has been launched. Such a course has been determined to include five individuals, four of whom are aboard this vessel at this very moment." Briscoll paused and asked the men to wait outside the large cabin.

David looked around and saw the windows were tinted dark — and that strong white light beamed from fixtures recessed in the polished ceiling. Window seats ringed the perimeter of the salon. The center of the room contained a large, oval, white table with matching chairs. The reasonably well-stocked bar, with four high-backed stools, lined the interior wall of the cabin and was flanked by two doors. Everything had a glossy, off-white fiberglass finish.

"To continue, ancestry or heritage is anything that lends class distinction to a group of people," Briscoll expounded. "Some groups, such as those comprised of people like your associate, Bill Steward, have very little, if any, inner strength. That is why my men approached him first. Unfortunately, the information Mr. Steward confided has involved you in my present business. My own heritage is direct from a family involved in discovery and examination. You see, my uncle was the curator of the Smithsonian. He discovered all of the data concerning the wreck of the sailing ship Century."

"He gave it to Dean Worely — or so I thought."

Why deny anything? David was exhausted, and the gold had definitely lost its luster. It also seemed they'd lost the gold. "Where is Mike Post?" he inquired.

"Again with the interrupting questions. Puleese, Mr. Warner, my associate removed the bullet from Mr. Post's shoulder. Being of similar blood types, you unknowingly gave him a transfusion. Yes, Mr. Post is, as you Americans say, all patched up and raring to go. However, the blow to the throat from the pistol barrel will require recuperation before he can again adequately express himself. As with you and Ms. Dubois, Post is going absolutely nowhere. Would you care for one more glass of water sir? I see your tumbler is again empty and I would appreciate undivided attention for what I am about to disclose."

After a couple of clinks and a gush, the bald man continued. "You see, Dean Worely is my father, biologically. Now in his eighties, he is still scamping around. In the nineteen-seventies, he hit it big with Shell in Trinidad and Venezuela. What with stock options and a good business sense, good chap Dean became a wealthy oil baron, but always remained the scamp." The big man stopped to light a cigar. "May I offer you one? They originate from Columbia, and I believe they're much better than the Cubanos. Some of my clients supposedly have genetically manipulated the leaf for more taste, and even less dryness with an incredibly mild aroma."

David declined. Briscoll inhaled and began again. "Dean was amorously targeted by my dear old mum and soon succumbed to her wiles and fiendish ways. I can only imagine what an ingénue like mother could do in her prime. She saw the adventure in Dean's eyes and his fortune in the bank. She probably acquired his affection with some very deft maneuvers. I feel the necessity to mention, I was born less than seven months after their wedding. Slightly premature, so they say." He struck a pose to demonstrate his size. "But I've since made up for that. Whatever, Dean was a loving father until he brought a gift to mother she hardly expected."

He inhaled deeply on the cigar and sipped his drink, seeming to want the drama to build before he continued. "Yes, father Dean tried the local tropical fruit once too often when he went out to a drilling site, which he did quite often. More than oil was getting drilled. One return gifted dear Mom with the clap. Shame on him for not taking precautions — and more shame for getting caught. Needless to say, the divorce was over before it began. Mother fought hard for her share of his wealth, and my enviable juvenile status didn't hurt the settlement. At least Dean had the foresight to give her only one hit. It was a gigantic alimony, for the 1960's anyway: a lump sum of almost a million and a half. Well, Mother decided the affair was so depressing and had smeared her good name stateside so badly, she headed for the Mediterranean. There she met Thomas J. Briscoll, who at that time wore the 'junior' moniker. Thomas was gallivanting across Europe, exhibiting his sire's wealth throughout the casinos and gala balls as one of the most eligible bachelors."

"Thomas J., my senior, married Mom and they became well entrenched with the jet set. Dear old father, Dean, assisted with occasional inside oil information, donated expressly for my education's benefit. That, coupled with Mother's insight, augmented Briscoll's father's West Coast fishing business and fortune by various other acquired interests. To the son of a previous marriage, Thomas J. was amicable enough to lend the family's name as he shuffled me from elitist prep school to elitist college. That procession of scholarly mansions created the connections I ply today. My fortune, rather our fortune — Palmer's, Mullen's and my own — is freshly created without stain of inheritance. Self-made, as 'they' say. Ahem," he puffed up his chest and said, "It is much more respectable, and certainly much more conversational, at cocktail soirees." He gulped his drink.

"So, Mr. Warner, that brings me to Carriacou, Island of Reefs. My father and uncle entrusted me with the evidence previously used to direct them here to seek the wreck of the Century. I have discovered further information, which almost certifies that wreck is here, and includes eight chests of the rarest gold coins and jewels, including the Stern diamond."

"A comprehensive search of Mr. Post's humble abode discovered the rubbing 'Century 1699'. It was amazing; a schoolteacher in backward Carriacou, a teacher with an obviously full after-school calendar, could do research which virtually equaled my own. Post had everything except a comprehensive manifest. It seems Mrs. Eva Hollenzock had just inherited a fortune from her Prussian rabbi father, Isaiah Stern. That fortune contained numerous pieces of fine jewelry with precious, well-cut stones in elaborately rich settings. Among the finest pieces was the Stern diamond. It also seems her husband, Malachi Hollenzock, wasn't as successful as Mr. Post's research depicts. He was a banker, but also quite the hustler, and had compiled a mountain of debt through bad business ventures. It was Malachi who yearned for a chance to start over in Barbados, very far away from his debtors."

"The receipts of the old Hebrew trading companies are better kept than maritime insurance records. In fact, some of those same family-owned companies are still in operation today, four centuries later. There even exist drawings and paintings of much of this lost jewelry. You may not be aware of the value of certified antique jewelry settings and quality gems, but it is presently through the roof. I am in direct contact with many of the major players of a circle awaiting the success of this endeavor."

"How many carats is this Stern reported to be?" David inquired.

"Almost a hundred." Briscoll replied.

He whistled, "Well, Mr. Briscoll, I wish you all the luck. I think it would be best for all interests if you took what we've already found as a token of our appreciation and we go our separate ways. It would be more advantageous to contract a professional, commercial diving team. Feliza and I are just amateur, recreational divers."

"Yes, you are amateurs equipped with the most state-of-the-art underwater detecting equipment the United States Navy could supply. The underwater communications you possess aren't on the commercial market yet, at any price. Either you pulled some strings or pried a door. No, my group has fully accessed the value of professionals versus you two and the dynamic duo was chosen. You already know the site, which keeps the information to the minimum of people."

"The L'Attrapis is very well accoutered and will now be used as the surface boat. It is equipped with a three-hundred cfm compressor that runs off a generator. You will air dredge the sand, and it will dump through a fine mesh screen suspended twenty feet above and twenty-feet down current from you. This vessel, via high-resolution underwater cameras, will oversee that screen, and your labor. So any escape attempt will be monitored. You will also not be able to hide anything for future retrieval. The mesh will grab all the gems, loose or mounted. With Officer Richmond a member of the group, we will be given adequate notice should the Grenadian Coast Guard be dispatched in this direction."

"Do we have a deal, partner?" Briscoll extended his hand to David, twanging a western John Wayne imitation.

"Like I said, Mr. Briscoll, thank you for saving our lives. Truly, I'd like to help and continue diving. I've never used a dredge and certainly Feliza hasn't. It would be dangerous and undoubtedly counterproductive. Please reconsider," David pleaded. "We can be out of here immediately, and you can have all the valuables we've found."

"Puleese permit me to make one thing clear," Briscoll returned. "We know of all the valuables now. Understand? All you have to do is point out where they are. I am certain that Ms. Dubois is ignorant to the location. Mr. Palmer's medical training also included injections of various serums to loosen the subconscious. She was delved deeply, and I truly believe she doesn't know. However, we did get a good accounting of what to expect and," he wrung his hands, "I'm overflowing with excitement. You will show us, or she and Post will suffer. Those previous proceeds are mine. You interrupted my search, Mr. Warner. Seldom do we enlist outside partners. Consider it good or bad luck. Accompanied by my two men, you will retrieve your finds later this evening."

"Once a decision has been made, it has already been talked through, and never have we changed a plan of action. I see no reason to lobby your cause. There is little danger with the air dredge. You will have a valve to instantly shut off the airflow. Ms. Dubois will fan the area directly in front of the suction mouth. You only need to watch she doesn't get sucked in…" he paused and added sarcastically, "as you obviously have been."

"Actually, you should consider yourself lucky you are an accomplished diver and are still a necessary instrument of this mission along with Ms. Dubois. Mr. Post, on the other hand, has little value as a researcher or a vendor. He will be the first extinguished if you rebel, attempt theft, or try to escape. To argue further is masochistic. Palmer and Mullen can be very influential!"

David extended his hand to shake on the blackmail. "Partners it is, Mr. Briscoll, but I suggest you pay off Richmond in one lump sum. If he sees what we've found his cost will increase."

"David…" Briscoll spoke in a very condescending tone as if to a child, "I'm on a first name basis with all my partners. However, none of them will ever instruct me as to what to do. I will deal with Lionel Richmond and he will be very satisfied with his share, as will you and everybody else. As to the current finds, those will be used to insure my investment of capital, equipment, and personnel…"

"I'd like to see Feliza," David interjected.

"In due time, at the latest tomorrow when you dive." As if they had been meeting in a restaurant he casually remarked, "Would you like the chef to prepare you something quite palatable? I've had your cottage floor scrubbed and the furniture replaced by this morning's dawn, so nothing will be noticed. A note was left for your workers, attached to your coffee pot, stating you and the lady went to get more equipment in Grenada, and should be gone for about a week. The note was left purposely ambiguous, so Steward would think it pertained to your diving project, and the men would expect your return with parts for the boat. The same message was communicated to Ms. Dubois' relative at the restaurant. All equipment, personal articles and necessary clothes were brought to this boat so you can be as comfortable as possible. However, studies have shown when male and female coworkers fraternize during non-working hours, production declines. For the better of our endeavor, we will keep you, and the lovely lady separated. That will ensure little conspiracies won't be easily hatched. Mr. Post has taken a personal leave of absence to visit his ailing sister."

"If she's been mistreated…" David muttered.

"Then you'll do what?" Briscoll challenged. "Don't we seem like gentlemen, David? Officer Richmond poured on and on about the lady's spotted, off-island reputation. But you didn't hear any of that did you? I must say she is an attractive piece, but definitely not our type. Presently

Ms. Feliza Dubois is sleeping, if you must know. She has adjusted well to our hospitality. Aryans — pure superior bloodlines — are my most desirable females. Here in this backward locale, there is more chance of acquiring a deadly virus than an intelligent conversation. By the way, I do look forward to listening to your exploits during future cocktail hours — so I can incorporate them into my sales pitches. The haughty-tot rich love a narrative to escort each item of antiquity, like a distinctive screenplay. Ms. Dubois mentioned sharks. That must have been one hell of a day, sharks above and below. What about having some dinner?" Briscoll asked in his persistent, motherly voice.

"Yes, Thomas, I'll eat," David answered.

Briscoll pulled a small device, which looked like a pager, from a waist pocket and spoke the word 'dinner'.

"It was exciting and I'm sure you had a great hand in the choreography. One request," David asked, "since she has mentioned the shark incident to you, we need spear guns for protection."

"No problem," Briscoll assured. "We don't want chomped divers. The rubber band guns will be dropped by weighted line to the bottom, uncocked. When you surface, you will swim directly in front of both cameras, displaying bare hands."

He sucked on the cigar and continued. "You'll find, David, we are very easy going, professional men — extremely determined to achieve the goals we set many months and thousands of dollars ago. However, because this profession can be stressful at times, you'll find astonishing, split-second reactions. I said we are both professional and gentlemen, but not necessarily nice guys."

A slight oriental man brought a tray with a cold soda and an enticing plate of food. "Chicken Kiev I believe, isn't it Conrad?" The server uttered something in a language David didn't recognize, nodded, and then quickly exited. "You will eat extremely well aboard the L'Attrapis. Breakfast is at 0600 hours. Lunch will be convenient to your decompression schedule, and dinner promptly at seven. Ms. Dubois will join for each repast."

David quickly consumed the meal, then burped and smiled slightly.

"That's it. Cheer up, my good man," said Briscoll. "Things could be considerably worse. Examine the consequences. You could be fleeing the murder of a government official — or you yourself could have become a rash fatality with your cohorts. Now you are in the lap of luxury, tended and cared for with the proverbial kid gloves. You will dive within the limits, but at least we have an on-board decompression chamber if an accident occurs. My group tries to anticipate everything."

"Now," he picked up his small transmitter again and whispered into it, "let Mr. Palmer show you to your stateroom and the areas necessary to your labors. Inspect your dive gear. If anything has been missed, please let my assistant know. If you are rested enough, please assemble the underwater communication equipment where he designates. If there isn't anything further, I think I'll indulge myself with a nap. It has been a tiring, hectic day." With that, the rear door opened and the smaller, darkly-clad man entered, nodded, took David's arm and directed him outside. There was no time for any final salutations.

Seconds of a bright afternoon were whisked away as David exited the deck to the mega yacht's interior. Each bulkhead hatch was wound shut as they passed. The vibration and accompanying noises of the engine, or generator, became more prominent. Behind the conference room was a hallway with a row of doors. The man silently opened the furthest forward hatch and pointed inside. It was a small stateroom with his clothes neatly stacked and toiletries resting along the small shower.

David surveyed the cabin and plopped on the tightly sheeted bed. The silence ended when the door closed and his guide offered, "I don't know what Tunaman told you, but we are mucho seriouso hombres, amigo. Swim or sink! If you don't produce, you and that black cunt are history. Speaking of history, where did you get the professor? You find him or the reverse?"

"Does it matter?" was the curt reply.

"No, not really. Swabby, let's get something straight. We are Americans, and we still like America, especially U.S. dollars. There will be no harm to you. You never know, you might take to this line of work and join us for another trek. Worry about yourself laddy, and don't confuse your personal issues with those other two characters. Believe me, either the bitch or the pony tail would sell everyone else down the river without so much as a blink to save their own ass."

"I'll take that to heart. Mr. Palmer, isn't it?" David extended his hand.

"Palmer it is." They shook hands as if it were a common custom between captive and captor. "One white man to another, never trust a spook or a bitch. The combination will spell disaster. Anyway, your gear is in the next cubical."

David sorted out two complete sets of dive gear with spares, and was informed the scuba tanks were kept aft where there was a fill hose near the dive platform. "Saves labor, carrying tanks is slave work. We reduce the effort; that's the thing we do best," Palmer recited. "This motor cruiser is one-hundred-and-ten feet at the water line of its tunnel hull. That design gives it great stability while drafting less than eight feet. The motors are two twelve-cylinder Detroit diesels with two backup ten-kilowatt generators that, with a few changes, can be used for propulsion. It has enough tankage to carry it tomorrow directly to the Med. Satellite, and computer communications link us to various sites the world over. Our water maker produces a thousand gallons a day if necessary. So, you can see all the labor-saving angles have been covered."

Everything was checked a second time and, to David's delight, his captors had overlooked the power head for the spear gun in his buoyancy vest's pocket, which still had two spare bullets taped to it. He tried to conceal his relief. Palmer continued his tour along to the operations center, where everything was monitored, explaining each panel with seemingly immense pride. Amid gauges for the two huge diesel engines, two generators, compressors, air conditioning and water makers, were the monitors of the surface and underwater surveillance cameras. The underwater communication console was attached to the underside of the desk and took very little space. A half-hour later, with several references to the manual, the unit had been tuned and ready. David was returned to his chamber to rest and instructed to dress for dinner.

The melody of the tune, 'What a Difference a Day Makes' ran through David's mind as he stood under the hot shower in the locked cabin. Briscoll was correct; this was the best of all options as an outcome of the situation with Richmond. The hot spray patted his back and soothed several aches. Palmer unlocked the door at six forty-five, and they joined Thomas J. with Feliza in the bar. Weak rum cocktails were served to accompany another speech from the tall, bald host. David and Feliza met half-way and embraced as her tears wet his shoulder. Palmer and Mullen smirked.

"Yes, I can see that spark of affection between you two. Admirable, isn't it fellows?" Briscoll commented, and then the three clinked glasses.

Feliza nodded to David but didn't speak. Her expression conveyed she was all right, but frightened.

"It's rational to be afraid — but again, please permit me to reiterate: we are your saviors. Always consider the end result." Briscoll came between the couple and placed his fatherly arms on their shoulders. "Drink up," he said. "Think positive and tomorrow we will have treasure to discuss."

The group followed through the aft starboard door onto a covered deck behind the windbreak of the upper steering station. The long, oval table had been set for dinner served from a nearby gas barbecue.

"Allay your fears. Mr. Post is regaining his strength in his cabin by eating a specially prepared meal that will easily pass his damaged esophagus." Briscoll explained.

Everyone ate, listening to Thomas J's one-sided conversation. "To our two divers' luck and good health." The three who belonged to the yacht raised their cups. "Mr. and Ms., let me explain in detail how you happen to be here. My associates, Palmer and Mullen, love to take a nightly stroll. It is something that persists from their military service days. They call it reconnoitering." The smaller, Palmer, graced a sly smile, while the bigger cupped his mouth and coughed a laugh.

"At my direction, they were planning to watch you lovebirds and learn of your recent finds. That was interrupted by the arrival of Richmond. As with any angels, they struggled to remain invisible, and waited to see if you could handle the circumstances alone. As the action peaked and the power teetered, they protected all three participants. No, make that four, counting Post. Mullen carries a tranquilizer gun that stung all three combatants and stopped the action. No noise, no blood, no struggle. Everyone was loaded into our inflatable and brought here to sleep off the drug. Mr. Post had successful emergency medical treatment to remove the bullet from his shoulder. His cracked ribs were taped. Officer Richmond had a rudimentary splint prepared for his elbow. I'm afraid the degree of his injury was beyond our medical expertise. After sedation and reasonable negotiations, he agreed to silence and treatment at the local clinic, which has a radiology machine."

"May I interrupt and ask a question of you, Swabby?" Palmer snorted. "Why wouldn't you cut a deal with the uniformed nig? You were going to kill him rather than give up a few coins. I got to say that really impressed me. But why were you doing it, for the lady or the gray pony tail?"

David chewed slowly, looked up from his plate and replied, "Stupidity more than greed. Honest, I just got carried away. She and I fought for that stuff and weren't about to give it up just because he said so. Everything went haywire so fast. One lie led to another; then there was no turning back."

"Yeah, Swabby, but what about after the nine-millimeter started doing the nig's talking? I saw you through the window. Hell, you just clammed up. The lady here blew her cookies after the teach caught a shot, but still, she didn't beg. That's balls. I give you a thumbs up," Palmer praised. "'Specially for a nig bitch."

Feliza's spoon clattered to her plate — yet she never uttered a word. Instead of glancing David's direction, she turned to Briscoll, who quickly added, "Palmer, please don't make our guests uncomfortable with racial slurs. Call greed for what is it, an admirable, ageless trait."

Palmer continued, "Word is you were some kind of patrol cop in the Navy. One of those guys who always pulls the plug just when the good time's about to start. I used to hate those spic-and-span types, strutting around in groups through Saigon in their pressed, white uniforms. So you must have made some good contacts."

This time, David didn't look up. "You got it wrong. I mostly jockeyed a desk with a lot of trips transporting prisoners, which others had apprehended."

"Sure." Palmer dropped the questions as the head of the table struck his cup with a spoon.

When coffee and cookies were delivered, Briscoll began again. From a polished leather portfolio case, he withdrew several prints. Laying them on the cleared table, he pointed, "This is the Stern Diamond, ninety-seven exquisite carats. As you can see, it is almost as big as half of a man's thumb. According to records, this gem was a gift from an Indian Caliph in return for a century of free passage through what is now Turkey, and all the way to the Baltic States. This jewel was supposedly delivered with an entourage of virgin female slaves. If you examine the setting, you will find it exquisite. I can tell by its great cutting and intricacies it was probably sculpted by a Hebrew artisan. And since it is gold, it will still be perfect. The diamond rests among several golden women intertwined, supporting the gem between their arms and legs."

More pages were deposited on the table. "Along with that mammoth gem are these." Pointing to one paper, Briscoll said, "This is the ruby of Bangkok, a mere fifty carats measuring three quarters of an inch in diameter. And these three are sapphires from the thirteenth century conqueror of Northern China, Temüjin, or as he is known to the Western, unscholarly world, Genghis Khan. Probably all three gems originated in Thailand. These five jewels will bring millions of dollars to our coffers. There will be no middleman expenses. When they are found, you will be rich. We will be richer. The dredge shouldn't damage any of the stones. Ms. Dubois, it will be your duty to brush away the loose sand with a ping-pong paddle that we will provide. If you pick up one of these, I personally will give you a kiss."

Feliza looked directly at him and gave a gracious smile. During the meal, she hadn't uttered a word.

"One more bit of information concerning our search," Briscoll droned. "There is a high probability this site is the Century's resting-place. My uncle first found reference to the wreck of the Century while cataloguing items as a neophyte researcher for the Smithsonian in 1953. Uncle Frank's interest was piqued when he found the journal of the court trial for the infamous Captain Kidd. Another journal referred to two members of the Century's crew who had survived the sinking. Sailors Allsop and Stricklind sailed with the Century from Europe, but were somehow captured with the notorious William Kidd aboard his ship, Antonio, in New York Harbor and sent to the gallows. They attempted to trade knowledge of the wreck site for freedom."

"My dear uncle was a grand researcher, but I located this only a few years ago." A small, old, bound book with gold gilt still edging the pages was unfolded on the table as Briscoll talked. "Justice Bergerman presided over the various indictments and kept minute notes of the testimony from all the supposed pirates. Once they were indicted for crimes involving the Century, Allsop and Strickland's testimonies made numerous references to a reef-surrounded island to the west of Barbados. Since it's written in the English longhand of the period, I had to have this volume translated. Each of the pirates told an identical story. They were repeatedly questioned and agreed the crew had scuttled the ship. They said all the wealth went down to the diamond. It seems the Captain of the Century, William Zane, enticed the crew to murder the passengers and put the boat down even before the beginning of the voyage. This was to be their version of a pirate pension plan."

Briscoll surveyed the small audience as if anticipating questions, and then proceeded with the story. "Sailing well south of Barbados, they headed to about 12.5 degrees latitude, where Zane had previously encountered a quiet, desolate anchorage inside a long, protective reef. They had already poisoned all the passengers and four of the crew, who hadn't been necessary for the mutiny. Zane knew he couldn't keep the Century so it was put down. This is how my father missed the wreck, believing it had to have been driven by a storm to its end upon the reef and sank outside. He never looked for it inside the reef. As lifetime sailors, they knew they could always be recognized if they returned to a European port. They decided to head for a location in the New World."

Briscoll read from the sheaf of papers as though he were addressing a congregation or a board of directors meeting. Every so often he'd raise his voice as if to smite with brimstone, only intending to emphasize a point he felt was important to all the listeners. "The four remaining crew: Captain Zane, First Mate Allsop, Boson Stricklind, and a Walter Gunness, took a sizable-fortune — a quarter-chest each, about all they could carry. According to the testimony of two pirates, they took coins that could be easily spent. The jewels were left with the remaining gold for their return in another vessel. In those days, native Amerindian divers could be brought to the site on a sloop — and in a few days, would have the treasure out of the hold."

"There's no mention they blew her up. That would not have made much sense. They sailed easily downwind in the Century's long boat to the Dutch port of Curacao, and caught boats elsewhere. The why and how of Allsop and Stricklind getting involved with piracy and conspiracy, with none other than William Kidd, seems nothing more than dumb luck. It seems the four separated and Allsop and Stricklind crewed upon the Antonio out of Santo Domingo, Hispaniola. Little did they know that her master Captain Kidd had been denounced as a pirate for capturing the Quedagh Merchant. To their dismay, the entire crew was placed in irons by the crown's maritime court when they arrived in New York Harbor. Kidd tried to buy his freedom with stories of buried gold on various islands. Thus, our two characters related this story. Each swore they could set a course and return directly to the diamond. However," he paused, "they were hung."

Briscoll received no questions. The short oriental gentleman quietly refilled the coffee cups. Feliza had dodged David's looks all evening. He assumed she was afraid she'd break down in tears if their eyes met.

Briscoll began again, "So, we have four murderers, two who escaped and two who were hung. The latter were disposed of either after they gave up the location or when they wouldn't talk." Pointing, he asked, "Mr. Warner, from your experience, does it seem the underwater wreckage has been disturbed by an earlier search? Ms. Dubois listed two portholes, several small bottles, an intact clay jar, a gold chain, a silver knife handle, a bronze rivet, six or seven white clay pipes, numerous lead shot, unrestored silver coins, and the three prizes of 1588 gold escudos. An anchor and a bronze cannon still rest down there. We will raise them on the morrow. Does that inventory concur with your own, Mr. Warner?"

"Sounds about right, give or take an artifact or two. Everything we have will be given to you tonight," David replied. Feliza had not mentioned three coins or the dagger, which were hidden where she hadn't seen and they hadn't looked. He knew Richmond and these two cowboys had searched his place from top to bottom, but hadn't been smart enough to find the crawl space in the attic. At this point, he didn't expect to make it through this ordeal without outside help, as no one in the room seemed like they wanted extra partners. Feliza, Mike, and David were definitely expendable.

"Tonight, Mr. Warner, you will accompany my associates Mullen and Palmer to retrieve these items — plus all the glass bottles, pottery shards, and encrusted artifacts from their hiding spot. Ms. Dubois will remain aboard the L'Attrapis so your actions will be efficient and harmonious."

"Needless to say, we are eagerly awaiting these items to discover if there are any further clues to precisely name this wreck site. So, again, I pose the question to you: does it seem like this site was disturbed previously?" Briscoll asked.

David cleared his throat. "I don't have enough experience with underwater wrecks, but we did have to pry the ballast apart. It seems the stones are as they fell. There has been only one dive with the metal detectors. I suppose there might be something definitive on the bronze cannon, such as a forging date. As I told you, we're neither expert salvage divers, nor historians. Mr. Post would be the man who may know more along those lines."

"Ahh, the importance of Mr. Post. It is quite the shame he is virtually silenced with a very sore voice box at the moment. I will take the items to him, along with a tablet and pen, when he becomes more coherent. On that note, I think we should now adjourn this discussion and retire," nodding to Feliza, "and you three musketeers should ready for your night-time excursion. I'm sure you will agree to provide transportation with your vehicle."

David mumbled an agreement and was then led to his cabin. On the bed were dark blue coveralls and a knitted watch cap that folded down to a full ski mask. At one in the morning, he was awakened to join black-faced Palmer and Mullen for their mission.

As soon as they were away from the boat, Palmer lit his first cigarette and began complaining to no response about smoking not being permitted on the yacht. He chain-smoked without caution during the entire trip. Once ashore, David's truck bounced to Mike's Outpost without meeting another vehicle.

Mike's place had been cleaned and set in good order, probably after an extensive search. With a few shovels turned, the footlocker appeared. The motor yacht was hanging peacefully when they returned with the artifacts. This, the day of David's resurrection, had been difficult. Counting his blessings, he slept well.

CHAPTER THIRTEEN

David ate a hearty, early breakfast to the background of CNN news received via satellite dish. Potential presidential candidates were competing for dollars and votes, and NASA had lost another space probe. Nothing changed. His new associates ate with the passion of the starving homeless, never uttering a word. With his directions, the L'Attrapis anchored above the wreck site more than a few miles off the shore of Eastern. Feliza was ravishing in her favorite glossy-white bikini and seemed cooperative while enjoying Eggs Benedict. Supposedly not a morning person, Briscoll didn't make an appearance.

By nine, Palmer had provided a quick instruction course in the operation of the air dredge. It was as simple as vacuuming a rug. Turn it on, point, and hold tight. If they saw something valuable, or big enough to clog the suction, they were to shut it off. Their instructor would be at the communication console in case any problems arose. He would not only be listening but also watching the TV monitors. Their first directive was to dredge around the anchor to free it. A gentle breeze held the motor yacht at an angle that obscured their splashing from island eyes. As cover, the yacht's tender, a small Donzi speedboat, would occasionally buzz around, sometimes dragging a water skier. With Officer Richmond as a team member, the government should remain uninformed and at a considerable distance.

The usual dive profile of twenty-two minutes was agreed upon. Feliza was silent until they donned their dive gear. She asked several questions, professed her fears of sharks, and was reassured the spear gun was already waiting on the bottom. David could think of no way to tell her of his discovery of the power head. As David dropped through the bright water, his optimism of regaining their freedom returned.

The white dredge tube was made of reinforced, four-inch PVC connected to a flexible hose of the same diameter. The suction end was secured by two small tanks that were flooded with seawater to facilitate handling at the prescribed depth. Those same tanks could be filled with air to ease lifting it to the surface. With one valve controlling the flow of air, the process seemed simple. A platform that resembled a trampoline was lowered from the underside of the yacht. In place of a mat was a fine mesh of woven monofilament with an eighth-inch grid. The yacht motored slightly, slanting away from the dive site and permitting the dredged sand to fall away from their line of vision. The continual rocking of the boat would sift the material — just as a miner might work a sluice to find gold nuggets along a river.

Once on the bottom, Feliza drew a dagger in the undisturbed sand and displayed a questioning look. David's reply was to give the traditional okay with his thumb up. She tried to write 'where' and again he only signaled 'okay'. Fearing the camera would notice, he shrugged while moving the hose closer to the huge anchor that only had one edge of a fluke visible. She knelt before him, ready with her ping-pong paddle.

The valve opened easily, but he wasn't prepared for the jerk upward that followed. The hose bucked like an untamed horse trying to unseat its rider. Feliza backed away with a frightened look. It took several hectic minutes for the operation to become more manageable. The procedure progressed effectively, and the suction began doing a good vacuuming job. Feliza brushed the sand vigorously about two feet beyond the nozzle while David aimed it. Every so often she would raise her left hand, signaling him to stop, while something was pulled from along the edge of the anchor and placed in the ever-present net bag. They hadn't detected this area because it was so close to the two large masses of metal. With their eavesdroppers sitting at the instrument console eighty feet above, the divers minimized the chatter. Constant sounds of heavy breathing filled the silence, casting an erotic undertone beneath David's otherwise somber moments. The dredge pulled the sand until it hit either planking or the hard-packed bottom, at about eighteen inches to two feet of depth.

At the elapsed time, they tied the dredge with the other tools, including the spear gun to the anchor ring, and started to the surface. As they ascended, the view of the area down current was astonishing. A curtain of sand filtered through the mesh screen and obscured everything. Fish darted in and out of visibility. The fear of the gray guys with the big fins replaced the lure of treasure in Feliza's eyes. For the first time since their capture, she hugged David close. Occasionally, a bigger-than-usual tail or fin would appear at the edge of visibility, which sent a shiver through both divers. Without a weapon for protection, while coming up the ascent line, the decompression was scary. It was certain their topside captors enjoyed seeing them as bait on the line. They never interrupted with anything helpful, but occasionally taunted the diver's fear with a sadistic chuckle.

Mullen, the gum-chewing muscle man, waited with a very visible, silenced pistol while Feliza and David disengaged from their gear. Palmer and Briscoll arrived during their fresh water rinse to ogle at Feliza's curves.

"Guys," was Feliza's first remark, "to ensure our long lives, you should put your heads together and design a safer way for us to surface. Those big guys in the gray suits are too erratic."

All three of the topside crew just leered. "Hey guys, start thinking with the top head and forget about the groins. Okay? It won't do this project any good for us to get bitten." She wrapped herself in a big white towel and continued. "There must be some way we can bring the spear gun up with us each time without you thinking we're going to use its one shot to conquer this boat!"

Briscoll was quick to respond. "Ms. Dubois, you must prove that the two of you are trustworthy before more privileges will be extended."

She growled back, "Well, big guy, extend yourself into that sandy soup just one time, and you'll understand what it's like to be fish food."

"Now, now, don't get testy. That tone will only be a negative influence during negotiations. Remember, we saved your cute little ass and can toss it back to either vicious island, or marine predators at our discretion." Very firmly, the bald man followed, "Both of you should keep that in mind. We shall examine several possibilities for your increased safety. You see, this is a rare underwater effort. We usually operate with both feet on the traditional good earth. If Richmond hadn't been so impetuous, the program would have permitted you to do all the risky, sub-aquatic labor and then relinquish the treasure to us at an opportune moment. However, that darkie's attitude has bonded our interests."

Looking at his watch, "According to our dive format, your surface interval after the first plunge should be for a minimum of seventy-five minutes. I suggest we further discuss this issue while viewing what you have in that net bag."

Briscoll carried the bag and proceeded toward the stairway. "Please join me on the upper deck when you have your equipment arranged for dive number two. There will be suitable fluids available to replenish your exhausted electrolytes."

Twenty minutes later, the muscle man ushered the divers to the upper deck area. Briscoll and Palmer were sitting amid an array of white plastic five-gallon buckets and were picking through Feliza's finds. 'Precious,' 'glassware,' 'iron,' or 'waste' labeled each bucket. Spread out on a blue vinyl sheet covering the dinner table was everything that had been buried in the footlocker from Mike's yard. Feliza took a glass of juice and handed it to David with the warmest of smiles. Even though their conversations had virtually ceased, her penetrating eyes seemed to be telepathic. Perhaps his psychic ability was confusing the message, but it helped make the best of a bad moment.

"Ladies and gentlemen, what we have is an unorganized archaeological effort. That in itself is not a bad thing. This venture evolved from your initial efforts," looking at the two divers, "which were very haphazard to say the least." Palmer never looked up from the pile of artifacts in his bucket. It seemed he was quite aware of how much Briscoll loved to hear his own pontificating voice. "Now we're engaged in an operation where nothing will be missed. At the end of the third dive each day, the mesh screen will be elevated and cleaned while you decompress. By the finale of this expedition, which we estimate will be in two to three weeks, each of you will be well versed in everything that arises from the sea floor."

For the remainder of an hour, bottle necks, pottery shards, brass spikes, and coins were inspected for age and origin. Briscoll had an array of books within arm's reach to substantiate each description. His voice described the artifacts. The bottles were, for the most part, green leaded glass that originated in Bohemia, now Czechoslovakia. That was the main location of glassblowing, second only to Venice. Blah, blah, blah.

The pottery was standard clay with the basic English brown glaze. Everything was produced during the period the Century had sailed. The square four-inch brass nails and the foot-long peened copper rivets were displayed in a large book concerning antique ships.

As David and Feliza returned to their equipment, Palmer escorted the entourage to a small, virtually invisible hatch in the engine area. A lab had been contrived to reclaim the encrusted silver items. In operation since early in the morning, two coins and the knife handle were subjected to ultrasonic blasting by sound waves, and the black scale was slowly disintegrating. One coin had a barely visible date of 1672, which pleased their ship's master.

"By now you see, my friends, the L'Attrapis came well equipped for this mission. Nothing was left to chance. This coin from your original find could prove to be worth a thousand U.S. dollars, if properly cleaned. Your mentor, Mr. Post, was going to send such incredible finds away, probably to be butchered by a pawnshop hack. It disgusts me — an intelligent duo, such as you, could be conned into believing such transference was necessary." The gold coins were displayed on a burgundy cloth. "You were working and risking your lives for the benefit of an old, worthless island blackie — and a self-confessed child molester. These gold coins are in excellent condition and will be snatched by collectors worldwide. All this can be done without outside support. You should be so thankful you are receiving our professional assistance. In the future, pick your associates better — or they will pick you clean."

"Well, Mike knew more than anyone else in Carriacou about the Century and the items we were retrieving," David attested.

"Aahh, yes, that is the correct term, Mr. Warner. 'Retrieving' — just as a trained dog would bring a trophy to its master. Not a respectable labor for you."

David bit his tongue and sought a pleasant tone, "Well, Thomas, it is lucky you came along to save us from ourselves. But this didn't begin as a full-blown treasure hunt with all the perils described in the fine print. In fact..." he stopped himself.

"In fact what, sir?" Briscoll blurted the question. His unmoving eye projected a chill. "I have read the contract that bonded your group. Ridiculous, if I may say so. You three remind me of that movie, 'The Wizard of Oz'. You, Mr. Warner, are seeking a brain; the black man wants courage, accompanied by the heartless child molester. And Ms. Dubois is just trying to get home again. Isn't that correct?"

Feliza never looked away from David's gaze. "That's right, Mr. Briscoll. I still want to go home. Away from this sand, sea, and sun." She was ready to wear the ruby slippers.

"My dear, when this is finished, you can call several states your home. Work hard and it won't be disappointing, that I promise. You'll attain the state of grace." Briscoll's voice started low but gained volume. "The option for double crossing us is the state of mourning!" The three laughed while herding David and Feliza to the dive platform.

"I have magnanimously decided you may ascend with the spear gun. However, it must be clipped to a line that will be readied and dropped ten feet below the surface. If you surface with the gun, cocked or uncocked, Mr. Mullen will shoot the bearer. Is that understood?"

Feliza murmured a gracious 'thank you' before they hit the water. David looked to the west and caught a distant glimpse of his almost-completed boat on the far shore. There appeared no way to signal. Even if Bill had been watching through binoculars, anyone on board the yacht would be hard to distinguish.

On the second dive, David and Feliza quickly attached two lift bags that brought the gigantic anchor thirty feet off the bottom. On their signal, the Donzi towed it until a fluke hit the deep channel's canyon wall. The bags were deflated and carried back to the brass cannon. The cannon was buoyed straight to the surface where it became the topside crew's responsibility. David suggested to Feliza to keep watch, because they could be crushed if the cannon slipped out of its harness and fell.

The dredging resumed and David's arms again felt a now-familiar pain. Holding the suction tube was strenuous work and would probably become much more difficult before their quest had ended.

Feliza's eyes were wide as she tried to watch the cannon at the surface and continue to safely brush the sand. Realizing the crew's attention was probably diverted from the video monitors, she used her fingers to make a 'kicking' signal. She was suggesting they swim away. David shook his head in the negative. The labors of moving the anchor and cannon had eaten up too much of their air. Full tanks would be necessary to make it even close to the shore at least a mile away. With the high-powdered Donzi as a search boat, and at least one crack shot aboard with a silenced rifle, they'd never make a surface swim of any distance. He thought about showing her the power head he'd hidden among the remaining ballast stones on the first dive, but realized she could possibly reveal it after another inoculation of the interrogation serums. His mind whirled as the suction pulled sand from about a quarter of the area where the anchor had lain. More items went into Feliza's net bag without a smile. At her side was the cocked spear gun.

With only eight-hundred pounds of air remaining, David closed the air valve and put the dredge to rest. His forearms and shoulders ached from the fifteen minutes of labor. Even when weighted properly by filling the dredge's ballast tanks, the tube jumped, heaved, and had to be fought every second to keep it controlled. His dive buddy had the net bag bulging with recovered items. Giving her a quizzical look concerning the contents, she shook her head denoting little of interest or value.

David grabbed the spear gun and they slowly rose to the surface, mindful of apparitions in the sandy cloud from the suction's outflow. The spear gun was not cocked and the trigger guard was clipped to a stainless D-ring, permitting it to dangle ten feet below the surface. When their flippers were thrown onto the dive platform, a grinning Mullen accompanied their splashes with the very audible cocking sound of an automatic rifle.

The brass cannon seemed smaller out of the water. It was still attached to a line from the power winch on a dinghy davit that doubled as a small crane. The cannon's brass didn't gleam, but it appeared remarkably clean resting on the white deck. The cannon was about four feet long with about a two-inch hole. The barrel was wrapped with a design of two intricate, winged dragons whose wide-fanged mouths met at the fire hole. Their scaly tails curled around the two mounting stubs, the art of destruction.

A substantial lunch of pasta was provided during the second surface interval. The lectures on the artifacts continued with the cannon being the center of a one-sided discussion. Briscoll sat very regally at the head of the shaded table. The artifacts that had littered the table earlier were not resting on the same blue vinyl, but now on the deck near the gas barbecue.

Briscoll began his dissertation. "The gold coins are Spanish Escudos, also known as the famous doubloons, which were the world's currency in the sixteen and seventeen hundreds — much as the United States dollar is accepted worldwide today. These three coins are the most valuable of the items so far reclaimed by this search. Each has a value of at least three times that of the cannon. With the date of 1688, and in virtually uncirculated condition, they are worth ten thousand U.S. dollars or more. I say 'uncirculated' because usually, there is a slight assayer's cut to provide purity, but for the most part, these three aren't even scratched. You see, in those days, to make change the coins were actually cut or chopped. That is where the term 'piece of eight' originates. The silver coins, which are still under treatment, are complete eight reales. Those reales are also termed 'cobb' dollars. The gold coins were smelted, but the silver was cut from bar stock and stamped by a serious hammer blow. Both of these coins were created after melting beautiful Amerindian, perhaps Incan, Mayan, or Aztec art."

"With the decline of the Spanish Empire after Drake's victory over the Armada, these coins became slightly less available, but since these are dated a hundred years after the Armada's defeat, their value increases," Briscoll preached. "It is pure conjecture, but perhaps before they set sail, the Sterns had collected on the debts of Spaniards preparing for the War of Succession and the restoration of Phillip the Fifth. The coins undoubtedly were minted in South America and convoyed to Spain for the express purpose of relieving the debts of the upcoming war. If these debts were not kept current, then the Spanish monarchy would descend into bankruptcy and lose the support of the wealthy European bankers."

The short Asian man refilled Briscoll's glass with white wine and then cleared the table. There were two other Asians aboard who did housekeeping and engineering, but they kept well out of sight. Probably Filipinos, David imagined them to be no more than paid slaves who communicated only in their native tongues and made no witness to any of the trio's activities. Briscoll was assuredly their savior, also.

Palmer fingered the gold chain Feliza had found. "What about this, boss? Isn't this worth more than ten grand? It's got to weigh almost a pound."

"Mr. Palmer, the coins weigh an ounce which provided the consistency in their monetary system. Of course, purity was always a question, as with our female diver."

Feliza replied with a sharp look that didn't faze Briscoll. He took the chain from the smaller man. "This chain weighs more, but has nothing that defines it as definitively from a certain date." Fondling the links, as though he could witness its past, he brought it close to his good eye. "The catch-and-link design is Italian, but that doesn't pinpoint when it was created. Buyers can always suspect it was a later copy."

Briscoll's explanation droned on. "On the other hand, the cannon can be dated from forging marks. It is a swivel gun, usually mounted at the bow or stern of a vessel. This was not intended to be a very accurate or powerful weapon. Thus, it was used at close range, mostly to dissuade boarding parties — or as a last act of desperation. We do not have an estimate of the Century's armament, but I should suspect that at least a few more of these beautiful weapons are lying below, along with six to eight cast iron monsters." He rose and directed his audience to the art of the gun. "The winged dragon has, from the beginning of time, been the purveyor of doom. The Chinese developed gunpowder in the ninth century from a mixture of charcoal, saltpeter, and sulfur. According to existing paintings, gunpowder was dispersed in bombs and dropped from balloons designed as dragons, to instill fear among enemies."

Feliza was nodding with closed eyes. This did not please our mentor who abruptly kicked her chair. "Ms. Dubois, you find no interest in my research? Perhaps I should apologize for wasting everyone's extremely valuable time?" The condescending voice changed pitch and increased in volume. "My dear, your time is my time." He glared at her. "At this moment, I own you! Don't forget that!" He shook her shoulder harshly while looking into David's eyes for a reaction, which never occurred.

After a long, drawn-out sigh of exasperation, Briscoll concluded the lecture with a look at his stainless Rolex. "I would imagine the water will keep you awake. Try to be attentive on the sea floor and find more gold! Whatever you do, take your time, or rather, take my time. But puleese, puleese try to save everything! There are suckers out there who truly believe this underwater trash is valuable! Am I understood?"

After a committal nod, David and Feliza began their third dive, which had become a routine, from preparation to turning on the dredge. They would drop through the crystal water as if riding an express elevator. In minutes, the operation would change pace as though they were suddenly lead-footed in a London fog. David wore an additional weight belt to increase his stability once the dredge started to gobble the sand.

Feliza kept fanning the sand despite her visible exhaustion. Her first action was to string the two rubbers on the spear gun and place it within her immediate reach. If she moved two feet, the gun went with her. They moved on autopilot and had no need to chat via the underwater equipment. She was completely at ease and too tired to sing or hum at this depth. Yet, eighty feet above, men were poised to terminate their partnership, if the routine notably varied.

Suddenly, she came to life, waving David to halt. He shut the dredge valve and watched her remove several clay pipes, some disks that didn't resemble any they had previously discovered, and two gold crucifixes. Once Feliza had cleared the sand pocket, he opened the dredge up again, only to stop at her signal. The suction had uncovered a slab of very black, smooth wood. Feliza nimbly fanned and ran her gloved hands along the wood to determine the edges. Despite their virtual enslavement, this find exhilarated them.

David's hands cleared one side to about a foot. He almost used the crow bar resting under the big coral head as his next tool, but then remembered Briscoll's loud-mouthed lecture about trying to keep things intact. David's bottom time was at fifteen minutes and his tanks had 1700 lbs. He figured his buddy had at least that much.

"Feliza." David used the underwater comms for once and it shocked her to attention, doing the same to whoever was sitting at the monitor, "I'm going to use the suction to try and get beneath it. Bring that net over."

With a stream of bubbles, the dredge came to life, pulling vigorously at the sand. It could have been only a big wooden beam, but his mind imagined a treasure chest. At nineteen minutes of bottom time, he reached its lower edge at about 18 inches. That made the cube two foot, by two foot, by one and a half: a hell of a lot of gold, if that's what filled it. The dredge undermined the box until it toppled. The wooden box fell, apparently intact, into one of the nets they had used to move the ballast stones. After attaching the lift bags, they followed it to the surface.

The topside crew members were drooling when the box finally reached the motoryacht's stern dive platform. Briscoll was holding the pistol, but it wasn't pointed as it had been the last time. The other two, who resembled the old comic strip characters 'Mutt and Jeff', were busy attaching the davit line through the green netting, raising a few shouts and curses. With gear off, the divers waited while the lift bag was deflated and the box was raised and swiveled to the upper deck. David was shocked to recognize his purgatory holding cell when a lid behind the yacht's exhaust stack was lifted to accommodate the box.

"Mr. Warner. See what your hell looks like, now that your eyes can focus." The tall bald man said to him over his shoulder as the box lowered. "This could be a big part of the payday." The box dropped out of sight. "Come closer, puleese, both of you." He raised a small lever and water started flowing from the lower vent. "Now you realize," Briscoll chuckled and spoke to David, "yours could have been a watery Hell."

Laughing at the humor David missed, Briscoll rolled on, "This compartment is used to secretly hold valuable items when we are underway. As you can see, or rather, can't see, there isn't any seam when this hatch closes. The stored items are hidden from the prying eyes of customs officials who think this is just part of the exhaust stack that runs to the stern of the yacht. We preserve those items either in air conditioning or fresh distilled water. Puleese, don't get your hopes up. This chest probably isn't filled with golden escudos. You ask, how do I know?"

Palmer leaned against the wall, "Yeah, Boss, you got X-ray vision or what?"

"Gold would be in a solid steel chest — or at least, there would be heavy metal bands around this one. Ahh, you are about to say the bands have rotted away. But my dear, hopeful comrades, this chest is smooth. No wear areas or rust stains. It is a traveling case of some sort, not for extreme valuables. There is no lock or hasp, my dear Doctor Watson."

David coughed and spit over the side. "I don't see any hinges. How's it put together — and better yet, how does it come apart?"

"Well, it is just as the modern fiberglass compartment we dropped it into; it must have an extremely well fitted lid." Their leader shut the valve with about three inches of water above the wooden box. Still suspended in the net from the crane, he took a magnifying glass with a slender penknife and looked at every edge.

Mullen's strength moved the box like a gyroscope until Briscoll raised his hand and started using the knife. "I would wager that the wood is walnut and for some reason, neither the boring worms nor rot have caused much deterioration. Mr. Warner, puleese assist my efforts."

He pointed David to a narrow trowel he had wedged in a barely visible groove two inches from one side. After he placed another trowel into the slit, he summoned Feliza, "Ms. Dubois, lend your sinewy strength." She moved to the box and locked her eyes to David's in an emotional stare as she applied pressure. Briscoll took a third leverage point, and with combined strain, the top gave slightly. After repositioning their levers, accompanied by three grunts, the box opened to reveal a pool of filthy muck.

Briscoll grabbed tongs from the barbecue grill and penetrated the sludge. Between the metal pinchers was a small statue. He took it and handed the tongs to Feliza. Another thirty-one pieces were removed, ranging from four to six inches in height. David peered over Briscoll's shoulder and through the magnifying glass to see that it was a miniature man wielding a sword."

"Yes, yes, yes." Briscoll would have been happier if it had been the gold, but not by much. He rapidly surveyed the other pieces, "Yes, a chess set, circa the thirteen or fourteen hundreds. I can say this will be the first item sold and will bring a high, no, an extremely tidy sum." He lifted the original piece. "Ivory, carved in the East with incredible detail. Look closely here, all of you: the sword held by this one is of gold and probably every other decoration is from preciously malleable gold. This will bring a fortune!"

The day was over for the divers. David's legs and arms became heavy as he leaned against the portside railing. It was close to five and that meant only another hour of light. It always made him feel old to be this tired and crave sleep before dinner. If he ate then he would have to stay awake for digestion. They'd only been down a combined sixty-six minutes, but the days were running hard and much too close together. These guys weren't about to give a day off for rest.

Cocktails were consumed and conversation excluded the divers. Feliza had gone below 'to freshen up' as women always say. David sat rooted in his chair, not moving or making a sound. The muscle man, Mullen, morosely perched at the rear with what looked to be a silenced Smith and Wesson automatic in his lap. Briscoll and Palmer talked incessantly as they reviewed each of the chess pieces. With his legs propped on the upper stern rail, David watched the sun drop behind Top Hill — and his head went with it. Luckily, this nap was permitted.

Another short Asian servant shook David lightly and pointed toward the table. The group of three sat chatting. He stretched and saw they had set up all the pieces and were playing. Briscoll was correct; it was exquisite.

That night's sleep was short, bookended by workdays. David had been too tired to even try to plan an escape. His small cabin had a center lock on the door. Even if he smashed the port, he might only get his arm through to wave.

At breakfast, as David consumed his third cup of coffee, Briscoll escorted Feliza. She sat close and grabbed his thigh. "How are you feeling, David? I'm starting out tired today." She squeezed again and gave him an inexplicable, wide-eyed look.

She might have confessed to being tired, but there she was with her billowing hair well brushed, and a slight blush of makeup on her cheeks. David could smell either body wash or conditioner. His small bath stall hadn't been equipped with anything more than a bar of Dial and a Bic razor. She looked good and bright wearing a pale yellow bikini. These guys must have transferred everything of hers from the cottage. He scanned the shoreline and felt some solace in the nearly finished Summer Breeze. It had been such a simple plan, to relieve stress by reviving his life sailing the Caribbean. However contrived, his goal was so close and still so very far.

"So, gentleman," David got their attention, "how is Mr. Post doing? What are my chances of visiting him?"

"Not much, Swabby," was Palmer's brief reply. It was too early to push the issue and excite everyone.

They splashed just after eight and again at ten thirty with only a few silver coins to show for their efforts. After lunch, they were returned to their cabins and permitted to nap. At two, David was roused and brought to the lower barroom to find Mike sitting, strapped to a wheel chair.

"Are you all right, Mike?" David asked as he approached. Mike was gaunt, wearing a robe that covered only his right shoulder. Gauze covered his left shoulder, where he'd been shot. That arm was in a sling and restricted under a wide, black, nylon strap. A massive purple bruise marked his Adam's apple. The areas around his sunken eyes were so dark, they too looked battered.

Mike kept trying to clear his throat by gulping, but finally just nodded.

"You see, David, we have done the right thing with Mr. Post. He was not available earlier because his wound was being treated with an IV of antibiotics mixed with morphine to relieve his discomfort. I thank you for being patient and not jeopardizing the fragile beginnings of our joint venture. Now, perhaps you will dive with more optimism and find something as valuable as yesterday's chessmen."

"Well, we're trying, as I'm sure you can see on the monitors. We aren't wasting any time or effort," David explained. "These first two dives have taken us halfway across the area where we'd moved the ballast. That means, in two more days we'll have to move the remaining stones. What's your plan for that?"

Briscoll quickly returned, "Lift and move back to this spot already dredged. This morning, we sorted through the residue on the suspended sifting screen and came out with five gold and thirty-nine silver pieces. I suspect at least one of the chests must have smashed open as the boat sank or as it decomposed."

"Does the maritime justice's journal mention anything about how the men figured to get their gold back from the watery depths? I mean, didn't they usually bury the gold ashore?" David asked. "That's the one question that has been in the back of my mind since the beginning."

"Perhaps you've read one too many Robert Louis Stevenson novels, Mr. Warner. Of course it would have been easy to do — but also easy for any of them to return and take everything without the others." Briscoll pulled a stack of papers from his leather case and shuffled through them. "Captain Zane, and I'm quoting according to the interrogation of Allsop, thought that putting everything down with the diamond would be safest. He felt the others couldn't come back without him. As he was making the decisions, it was his call. I'm sure they expected to return within the year to find the hull still intact. Well, here we are three centuries later, hoping they never made a successful recovery voyage."

Palmer moved to wheel Mike into the sun. "Well, Swabby, your amigo here is going to get some sun today to brighten up his dull color. He looks like death warmed over. He'll still be getting his nourishment alone. You and girlie do your water thing and we'll see he gets back into shape. By the time this mission finishes, all of you will be in prime physical condition. Not that the Sambo bitch needs anything except a tune-up now, but you'll be ready to spend some of this money."

Briscoll chimed, "Only if Mr. Warner gets off his ass and finds more of it. To date, my accounting of finds totals just over a hundred-thousand dollars, which is barely the break-even point to cover expenses. I suggest you reapply yourself with the dutiful Ms. Dubois and search like never before. Let me remind you, minutes are passing."

Fifteen minutes later, the dredge was churning the bottom again. Feliza was unusually cheerful, humming through the comms while fanning the sand. It came to little avail as she filled the bag with artifacts of little visible worth.

Almost to the edge of the remaining ballast, they uncovered two huge, heavily encrusted iron cannons. Along with the rusted iron artillery were thirty or forty six-inch, cannon balls. After inquiring through the comms with the boss above, the decision was to harness and float them to where they had deposited the anchor. This project took the remaining air and bottom time.

On the surface, they received another severe lecture as the leader rummaged through Feliza's bag. "Two silver coins, that's it for the dive? What the fuck are you doing down there? Yesterday was a good payday, but today's a joke!" Briscoll loudly ranted. "Don't try to hide anything down there for a later return. You saw what happened to the original pirates. History has a bad habit of repeating itself."

Feliza softly asked, "What about the two cannons we found today? Aren't they worth a good bit?"

"You may be beautiful, my dear Ms. Dubois," he replied curtly with little patience as he ran his hand through her overflowing curls, "But you are not very smart. Those iron cannons would have to be processed with reverse electrolysis for an estimated two years to repair the salt damage. Only then would the rusting halt. After all that effort, even though they were forged in the early sixteen hundreds, the two might bring five thousand combined, perhaps as decorations for a nautical motif restaurant. That is definitely not worth the effort. The weight of the cannons would be at least a ton each and would cause a serious list on the L'Attrapis. No, they can remain on the bottom. If you want them for that hovel of a restaurant that you call The Fort, we can arrange to include them in your share."

"No thanks. Only if I can wear it or put it in my suitcase when I leave, otherwise, I don't want it," she said, shaking her head free of his hand. "What about the cannon balls?"

Palmer laughed, "Leave it to the bitch to worry about balls, huh, Tunaman?"

"My dear, sweet, sweet woman, you pay attention to so very little beyond your appearance in any nearby mirror. If those balls had a stamp on them saying Century, then we could cash them in. But now, as with the gold chain, they could have come from anywhere at any time period. The iron cannons undoubtedly have some marking of recognition and could be ascertained as part of the ship's armament, but are too cumbersome to accommodate on this vessel. The balls, however, could be from Timbuktu at the end of the eighteen hundreds. It is simple to remember that anything that has a date is worth much more than that which doesn't! Puleese, puleese! Store this information inside that cute little brainless head for later retrieval, so I don't have to fucking say it again!"

Feliza's eyes flamed at the insult, but she bit her lip and sat back in the chair. Cocktails were served and dinner followed quickly. Not totally exhausted, David lay on his bunk staring at the white ceiling, attempting to find any way out of this predicament. L'Attrapis' crew always had the upper hand, no matter what he concocted, as long as Mike was held prisoner. The easiest scenario was for Feliza and him to drop in the water with fresh tanks and just head for shore as quickly as their flippers would push. Once there, they could be somewhat protected among the men working on his boat.

The downside was Richmond's complicity with the Briscoll boys. They would have plenty of time to dispose of Mike. Dead men tell no tales. Richmond could easily flash his authority in Eastern, arrest the two of them for questioning, and detour any investigation far away from the motoryacht. Once they were within his grasp, he knew Richmond would take extreme pleasure in settling the score for his broken arm. Every strategy came out lose, lose, lose for the good guys. As long as Briscoll was holding the main card, Mike, they weren't any better off than the pawns in that chess set — to be moved and sacrificed as the king desired.

Another option was for Feliza to escape alone, while he returned to the boat to fight the three of them. That meant the opposition would be watching and waiting. They couldn't create an elaborate ruse of her being sick on the bottom, or anything else, without getting some private time together. The bad guys were making certain that would never happen. If David escaped at night by breaking the cabin door and swimming to shore, who could he turn to for help? There was no proof of any conspiracy with the immigration officer. If he called Shremshock, the Chargé d'Affaires in Grenada, it would take literally hours, if not days, to circumvent Richmond's actions. That was if Shremshock responded at all, since he was trying to keep the surface of his small pond smooth and quiet.

Amy, dear precious Amy, might be some help. David had left her swinging in Feliza's breeze. He believed Amy would do whatever it took, short of what it would definitely become: an international incident. Future in-law or not, the Admiral's career wouldn't permit such a smudgy mark of involvement with kidnapping and illicit treasure hunting in another country. No, the United States would claim no knowledge, and David would be the one left to hang. Amy was still expecting a plane ticket to be delivered to her office in wintry Washington. For once, it was best he'd procrastinated and not even purchased her passage, keeping her far away from this danger. She and her parents had become a second family. Although she might be cursing his inattentiveness, at least she was doing it from a safe place. In his dreams he had her in the safety of his arms, only to disappear with the wake-up knock.

\\\\\\\\

Following Palmer up the interior steps, David noticed the weather had changed, with a good wind chop building a ring of foam at the reef's edge. L'Attrapis hardly rocked on her two separated hulls. The night had given him renewed strength and the steaming caffeine somewhat upgraded his optimism of escape from zero to remotely possible. The Mutt and Jeff duo wore their usual full-sleeved, dark blue jump suits and ate without comment, occasionally laughing at a cartoon character's antics on the wall television. Mullen left and returned with Feliza ten minutes later. Wrapped in a vivid purple sarong, the island girl appeared more relaxed and refreshed. She seemed ready to revel at a beach party, rather than sit on the ocean floor and dust with a paddle.

The early morning stayed pleasant, free from Briscoll's patronizing voice. If David closed his eyes and combined all the aromas and the sounds of the slapping sea with his imagination, he could fancy himself on an expensive vacation among the rich and famous. They might become rich, never famous — but perhaps notorious.

Before the day's labors were initiated, while still buttering toast and smearing marmalade, captors and captives were almost equals. The two men enjoyed the first-class lifestyle and served their leader, but visibly had similar feelings about his demeaning attitude. They were well paid to cater to his whims and efficiently solve problems with tact, without clues or compunction. It was a good bet there were few living witnesses to their abilities. The last cup of coffee brought enough enthusiasm to David for him to slightly believe that he, Mike, and Feliza might become the exceptions to make it through the gauntlet of greed.

Every time David saw Feliza, she had transformed a bit more — from the barely-tamed island creature who had easily seduced him, into a lady of relative leisure who might actually belong on a yacht such as L'Attrapis. She ate with an undaunted appetite, mannerly consuming eggs, waffles, and ham. No longer did she flaunt her bestial femininity, and growling objections, but instead demurely batted her eyes and kept her thoughts safely private. She must have realized any argument would be to no avail. For safety, it was better to be an attractive and quiet woman.

The compressor roared and transfused life into the dredge while David and Feliza shivered into their damp wet suits on the large dive platform. Palmer shared no words of motivation, just coughs interspersed with yawns. Mullen was the typical mute guard, standing in the corner, lovingly dragging his big thumb across the serration of his handgun's hammer. He stood at six-and-a-half feet and wore a blue jump suit adorned with a matching blue headband to control his gray ponytail. Along with his waxed, handlebar mustache, all he needed was an electric guitar to fit a scene from the rock and roll sixties.

Now, years later, exhaust bubbles were as close as it came to music for the crew. Sometimes, it resonated like a four-string base, and other moments, it was a searing lead guitar, rattling off as eardrums equalized.

They plunged off the platform and into the bay without hesitation. To stall or complain at any instant would have instigated a situation, which the divers couldn't adequately debate or win. David's dive buddy's persona glowed with an incomprehensible satisfaction. He'd seen that look before when it was directed to him, but now she was oblivious to almost anything external. It was as if she wore a hidden set of headphones, listening to that different drummer people always spoke about.

The relentless moving of sand throughout that day brought five more gold coins to the L'Attrapis coffers and pleased everyone, but no reprieve was yet in sight. After each dive, it took longer and longer showers to get the sand out of their bodies. The palms of David's hands were showing damage from being immersed too long handling a constant vibration. The skin was just wearing away at the friction between the dredge handles and the woven plastic gloves. His 'employers' had been so gracious to provide an ointment that David vigorously worked into the irritated, flaking skin.

Briscoll sat silently, reviewing all of the research material, which was spread around his seat at the head of the table. Various pieces of pottery or glassware secured each page against the breeze. He had a desk lamp pulled close and was inching his finger line by line as if something were lost. David sat in silence enjoying the starry, moonless night. The moon was waning and wouldn't rise until after midnight.

Mullen tapped David's shoulder to alert his attention to an infrared scope he was using to spy on the Eastern neighborhood. This was probably his usual nightly entertainment — but this evening, David was awake enough to participate. Letting him view was either an act of camaraderie, or an attempt to impress with the types of equipment they had. As David put his eye to the long green tube, he clearly saw groups of Eastern's residents strolling the main street on a typical Saturday night.

Mullen grabbed it to sight and lock it on a specific target he had found so interesting. There in the scope's radiant darkness was Richmond with his white arm cast glowing just beyond his official shirt. He had parked the Land Rover and was walking down the beach. Palmer joined at the starboard rail with night vision binoculars.

"There's your buddy, back on the same beach. What do you want to bet he's up to no good? Guys like him always bring to mind that Eddie Murphy line from the movie 48 Hours. The white man's worst nightmare is a darkie with a badge and a gun." Palmer didn't pronounce 'darkie' with any extraordinary fervor. The word to him was merely descriptive of people of color. He seemed to rebuke any authority except his boss's and certainly couldn't relegate anything close to equality — and definitely not supremacy to these island dwellers, with or without formal uniforms. "Watch him; he thinks he's invisible, just sneaking down the beach. I trust the mosquitoes will eat his black ass alive."

David didn't bother to mention there usually was an onshore breeze that made Eastern much more habitable than the lee side of the island. But he could always hope the sand fleas would decimate the immigration officer's bare ankles. Mullen took the scope back and grunted something close to an affirmative. Both men became agitated and finally Palmer railed, "I told you so, Swabby! That guy's up to no damn good. Let the man see through your scope. Tony, me boy — if it looks good enough, we'll take a jaunt tonight and get some of that for our own selves. Once one of these dark girls is spoiled, I figure she's up for grabs."

Reluctant to give up his vision, the big man finally stood back from the clamped tripod and pointed to David. He sighted the scope, and there was the prissy immigration officer, with his pants down, rapidly copulating with an unseen female bent across an overturned fishing boat. Sickened, he knew who it had to be, but watched anyway until the grand finale of rapid thrusts. The dark girl rolled over and straightened to reveal herself as the no longer demure Rochelle.

"Ain't it amazing, just simply amazing, what a one-armed man can do when he sets his two heads to it?" Palmer squeezed out between lurches of unadulterated glee. These men were overjoyed at catching a secretive glimpse of another man who suffered from a serious character flaw.

Nothing amazed David anymore — and certainly, it didn't deter his appetite for dinner. At least Feliza had been resting below decks and had missed all of the gutter remarks Palmer could muster. She arrived, apparently unescorted from her cabin. David wondered if Briscoll believed she wouldn't escape alone. It was heartwarming.

Dinner conversation returned to the wreck after Palmer asked Feliza pointedly about her family ties. His and Briscoll's voices droned on about coulds, woulds, and shoulds. David's imagination took over again and he began a private inner-conversation. Perhaps it was their first step over the line, searching and locating the wreck illegally, that had spawned a moment like this between island relatives. He chewed a delicious grouper steak while mulling that thought, rationalizing that everything had happened independently of his efforts. It would have all happened anyway, so lust and greed must be an integral part of everyone, everywhere. Eight to eighty, everyone was greedy and crazy, but his part had to cease if he wanted to flee with what sanity remained.

CHAPTER FOURTEEN

In Washington, DC, the month of March began like a pussycat. The temperature had risen to almost sixty and spawned a false hope of an early spring. Everyone's mood dipped with the thermometer after a late season storm roared in from the North Atlantic and dumped ten inches. The thick, icy crust had been scraped from the concrete to form a border ridge on each side of the walkways. It was boots and gloves weather. The cleared path was narrow, which meant if three people happened to congregate, at least one was destined for wet, chilly ankles. The sun made infrequent appearances that never lasted more than a quarter of an hour. The usually dark sky cleared from a charcoal morning, to a less ominous light gray at noontime, to the evening's dismal dark smoke that haloed all the streetlights.

Bundled in her long, Navy-issued coat, Lieutenant Whistlow leaned slightly forward against the stiff breeze. A billowing knit cap contained her fashionably short blonde hair. A matching wide, white cable-knit scarf made her slender, red chapped nose very visible in the middle of the exposed three inches of her face. Her steps were heavy due to the unfeminine felt-pack and rubber boots that satisfactorily traded style for warmth. Noontime workouts at either the squash or handball court kept her figure free from seasonal fluctuations. She was five-seven and knew she had more appeal to men when wearing thin, red heels with gossamer silk, rather than the present dapple-brown galoshes and thick wool.

Amy was dieting, exercising, and shopping in order to increase her appeal to one man: David Warner. They had been lovers and that emotion couldn't be easily displaced. He was drifting away, but he could still be landed if he'd simply give her a chance. David had called only twice, but that was weeks ago. Neither of the access numbers he'd provided yielded any response. Mike Post, the computer teacher, didn't respond to e-mails and his school reported he was off island on personal leave. The Grenada Embassy had assisted with the transfer of equipment, but since then, Amy had heard nothing.

Obsessing wouldn't help. The Admiral's daughter longed for the shared intimacy that was missing, even though there were hundreds of men who would love to file an application for a chance to win her affection. Since David left, she'd found it difficult to reconcile that he might not return. Her father had warned her, early in the relationship, against jeopardizing her career in an emotional involvement with other naval personnel. Now she couldn't remember if it had been she or her father who had first been taken with the shy warrant officer. They had romanced ever since the time he walked into a computer information class she was teaching. Then her dad had singled out the unassuming, young officer to assist his office in everything from crises management to slicing golf drives.

Dear old Admiral Dad kept David in tow and a lid on his daughter's relationship. Amy wasn't sure if he felt publicly it might damage careers. The Admiral permitted good doses of affection, yet David was never close to his daughter for long periods. Her father had wanted a son — and perhaps David provided that type of companionship. There had been times she knew both father and daughter were competing for the warrant officer's time.

Amy was an information specialist with the Chief of Naval Communications for a father. With all the United States Navy's power behind her, Amy couldn't communicate or retrieve any information concerning David's present location. Everything frustrated her. Phone calls to the local police on an island named Carriacou provided no assistance. They knew of him and his boat, but he hadn't been seen in town for several days. The police claimed that getting transport was difficult to check his house, but promised if they saw him they'd pass along the message. The Caribbean policeman offered a comment that translated: it wasn't worth worrying about since vacationers like David often took off on sailing trips without a moment's notice.

Unbundled in her office, Amy's attention span was consumed by the mental image of a darkly tanned David, lying on a beach full of swaying palm trees. Well, Amy thought, damn him anyway, to be playing in the warm surf while nothing but a chilling breeze blows up her skirt. It wasn't like him to make an offer and then forget. It wasn't like him at all, but who could measure the changes that life on a tropical, one-horse island may have caused. It was a certainty David would welcome her once she got there. Worst-case scenario, she might get sun burned.

Searching the Internet for travel arrangements, Travelocity showed three legs to the trip: first to Puerto Rico, then to Grenada, and on to Carriacou. Commercially, it couldn't be done in one day, and time was of the essence. A few more mouse clicks and she found a military transport going red-eye to San Juan, hopefully with an empty jump seat. A puddle-jumping turbo prop leapt directly to Grenada from San Juan, just in time to catch the afternoon ferryboat from the capital of St. George's for Hillsboro, Carriacou.

A lengthy vacation was no problem, since her department owed her plenty of comp time. There were plenty of seats on the flight to Grenada, even in the middle of a stateside winter. The ticket price was the same with either twenty-four hour or two weeks of notice for a traveling naval officer. She pushed a button on her desk phone.

"Dad?"

"Amy, how's your day behaving?"

"I'm taking a vacation," she blurted. "This weather has me pretty down."

"Really? Let me guess, you found a resort on Grenada that has an available room."

"Something like that. It is a combination of late winter blahs and a feminine premonition. I think David has some kind of problem. I haven't heard anything from him or anybody else on that rock he calls home for weeks," she plied.

"All the more reason to stay put. Light a fire under the local authorities to look for him. Don't get involved in something that is out of bounds. Remember, no matter where you are, you, all service personnel, are ambassadors of this country."

She could visualize her father beaming at that statement. He'd written it for a commencement ceremony four or five years ago and had placed it in his 'ready to use' repertoire. The world couldn't exist without the Navy — and the Navy was his world. It wasn't hers. Amy had tried to be all her father wanted, but now, at twenty-eight, it was her turn. She couldn't write off the time spent with David that easily.

Her sights were set on an invisible target.

"Dad, I'm sure information will be channeled adequately while I'm away. I'm due about three weeks of comp time, and I really need to get away."

"Three weeks?" He was surprised.

"Dad, it is winter and I'd like to go somewhere warm and unwind. The naval machine will still operate, and I will never be out of reach. I'll keep you posted." She promised.

"Well, Lieutenant, leave your desk tidy. I'll miss you, Amy. Talk with your mother. Be careful and promise you will stay in touch."

"I promise. I'll call you before I leave." She punched another button. "Jakowski, this is Lieutenant Whistlow. I'm going to need a jump seat or better on a flight leaving for San Juan, in the early morning, two days from now. What can you do?"

Amy could have tapped her keyboard and done it for herself, but that would have stepped on Helen Jakowski's toes. Her Tuesday squash partner worked at the naval air distribution center at Reagan International Airport. It was her responsibility to know the location of every plane of one entire division.

"Sure, Amy, you really are going down south? Lucky you! How come I never have boyfriends in the Caribbean?"

"Yes, you do, Helen, but they are all restricted to their quarters on carriers," Amy laughed.

"Guess you're right. You want one heading out Thursday. What time do you want to get there — counting on good weather?"

"I've got connections that leave either at nine-hundred or thirteen-hundred hours. You don't have anything heading for Grenada, do you?"

"You're not that lucky. We have one heading to San Juan, but that would get you there after dark. Be at Bay 17 Thursday, at zero-two hundred hours. Wear everything you've got that's warm. If you want a really warm seat on that plane you can try out the wolves' lair in the cockpit. Those guys make it live up to its name."

"You're going to make me blush, Helen. I'm headed south and will hopefully get all I can handle. You remember David, don't you? Well, I'll be there at two, so that'll get me in there at around seven."

"No, you'll be going from daylight savings time to Atlantic Time, which is an hour later, so it'll be eight. So, you're going after that quiet one? Good luck. What do you need on the return — or, do you even want to know? There's a flight coming out of San Juan or Rosie Roads up here every day. If you could hold off until Friday, I can get you on a trip that's dead-heading to pick up Admiral Hauser. You could be the stewardess."

"I haven't had a real vacation in two years, and I don't want to waste time getting there. I've got my heart and my mind set on getting there yesterday."

"It's not only your heart and mind that's set, girl. Be there — I have you on the manifest."

"Thanks, Helen."

"Bring me back a souvenir, a nice bottle of rum, sweetie." "That sounds like a deal. See you."

Moving the ballast stones didn't produce much more than extremely sore muscles and scratches. The rocks were moved to where they had already taken the stones ashore. That area had been searched twice with the metal detectors and then dredged. Four more gold doubloons and a couple dozen silver pieces of eight did not make anyone ecstatic. Feliza and David carried each rock at least twenty feet. The Donzi would have been conspicuous moving the loaded nets short distances several times in a half-hour. Their brute labor was the only solution. Each dive only moved twenty stones. After four days the wet suit arms had been scraped away, and Feliza and David both began wearing blue jumpsuits provided by their mentor.

When they had started moving the first stones, their optimism was boundless, their bodies fresh. But at the present point, the bottom time was compounded with no distraction from the grind. David and Feliza spent each day either in the water or waiting to dive. During their free moments, which would have been better spent dozing, they listened to how unproductive they were. The days were long, and seemed longer. At the end of each day they had to clean off the sifting screen into buckets for the boss to scrutinize.

"Ahh, my divers!" David raised the brim of his hat to see Briscoll strutting across the deck, flanked by his team. "The dynamic duo, my extraordinary aquanauts. I have spent this morning organizing and accounting the finds you have made, both past and recent. The list of your recent finds is very short, while the list of the finds made before combining our efforts is very long."

His fleshy arms rose and parted as he began to sermonize. "Why would that be? I ask you, why would you be finding more then than now, especially since you now have the best equipment money 'can't' buy? It is an intriguing question. If you two will permit me to postulate, it could be because you are not bringing your finds from the watery depths. Instead, I believe you are hiding them below for some future reclamation, after the L'Attrapis has departed. Let me make this point perfectly clear. If we depart without suitable bounty, you will already be among the dearly departed. Do I make myself clear?"

David watched as his one good eye moved rapidly, waiting for a reaction that never happened.

Briscoll paced as he talked. "Please don't misconstrue this as a threat — or that I am condemning your veracity. You must consider this as an audit of an investment. It is merely good business sense. I warned you previously not to attempt to hide anything. To certify you both are working with good intentions, Mr. Mullen will take the plunge with your detector and check the areas you have already surveyed. If he finds one coin, one piece of jewelry, your punishment will be severe. However, it will not be so severe that you will be unable to perform in my service. Mr. Warner, I promise you that Ms. Dubois will suffer the brunt. Tell me now if you are holding out on us, so we don't waste Mr. Mullen's valuable time." He instructed the guards to lock David and Feliza in their cabins while the mute checked out their honest efforts.

Two hours passed with the only fear being the big man would discover the power head. Days earlier, when they had begun relocating the ballast pile, David had moved the stainless tool to the underwater slope that had become the deposit for the anchor and iron cannons. It was a relief, and could have been considered a reprieve, when Mullen surfaced after finding nothing of value in the sandy bottom area except a few discarded musket balls.

Pious Briscoll was at a loss for words as he tried to do something he professed to be lousy at, making an apology. Silence was at the top of that night's dinner menu.

Following the afternoon's threats, Feliza stayed safely in her quarters when they weren't diving. Palmer and Mullen devoured her with never-ending stares accented by crude comments. She hadn't talked to David with more than a five-word sentence since they'd been shanghaied and brought aboard L'Attrapis. David was the extremely lonely recipient of only a handful of her seductive glances. Her expression changed, having become much calmer and more demure. She ignored all attempts to be drawn into a match of insults concerning her race, her island heritage, or her supposed livelihood while in the states. Her assertive, extra-sensual persona wisely converted to a sheepish, uncertain woman who seldom met others' eyes. David believed she consoled herself with thoughts of the dagger and coins hidden at his cottage.

Five days following this incident, Briscoll left the boat for points unknown. Life felt much quieter. Mike was kept on lock-down, but Palmer permitted another short meeting to reassure David. The physical wounds were healing, but the flash of Mike's eyes and his cynical smile had disappeared. The ordeal dealt a severe blow to his already shaky psychological equilibrium. There was little doubt, if he came through this, he'd have to start over. David hoped they'd all at least have a decent nest egg to make their new beginnings. All hinged upon them finding more, and more, and still more. They'd have to retrieve the mother lode before they'd see any share. Their lives were tethered in the balance.

Palmer was almost likable when soothed by nicotine, less of an irritating asshole. Neither he, nor the giant beach boy, made any attempt at civility. Since Briscoll had gone, the rank of commander had fallen to the smaller man. Anything needed to keep the project moving was usually quickly provided. Palmer stayed out of the sun and remained fully clothed. He always wore a hat, and never swam, even in the heat of the day. Now David understood why they had been so hard to locate on Carriacou. Money bought necessary silence — and unless it was night, or a rare occasion, they never left their domicile. The two remained almost invisible. If he had met them on the street, he wouldn't have categorized them as harmless — but certainly not dangerous. They were an eye-catching duo, yet easily forgettable.

Mullen sat eating candy for hours, sunbathing on the aft deck and staring out at the weather horizon. The automatic pistol was always stuck into his belt. The rifle that had perforated Dolly was concealed somewhere. The shorter man was undoubtedly armed, but his weapon remained hidden.

Even if David and Feliza had had an opportunity to conspire and plan an escape, it was uncertain what they would face. The big man tanned to bronze and would occasionally get into the water to help them at the end of the day by emptying the sifting screen — but only if his cohort aimed the pistol.

The other crew became more conspicuous, which might have had something to do with Briscoll's absence. Conrad was the chef and general housekeeper. He had a slight muscular frame and was maybe two inches shorter than Palmer. He was definitely of Asian descendent; David guessed Filipino. Quiet and subservient, Conrad would stand rigid behind the head of the table at mealtimes. He waited with darting eyes, and hoping to further secure his position by catering to the bosses. Asians mature quicker and age slowly; Conrad might have been a seasoned thirty-five. The other crew members were definitely in their twenties. The one with a bushy-top, shaved-sides hairdo, was the mechanic. He reminded David of a miniature Will Smith, so he mentally labeled him 'Willie'. Having seen the spotless portside compartment, which housed one of the two twelve cylinder engines, he imagined Willie spent his days wiping and tightening, never mingling. He was living better than he'd ever dreamed. L'Attrapis was a heaven afloat for these men — even if they lived together in an eight-by-six cabin slightly above the bilge. David had only seen the third crew member once, another young male collecting laundry.

David managed to convince himself that things could be worse, and realized everything could change in seconds. Their hosts were sociopaths; predictable only to the extent that their reactions would be violent. His small, sterile, white cabin had no distractions, such as books or music. Time spent there was much like what he would expect of a first-class solitary confinement. The lock on his cabin door was a twist bolt that slid into both sides at the jamb. The cabin had been designed for imprisonment, since the interior side of the door had no knob. Either 'Mutt' or 'Jeff' escorted David from it at six a.m. and returned him again to his quarters after dinner. The rest of David's day was spent in their presence, or locked up. It was an easy choice: fresh salt air with the fiends definitely offered a better environment than being left to his thoughts in the sterile cabin. Feliza took the other option.

During the first days aboard the L'Attrapis, David was subjected to several impromptu inspections of his dive gear, bathing suits, and cabin. Those searches were for valuable artifacts he might have hidden. They had at least permitted him the respect of not examining his body cavities, probably only because neither Mutt or Jeff wanted to perform the task. He wondered if Feliza had fared so well. Minus bald Briscoll's supervision over the two guards, everything had become slightly lax. Escape was still impossible while they were holding Mike, but it seemed like a good time to secret the power head aboard. David chose not to tell Feliza anything about it, since she might be subjected to another dose of the boasted interrogation drugs. She might also place too much false hope in the small, stainless cylinder.

During a late afternoon dive David slipped the power head from the anchor pile into a pocket of his buoyancy vest. As they ascended, his dive partner kept a vigil for sharks on the cloud of disturbed sand, and David pretended to have a serious itch. As he scratched, the forty-four-magnum casing was wedged into the crotch of his spandex trunks. At the surface he feigned a stomach problem and was quickly led to his cabin. Hiding it there was another problem, but what did he have to lose if it was found? He pulled some foam from his single pillow and slipped it into the spongy pocket.

How to use the power head was another problem. To detonate on the spear, it had to make contact with a body. That was out of the question — since the spear gun remained locked when out of the water. The thrust would have to be incredibly strong against anything not rock solid.

With a mute counterpart, Palmer sought David's ear as a sounding board. David never said much, which made Palmer happier just to rattle on, uninterrupted. The man was wound tight, and seldom said anything that might provide a view at his inner workings. As he chain-smoked cigarettes, he'd chat to the accompaniment of David's nod or shrug. David received only curt answers to his few questions, and after a week he still had no idea where his guard called home, nor about any of his personal history. However, David did receive lectures on the world according to Palmer: politics, economics, and any other philosophy that might get stirred during the day. Satellite CNN provided most of the stirring. Between dives, David's usual position was to recline with the brim of his ball cap pulled low over his eyes. It could be worse, much worse.

David's main question was, "How would they ever know if they were missed?" The boys were completing Summer Breeze and anyone who came close to this motoryacht was waved off. Every so often, while the boss was aboard, the Donzi would disappear, presumably to get supplies. A motoryacht such as the L'Attrapis would have a huge larder. Bill Steward would realize a problem later, not sooner. Aunt Bernadette was another possible help, but whom could she call for assistance? Feliza's wild nature might delay any summons until Bernie really started to worry.

\\\\\\\\

The air transport left at three in the frosty morning. The cargo area of the C-5 Galaxy was unheated. Chilling breezes seeped from numerous leaks in the fuselage. Helen Jakowski had warned her against getting comfortable with the flight crew. Amy presented her credentials and transport permit to the copilot without lowering the hood of her ski parka. The formless, blue coat worn with matching mittens and ski pants obscured her shape. Not accustomed to late nights, she refused coffee and conversation in the cockpit, and instead curled up, safety-belted across the only two bulkhead seats. Sleep came easy. The loud base drone of the four-turbo props drowned out everything except dreams. Amy was ready for tropical warmth.

At six in the morning, she awakened to a tight banking of the airplane. The transport had luckily caught a tail wind, which pushed them south. They arrived three-quarters of an hour early. As the plane descended, Amy quickly realized she was now overdressed. After a pull on the two laces and three zippers, the bundled passenger regained her beauty. As the crew prepared for landing, they were surprised at their dozing passenger's refreshed transformation.

When the heavy outerwear found a locker in San Juan International, Amy became a usual, pale traveler in search of a tropical tan. It was only eight, Atlantic Time, and nobody would be sitting at their desks in Washington for another hour or more. From the enormous wall television, CNN reported a disastrous cold wave had settled over the northeastern US. The same monotone voice relayed the penalty fines of two NBA players before the boarding call for Grenada flight A-11 was finally announced.

Amy felt she was almost there, wherever Carriacou was.

Arriving at Grenada's lush green Point Saline Airport, Amy was hustled to the port of St. George's in a plush taxi van. Grenada was even warmer than Puerto Rico, almost stifling without a breath of breeze. The taxi stopped often along the beautiful harbor drive and picked up additional passengers on the way to the town wharf. Red, clay-tiled roofs and clean, white walls surrounding the natural, heart-shaped bay made Grenada's main city of St. George's a definite Kodak moment. A continuous point of land stretched north from a beautiful long beach, 'adorned' with the ruins of several buildings — which the van driver volunteered had been destroyed by the American troops when they attacked in the early eighties. These hills formed a protective wall with a natural cut facing west that made a perfect, narrow harbor entrance. The sea beyond the brown cliff barrier deepened through several shades of blue.

The Lexus, a wooden ferryboat, had little in common with its namesake luxury automobile. The ferry was at least eighty-feet long with what appeared to be telephone poles for the main mast and boom. Its hull was painted a bright Chinese red. The big motorsailer had passenger seats on the open fore deck, directly behind the steering station and inside a large air-conditioned stateroom. On the deck was the same cargo that had moved along that route for centuries. Wooden barrels of rum from Trinidad and cages of squawking, white chickens crowded among noisy, hobbled cows and goats. Black men, glistening with sweat, shouted at women passing along the cobblestone streets jammed with cars and trucks. Continually chattering school children in blue uniforms strode over cleated ropes and dodged cargo swinging from the boom.

Amy coated her skin with sunblock and relaxed on a wooden bench on the Lexus' topside. She noted the two clocks on churches along the town's hillside were accurate. The ferry's three o'clock departure left little time for anything except a sunbath. Mothers and inattentive children straggled aboard with cardboard boxes of belongings secured with rope. As the volume of surrounding conversations increased, any hope of a nap in the warm sun dissolved. On the starboard side of the passenger lounge, a young brown-skinned girl with overflowing nylon dreadlocks and complementing inch-long, decaled acrylic nails, sold beer and soda. Not much of a drinker, Amy quenched her thirst with a brown bottle of local lager — and celebrated her anticipated meeting with David by a quiet burp. She found what little sea legs she needed and took a place to watch the general Caribbean melee.

A few minutes behind schedule, the ferry's hull shuddered and creaked as its gigantic diesel heart began to turn the propeller. The Lexus lumbered away from the concrete abutment and reversed through its own billowing black cloud of acrid exhaust. Children found their parents and sat, quietly enjoying a chance to doze.

Passing fishing villages of crumbling, gray stucco houses on Grenada's west coast did little to relieve Amy's restless feeling. A dozen gorgeous, uninhabited islands north of Grenada didn't help relieve the frustration either. Occasionally, the ferry would come near a small boat with a few men drift fishing. Amy was either all or half of the white people on board, which gave her the privilege of curiosity. The few local women who spoke casually with her were Grenadians traveling to visit relatives in Carriacou, but didn't know much about the island.

A tall, very thin, elderly man with twin tufts of old-fashioned gray mutton-chop sideburns and a matching mustache volunteered that he knew Amy's friend in Eastern. The slim man wore a white shirt with an orange, square-ended, knitted necktie and introduced himself as Wendell Cronen. He was a good friend and neighbor of Bill Steward, who was building her friend's boat. Wendell told Amy he'd just visited Grenada to pay his land tax, since he didn't trust the local collector.

Wendell had met David several times in local shops, but they weren't friends. Amy smiled when she learned her American companion was nicknamed SP, for shore patrol. She plied the elder gentleman with a beer and in return, was regaled about how Carriacou was changing — rushing foolishly into the future. Wendell related presently there were at least a hundred automobiles on the small, thirteen-square-mile island, populated with almost eight thousand people. Coughing loudly and spitting over the port side, the man told her how basic life used to be among the fisherfolk. Wendell described Carriacou as having only four real villages and about a dozen crossroad settlements. Hillsboro was the center of government and it had the main dock where they would arrive. He looked at his watch, pointed to the island far off the starboard bow and said, "Be dere in a nudder hour."

According to Wendell, the main city was too busy these days with ice cream stores and travel agencies. He couldn't imagine that people could sit in an office, close to home, and plan to travel to England without ever talking to a ship's captain.

Wendell continued to tell Amy that Eastern, where David lived, was still a quiet, traditional fishing village protected by a reef. Amy asked him about the boat building and the explanation required another brown bottle. Wendell stated the inhabitants were all descendants of Scottish fishermen who had brought salted cod south to the plantations in the seventeen hundreds. His red-tinged eyes gleamed as he testified he'd been raised on salt fish and still loved it although it wasn't very salty anymore. Carriacou salt fish was famous throughout the Caribbean.

Wendell promised Amy would love Carriacou, and the village of Eastern. Most people born there were light-skinned and kept to themselves. There were even some families with red-haired members. Just the opposite was West Bay with its population of dark African descendants, who had quit fishing and were now baiting their hooks for the tourists who loved the beach and hot afternoon sunsets. From Wendell's home in Top Hill, which was also the best place on the 'whole damn island,' you could watch the sun rise from the sea and set beneath the waves.

Unaccustomed to alcohol, the motion of the boat, the hot sun, and the salt air, Amy began to feel the effects. The old man's smile was dazzling with a mouth full of take-out teeth. After the third beer, his thick tongue was constantly licking his lips and mustache. His fourth beer emptied quickly as the discussion turned political.

"Ya knows, yous Americans, always gots to be stickin' yous nose in everywheres it don't belong." Wendell sat heavily and sighed. His diction was slow, precise, and clear — yet very much of the islands. "Hell, I listen to the BBC every night, and it is amazing what dat country of yours is trying to do. Now, no offense dearie, but dat president ought to leave de Arabs and the Caribbean to their own self. Hell, dey crushed de banana business on all dese islands." He drew attention as he swung his arms around and got louder. "I tink we ought to tell them to stay away. Not you, dearie, but them guys always coming around, figurin' someting next you need. Old woman is always sayin' she needs dis or dat, but done well without it for de past fifty years. Now all of a sudden she see it on the damn tele, and it is gonna make her life easier. Well, don't make my life none de easy. I gots to figure outs how to scratch it up somewhere. It ain't makin' my life more easy, but that woman being unhappy, can make life rougher."

Amy laughed, "I agree. I think the USA has so many problems of our own that need attention; that's where it ought to focus."

"Well, dat USA ain't been nice to us since we invited old Fidel to come and speak. Now that country of yours don't help us wid one red cent. Lucky the Arabs and Chinamen got enough to help. Now our government, let me tell you, dat's someting else. Yous got's a government of movie stars, but we'se gots personalities without abilities. Dese guys give you a smile and tell you to go out and buy another bowl, because tings is gonna be so good dat the ones youse got is gonna overflow. Yeah, but once dey gets a seat, only their bowl's and dere family bowls be overflowing. Dis whole Caribbean is gone to Hell. Some of dem islands are loving the tourist, but dey don't want the outsider to stay after vacation. They want him gone so dat dey can keep their island for dem own selves. Yeah, dey never figured that dese islands is such small tings, and when lots of people start trampin' all over dem, sooner or later that European, or Canadian, or American is gonna want to stay and do business. Guess what happens next?"

She bit, "What?"

"Well, dat outsider does better business than de local! I tell you so. Soon de local dat loved the tourist, hates him! Ain't dat sometin'? You bring him in, take his money and den lose your job. Den you start comparin' your life to deres and it don't look so good anymore, dat island life. So now de young are all de time angry. Some de udder islands is doing dis eco stuff, countin' the numbers, and not harming this island. My, my, my, same ting happen, I tell you so. Here our people do goats, fish, grow some corn, and rent out some rooms to travelers, but de government can't make up its mind what's to do. Should dey be farmers, fish, or expect the strangers to keep comin'? Dey tink dat doing nuthin is better than doing somtin wrong. So deys do nuthin and where does dat gets dis Island? Nowheres! I tells you, nowheres at all."

"Well, maybe you're right, but they are right also," Amy countered perfectly. "People seldom can see the future results of their actions. Have you ever been to the States, Wendell? It is a really different world up there. Everything moves so fast. What's new today is old tomorrow — and nobody knows anyone anymore."

"Don't think dat I'd like it, dearie. I been as far north as St. Maarten and south to Trinidad when I was young. Dat sailin' around is for younger men. Me give it up bout nye on ten years now. No dearie, I like it slow where I knows my neighbors is my friends and been my friends for all dere lifes."

"Tell me dearie, what's dis infermet ting I keep hearin' about?"

Amy promised a continuation, but excused herself and headed for the ladies room. She looked in the mirror and saw a broad, beer-induced grin stretched upon slightly reddened cheeks and exclaimed, "I'm really on vacation!" Upon her return, she bought Wendell another cold one but abstained herself. The three beers were having an undesirable effect on her bladder. She sat down and enjoyed fifteen minutes explaining the information highway to a man who lived on an island that had only had electricity for ten years. Then, she steered the conversation back to his neighbor, Bill, who was working for David.

"Aw Billy, yes, Bill Steward and me was raised together," Wendell slightly slurred. He sighed deeply again. "Yes, well I can bring you to him if you wants to get a taxi, or we can wait for de bus. Hell, I tink your friend lives close to where dey's buildin' dat boat. If I'm right, dey's 'bout finished wid it. Ready to launch. Be a party. Always is when dey christens a new boat. Billy must have built least a hundred boats in his time. Yeah, dearie, I can take you right to Billy." With that, he drifted off, head on chest, and the last beer clenched tightly between his legs. Twenty minutes later he awakened and drained the bottle as the Lexus tied to the dock.

It was only minutes past five and Amy was sweltering with the dry heat collected from a bright blue, cloudless day. The warmth radiated from the dusty asphalt street with little shade along the main boulevard, which ran west toward the visible sun. Amy pulled her ball cap further down to protect her nose. She wasn't certain if Wendell was being a gentleman as he grabbed her arm, or merely steadying himself as he shuffled along, permitting her to carry her own bags. The herd of travelers and animals were met by a clamoring array of taxis, trucks, and small, smelly outboard boats. The event was noisy and impolite with passengers pushing and rushing through the crowd as if they might miss something or be missed. At the street, Wendell steered her left and down a few blocks to a huge, old mango tree, loaded with dangling blossoms. The old man creaked as he sat down on a cement block and offered her another block to wait for the taxi van to Eastern.

Even though she sat beside the window in the crowded, after-work bus, there was little air. Dust billowed from the road and small, dried, yellow leaves lined the ruts. Wendell commented that Carriacou was drier than usual. Their route went through countless turns, moving up a slight grade and then switching back and forth on the descent. The only hill she'd seen couldn't have risen higher than a thousand feet, and the lack of elevation could explain the scarcity of rain. Grenada, which had more than twice the elevation, was lush green. Carriacou was an arid, overdone golden-brown. Emaciated cows with their hides loosely stretched across protruding bones wandered the roadsides, chewing anything green they could find.

"Yous see dem cattle? Not too many years ago, dem cattle and donkeys was the only way to get up and over dis. Dat's why deres so many turns. If you needed something, chances were it was easier to go round by boat. But us dat lived at Top Hill, we'se always has to walk. Wasn't but two government cars on all of Carriacou till I made my second, no third boy. Dose two trucks were ambulance, police, and for buryin'. And I swear dey's still runnin'. Anyways, 'bout dese cows: well now dere owner don't have 'nough to feed dem so dey range. Now if I lived down here, which I never would, I'd take a chunk off every one of dem damn cows dat eats my garden. Yeah, de people dat live here has to put up with such nonsense. Dese cows probly belong to some big-time politician that's already eatin' off dese people hisself! Take a cutlass to dere big dumb ass and chop it once; den see who's cryin. My friends had all dere pigeon peas eaten while dey slept one night. Cows fat as hell smilin' in de morning. Me, I'd had a beefsteak for de first meal. 'Bout half dem stupid cows dies every summer anyway from no water. Den dey stink from Hell to high heaven! Damn cows."

The van passed several small, one-room, grocery-bar combinations with grizzled, barefoot men in ragged clothes sitting on wooden benches and leaning against the faded walls drinking beer. Several different plywood stores were built side by side and were probably selling the exact same items at the exact same price, or so Wendell professed. Finally, at a tee in the road, the van stopped in front of a larger, blue store. Working men got off with sacks and parcels of hand tools. Hefty, dark-skinned women wearing coordinated outfits, who worked at Hillsboro offices, arrived back at home with not a hair of their very creative hairstyles out of place. As Amy removed her cap, the hair did not spring back. Her own hair was pasted to her forehead and neck with sweat. Amy watched as almost every passerby continually mopped perspiration with a washcloth. Her tank top was sticking to her, which was a problem because she hadn't worn a bra. With a bag on each arm, Amy struggled to shield her breasts from public view. She'd imagined the Caribbean would have a bit more of a relaxed attitude, instead, she attracted the shaming, clenched-lipped stares of local women and the shameless grins of muttering men.

Wendell led her from the van into the shade of Elsa's Beer Garden. Elsa was a big woman, crowned with a large yellow shower cap. She wore a bright orange-and-green muumuu that could've easily doubled as a couch cover. Elsa sprawled across an entire corner in her over-stuffed chair with her enormous legs propped up on an upside-down plastic bucket. She was watching The Young and the Restless. To her left sat two chunky schoolgirls in matching, blue-plaid skirts. They all appeared hypnotized by the plot. In response to Amy's request, Elsa lifted the cooler lid in a practiced motion, retrieved two Heinekens and accepted the money without taking her eyes off the small black-and-white screen.

"Now, dearie," Wendell continued, "Dis what we call Peacock's Walk, just on the outside of Eastern. Dere was some crazy Dutch farmer dat brought peacocks here to breed. 'Magine dat! Nows Elsa and her brood do all de struttin'."

"Do we have to wait for another bus to get to Eastern?" Amy asked.

"Nah dearie, de udder side of de road and dem three streets is de whole town wid de beach beyond. Dat where your friend lives. De bus don't go down into the town unless dere's real old persons riding."

Amy looked at the man who looked every bit of a fit seventy.

"How old are you Wendell?"

"Not dat old anyways. Me seen seventy already, but mommy and papa still breathin', theyse not met ninety yet. It's for dem that need to get dropped off close to home when's dey come back from the clinic or de bank. Come, we walk with dese."

Each with a beer in one hand and a bag in the other, they sauntered along the hundred-plus yards of sandy track to where a good-sized white boat was pulled up on the beach. At a quarter to six, the mosquitoes had begun to dine.

Amy swatted one on her ankle and cursed the insects. "No dearie, dose ain't skeeters. Deys no-seeums, little tings dat must be nuthin, but all mouth." Amy opened her bag and retrieved some pleasant scented pump spray. "What's you tink we used for dem bugs for years, dearie? What you tink?" Her answer was a shrug. "Nuthin', nuthin' at all, but we'se never had a problem with them up at Top Hill where de breeze blows most all de time. My daddy always said dere was bottom-land folks and hill folks. We gots de breeze, and dey gots de sea." He swiped at both his ankles by swinging her bag. "Damn bugs!"

"Dis your friend's boat," Wendell said, pointing to the boat and then to the first little house, which sat alone just on the other side of the beach road. "And dat's Mr. SP's place and his white truck. Bill, Billy Steward, where's you at? I gots someone here wants to chat wid you." A pounding noise and some type of music emanated from the boat's interior.

The exquisite tropical scene enveloped Amy in a flash. There was so much beauty crammed on the edge of this incredible bay. She now understood what had attracted David to this spot. His cute cottage was tucked between stunted, dried tan corn stalks and deep green sea grape trees. It looked like a movie set where Lauren Bacall was about to whistle.

Amy immediately saw the sleek boat was heavily built from thick rough planking. Sleek and sturdy, she thought, just like David. The foot-thick keel rested on even larger blocks of wood and its brilliant white hull, propped with straight poles, dreamily reflected some of the sunset's rosy tones. The darkening blue sea was flat and calm with a dozen or so boats of various types lying slack at their moorings. Tall, untrimmed palms made the white sand beach wondrously majestic.

Distant, in the fading daylight, were silhouettes of several small islands and big yachts. Evening stars were just beginning to twinkle.

As much as Amy hated to use the word 'awesome,' no word could better describe David's boat. It appeared long and strong, yet somehow delicate. Her own sailing lessons had begun in a tiny, fiberglass sunfish and progressed to a twenty-foot Soling on Annapolis Bay. She had sailed with prospective suitors and friends of the family in their beautiful, floating, electronic-equipped weekenders. This boat, however, was at the other end of the scale — a utilitarian tractor, distinctly not a Ferrari. The beach work area was littered with pieces of well-used sandpaper, hardened paintbrushes, and a multitude of small chunks of wood. Two, rusty, fifty-five gallon drums were overflowing with trash. The pungent odors of oil paint and thinner combined with fresh pine sawdust — formed an irritating aroma. Contrasting the modern refuse pile was a wall of dark gray stones, neatly stacked between the next two palms further down the beach.

Wendell knocked several times on the hull, while Amy stood back to embrace the smooth, flowing form. The foredeck progressed upward to a beautiful, varnished bowsprit. The small stern swept in behind the cabin top to the helm where the large wooden wheel was mounted to an old-style brass binnacle. The tall, thick mast was stayed with bright stainless shrouds. Amy's gaze fell upon the cabin, where a round dark face, almost totally encompassed with gray hair, appeared. The beard and hair were a slight shade darker than her present companion's and ran around the face like a helmet with only the high cheeks, nose and forehead uncovered.

"Wendell Cronen, what yous knocking so loud for?" the bearded face inquired.

"Bill, I was comin back up from Grenada today after payin' my land taxes on de Lexus, and meets dis here American woman who came all dis way to see Mr. SP. So I brings her here. Miss, what's your name?"

She approached to shake hands as Bill descended a wooden ladder. "Amy, Amy Whistlow. I was in the Navy with David, or, Mr. SP, as you call him. In fact, I'm still in the Navy," she said almost nervously. "Is he around?"

"Well, Amy, me think SP talked about you." Bill took her arm and led her away from Wendell. "Yous the lady sent all that information."

"Yep, that's me," she replied proudly. "I came to see if he put it to good use."

"Well, yeah, he did, but took off somewheres 'bout two weeks ago. Me thought he might a gone to Grenada, or to the States to see you. Me haven't seen him for a while," Bill rattled on. "A note on the coffeepot say he headed off. Just been finishing his boat, Summer Breeze. We'se close to it now. Really wish he'd get back. What he tell you?"

Wendell walked up to join the pair, only to have Bill put him off. "Thanks. Appreciate you brung her all the way down heres, but she and me gots some personal things to discuss. If yous wait another half hour or so, me'll get yous a ride back up the hill." The older fellow shrugged and reclined against the nearest palm.

"Amy — Amy, right?"

She nodded.

"Guess you expecting same as me, to see SP?" Bill escorted her to the side door of the small house, which opened into a nice, cozy kitchen. Bill was considering the brawl that would erupt if SP's darker woman encountered this lighter version in what each considered her own territory. Certainly, SP would take a real beating from both of them. He eyed this stateside one under the unshielded ceiling light. She looked fit, trim, and ready to go.

Amy asked, "Do you know Mike Post, the teacher here? Where is he? Did he and David leave together?"

"Well, young lady, me knows 'bout everything concerning this present situation, 'cept where everybody at." He opened the refrigerator and got himself a beer, but Amy opted for cold water. "Me start at the beginning. In fact, me the beginning of this mess." It took fifteen minutes for Bill to recount everything he knew concerning the teacher and SP, while managing to leave out the other female in the story. "They could have found all the treasure."

Bill tipped the beer again and continued. "That's when he disappeared. Figured he gone to Grenada, or somewheres to get more equipment. Like me say, me quits on the deal when the little boat get shot up. There was no reason to stay in touch with the teacher. Didn't even knows he was gone. Guess that means all of them somewhere else. But what are yous gonna to do now? Guess yous should stay here, since this where he'll show up sooner or later. Me gots to take the men home. If yous want the truck, yous can drive us. Otherwise, be back here bright and early."

Amy declined due to weariness, and the prospect of dangers on the roads of Carriacou. After rinsing her face at the kitchen sink, she examined the remaining two rooms, switched on the radio in the living room, and twirled the tuning knob through a half dozen stations. None satisfied her. She hit the power switch. The digital clock read it was only seven, but Amy was ready for an unexpected lonely bed.

CHAPTER FIFTEEN

Almost eleven hours of unexpected, solo sleep brought Amy Whistlow back to top physical form, yet her psyche was wrapped in confusion. With nervous energy, she opened the house to the cool, fresh morning. Unshuttered, the brisk sea breeze swept away the mustiness of the cottage. The small place had felt like a tomb at night, which amplified her depression. She scanned the rooms and saw very little evidence of David's presence. The walls had no pictures. Even the dresser top was clean of pocket change. No newspapers, mail, or keys were on the kitchen counter.

The front living room ran the twenty-foot width of the small house. She'd never seen a home like this before: constructed and painted sky blue, yet unfinished inside, without plaster or gypsum. The floor planking was a deep brown, covered with two golden woven mats. It was adequately furnished with two sturdy, reddish-stained, wooden armchairs embracing faded-orange cushions. A matching, small table had a neatly squared stack of boating magazines and catalogues shelved underneath. David seemed to be living meagerly — attempting to minimize the number of possessions he would soon take aboard his boat.

Where she had slept was surprisingly orderly for a man with a history of pitching his worn clothes in a corner. The bed table held nothing but some aspirin and cold pills. Amy was relieved to find the closet held only men's clothes. She had been prepared to leave if her curiosity discovered feminine articles. The medicine cabinet in the bath was neatly organized from disposable razors to deodorant.

The kitchen was stocked with necessities to the extent that she'd expect of a bachelor in paradise. The fridge held little except beer and half jars of various condiments in the door. There were sardines, canned soups, and veggies, with some packaged noodles on the shelves. Onions and garlic hung in wire baskets above the sink. In the lower cabinet was a half-bottle of light brown rum and a full bottle of vodka with three liters of tonic. She found coffee, prepared the percolator, and strolled outside to the front porch while it bubbled.

The porch's one chair faced Summer Breeze and the north point of the bay. Sea grapes grew to the road and blocked the approaching sunrise. With a cup of café Negro, too hot to sip, Amy slipped into the chair and tried to recall David's essence. When they had lived together for a short time, she could almost anticipate his reaction to any situation. During the four-year relationship, they traded inner secrets and knew each other. Really knew each other. Her situation with David was a gap, not yet a divide. Amy was prepared to do whatever was necessary to build a bridge. That even included quitting the Navy.

The complete seascape panorama was lovely with his boat at the center. Knowing the man she loved had chosen such an adorable vista, and sitting in his same seat, brought Amy to tears. She sobbed through the first sip of coffee. Still early, infrequent barking dogs, roosters, and a few babies provided the only background sounds. A tiny mosquito buzzed as she wiped her eyes.

"Where are you, David? Something you've left here should tell me where you've gone."

Forty minutes went by in a daze of good memories and possible solutions. The treasure provided the only plausible answer and Bill was the only one who knew about it. People don't just disappear. That only happens in paperbacks. Amy wouldn't know what could be missing from David's cottage, but Bill might. The boat builder had said they talked almost every late afternoon. The cottage felt strange to Amy. It was too neat for David Warner to call it home. She sighed deeply and quickly toyed with the thought of involving her father. He'd send in the cavalry, if possible, with all the favors and muscle an admiral could muster. No, that would produce too much attention.

The treasure hunt was obviously illegal. The Grenada government, if told after the fact, would want much more than a percentage and just a mere ounce of flesh. The island would scream bloody murder for the theft, even if they hadn't known the treasure existed. But if treasure was the cause, then it should also produce a solution.

Bill parked the small pickup beside the house after he'd dropped the men at the boat. "Had a good night, Amy?"

"Slept soundly. Bill, I'd like to talk to you some more if you can spare the time." She stood and stretched. Dressed only in a one-piece bright yellow swimsuit, cut high at the thighs, she commanded Bill's attention.

"There's coffee. Help yourself."

"Well, the men know what to do. Let me check a few tings and see if they need supplies. Then me come back and share another pot of coffee with yous." Bill walked toward Summer Breeze, shaking his head and thinking how anybody could leave a woman like that alone. It was then he realized what he had tried to hide — SP had to be in big trouble.

Amy's cold shower countered the now high and heated sun. It was about triple the temperature of her stateside home. Dried, in shorts and a T-shirt, she prepared another pot of the aromatic brew. A few almost-stale crackers and refrigerated jam were the closest thing to breakfast. She sat at the porcelain and metal kitchen table trying to blank her mind with the distraction of the percolator.

Bill broke her trance knocking at the screen door, "Coffee smells good." He poured a cup and sat. "What do yous wanna to do today, Amy?" Bill made an extreme effort not to use the island dialect, to remain calm, and to talk slow. He felt the island patois would make him sound ignorant to this beautiful stateside woman. "Me help any way possible. Me wasn't only building Summer Breeze for SP, we's friends, good friends. Told yous last night, when me was beat up, he took good care of me. If kept me big mouth shut, and kept to building boats like supposed to, none of this would happened. SP didn't knows nothing about the wreck. Teacher did, way before we'se ever met. He had all kind of facts."

"Where does Mike Post live? Not that it would do me any good to know, as I'd be lost once I was out of sight of Eastern."

"Oh, there ain't that many roads on Carriacou. Sooner or later yous find it by asking people. Everybody speaks English here. But we can drive there together."

"Bill, I don't want to drag you away from the boat work; then David will be angry with both of us when he returns."

"Amy, yous know SP better'n me, but me never seen him upset over anything. He'll understand when we see him again." He leaned forward keeping his cup cradled in his strong hands. He whispered, "Me think you are right. Something musta happened to SP. Don't wanna get yous worked up," he confessed sheepishly. "There was a woman, a local woman diving with us. Fact is, the way SP tells it, was she who found the wreck. So, after dropping off the workers last night, me went where she worked.

They haven't seen her for longer than SP been missing. Me seen both of them coming back from diving early in the day and go out again in late afternoon."

Bill peered over the cup as he slowly sipped his coffee and waited for Amy's reaction. "Day before, SP and me went to Grenada. Picked up the stuff yous sent. Next day, Wednesday, was first time they suited up to use it. It was also when me told them me want out. Treasure and Grenada was one thing, but getting shot at was something me wants absolutely no part. Since yous here, me can only think of three possible things that happen."

"What?" Amy waited for the older man to reveal his troubled thoughts.

"Well, a day before we goes to Grenada, like me said, to get dis dive stuff, SP didn't say nothing about other plans. He would have told me 'cause we was still partners. Hell, even after me want out, SP still figured me a partner more than just building the boat. Sure he would have said something about going off island. If Grenada government caught them, something be on the radio or tele news. Woman's always got it on at home. Second, if they goes up to Florida to sell the stuff we found, like teacher said he could do, they had for sure told me to have somebody look after the houses since all the craziness that's happen 'round here lately. Believe me, SP and that girl were scared real bad by them bullet holes."

"Wait a minute, Bill, you said before that she was a woman, but you just called her a girl. Is this someone that I should consider competition?"

Bill had become excited and his mouth sped past his brain. "Well, Feliza..."

"Feliza, Feliza? What kind of name is that? Feliza?" Amy chirped.

"Well, Feliza," Bill took a couple of deep breaths, refilled their cups and continued, "Feliza is the daughter of the man me first searched with for this wreck. He's dead now. Years ago, she went to the States with her sisters to get more schooling. Hell, me didn't even knows she come back. Truthful, that girl's not quite as good looking as you, but she's still a looker. SP and her began diving together, 'cause one day she sort of saved his little boat, one they was shot at in, from floating on the reef." Bill was talking quickly as if this confession was a gas pain. "So, they dives together. That's about all me knows about that. Me no know."

"Amy, SP was always talking 'bout you. He was happy you was coming here." Bill looked at her and saw her staring blankly at her full coffee cup, wearing a deep scowl. "So, me was saying, third thing might be an accident. They came back from diving so me knows they was here Wednesday night. Boat's here. Could been an accident like those bullet holes."

"Bill, I'd like you to take a look around and see if there's anything of David's that out of place or missing."

Bill walked around opening every cabinet and the closet. "Well, what me sees is two things: too much stuff left to have packed a bag for more than overnight. Second, there's no dive gear other than those tanks outside. Me never thought it proper to inspect his house while he was gone, but now you woke me up! So what we'se do now?"

"Dive gear? Are you certain you saw them return on that Wednesday? Could they have dove from some other boat? Is it possible they could have drowned?" Her questions rattled off.

"Empty tanks and boat here, so they didn't drown. Yeah, SP took real good care of that diving equipment. Every night while he was filling tanks, everything else would get a good rinse." Bill rubbed his furry jaw. "Yous knows everything is missing, both sets with all of that new stuff you sent. If someone local had seen something, they say so. Anything that happen here is news and woman be chatting it up all over the place. If a boat or another native missing, somebody be looking," Bill blurted out.

"Well, you said this Feliza girl-woman is a native and no one cared to look for her?" Amy quipped.

"When yous meets Feliza, yous see that she can take care of herself. Plus, she apt to just float around here, there, and everywhere. Supposed that now she here to enjoy the quiet life after living in Las Angeles. Her aunt never knew to expect her home, only at work. Now she ain't showing up to help, so her Aunt Bernadette's worried. But no one wants to have police looking for someone that might be making some kind of trouble. So Bernie's been quiet and just worrying at home."

Amy closed the bathroom door but spoke, "Where are the police? Where do we make a report?"

"There isn't that much of police on this little island. Immigration officer doubles for police to save money. If he decides he needs help, then he calls in proper detectives from St. George's. Anyway, he's in Hillsboro."

"Get your men squared away, and let's go to the teacher's house to see what we can find. Then on to the local constable." Amy requested.

"We can leave when yous ready. Pick me up at the boat."

Amy finished freshening up and applied make-up with bright red lipstick. Another woman, an island girl who she imagined as a dark-skinned, barefoot vixen, was trying to steal her man. "Let her find someone else. David is mine." She puckered and used a tissue to shape the bright red on her lips. "Damn you, David, damn you, wherever you are! But I'll find you, if not for anything more than to squeeze your balls so they won't be good for anybody else's pleasure or your own! And woman," she raised her clenched fist, "when we meet..."

The Outpost's chained gate was slightly more secure than the locked door. They parked and explored the interior of the landlocked sloop. This added nothing more to the mystery, except both David and Mike Post were very neat and organized. Bill found the location of the buried box was smoothed over. Digging, he hit nothing but sand. "Don't believe they would move it less they was gonna to sell stuff."

Amy hadn't found any research concerning the wreck either. Not even what she had sent. There were no CD's for the computer. Mike Post's wardrobe was full and two suitcases rested in dust on top of the closet.

Chattering continually about all of the things that had been in the buried box, especially the gold coins, Bill drove to Hillsboro. Officer Richmond sat placidly behind a large desk. Other than his right arm in a cast, he was perfectly attired with a starched white shirt adorned with gold nametag and other service medallions. "Why, Miss Whistlow, an honor, I'm sure." The young officer extended his left hand while Bill tried to stand as far out of view as possible, in the few midday shadows.

"Sorry to barge in like this; I know how busy you are, officer. My driver," she nodded towards Bill, "says you are a one-man operation in Carriacou. Must keep you very busy."

"Yes, it does," he said almost serenely. "It was I who spoke with you over the telephone. As I said then, there is no reason to worry. Mr. Warner loves to sail, and probably caught a boat to Grenada."

"Wouldn't he have to check out with you?" Amy questioned.

"As I said, he probably headed for the mother island where he could have dealt with another officer," Richmond offered. "It happens all the time. An acquaintance, new or old, sails south, and off they go. I know Mr. Warner, but haven't seen him for weeks."

"Do you know a Mr. Mike Post who teaches school? There's a Feliza Dubois also missing. David mentioned to me he knew them. It turns out they haven't been seen around either." Amy replied.

The officer puffed up his chest, sighed loudly and visibly swallowed hard. He hardly expected the American to tell this woman of his island playmate. He placed his manicured left hand on the desk, and his well-polished shoes seemed ready to push him out of his seat. "Mr. Post left by plane weeks ago. I personally cleared him. Ms. Dubois left also. They did not leave together." He almost stuttered the 'd' of did.

"Where were they going? Could I see their exit forms?" Amy began to pace as Bill walked out into the sunlight, hoping that she wouldn't shake a wasp's nest.

Richmond finally rose, stretching to his full height without moving his feet. "Miss Whistlow, I believe you said you are in the United States Navy. Is that correct?" His voice showed irritation.

"Yes, sir," she said routinely.

"Miss Whistlow, as unbelievable as it sounds, the United States has no authority in Grenada. Those immigration papers are not subject to inspection by anyone other than my superiors. If that's all, we can conclude this meeting." Richmond was annoyed.

"Excuse me, I didn't mean it to sound like it came out," Amy persuaded. "David is a close friend and I'd like to get any information that might provide some clue to his whereabouts. I'm sorry if I offended you at all. David didn't have a large circle of intimate friends here on Carriacou or elsewhere. I just thought that those two might know where he went. I certainly didn't mean to step on your toes. Please accept my apology."

"Certainly, no offense taken. An apology from a beautiful woman is always unnecessary." Richmond folded himself back into the wooden swivel chair, again without moving his feet. "Hopefully our paths will cross outside of these walls at a more civil function. Where are you staying?"

"In Eastern, at David's, for the next few days. If he doesn't show up, I may as well return home."

"Well, Miss Whistlow, I'll inquire in an official capacity. If I see Mr. Warner, I'll be sure to tell him you are on the island."

Amy nodded and thought Richmond smirked during the last sentence as she walked outside to join Bill leaning against the truck. Inside Richmond crossed his leg, which began to shake to some unknown rhythm as his good hand drummed a pencil's eraser on the desktop. He would see Mr. Warner and Ms. Dubois soon. Mr. Briscoll would be happy to pay for information about someone searching for his divers.

It was Friday and government payday. The warming streets were crowded with shoppers, school children, and pensioners. Bill tried to raise Amy's spirits by being a local tour guide and suggested lunch, but Amy declined, opting to shop for a few things at Carriacou's largest store. Bill mentioned fresh vegetables should be bought when they were available, which was now. After being pushed and shoved by locals who pursued the few fresh goods that remained, and with the truck's bed filled with enough supplies to last a week,

Amy and her driver bounced back towards Eastern. Bill chattered on, waving and helloing almost everyone they passed — but Amy remained mute, lost in thought.

At the last turn before heading out of town, Bill brought the conversation back to the problem at hand. "So, what you gonna do now that you've put the government on the alert?"

Amy sat in the passenger side and quietly remarked, "Well, I certainly don't profess to know much about men, especially not West Indian men, but I have a feeling Officer Richmond knew more than he was saying. I couldn't believe how he went ballistic when I asked about the two immigration-exit papers. He could have easily shown them to me without such an uproar."

"Well, yous right, yous don't knows West Indian men. We'se don't take kindly to outsiders, 'specially woman outsiders, asking about business. Richmond puts up with outsiders everyday asking stupid questions and doing even dumber things. Yous think he be 'customed to it by now. No reasons to bark at yous like that. Knows everybody on this rock, 'cause that's his job. But boy's really so full of hisself in that starched, white shirt, about to make me get sick."

"That's what I thought. Most times men play along and flaunt their importance. Unfortunately, now we'll never know where Mike and the island 'wonder woman' took off for, if they did. Somehow this mystery keeps getting deeper."

"Sweetie, don't be making something out of nothing. There's enough here already to be worried about. You see that guy, he don't want to get anything dirty, 'specially his hands. Never did a hard day's work. Just sits there, pushing a pencil." Bill assessed.

Amy was angered by frustration. "Bill, you have to have all of the pieces or facts to find a solution. Didn't you ever do one of those jigsaw puzzles? You always have to put the border together first, then fill it in."

"Maybe this puzzle don't work that way. Maybe we'se has to work from center out. We'se knows the center is the treasure. Has to be. Why else would all three people involved with it be disappeared? There is one thing now at center. A big yacht anchored near to where SP was diving. Never went to see the wreck, as me feel a bit too up in years for swimming underwater. But for a while now, dis big expensive motorboat been setting real quiet, close where that wreck is. Now maybe that's a coincidence, but it could be worth checking out. Big yachts come to Eastern all de time, just to sit out of the way."

"Should we return and ask Officer Richmond about it?" Amy asked, perking up a bit.

"No, me don't think so. He's had enough of yous for a while." Bill laughed. "Hell, he almost broke out into a sweat. No, think best if we'se keeps this between you and me and keep watching over our shoulders. Well, when SP was driving anywheres, he was always going around to sees if anyone was following. Me no know, so me start doing the same."

Rather than taking the direct route back to Eastern, Bill drove Amy past his home on Top Hill while her store-bought ice cream melted to a less-than-delightful goo.

An hour later at the cottage, over perspiring glasses of ice water, Amy asked, "When was the last time you saw Mike Post?"

"Well, that Sunday when we was all moving rocks. We took a lot of goodies they found to his house. David drove me back."

"David dove again after Sunday?" Amy asked.

"Yes," Bill rubbed his chin, "Told yous all of this, but they dive Monday. Thought they was crazy after being chased by sharks and getting shot at. Hungry for that gold."

"Were they finding anything?"

"Sunday was a real payday when me called it quits. Gold coins! Yeah, gold coins and Feliza decide to keep hers to herself. She and Mike just don't see eye to eye. But that girl always had it rough to keep her young sisters going, after Raymond drowns. She had little to keep her own self going, except a strong will with a real nice mirror reflection. So, she wanna hold on to her share."

"What about the next days they were diving?"

"Well, that Monday at lunch they only gots two more gold coins, and a bit of other stuff. Now one day after we'se comes back from St. George's with that stuff you sent SP, well, they was both beaming. Can still see that girl swinging her happy hips, humming a good song. Yeah, think they found something real good that day, but by then me was out. That girl was not sharing another thing she didn't have to. When we was together those few times, she never said but three words to me: hi, goodbye, and thanks. Now, that better than a lot of the words she put to the teacher."

Amy paused and refilled their glasses. "Did they leave to take the things they had found to Mike's?"

"Let me think about that...?" Bill rubbed his jaw. "Monday night, no. Tuesday we was in Grenada. Me had the truck that night. Let's see... I remember that girl just humming that song. No, they didn't go anywheres while me was here."

"Anywhere?" Amy scowled.

"Look, it ain't what you thinkin. SP and her was, was ..." Bill wrung his gnarled hands.

"Was what?" she snapped.

Bill looked down at his gnarled feet and cautiously picked at his big toenail. His sheepish look said what she didn't want to hear.

"Well?" she waited.

"Well, guess they was working close, and staying here for protection. Figured if they was gonna be back to back, somebody might have a harder time sneaking up."

"You sure it was back to back? Sounds to me like David and Feliza were rubbing bellies." Amy surprised herself as Naval Academy slang popped out.

"Me no know about what they did inside here, but never seen any hanky and panky while we'se on the boats. That girl work nights after she'd dive all day. David would take her, or she catch a transport."

"I don't care what they were doing," she lied — and it was obvious.

"If they found something and didn't take it to Mike Post's, then it must be in this cottage."

"Or the truck," Bill responded.

"OK. You do a good check of the truck for coins and I'll go through this place."

Amy started in the kitchen, shaking out flour, cornmeal, and oats. She shook spices and pulled the drawers. Pots, pans, cups, saucers, everything got rearranged. The chairs and table had no hidden wealth. In the bath, her technique was repeated as she even lifted the toilet tank lid and seat. Gold coins could be secreted anywhere. She unraveled the whip-stitched seams of the living room furniture cushions, but she found nothing in the foam.

Remembering Sherlock, she looked for the obvious to no avail. The light switch covers and receptacles were too small, and the lights had neither shades, nor large enough bases. She had saved the bedroom for last. Bill reported futility and returned to the workers at Summer Breeze. Amy sat on the edge of the bed. Pillows and mattress passed inspection. Every shoe was checked. Paperbacks and magazines were shook without a find. Finally, she removed every item of clothing from the closet and went through each pocket. Leaning back on the bed, she looked around the room. Then, as she started to doze from the day's efforts, it hit her. All the rooms except the bathroom were open to the roof. For privacy, or for some other reason, the bath had been given a ceiling, which ran from the bedroom closet wall to the kitchen, creating a crawl space.

With renewed intensity, she removed the hanging clothes a second time. Always prepared, she found a flashlight in her shoulder bag. The walls tapped solid, but the top panel moved when she bumped it with the broom handle. Not bad, she thought, the panel went beyond the room's dimensions — so there were no visible seams at the edges. If you weren't specifically looking for a trap door, you'd never notice it. She brought a sturdy kitchen chair into the closet and stood looking around the dark crawl space — finding wispy cobwebs, but nothing shiny. Never one to be afraid of crawly things, Amy stuck her hand in between the bath and closet wall to find an oily rag stuffed into the gap. Her gasp was loud as she felt the weight of what had to be an automatic pistol. It was the well-blued .380 that David had owned as a backup for years. They'd target-practiced together with it many times.

Reaching further, Amy's next gasp was louder. Another very heavy, dry cloth was wedged tightly into the two-inch wide partition. She could feel something like a handle and worked it back and forth until it came free. Even in the dim light, a glimpse of the golden dagger knocked her weakening legs from the chair.

"Holy shit, David, you weren't kidding about treasure." The bed claimed her again. She leaned against the pillows, the automatic in her left hand and the dagger in her right. "If people are after you, they are after this." She felt the weight of the knife balancing in her hand. "David, this is worth thousands. I hope it didn't cost you your..." Her eyes clouded at this sobering thought.

When her trembling stopped, Amy returned to the chair and retrieved the remaining bag to discover coins and another solid gold object. "Well David, if you stashed these out of sight, it must be for a good reason. You knew someone was going to steal it, either the bitch, the crooks that shot at you, or the government." She chewed on her fingertips. "If they have you, sooner or later you'll have to tell them to save your own butt, and they're going to come here for the gold. Bill was right. This puzzle starts at the center — and this is as close to dead cen..." she caught herself mid-sentence and coughed, "This is about as close to the heart of the matter as it gets. David, I know this island woman lured you; I just know it. It is just not like you. You're shy — and I love shy. So, I'll put this in my secret place, which will make me the center of things." She racked a cartridge into the pistol's chamber. "I promise I'll make the best of a bad..., a very bad situation."

Once everything was again neat inside the cottage, Amy dozed with the pistol and valuables beneath her pillow. In the late darkness, accompanied by a small cloud of mosquitoes, she quietly buried the precious items in the crotch of sea grape roots just across the road. She carved the tree with AW + DW. The Walther weighted her black leather belly bag and would never again be out of reach.

Boat-builder Bill didn't need to know everything about her discovery inside David's closet wall. The next morning she had coffee and toast ready for another conference. Crusty, blackened silver, two gold coins, and a beautiful ring rested in a bowl centered on the white metal kitchen table.

"There seems to be enough here to make somebody return," Amy said, filling Bill's cup while he fondled the wealth.

"Sure enough, but who gonna return? Will it be good guys or some others? Been thinkin' about being at center. Somehow, we got to draw in those bad guys to where we want them, when we expect them," he mused as he blew on the steaming liquid.

"Sounds like a plan."

"Well, me ain't smart. SP with his experience couldn't locate those villains after they beat me up. So, don't know what me could do, would be better. But that big motoryacht sitting just inside the reef could be where they are nested. It weren't there until maybe a week or so ago. Definitely not there when I was beat, or when we'se was moving those rocks. Me no know. Haven't given it a lot of attention, but nobody come ashore to Eastern from it. That's strange. You see, Amy, we'se used to big yachts coming around. Sometimes rich owner wants to see how the poor Caribbean fellow gets by. That makes 'em feel richer. If the owner is back to wherever he belongs, and just captain with crew is on board, they sit out there saving money. Oh yeah, me see these guys just sit there to eats the boat's galley empty. If they was at a marina, like in St. Maarten or Antigua, they's be spending lots of cash chasing thrills. Yeah, me knows that life. But if it is the owner, or just de crew, they would come ashore here one time or another. Hell, can't stay on the boat forever. Sure can't spend a lot of money in Eastern." Bill took a gulp of coffee and finished, "If it was expensive, none of us could live here."

Amy remained silent, taking an occasional delicate sip. Her right hand caressed the emerald ring. Absently, she slid the ring onto her marriage finger. It spun easily, having been measured for a larger hand.

"Well, Amy, what do yous suggest for the next move?"

"Hmm," she pondered, shaking the bowl of treasure, "Rats have to smell the bait to get trapped. Do you have any fine wire?"

"How small yous need it?"

She lifted one of the gold escudos. "I need to attach this to my neck chain."

"Got what called seizing wire. Stainless and can twist without breaking. Also got some real fine copper wire for tying bait to hooks. Wouldn't see that at all. Why? What you thinkin' of doing?"

"I'm thinking I'd like to wear one of these coins." Amy posed.

"Huh?" Bill couldn't comprehend how a woman could think of

jewelry at this moment. But he reasoned she was an American.

Amy continued. "I'm going to watch that motorboat today and tomorrow. If they are doing anything, I'll see it. Then I'll let them see me. Do you know anyone who has a flashy speedboat that would take me out there Monday morning?"

He immediately thought of Allister Hope's Formula. "Yeah, pretty certain that can be organized. But if they is bad guys, you sure you wanna get close?"

"So close," she lifted the coin and held it between her thumb and index finger, "they can smell the money."

Bill took the truck and Amy found a wide spot of empty beach that permitted an unobstructed view of her curves in a skimpy, black bathing suit. If they could see her, she could see them. Maybe her spa-trimmed body would be attraction enough. Through binoculars she saw two men sporadically appear at the stern and upper deck. The yacht pointed away from the beach in a southerly breeze. It could belong to the tall, tank-topped, pony-tailed man whose bronzed bare shoulders were visible above the back of a green canvas deck chair. He might have been an aging rock star who seemed devoted to reclining in the direct sun at the stern of the beautiful cruiser. The other shorter, fully-clothed man stood and smoked in accompaniment. Then he scampered nervously along the upper decks. Twice she saw flashes from that upper-deck railing, which could have been the reflected glare of field glasses watching her. Once, an even shorter man wearing a white uniform brought the other a drink. That made three aboard.

The wind changed direction for a few minutes and the yacht swung so the name L'Attrapis' was visible on the stern above an ample dive platform. Her French translated it as the 'catcher,' but the owner probably had a more personal definition. She mused that the twin-hulled yacht would make any seriously upscale Mediterranean marina proud. The boat swung away from the beach, but not before she saw two divers pull themselves from the water. The anchorage was almost a half-mile distant, but she could see the divers were wearing unisex, blue coveralls. The wind moved the stern out of view. She thought she glimpsed one diver undress revealing a dark, bikinied body. "Aha! So you must be my competition! Bitch!" Amy exhaled with her breath. "Come on David, give me a little peek." The other diver remained out of sight.

A strong breeze came from the south swinging the stern away from her sight. By afternoon, the sun was overriding her lotion. A swim in the sea didn't make it comfortable. She retreated to the cottage porch, which still offered a view of the mysterious yacht.

"It's like the old slight-of-hand magician tricks," she mused. "Keep everything visible. Have the audience distracted and thinking something much more devious is happening. That's it!" Amy had formulated a possible plan of attack.

"Shell game," she said as Bill rolled the truck alongside the cottage.

"Me gots yous the best-looking boat Carriacou has to offer. It's one of those go real fast, Florida boats. Friend says that he and it are at your disposal. Mr. Hope knows SP and will do anything to help."

"Bill, this could be dangerous. If we are correct, and that boat has kidnapped David and," she paused to sigh, "Feliza, then those people already have broken laws almost as serious as murder. They probably won't care about breaking a few more."

"Listen, me knows how dangerous this is. Been dangerous since them bullet holes. Didn't tell me friend Hope about all the details, but he got a feel for the situation when me say SP disappeared. We'se island people don't try to clean up a mess less we'se can clean it all up. Me and Hope ready to do some cleaning."

"I've been thinking about strategy and I have a plan. I'll need you to help on some fine points."

Bill listened and suggested a few additional maneuvers.

Amy watched the yacht throughout the evening and after nightfall. Nothing seemed out of the ordinary. The upper deck was dimly illuminated until slightly after nine. The magnification of her glasses wasn't powerful enough to discern faces in such extreme, low light. There might have been one more man visible, but she couldn't be certain. It might have been just a wishful thought.

The next day, at the beach again at eleven, Amy saw the motoryacht's chase boat return. From her vantage point, she could see clearly as the tender tied to the starboard side. The man, treated with the assistance given either to the owner or a guest, wore white shorts and shirt.

The shorter, bearded man talked to the bald man until they disappeared from sight. That night, there were no lights glowing from the upper deck.

CHAPTER SIXTEEN

The next morning, Amy's shower failed to rinse away another lonely night of worrying about David. According to Bill, Summer Breeze was only days from completion — then a launching party followed by sea trials. His arrival with the boisterous workers shortly after dawn was a good substitute for an alarm clock.

Two hours later the white Toyota rumbled again into David's driveway, trailed by another, newer four-wheel drive truck. A slim, silver-haired gentleman, wearing a well-pressed tan work shirt and pants drove the second truck. He was so well groomed Amy thought he must be another Grenadian official Bill had sought out to assist in solving the mystery.

A light knock brought her to the side screen door. "Amy," there was a long pause. "Well Amy, me embarrassed to say me don't remember yous last name, but this here is Allister Hope."

"Bill, I never mentioned my full name." She stuck out her hand and it was met by a firm grip of a rough hand. "Amy Whistlow, and I am very pleased to meet you."

"Likewise, I'm certain," was the perfectly enunciated reply. "Please call me Hope."

"Well, that sounds good, since hope is exactly what I need." Amy returned to the kitchen table and without asking, poured three cups from the steaming percolator. As she placed one in front of Hope, she asked, "You are with the Grenadian government?"

Bill laughed, "Allister has relatives in every department of the government, but this is the man with the classiest and fastest boat in all these islands."

The silver-haired gentleman shrugged and countered, "I'm very proud to admit what Billy Steward says is partially true. I have a Formula speedboat that may not exactly be the fastest, but it's legal — and I only commit to perform legal tasks. Perhaps faster vessels are in the area, but their owners tend to perform nefarious and much more dangerous errands. May I ask what use you desire of me?"

Amy smiled, viewing the three pairs of bare feet beneath the table.

"Has Bill told you anything?"

Bill lowered his cup and mumbled, "Don't feel it was me place, saying something out of turn."

"Mr. Hope...." Amy began only to be interrupted.

"Just Hope is fine. The 'Mr.' sounds a bit too proper."

"Hope," Amy replied — and then turned to look out the window as she felt her eyes beginning to cloud. She coughed and began, "David, you know him as SP, lives here. He invited me for a visit. We are old friends from his Navy days." She had to wipe away a single, disobedient tear that dripped down her cheek. She cleared her throat again.

Both men shifted their eyes down to the floor as Amy continued. "Well, damn it, David is gone. I think he might be on that cruiser anchored near the reef." She pointed as the tears began to flow. "I don't want to cry, but I don't know what to do."

"Young lady," Hope said softly, "please retire to the lavatory and take all the time you feel necessary to compose yourself. Bill will inform me of the pertinent details."

"No, no, I'll be all right." Amy rose, and steadied herself on the gas range, as she used a paper napkin to dab at the corners of her eyes. She feared Bill would reveal more than the essential facts. "I think, or rather Bill and I think, something terrible has happened to David and Feliza Dubois. They haven't been seen anywhere for more than two weeks. According to Bill, that motor cruiser appeared just about the same time of their disappearance."

"Pardon my asking, but why would they be aboard that motoryacht?" Hope inquired.

"I know it is kind of vague," Amy answered, "and this could be completely wrong, but we're out of any other possible clues unless they were seriously harmed. I don't want to consider that possibility. I saw two divers in blue coveralls on Sunday when the wind shifted slightly. One of them was a dark girl with bushy hair. I've never met Dubois, but it sounds like it could have been her."

"She's been watching that boat constant," Bill chimed.

"Well, my dear," Hope responded, "Doesn't it seem probable that if SP is aboard and diving, he would come ashore to meet you?"

Continually dabbing her eyes, Amy almost choked as she fought back more tears. "We…no, I think he was…no…they were kidnapped."

"Wait a minute!" Hope pushed back from the table. "Wait a minute. If you aren't jumping to a conclusion, then there are local officials much more suited to pursue such a complaint than myself, a mere boatman." Hope turned and stared at Bill. "What are you trying to involve me in Billy?"

"I've been to see those officials," Amy said sadly as Bill nodded in agreement, "with no success. What I want is to be taken to that yacht in your boat." She almost smiled. "I'll try to use my feminine charm on the captain to get an invitation aboard. With your speedboat, I can portray a wealthy vacationer who was abandoned by her supposed host, SP, and is looking for a thrill before returning to my stateside home. Do you have water skis?"

"Single ski only, but maybe I'm misunderstanding this situation." Hope looked at Amy squarely as he continued. "You think the powerboat kidnapped SP and the other girl, and is making them dive?" Hope's eyes widened in astonishment. "So you want to put yourself in danger to rescue them? I don't like that strategy at all young lady. It is way too risky." Hope leaned back in his chair and asked for another cup of coffee.

Bill jabbered quickly in the local dialect. "Hopie, there been lots strange things 'round here that only few knows about. Me took a whooping from some guys one night, about a month ago, for no reason. There's been other times that just don't seem right thinkin' back on them. This big pleasure boat show up and the two of them, SP and Feliza, gone. Yous knows SP and Raymond's eldest daughter can both swim real good so it ain't like they drown. What Amy wanna to do is right, but me wanna to do something more, so that boat don't get away."

"Billy Steward, are you out of your mind? Wait a minute! Wait a minute! I don't think I want to be involved in any behavior that may result in damaging a vessel for no good reason. Listen to me!" Hope stood and stuffed his hands into his pockets and rapidly posed his questions. "Who owns that boat? What if the captain takes offense to my boat nearing his mooring? What if he really does have SP and this Feliza, and then you arouse suspicion, causing them to leave? There isn't any Grenada Coast Guard boat that could catch that hull. And why don't you go to the government and have the Coast Guard check that boat?"

Amy replied, "We spoke with Richmond, the immigration officer.

Honestly, I never asked him to inspect that boat. Considering his opinion concerning sharing immigration information, I assumed his doing an inspection, requested by me, was an absolute no-no. That is why this avenue seems to be the only way. Please help us."

"I'll do what I can," Hope offered, "but, young lady, I'm not involving myself with anything that even remotely seems like it may be outside of the law. Do I make myself clear?"

"Mr. Hope, I would never ask anyone to break a law, but I've been watching that boat through binoculars and it looks as though they are diving every day. I'd like you to permit me to charter you for water skiing. You drive the boat and pull me around the bay. After a suitable period of time, we approach the yacht and pray my yellow bathing suit is attractive enough."

"Amy, me didn't say nothing 'til now, but me wanna clog the engine fresh water inlets so they has to wait for repairs." Bill presented.

"Wait a minute! Somehow those two sentences don't mesh. Amy, you say no laws will be broken and my old friend Bill Steward is saying he wants to disable another man's boat, a boat that belongs to a man whom we've never met!" Hope outstretched his hands palms up, as if he were holding a weight, "What is this all about?" Hope posed the next question with a very haughty attitude. "I'm not stupid. First, I transport two crates of suspicious equipment stenciled 'Property of the U.S. Navy'. I know David Warner was in the Navy stationed in Washington, D.C., the capital of the United States. So, tell me, this is an espionage mission? Am I correct?"

Amy saw a gray area. She decided not to define it and tuned her approach. "Mr. Hope, I work for the Navy in Washington D.C. I sent David that equipment to be tested. That part is entirely legal and above board. However, I," she lowered her voice, "think someone abducted David to use that equipment."

"What type of equipment is it?" Hope posed.

"I don't want to involve you in this other than as a legitimate boat rental by a tourist," Amy replied.

"So, it will be an everyday boat ride where Bill Steward cripples a million-dollar power yacht! Yes, that certainly sounds completely legitimate." Hope laughed.

"Bill, how do you plan to do that anyway?" Both Amy and Hope said in near unison.

Bill grinned, "Plumbers Mate. Me'll just squeeze that putty that seals plumbing into the through hull inlets, and dem diesels will overheat quicker than sheet. Oops, pardon my French."

"How did you ever come up with that tactic, Bill?" Hope asked. "How deeply are you involved with this espionage?"

"Me ain't involved with no spies. SP is me friend besides me working for him. Engine thing me used once or twice before. Years ago, someone been pulling me fish traps, stealing fish on a regular basis. Actually, it was while captaining yous first boat. It was like they knew our schedule and would rob me fish the afternoon before the boat landed. It was always after a four-day trip to Grenada. When me pull dose traps day after we gets back, there wouldn't be enough to feed a cat, let alone Cecilia and children. So me lost out on the work, bait, fish, and money spent to buy other food. Me was losing all the ways 'round. Once, for sure it was Lalou, that French bastard from Petit Martinique who had a four-cylinder diesel in a fast little skiff. Me saw him putting away one night in me fishing grounds when sailing yous first boat back a half day early from Grenville. Me never forgot. It was on a full-mooned night. Me waited awhile and picked the right night when those Petite Martinique boys was all partying at a wedding. Drank a few beers with them and then say goodbyes. Just after me gets to the dock, me slip in the water. Take only a second to wipe a piece of paper with that gunk on, across his hull. It plugs up his intake. He don't go anywheres for a while. Dumb French frog didn't have no gauges, so it overheated, blowing the head gasket, or so me hears. Guess he thought a lot of people didn't like him much, 'cause he never blame no one particular." Bill grinned through his close-cut beard.

"Billy," Hope slapped his shoulder. "I never would have believed you had a bad thought in your life — but truthfully I never cared for that Frenchie either. How do you plan to get under that boat? I'm interested," Hope turned to Amy, "because, young lady, this is turning into counter espionage. You are no longer a young man, Mr. William Steward. I don't think it would be wise to contemplate swimming back to Eastern from as far out as that boat lies."

"Me no pup — and this old dog might have gray whiskers," Bill pulled at his chin to Amy's delight. Her eyes were red, but she was again smiling.

"Yous never seen one of them cowboy movies where the injuns attack the covered wagons? That was one of first things we used to watch on Wednesday nights when we first gots black and white."

Bill jumped up out of the chair and crouched like someone was shooting at him. "See, this trick only works if Amy gets on that floating palace and decides those guys are crooks." Bill pompously continued. "Well, me believe anyone who can afford some pleasure boat like that must have done something illegal. So Amy, me been thinking 'bout this being a rescue en all. If you get aboard the palace and back on Hope's again safely, think you could tell if they was bad guys?"

Amy took a gulp of coffee, pursed her lips and sternly assessed, "I'll know."

"Good, that's all this plan takes — 'cause me don't want to go screwing with some rich daddy that's taking the family for an outing. So, yous give word to Hope, but yous gots to leave something on that yacht. Gots to look like you forgot it. Then me roll into the water and be between the Formula and yacht. If you nod okay, me smear the cooling water ports with enough putty they be pulling part hoses for least a day."

"But won't someone see you get in and out of Hope's boat?" Amy asked.

"It'll be tricky, but if yous swimsuit's exciting as I guess it is, every eye will be on yous. Me be hiding under a piece of old tarp like one of those covered wagons. Those poor injuns never had a thought there be so many guns behind that canvas. Then me just roll over the side and hang by our boat. Take a minute to make my way between the two boats. If me can't hold my breath long enough to smear two ports and gets back, all those days diving conch as a boy are wasted."

"But you still have to get back in my boat without the crew of the other boat seeing you," Hope finally seemed eager to join in on this wacky maneuver.

"That's where the second part of the wagon train stuff comes into play." Bill was really excited, taking a stance like he was firing a rifle. "Remember how those injuns would ride them horses, shooting under their necks?"

Amy looked at Hope and then back to Bill, "I still don't get it."

"Yous see, it surprises you 'cause it's so simple." Bill crouched low with his arms spread wide as if he were telling a story to his children. "We drag a line on the side of your Formula that's away from the yacht. We practice it before, so it is the proper length with a loop and a ski jacket. Me wear the jacket, hang on, put my foot in the loop, and stay out of sight on the side as you motor away. Then when we'se out far enough for them not to see, yous gets ready to ski again and me gets back in the boat. But you gots to go back inside dat yacht for something and gives us the sign. Otherwise, we mights be making big trouble for ourselves."

"I can do that. In fact, what I'll leave will bring all the attention we need," Amy smugly replied.

"Aha," Hope sounded skeptical. "Have either of you considered the consequences for SP, and the Dubois girl if they are still on board? An action such as this might be dangerous beyond this group. It may even bring harm to a friend."

Amy cleared her throat. "Mr. Hope, please don't think ill of me, but I know David Warner. This is not like him at all. He told me exactly when to come for a visit. I know, or rather, I can feel that he's in serious trouble. His absence, coupled with Dubois' and another friend, has to make you wonder. There's a little more to this, but honestly Mr. Hope, it's nothing bad and I really don't want to involve you beyond just the boat rental," she pleaded.

"Alright. This has something to do with that U.S. Navy equipment I delivered from Grenada. Some group has commandeered that equipment and three people to use it. Do I have that correct?" Hope said.

She looked to Bill and received an affirmative nod. "I sent David that equipment," Amy uttered as her voice demonstrated another oncoming bout of sadness, "It was used one day and then they disappeared along with it."

"So you're with the Navy investigators like SP was?" Hope asked.

"Sort of. David's a good friend of my family and I sent him the newest equipment to test. I feel it might be my fault all this has happened. If I'd have never sent that stuff, he might now be sitting at this table. International thieves may have gotten wind of it. It is my responsibility and I'd at least like to try to help him out if possible."

"Alright young lady," Hope said in a fatherly tone, "Bill's scheme seems a bit crazy, but I'll go along and risk it. Eastern is a sweet place —

and as far as I know, there's never been a problem such as this. We can't have international criminals lounging at our village. I think it would appear better if you drove to my dock early tomorrow. That will give Billy Boy plenty of time to organize his cowboy and Indian routine, young lady."

Amy took his extended hand and clasped it tightly between both of hers, "I'll do whatever I can to help. The United States of America has been good to everybody. I can help keep the world safe," Hope said, swatted Bill on the shoulder, and departed.

"There ain't no finer person for help, Amy," Bill grinned.

"Bill, this could get dangerous. I'm very wary and maybe you ought to forget about your putty thing."

"Listen," Bill looked sheepishly at his hands folded in his lap, "me was so ashamed when me backed out 'cause they was shot at. They, not me! But it was me that tremble. Now can't live with being so timid. Me need to do this."

"Here's what else I've been planning." Amy left the table and returned a few minutes later. She had fitted one of the golden Spanish coins with fine copper wire as a pendant onto her gold chain. The emerald-and-diamond ring was on her finger.

"Wow!" Bill exclaimed. "Blind man couldn't miss that coin. Careful that it don't get you grabbed out there."

"I don't think they would be that stupid. They must have needed David and Feliza with the equipment," she spit out the second name, "and taken them after dark. Mike Post's disappearance is something that establishes the bad guys are competitive treasure hunters. My guess is they needed divers and the divers I saw are our two friends. Mike must be with them because of his research."

"Bad guys already grabbed the treasure that we'd found and buried at the teacher's house," Bill added.

"So?" Amy assuredly quipped. "I don't think they'll take on two local men for a bit of jewelry. I'm hoping they'll come back at night for it."

"What?" Bill looked aghast.

"Bill, remember when you said you wanted to be the center. Well that's what I expect to happen."

"Gold's sugar to a lot of flies." Bill chimed. "But what are yous gonna do when they gets here?"

"I have David's gun," Amy said decisively.

"What?" Bill stared at her in shock.

"It was with the remainder of the treasure. I want whoever wants the gold to deal with me."

Still in shock Bill gasped, "A sweet-looking woman like you could shoot it out wid bad guys?"

"Bill, I am Navy-trained," Amy said mundanely. "I excelled in basic training with special courses during my four years at the Academy." She added confidently, "I'll fight and do it well. There cannot be many people on that motor yacht. I'll have to deal with two or three at the most — and I'll have the element of surprise."

"Amy, me'll help," Bill blurted. "Me no know, just what you want me to do? You went to the United States Naval Academy?"

"Yep, and I teach there now. Are you sure you want to take the risk? I really believe if I surprise them, I can do it alone." Amy gathered the cups and wiped the table. "They won't know my talents. And I will probably be seeing my opponents first, up close on that yacht. That way I'll know how many there are."

"Me'll help." Bill was bouncing nervously from one foot to another. "Can't let you battle those men alone. If you hadn't say nothing, well that's one thing; but now that you tells, me gotta help. What kind of man would me be if me didn't?"

"A safe one," Amy returned curtly. She quickly added while looking Bill in the eye, "If you consider the danger and decide to help me, I won't refuse."

"Done considered and decided — or wouldn't have opened me big mouth. Just tell me what to do."

They spent the remainder of the morning plotting a trap. Then Bill returned to the Summer Breeze, and Amy hit the beach with her ever-present binoculars. The sun was cooperating with her expensive tanning lotion. In three days, Amy's skin was glowing and her hair was almost luminous. With broad-temple sunglasses, she could be a 'mover'. In the high-cut, pink two-piece bathing suit, she was definitely a 'shaker'.

The following morning, Bill drove to Hope's dock at West Bay, arriving just after seven. Anxious about the day, Amy awakened before dawn. She had highlighted her natural beauty as much as possible with waterproof makeup. The elastic of a visor embossed 'Scandalous' controlled her hair. That was the word Bill's wife would have used had she seen the vacationer dressed in a short, mid-thigh, light-green, belted jacket covering a yellow, one-piece bathing suit of slightly more material than a two-piece. That combination could put the bubbles back into a flat soda.

The morning was comfortable since the tropical sun had not yet roasted the air. Amy hadn't previously traveled farther than Hillsboro, but little changed along the rutted roads to Western Bay. After climbing out of Eastern, the light green vegetation deteriorated to tan, then gold, and finally after passing the airport everything became a crisp, harsh brown. There was little conversation as both the driver and passenger had thoughts of their love ones and the real dangers ahead consumed them.

The white truck clamored around a bend and the deep blue of Western Bay came into sight. The road worsened and Bill had to shift from second into first, slowing to dodge bigger and more frequent potholes. Dry, cracked mud, scraggly trees, and litter bordered the roadside. Used tires and plastic bottles that had rolled or blown to the ooze of rainy months were now cemented.

"Filthy people in this village. They blame visiting boats for spreading garbage just as they spread dollars." Bill pointed toward the mud flats, "This is the mangroves. When me young," he laughed, "would come all the way here to get oysters that grows on the roots."

Bill spat loudly out the driver's side window. "Now, you see them houses on the high sides? Well, they tinks they gots it so good. Made their money overseas — built big house with never a thought about waste water draining to this mangrove. Now you eats one of these oysters, you gonna be sick, real sick. So again, it's few big deals that cost all of we. Me no eat no crab that lives in this filth no matter how much corn me feeds it."

"Corn?" Amy was beginning to slightly relax.

"Yes, corn. Dat's what we feeds crabs after catch'em to get rid of all the poison. Damn, don't you knows that crabs eat all kinds of junk? If you boil'em up without that, oh my, the water smells so bad you can't use it for no callaloo soup. So bad, that no dogs would lick a bowl with that."

Bill continued, "We was always rivals with these peoples whether it sailing, fishing, or liming. The Eastern Bay people always the best."

"Liming?" Amy realized she was getting a lesson in Carriacou culture while diminishing Bill's anxiety.

"Liming is what we does very best. Relax with a drink in the shade. Call it liming cause in the olden days, Brit sailors used to have limes on board ship to fight some disease. Well, getting those limes was best job on that boat. So the rest of the crew envied the boys that went ashore to pick them limes. They pick awhile and sits in the shade awhile, but they is off the boat and that the main thing. That's the way liming was born. Now everyone that's just hanging out is liming."

"Bill, when this is over, I'll treat you to the best liming you ever had," Amy offered.

"No, no, no, Amy." The nervous patois accent kept Amy's spirit high as they parked in the shade of a huge sea grape grove close to a sturdy concrete dock. Bill looked in the truck's mirror and straightened the collar of his ragged shirt. "Me who'll give you and SP the best liming party that you can imagine."

Amy grabbed her towel and shoulder bag that concealed the Walther pistol. Allister Hope was dressed the same as the day before, but she could tell from the lack of wrinkles it was fresh attire. A tan cap with a gold emblem reflecting the morning sun covered his light gray hair. His pearl-white boat also gleamed. Such a pleasure boat was common on the Potomac, but it shocked Amy to see such an exquisite and expensive craft in the outer reaches of Carriacou. She estimated it to be thirty-feet long or better. The bow area was clean of obstructions, except for a pair of cleats at the very prow to attach dock lines. Another younger man, also uniformed in tan, shuffled red fuel cans to a similarly-attired third man who funneled diesel into stern tanks.

"Good morning. I expect my Formula is adequate for your charter, young lady and sir." Hope and Bill tipped their caps simultaneously and laughed.

"Mr. Hope, when Bill recommended you, I never imagined your boat would be so, so…" she fought for the correct word, "so incredible!"

Hope looked away shyly, but proud eyes glowed from under the shade of his cap. "Next to my family, this is my pride and joy. I bought her brand new in 2012 and I don't let anyone but myself touch the engines. Worked my entire life in boats. Now I can finally afford what I feel is the best." He turned to the man at the stern who was refitting the deck fuel plug. "Finished fueling?" The young man never uttered a sound and waved a thumb up as he retrieved the last two empty plastic jugs.

"We're off," Hope said and twisted a pair of keys. The sparkling craft instantly roared. Amy held Hope's extended hand and climbed down into the plush-padded, white interior. Bill waited on the dock holding the two lines. At Hope's nod, Bill leapt aboard and the engines purred, reversing from the dock. The speedboat's interior had two pairs of circular seats capable of holding its occupants very secure while underway. A varnished hatch, which led to the bow's cabin, separated the first two seats of the skipper and navigator. The dash panel had rows of gauges. Behind the second set of seats was a spacious, open area big enough for sunbathing. The stern engine compartment ended at a dive platform with a small, metal folding ladder. While idling, or at the present low rpm, normal conversation was possible. Amy imagined the thunderous commotion these diesels could produce when the throttles were fully engaged.

Hope did nothing to disturb Western Bay, which held more than a dozen sailboats with sterns stenciled with far-off homeports. Bill stretched a second, handled, blue nylon ski rope loosely to the rear cleat and tied it to the stern line with a bowline knot. "You ready for a morning bath, Billy?" Hope called. "Please try not to scratch my pride and joy."

"Let's try dis," Bill said as he removed his shirt. Wearing an old, black rubber dive mask and a dark-green ski jacket, he splashed into the water without a bit of gracefulness. After attempting to hold on, concealed from view by the high gunwales, he signaled and climbed back aboard. "Need one more loop; the water, even at low speed, pushing me back."

Bill made another knot, tried it, and was elated with his success. From the water he shouted, "Give a bit of throttle, just like yous was pulling away from that floating palace."

As the throttle levers pulled down, the bow lurched up. Bill became invisible. A worried Amy checked on his condition. Peering over the side she saw that the force of the rushing water held Bill perfectly extended between the two loops with his back pushed against the side of the hull. She shouted a questioning "Okay?" — which he answered with a bearded smile.

The boat slowed as Bill pulled himself in. "Feel good?" Hope asked.

"Do all right as long as yous don't push it too fast." Bill secured the line and placed his dive mask and ski vest under a white, leatherette tarp he'd unfolded. The dashboard's dominant speedometer registered about twenty knots as they cruised past the Hillsboro government dock.

"Amy you want to try the water ski? We'll be in Eastern Bay in about five minutes," Hope asked without turning.

"Sounds like a good idea. Hope, I've been water skiing for most of my life, but take it easy. Not on me," she had removed her light jacket and posed with her right hip thrust out, "the men aboard that motoryacht must see my features. Remember, I'm the bait." The gold coin dangled between the deep separations of her breasts.

Hope fitted mirrored sunglasses from his shirt pocket, pulled the brim of his cap lower, and turned, looking as if he belonged on the set of the old Miami Vice program. "I'm at your disposal, young lady."

Amy rode the ski over flat water and through the speedboat's wake without a problem. Bill disappeared under the Formula's matching tarp as they rounded the north point of Carriacou. In the quickly closing distance, she could see the big powerboat through the Formula's spray. Hope took the first ski route outside the reef in open water. The slight wind chop had her minimal suit plastered against her willowy frame. She was continually conscious of the coin on her neck chain.

After two more passes beyond the reef, the white boat made a wide circle and came through the passage into the flat water where the twin-hulled yacht was anchored. Amy pulled her right arm up and glanced at the gold Seiko. It was eight-thirty. She placed her weight further back on the ski creating a rooster tail of spray almost her height. She imagined her figure would distract anyone from menial chores. That was almost what was happening aboard the bigger yacht. She could see two people in blue coveralls were interrupted by a larger man and led into the boat's interior. A shorter man was draping towels in an attempt to cover something just above the dive platform.

Every time the Formula abruptly changed direction, Amy leapt across its wake. From that angle, the white speedboat looked mystical, sparkling amid the sun lit sea spray. Hope steered perfect figure eights, wide loops, and tight circles. After thirty minutes of whirls and turns, the boat slowed, permitting the skier to pull herself to the boat.

"Whew," Amy took a drink from the offered water bottle. "So, have you seen anything going on at the yacht? I saw the two jumpsuits again. Bill, are you hot down there?"

He didn't respond, so Amy pulled back the white leatherette to discover Bill asleep using the ski jacket for a pillow. Hope laughed as he shook the sleeper's shoulder. "Hey Bill, you okay? We've been calling you."

"What? Oh, me okay, but thanks for waking me. No much sleep last night, probably 'cause of thinking about today. Vibration of these big supercharged diesels is like a lullaby in that warm shade." Bill rubbed both eyes and smiled. "So, yous ready?"

"That's why I stopped. Amy, I haven't seen anyone on deck since those four at the stern. But I'll bet they've been watching from within. Those ports are so dark that even if they had a spotlight on inside, we'd never see it. I make it to be about a hundred feet. Could be an Italian design? Never saw or heard that name before around the main ports. A big, sleek cruiser like that is usually a common subject of conversation with the sailors. It has a catamaran-type hull to better cut the waves and keep stability." Hope shielded the side of his face with his hand. "I'd imagine she could cruise somewhere in the forty knot range. I like the small Donzi it carries for a tender. Most people around here would feel blessed to have it alone."

Amy reached into her bag and found the emerald ring. Looking up, she said, "Don't like to take a chance with my good jewelry. Want to bring me in on the port side? Where are your fenders?"

Hope opened a panel on the starboard side and grabbed four white-vinyl cylinders on a single line. He wrapped one end to a cleat just ahead of the windshield and the other to the starboard stern. Hope looked at Amy and asked, "Are you sure you want to go through with this? Now's the final time to decide."

"Unless you've changed you mind, let's go," Amy declared.

Bill said from under the tarp, "Do something. Getting real warm under here."

The Formula's engines rumbled across the bay to the L'Attrapis, the only break in the continuous blue of the east horizon. At a distance, it appeared to be a sizable boat, closer, it was big, but as they closed to the smooth side, it grew huge. As they crossed the stern, Amy realized it was wider than the Formula's length. Surprisingly, the dive platform was actually the stern transom folded horizontally. There were two open upper decks. The lower deck was equipped for entertaining and the top deck apparently had a small steering station backed by another open section.

Hope sounded a horn and brought his boat in close. A slight, dark-haired man with a trimmed chin beard appeared at the second deck and waved them off. He wore a long-sleeve burgundy shirt and matching long pants, topped with a white Panama plantation hat. "We don't want or need any. Keep away."

Amy stood in the aft area of the Formula and whined, "I just love your yacht. It's so big. Please, can I come aboard for just a minute?" A man watching from the upper deck would make it impossible for Bill to slide into the water.

"No! Stand off!" came the small man's answer.

Amy leaned forward on the Formula's starboard gunwale, making certain that the golden pendant was visible. Hope brought the boat to a quiet idle. "Please, could I use your toilet? It's a girl thing."

"No, take your feminine problems elsewhere. Does this look like a floating flusher? Get out of here!" As he said that, his head cocked and he nodded twice. The hat and beard had obscured a tiny communications headset. "Wait," He made a beckoning gesture with his hands. "Come on in. Throw me your bow line."

A larger, round-faced man appeared on the stern platform attired in loose white Bermuda shorts and a matching polo jersey that displayed his plumpness. He wore a hat of the same type as the burgundy man. A deep voice broadcasted with perfectly British enunciation. "Puleese excuse my first mate. He has my orders to turn away any visitors for evident reasons." Without explaining further, he extended an arm to steady Amy's exit from the speedboat. "Good morning, my lady. I am Thomas J. Briscoll and my motoryacht, L'Attrapis, is at your disposal. Welcome."

Amy crossed the space between the boats. She extended her ringed hand to the broad-shouldered man. Rather than shaking it, he lifted the hand for a lingering, gentlemanly kiss. "And you are?"

"Amy Whistlow. Could I use your bathroom for just a moment? That's what I really need." She squeezed her legs together in little-girl fashion. "I really have to use the toilet, and I discovered our boat's facilities are out of order. I never was a girl scout — and even though the boat captain offered the entire Caribbean Sea, that's not my style."

As Briscoll turned to lead her inside, Amy saw the valve of a scuba tank extending beyond the yellow towels meant to conceal it. She jumped when a big-muscled, pony-tailed, older man opened the right half of the rear door. "Dear me, my lady, I can see you are all about style. Oh, excuse me again. This is my second mate, Mr. Mullen, who is always at my side. These days you can't take anyone, or anything for granted. The yacht's salon head, or rather, the toilet, is this way."

Amy entered through the heavy double doors into a chamber comprising the entire width of the boat. The doors were thickly made of some sort of modern composite material and had a large locking apparatus that probably offered a watertight seal. The interior of the yacht was not what she had expected. It was large enough to have been a ballroom without a chandelier. From it, the sea was visible and uninterrupted through darkened, curtainless windows. If she had to decide on a one-word description, it was 'disappointing'. Instead of rich wood paneling displaying tasteful art, the walls, ceiling, and floor were slightly different shades of white, void of plants, photos, or paintings. Integral white upholstered window seats bordered the interior. Everything sparkled, with barren cleanliness, rather than personality. Against the far interior wall, racks of ascending liquors along a mirrored bar bordered a huge flat television screen. The accompanying counter had four fixed seats flanked by two doors. Eight high-backed seats, with matching padding, surrounded a long, white oval table in the sterile chamber's center. The lighting came from four rows of small recessed spots. Amy gracefully passed through the featureless room — which reminded her of a conference room at a hospital ward.

Out of the corner of her eye she saw the tall, pony tailed guard move slightly. He shifted his hand away from his waist, as if to point. The owner touched Amy's arm and opened the door to the right of the bar. Immediately to her right, the door bore a brass plate engraved 'WC'. It was a powder room, again bland without decoration. Amy began to wonder if this was a budget yacht, and she laughed to herself as the two words were silly opposites.

The broad-shouldered owner waited to escort her exit. "It is a maze aboard L'Attrapis. One can get lost. Would you care for something to drink?"

Amy had hoped he'd be a courteous and curious host. He reached the back of one of the table's chairs and offered her a seat. "Thank you. Yes, I'd like a brief intermission from the sun and physical strain of enjoying a Caribbean vacation. I arrived in Carriacou last week and saw your boat anchored here. My imagination went wild wondering who could own such a beautiful craft — a sheik or royalty?"

"Hardly. What would you like? Perhaps a soda — or, since you're on holiday, a bloody Mary, or a screwdriver might be in order." The owner stared at Amy with strange, pale-blue eyes that moved out of unison. His gaze made him appear as though he was always listening to an inner voice.

"You're right, I am on vacation. I'll wager you make a good bloody Mary. I'll have one." She reasoned that drink would take some time to prepare and ingest, allowing plenty of time for talk — and for Bill to get into the water.

He laughed deeply, "Would a gentleman offer a lady an inferior bottled concoction?" He reached to his belt, touched a red button on a paging device, and ordered two drinks.

"I don't mean to impose further, since the conveniences were what I really needed." Her mind imagined the scene outside with the placement of the other guard. Bill would wait for the signal from Hope before he left the tarp, and Hope would surely wait until there was absolutely no chance of being witnessed. "Do you suppose the boat driver could get some water? I chartered a ski trip this morning and forgot where I was. I expected sodas and a working bathroom. But this is Carriacou."

Amy's eyes followed the pony-tailed guard as the owner again spoke into the intercom. He sat close to the rear doors, and relaxed on a seat next to the window. He was on the side where the Formula was tied and his eyes watched every movement. He wore a blue bathing suit wildly printed with white lizards that reached just above his knees and a light blue, sleeveless ER scrub shirt draped over his waist. She thought it probably concealed an arsenal of weapons. The suntanned man looked close to fifty, yet could pass for forty or less, due to excellent conditioning. Prominent veins emphasized his bulging biceps. The immaculately groomed handlebar mustache was inches below his official 'Men in Black' shades.

The smaller man who had been the upper-deck guard came into the room and whispered to the owner. Amy gulped air. She had no avenue of escape if Bill had been seen. But it was a false alarm. The owner instructed the short man to trade places with the ponytail. The larger guard took a liter bottle of water from an under-the-counter-fridge and exited toward her boat. The smaller guard remained. He exposed only a small portion of his face. His beard, comprised of broad-angled sideburns and the trimmed 'V' of a goatee, was impenetrable. His loose clothing could have easily hid at least one pistol. He didn't bother to take off his hat, but the owner had removed his, revealing a completely smooth, shaved head. Amy slightly shook as she mentally likened them to a not-so-funny version of the Three Stooges.

The door to the left of the bar opened and a white-shirted Asian man entered with three glasses of tomato juice on a tray combined with a plate of carrot and celery sticks.

"Amy, is it?" The big bald, round-faced man asked as he moved behind the bar. "Russian vodka, English gin, or virgin?"

"Vodka — but light as I want to be able to get back up on the ski. I'm embarrassed about not remembering your first name. Mr. Briscoll, thank you."

"No Amy, thank you for brightening what would have been another boring day." He handed her a drink garnished with a leafy staff of celery and a carrot stirrer. He served the smaller guard, and then joined her at the table to raise his tumbler in a toast. "It is Thomas J. Briscoll. I must sadly admit seldom does L'Attrapis have such an attractive visitor and such a good skier. I must also confess to having watched you cruise the circumference of this bay. The usual fishermen call displaying their unchilled wares, and, infrequently, a dissolute fruit merchant will row out with grizzled citrus and brown, over ripened bananas — but watching your skill certainly outweighed listening to CNN or the BBC. You," he paused and sipped his drink, "are beautiful. Is that your boat? Oh that's right; you already said it was a charter. I haven't seen that boat anywhere else."

"Oh, then you must have been in the Grenadines for a while?" Amy posed.

"No. Actually, the boat has only been here a few weeks. I brought

L'Attrapis from Florida. We are businessmen seeking a retreat from the mainstream." He turned to the guard, who sat looking beyond at Hope. "And you, Amy, what power could bring an elegant lady to such an unknown territory as Carriacou?" He reached to her right hand resting on the table, "You could be the Queen of Carriacou."

"You flatter." She permitted him to hold her hand and eventually, he fondled the ring.

"Married, divorced?" He politely looked closer at the ring. "Somebody loves you. Aren't you taking a chance wearing it in such a sport?"

"You've caught me," Amy said as the hatted guard shifted to a more attentive position. "Thomas, I slipped it on when we pulled up. As we Americans say, putting on the dog." Her thoughts tumbled rapidly as the discourse headed in the right direction. She leaned forward, relaxing her arm, which gave him better access to her hand, but also brought the gold coin close within his view. "Actually, the ring is what brought me to Carriacou. An old friend Fed Exed it to me with an airline ticket." She turned and primped a profile, batting her eyes. "How could a girl refuse?"

"Well, Amy, as I said, someone loves you — and he must be quite a catch." He lifted the hand closer. "This is an antique. Oh, by the way that's our business, antiques. This is very old, perhaps four or five hundred years. Cast in the Middle East. Jerusalem would be an educated guess."

"Thomas, thank you. I recently received it and hadn't yet had it appraised or sized." She leaned closer and thought the suspended coin touched his other forearm, but he didn't remark. "What do you think it's worth?"

"My dear, that might be construed as rude. We won't have such chatter over cocktails." Releasing her hand, he changed the subject. "I'd love to invite you and your suitor for dinner. I'd love to know how he came by such a beautiful piece," He slightly accentuated 'piece'.

"I'd love to come; however, it seems my friend is gallivanting without notice, and is participating in a sailing regatta or something of that sort. I am left to my own ends — and this isn't the first time he's done it." She rolled her hand a few times, flashing the ring and said, "However, I can forgive him."

"I find it strange a man would abandon you, especially after impersonally sending you such a grand bauble."

"Oh well, David has always been strange," she pointed to the furthest starboard window, shook the ring loose from her finger, and quietly placed it under the edge of her drink's garnish saucer. "See that wooden boat? He's having it built." The guard shifted his position. "I'm staying at his little beach house just to the left. Thomas, when could I come for dinner? It isn't as if there are a lot of dining options on this island."

"You met my chef, Conrad, earlier. We are very particular of our foods and their preparation. Rarely would I ever care even to sit in one of these vermin-infested establishments. Tonight, and every night until you leave, I'd feel privileged if you would join and share my table."

The seated guard rose and whispered something directly in Thomas' ear. The bald man replied with a vehement, one-eyed stare, causing the short man to retreat to the stern deck.

Amy's response to the invitation was apologetic. "Sorry Thomas, but not tonight. I am going with a local couple to the Old Fort Restaurant. I hear they have excellent seafood." She looked at the smooth head of her host and anticipated a quick reply that didn't come. He reminded her of a young, polite Uncle Fester of the Adams Family. Thomas seemed suddenly deep in thought. She continued, "But the next night would be fantastic. I'm stuck trying to enjoy the Caribbean alone until David returns."

"I'm sorry. I was momentarily distracted. My associate reminded me I could be possibly offering something I'm unable to fulfill. The hatted gentleman just mentioned an email, which we received earlier. It may dictate our departure from this paradise to conclude some other pending business. If we stay, I'll send our boat to notify you."

Amy drained the red drink. "My compliments to you, Thomas. I'd better return to skiing since I'm paying for the time." She rose and he followed her to the deck. The pony-tailed man was standing in the shade of an upper deck support. She looked at Hope, nodded and said, "Are you ready?"

Hope smiled, returned the nod and only uttered a very short, dignified, "Yes, Miss."

Just as Amy was about to leap the thin distance between the watercrafts, she added. "Oh damn. Excuse me, Thomas; I'm so unaccustomed to that ring. I must have been toying with it and left it on the table. I'll get it."

Briscoll turned quickly and headed inside with Amy close behind. "You should take better care of such fine jewelry, Amy." She felt her skin crawl as his slightly imperfect blue-gray eyes pierced hers. "I certainly wouldn't leave such an expensive piece unattended." He again accented 'piece' as he slipped the emerald ring on the proper finger, with the exaggeration of a man kneeling before a princess. "As I said, I anoint you, Amy, Mermaid Queen of Carriacou."

Amy forced a giggle and struck a pose with her hands wrapped and twisted at breast level, showing off the ring one last moment. "Thomas, you are such a gentleman." She leaned forward and pecked his cheek, which immediately burst into a deep blush.

"Thank you again."

The two guards observed from the double doors.

Amy thought to herself that it was easier to distract them than she had anticipated. Her watch read ten-fifteen. Bill had plenty of time to perform the dirty work. "Oh, do you SCUBA?" She asked asked the tall ponytail who offered no reply.

Briscoll pulled one towel, revealing the two sets of underwater gear. "Actually, my taller friend is the only one of us that likes the water. Our maintenance crew adjusted the L'Attrapis rudders earlier this morning in anticipation of departure." He gave her another penetrating look. "You may have seen them in the blue uniforms."

Amy turned and walked to the deck's edge near the Formula. "I don't see much when I'm on the ski except this beautiful boat's spray. By the way, how many crew do you need to manage L'Attrapis?"

"Less than you would think. I always captain her myself with these two," he paused, "gentleman."

"Well, thank you, and I do hope we see each other again." She stepped gracefully into the race boat. "Ready?" was directed at Hope — who simply nodded and stood by to release the bowline.

The small, hatted man held, and then loosened the stern line. Briscoll bowed at the waist and said, "I truly expect to alter our schedule so that I can validate my invitation, Amy. Expect to be a guest aboard Chez L'Attrapis tomorrow evening."

"I'll count on it," Amy said, staggering slightly unbalanced as the diesels pulled away from the big white yacht. She waved and coiled the stern line before sitting in the forward passenger seat.

Hope was grinning ear to ear. "Well, Miss, I'm dying to hear how that yacht is decked out. So you think they are the bad guys?" He turned his head and looked at his port side, which only revealed a single, blue nylon line crossing the metallic white gunwale. He never stopped grinning as the Formula cut a slow wide arc to the right through the placid turquoise surface. Far inside the shallow depths of the south reef, Hope slowed as Amy lathered herself with sun block. At a few hundred meters away from the L'Attrapis, they knew that good binoculars could easily watch their moves. Amy and Hope moved with the intent to shield Bill's reentry. Hope pretended to be readying the ski directly behind Amy, while really pulling Bill into the boat. Bill slid to the carpeted deck and covered up with the white tarp.

"How'd it go?" both men said in near unison.

Amy stretched her ski line in easy loops across the engines' cover. "I hope I gave you enough time, Bill."

Bill pushed two crumpled pieces of wax paper coated with gray sticky putty out from under his shelter. "Plenty time, Amy. Plenty time." Bill was excited again, rattling in the local dialect. "Them ain't going no wheres. Me hears that guy's voice and knows it was he who wanna build a boat. A baldy, right? "

"That boat is about as bald inside as he is," Amy reported. "He wanted you to build a wooden boat when he has that monstrosity?"

"He comes just after we lay the keel on SP's and wants me to stop to work for his bald ass. Pardon me,' Bill said. "Then about month later, two guys bruise me 'board Moriah. Chance, me no think so. Thinks they all rats. Big rats. Now they in our trap. Let's get out of here quick like. Those engines gonna overheat in a few minutes."

"We'll see, Bill," Amy said as she removed the neck chain and ring and strapped on a ski vest.

Hope watched as she used the rear ladder into the water and slid into the ski's rubber foot boots. The Formula stretched the towline taut. Amy yelled, "Give it a shot and go back past the boat. Let's ski back to your dock."

CHAPTER SEVENTEEN

Feliza and David had been about to splash when Mullen motioned excitedly with his hands, shut off their air, and roughly pushed them back to their respective cabins. The dive was canceled so quickly, they didn't have time to shed the blue coveralls worn as dive suits.

This shutdown was a first — and must have been instigated by the approach of an unwanted visitor. Again, it seemed a no-win situation for the couple. If they did survive a rescue attempt, they would probably be implicated with the crew of L'Attrapis for illegal salvage. But in this desperate moment, an ending with only legal consequences would be the least of all the possible evils. This brought a smile to David's face. It couldn't be too bad of a situation because Briscoll must have thought he could talk his way out. Otherwise, they'd have weighed anchor and headed for open seas.

His cabin door was slammed and locked, and David returned to his continuous contemplation of where everything had run amuck. The blame fell on that fateful crab he'd found on the first dive with Feliza. That damn crab probably would cost more than their lives. Where would they all be if he hadn't seen those wood ribs when he tried to snare dinner? David balled his single thin pillow, covered his face, and screamed to no avail.

Mike had appeared only once during a short lunch break since Briscoll rejoined the yacht. His shoulder seemed better, yet he shared the same dark, quiet mood as Feliza. His skin looked gray in the shaded sunlight and with several days of beard growth he looked destitute, which was probably not far from the truth. He still had trouble speaking above a whisper due to throat damage from Richmond's backhand. At least he was still alive, drawing ragged breaths, which lent confidence to Briscoll's promises.

David lay on the bunk with his pillow, controlling the darkness over his eyes. He'd heard a powerful engine come alongside, and crossed his fingers it was the Coast Guard — or some other law enforcement agency that hadn't already been compromised with an advance to their income. It would be difficult to see Richmond gloating and not at least try to rip off his head. The engine stopped and then restarted about forty minutes later. His heart and expectations sank once again as the decreased exhaust resonance meant the boat had pulled away.

Scarcely fifteen minutes passed before the air conditioning quit. David tried the two cabin lights and discovered they didn't flick on. This meant something must have happened to the generator. His cabin was close to the entrance of the starboard engine compartment, so he tried to listen through the door. The door was thick, which meant the curses that he heard coming from Palmer's mouth had to be loud. The small cabin had no ventilation other than A/C. David relaxed on the floor, which was still cool. He was happy this problem couldn't possibly be designated as his fault.

David must have dozed until his door opened, because his digital watch read just after noon. Mullen didn't wait. He reached in, grabbed, and pulled David to his feet. He was pushed down the corridor to the main room. There he joined a frantic Feliza and Mike. Both were bound to their seats, held secure at their arms and legs with gray duct tape. Mullen held David down into another chair at the table, while Palmer taped his arms to the chair, making a final pass around his midsection. He was stuck to a swivel chair mounted to the floor.

Duct tape doesn't easily break and David was helpless to rip it. The double doors at the stern were open, which helped reduce the heat. The dark side windows were sealed permanently. Without air conditioning, there was no ventilation — a major oversight by the yacht's designers.

Feliza strained and her neck veins bulged as if she were trying to forcibly levitate. Mike sat limply and stared at a place on the table. He appeared totally resigned to the hellish situation. David's island woman entreated him with one of 'those looks,' which he translated as despair. After Palmer and Mullen finished securing David, they flanked their leader at the head of the table.

"Ahh Mister Warner, I take it your easy morning with no diving has agreed with you," Briscoll snipped.

As the words rolled out, David could feel it coming. Briscoll's one good eye watched them like a father unhappy with his children — but certainly not afraid to mete punishment.

Sweat was beading on Briscoll's naked head and his white, short-sleeve shirt displayed a generous mound of sloping gut. Palmer nervously made a pen twirl elliptically between his index fingers. Mullen, as usual, unwrapped a piece of candy and sat on the edge of his seat paying attention to everything. Both were ready to follow orders.

"Well, I'm glad you, or rather, should I say, we got this little break in our usual schedule," Briscoll continued. Palmer nodded several times in agreement, but continued to watch his pen twirl. Briscoll stood and leaned forward, placing his hands on the table. "We had a little malfunction this morning, which is why we have these doors open permitting insects to enter. The malfunction permitted us this brief respite. Perhaps we should be thankful for this moment." Then, with a beaming face, he added, "I know, I certainly am. I'm just so, so happy."

Briscoll came closer to David with his hands clasped behind his back, which pushed his belly out even further. "This interlude was time well spent re-interviewing Ms. Dubois concerning your previous finds. It happens she forgot a few items: a couple coins here, a couple of rings there." The velocity of his breath took on a new dimension as he came so close to David's face he had to turn his head. He spit the next words livid with rage. "Where is it, Mr. Warner? I warn you, do not toy with me now! This is a very bad thing you have done. Why did you keep the coins and the rings? Now, where are they?"

If David gave them the treasure of the knife and the mirror with the remaining coins, they were done. They'd have his Walther and their fate would be decided. This moment was their last chance. Tears rolled down Feliza's cheeks as she bit her pursed lips. She dodged David's stare.

"Let's deal, Briscoll," the sentence just came out, "I give you the stash and you cut us loose. Then, all of us disappear into the sunset. We go ashore with you and stay. You get what you want and we get what we need."

Palmer rose automatically, put the pen into his shirt pocket, and leisurely stretched. Briscoll recoiled from David's face and pointed toward Mike. Palmer reached for a clear plastic bag folded on the table.

Briscoll spoke after each of the trio had been repositioned. Palmer was behind Mike, while Feliza got Briscoll and David got the large muscle man. "Deal, shall we make a deal? Mr. Warner, do you really think this is the first time such a deceitful act has been perpetrated against us?" He paused and placed his hands on Feliza's shoulders. "Ms. Dubois is such a beautiful creature." He pushed his face into her spewing curls. "It would be a shame to disfigure her."

Mullen's huge hands were now on David's shoulders. Briscoll calmly continued, "You want to play poker just because you hold the kitty, but truly have no cards. I'll call your bluff and raise you one dead school teacher."

Palmer casually flicked the clear bag open and revealed a draw cord. He covered Mike's head with the bag, which immediately looked shrink-wrapped. It happened in a split second. Mike's eyes widened and he seemed to revive as he realized the extreme danger. He tried to scream, but only gurgled and coughed.

"Shall we bargain now, Mr. Warner? Or, do you expect your navy to rescue you? Time is running out." Briscoll held Feliza's head toward the spectacle, just as Mullen forced David to watch. He nodded and Palmer released the bag. Mike coughed loudly sucking in a huge gulp of air.

Mike's eyes were no longer docile, but wide and terrified. He rasped, "Tell them. They know. She told them."

"Yes, she did indeed tell us. So shall you." Still holding Feliza's head firmly, the bald man continued, "You see, Mr. Warner, I have no faith in you. In fact, I never did. It is evident you are a coaster, just rambling through life. It is also evident your back has never been against the wall. Your parents nurtured you and then the Navy. Have you ever stood on your own legs? I think not."

"You're right, Briscoll; you do have all the cards, but what do you lose by releasing us?" David pleaded, "You'll never find where I've hidden it without taking me along. These two oafs searched my place and didn't find anything."

"Oh really! My two associates might have overlooked a spot, but now you are here to give meaningful direction to their next search." He nodded to Palmer — who resumed the bag torture.

Mullen held David's head. He shut his eyes, but still heard every second of Mike's gagging death. David shouted "Alright! Alright!" But it didn't stop. Mike couldn't move more than straightening. He strained his neck upwards, as if to pass through the plastic enclosure. David could hear Mike's feet stamping hard on the solid floor. Mullen put his right hand on David's forehead and forced his eyelids open. Mike's eyes stretched ghoulishly wide. His mouth froze with his lips uncurled to reveal a swollen tongue. Palmer seemed unconcerned with the dramatics and just held the plastic bag's draw cord from behind Mike. The small, bearded man watched

Briscoll for a signal that didn't come.

The warm room held the stench of murder.

Briscoll broke the silence. "You see, Mr. Warner, this has all happened before. We know the routine. You lie and waste our time, until our patience expires. With the unmistakable sad expiration of Mr. Post, you presently question what devious procedure may await the beautiful Ms. Dubois and yourself." Briscoll paused and fluffed her hair. "You are wondering, aren't you? Can the gold still buy you your freedom? Of course! Certainly! If it is there and my men return safely, you may swim as we disappear." He paused and coughed into a clenched fist. The bald man's tongue pushed at his lips and cheeks — occasionally making an appearance. His one good eye was stretched open.

"That is, if my damn generators get back online, we will disappear. If I had my generators, we could refrigerate Mr. Post and at a later time, provide a more proper burial. So, spare her another example of our determination, and puleese confess. Consider Post a debit. Don't enter Ms. Dubois in the same ledger column."

"Okay! I said okay! Mike didn't have to die!" David gasped for breath as he fought the urge to retch.

"Ahh, but I disagree," Briscoll droned. "He was a waste of this planet's oxygen. Must I remind you? It is only my opinion that matters at this moment. I am presently your judge, your god." He looped a wide black leather belt over Feliza's head and she went wild, crying for pity. "Render your golden, graven images — or we will sacrifice this beautiful maiden."

David shouted, "Stop! Stop! It is on top of the right closet wall! You just have to push up the ceiling!"

Palmer quickly uttered, "No tricks, swabby. There will be no booby-traps if I stick my hand up in there? If we get so much as a splinter, you'll wish you had the sweet death Post just got."

"There shouldn't be a problem, but why don't you let us go along?" David pleaded.

"Don't be ridiculous," Briscoll added. He thumbed open a pocketknife and placed the point to the corner of Feliza's left eye. "You can't have that much hidden. These two won't need any help returning with it." He laughed at his absurd joke.

"Really, it is all there in the space between the walls." David couldn't say it fast enough. "Really, it is there." A monstrous outcome, such as this, had been lurking in the recesses of his mind since the traumatic night with Richmond. Greed had over-ridden good conscience and born this sour, distasteful fruit.

"What's in the closet wall?" Briscoll moved the knife to the inside of her bikini top. Feliza squirmed and pierced the fetid atmosphere with a shrill shriek. Blood started to drip down her chest. He lifted the blade. Its edge was red. He swiveled Feliza and held her chin, looking straight into her eyes as if he were a dentist. "The way I did that didn't really damage your merchandise, sweetheart. As you will see, the slice is covered by even this tiny triangle. Isn't that correct, Mr. Warner? A small scar can be hidden." He put the knifepoint again to the corner of Feliza's eye. "With one eye, you probably wouldn't see the mark at all."

"Stop! Briscoll, please stop!" David wailed. He was completely defeated. "It's all there: coins, jewelry and the dagger! You'll find my pistol first, at the top. The treasure is beneath." He wanted to talk — and to cry. His head swung low as he rocked side to side.

"Oh, coins and jewelry? What jewelry? List them so we'll know we got it all," Briscoll said almost nonchalantly.

"There are twelve gold escudos. Four rings — two plain, two jeweled — a golden dagger, and a hand mirror. I think both are solid gold with jewels. There are a few other things of value. We found all that the afternoon you captured us with Richmond. We didn't even have time to closely inspect them." David wanted to keep talking, but sobs were capturing his voice.

Briscoll knelt close to Feliza — so that her eyes couldn't elude him. "Tell me about the dagger and mirror." He said and then slapped her so hard her head sank limp — but it was David who gasped. "This is the first I'm hearing of them. They sound quite valuable, don't they? Yet, you left them in your lockless beach house?"

Briscoll violently shook the sobbing Feliza. "Keeping secrets from me, my dear?" He slapped her again and she spat blood on his white Bermudas. "I thought I could trust you." There was a long pause as the bald man studied her whimpering — and then he continued, as if it were a second thought. "Trust both of you."

He took the penknife and cut the tape that secured her arms, moving backward to avoid her flailing arms. Palmer stopped the scene by placing the cold, steel barrel of an automatic pistol against her temple. "One more move, tarbaby, and I promise I'll fuck you while you're bleeding to death."

"Mr. Warner, your arms are also going to be released, but your midriff will remain taped. If you present any opposition, Ms. Dubois is history." Both their arms were cinched with large white nylon tie wraps. The tape was then cut, which permitted David to be pulled to an upright position. Briscoll dragged Feliza out through the door to the corridor of her cabin.

Palmer pointed to Mike's body, slumped from the chair onto the table. Mullen removed the bag from Mike's head and then cut him loose from the chair. The pony-tailed bodyguard then threw the corpse over his shoulder. Palmer eyed David with cold distaste as he said, "Put the teacher in the dink. We'll drop him when we go ashore to the swabbie's."

Palmer sat in Briscoll's seat and rested his elbow on the table to better stabilize the square black, nine-millimeter pointed at David's chest. Palmer chatted as if they were passing the time while a waiter brought a menu. "Swabbie, you amaze me. At first, I thought you had genuine granite balls. Now you make me laugh. You know the old adage: 'two people do not a secret make?' You let that black cunt wind your clock and you still out-greedied that worthless black bitch by hiding the good shit from her. That puts you up a few points on my scale. But to give in, when it's down to the darkie getting cut after your own kind gets whacked, is pathetic. If it had been me, I'd have taken it to the cold earth. Yes, same with my silent buddy there. That's how he lost his tongue, by not using it. Now you got to live with the consequences." He laughed, "I'd think a greedy bastard like you won't toss and turn much dreaming about the child-molesting teacher's fate, will ya?"

"Palmer, how can you live like this? You three are barbaric." David buried his face in his manacled hands. "You are no more than animals."

"Yes, we are." The mustache and trimmed beard parted in a smile. "Desire and practice, swabbie. Desire and practice. I supposed you and your stingy bitch are more evolved than us, the animals. Here comes Mullen. Get your lily ass up and don't give us a problem getting you back to your cabin. Otherwise, Mullen will carry you, maybe to your cabin, or maybe to our dinghy."

David was pushed along the hallway and shoved into his cell. "Oh yeah, swabbie! Remember what I said about two people do not a secret make? I hope you didn't think I was referring to your nig bitch not being able to keep it quiet. Nah, no way," Palmer chuckled. "I was talking about me not being able to keep a secret. This will really get you swabby. Some white cunt brought this all down on you. Yeah, your white bitch arrived in a go-fast boat wearing one of our gold coins and a really spectacular ring. Cute, but stupid. She came out here, probably doing a Sherlock for you, her one and only. She somehow fucked up our generators, which is why we are on auxiliary twelve-volts now."

David was listening face down on the floor — until Mullen roughly rolled him over so they could benefit from his expression.

"Yeah, she said her name was Amy something-or-other. You sent her a ticket with a coin and ring. Big spender, aren't you?"

David cringed and tried to kick the closest legs. Instead, those same legs forced the air out of his chest with one well-placed jolt. "Don't! She doesn't know anything!" David pleaded.

"Looks to me like she knows about the same as the nig. Tell you what, before we're through, I'll sample them both and give you a report. We are going to visit her tonight." Palmer laughed until he coughed — and then slammed the door.

\\\\\\\\

The three men sat somberly at the table. Briscoll sipped vodka on the rocks, rattling the ice in the tumbler, as he stared out the open doors. It was two in the afternoon, the hottest part of the day. The slight waves barely made a sound as they lapped against the hulls. The big, hairless man uncharacteristically squandered his shirtless bulk by resting his legs on the next chair. His shaved head, which had deepened from pink to rose, perspired profusely. A white, silk handkerchief, big enough to be used as a scarf, continually wiped and dabbed. He refilled his drink from a decanter on the table.

Palmer and Mullen drank hot coffee. The long, white table was in disarray, covered with the ingredients for a straight cocktail and everything necessary for a good, stimulating cup of instant coffee. Two wide-brimmed Panama hats joined the mess. Palmer had unbuttoned his maroon shirt for the slim chance to be cooler, but it only revealed his washboard abdomen covered with more scars. An automatic pistol stuck out of his beach pants. He relaxed, resting his jaw in the palm of his left hand while the fingers of his right hand drummed on the tabletop. Mullen refilled both cups and sat with his head tilted to the ceiling, eyes closed, as if he were praying. He never moved again during the conversation.

Palmer blew on his cup, then sipped and spoke. "So, Tunaman, what's our take if we pull out now?"

"Not enough to make it worth this unbearable heat. This expedition won't finish our business as originally expected. We will have to do one more little adventure, maybe to Peru or Argentina. But come on, we really don't do this for the money!" Briscoll sounded like a cheerleader. "It's the quest! We've brought in maybe three hundred thousand. If the dagger and mirror are spectacular, it could push that figure up to a million-five. Unique knives always bring a tidy sum," the big man reached for the ice bucket, "but it will still be a paltry amount compared to what we would get if we were liberating eight chests from this oppressive sea." Two cubes clattered into the clear tumbler.

"Well, better our pockets suffer than our necks," Palmer quipped with a grin. "I say as soon as our boys from Manila clear whatever that shit is out of the generators' raw water system, we get the fuck out of Dodge. In fact, why didn't we pull anchor an hour ago? If these jungle bunnies find our dead professor, we'll be testing the strength of a thick rope!"

"Ahh, for once the roles are reversed. Usually it is Palmer trying to squeeze the final nickel from a project and I," the big bald man laughed deeply, "Thomas J. Briscoll, want to depart safely. A few hours can't make much difference. The mechanic reckoned the entire system on the port 10Kilowatt would be stripped, cleaned, replaced, and running by dark. You get the gold from Warner's house, and we disappear to parts unknown."

Palmer pulled at his beard and said pensively, "Yeah, Tunaman, you sit here and play with Afro pussy, while me and Tony does the dirty work again. I got a feeling the blonde's got something waiting for us. It had to be her who damaged the L'Attrapis."

"Yes, I'll sit here," Briscoll returned sharply. "That's exactly what I'll do — and wonder how two specially-trained, very experienced men, wide awake, permitted someone to get out of that Formula and back to it unnoticed. If the American woman did it, I ask you, how is it we didn't see it? She only left my sight while she went into the head. I stood outside the door. You both watched the boat and the captain. I can't believe someone got towed underwater, or jumped in unnoticed. If I had suspected you two were so inept at securing our perimeter I would have had the underwater cameras operating constantly instead of just when our divers were working."

"Inept? So you think me and Tony are inept?" The triangle beard was frantically groped with his right hand. Palmer said as he turned to find Mullen, who was still staring upward with closed eyes, "Tony heard that. And I have to admit, it stings. It hurts our feelings because you made a mistake in letting anyone near while we're doing business. First rule since old times: look out for Trojan horses, especially bearing big tits! Tunaman, you just can't admit you made a stupid mistake!"

"No," the bald man growled, draining the remainder of his drink. Briscoll slid the glass across the table until it clinked against the decanter. "I'm not stupid. There isn't much we can do about it now, except make her pay for the damages with considerable interest. The occurrence of Amy's arrival and our vessel's slight disability are certainly not coincidence."

"Not coincidence? Is that what you'll say when we hit a fire fight on the beach of this podunk village?"

"There will hardly be a firefight, Palmer. You forget Officer Richmond is in our pocket. He gets paid to gather information and he seems to love money. We knew Amy Whistlow checked on Warner, but her immigration papers show she came alone. The only company she had was the old native shipbuilder. We both know that old man doesn't have the courage or stamina to swim out here from the shore."

"What, Tunaman? Seriously, I think that black cunt has put a voodoo spell on you! Your mind is clogged with a bunch of frizzy little hairs! If the blonde called in a team of Seals, why would they clear immigration?" the short man snorted.

"Now who's jumping to conclusions? I think you're becoming too stimulated on caffeine. Why would a Seal team come to Carriacou? To rescue a retiree and a bit of equipment? No way!" Briscoll barked.

"Oh, you better keep a lid on the booze! You know this project is already compromised. And it has been shaky for weeks." Palmer rose and leaned across the table speaking directly into the big, bald man's face. "If we had let Richmond kill these three, our problems would be over. We'd have brought in a pro dive team…" Palmer was interrupted.

"Stop right there!" Briscoll pushed himself up from the chair at the table and stated, "I explained the rationale of holding these people and you both agreed. If Richmond had been permitted to continue and kill them we would be out all of the money Warner and Dubois so gladly handed over. I'll admit they haven't found much since we grabbed them. With three murders, including two dead Americans, all of Grenada's police would now be crawling over this little village. Instead, we have one woman asking a few questions about an old friend, rather than a bevy of professional, international investigators. Richmond would have given up the treasure the minute he was arrested for the murders. This site, above which we are now floating, would presently be a Grenadian national park. Believe me, I have thought this through to the minutest detail — however, I did not expect Amy Whistlow would be so capable, so utterly capable. It was obvious she was showing her jewelry to either bait or impress."

"Well, that yellow coin hanging between those fine tits sure grabbed my attention. I'm certain Tony would agree — and she had your tongue dragging on the floor, Tunaman." Palmer said as he turned and stared out through the open doors. "We'll be ready for tonight. I'll be watching for that bitch to leave the cottage. You keep the Manila monkeys turning wrenches so this barge can be underway the instant we return."

"You know Palmer, we've been friends and associates for almost three decades. During that period, you've found my foremost, special ability is to be a good reader of people. I believe the American woman is naïve and demure." Briscoll joined the smaller man and draped his arm over Palmer's shoulder.

"Like I said, Tunaman, you got cunt on the brain." The short man shrugged off the limp embrace and waved his hands in ridicule. "Yeah, you read the black bitch as a sure thing to save her ass by telling us every detail of the treasure they've already found. But she holds out! Then you figure that the swabby will give up the gold to live out his pension happily. But both proved to be as greedy as Scrooge! So, just when did you become so adept at reading people? Me and Tony is who you read right! We do our jobs. And agree with your plans most of the time, but tonight I feel the outcome is not going to be good."

Briscoll tried to lighten the moment by laughing as he said, "I think you can get the professor to agree with you about the outcome. Wrap him in our workers' weight belts, and send him to Davy Jones before you go to Warner's. Drop his body on the outside of the reef. The current and the sharks will do our clean up."

"They may help, but it's always me and Tony tying the loose ends and sweeping your dust under the rug." With that, the short man buttoned his shirt and headed to the upper deck in hope of finding a breeze.

\\\\\\\\\

David lay on the cabin floor, nursing sore ribs, until he dozed from the heat. The air conditioning woke him when his sweaty clothes became clammy. The digital watch read 6:30. He tried to extend himself on his toes, but his ribs kept reminding him of Mullen's foot. That kick to his ribcage was one more in a long list of scores to settle — if that time ever came. He used all the strength of both arms to grip the inside of the small oval port. He was able to stretch, just enough to be able to see out the cabin's small window. The inflatable dinghy was still tied to the stern with Mike's body bundled in black plastic. The day's tropical heat must have made the corpse rigid. He heard the sound of the electric winch, before the small eighteen-foot Donzi dropped into view, and he wondered why they were readying their chase boat. His perspiring hands lost their grip on the edge of the port, and he fell backward, cringing with pain.

So, it seemed they were going to dump Mike and then hit Amy at his cottage. He knew she was competent in martial arts. Amy was so proficient she'd easily kicked his butt a couple of times when they were fooling around. But this was a serious life and death test with these monsters. If she had the gold, as they said, then she must have the PPK. David only hoped she realized the danger.

What could he do with only the power-head? Every time he had the chance, he'd inspected the outside of the door, and tried to estimate the approximate location of the center locking mechanism. The watertight lock was probably a basic ratchet, and presumably used a heavy spring to hold the locking tooth against the center gear.

The door wasn't made of wood, but of some sort of modern epoxy, probably coating a dense foam core. His one and only chance was to slam the power head against the door, hit the gear or the spring, and bust the lock like in the old movies. David wasn't certain if he'd still have a hand afterwards. If something in that door didn't give, he was sure he and Feliza would be joining Mike as fish food. That seemed the likely outcome when the maniacs returned.

The escape would have to wait until the Mutt and Jeff duo started ashore. That would pit David against only Briscoll and the Asians. Those three Asian crewmembers didn't seem like part of the mayhem team, but the L'Attrapis was their bread and butter. Men have fought hard for much less. If he could free Feliza, then the odds would be better. They could escape to help Amy ashore, first kicking Briscoll's ass. After taking weeks of abuse, he imagined that Feliza might kill one of their three captors with her bare hands.

The small shower in his compartment was the only refuge to help David think through this attempt at freedom. On the small bunk lay the four-inch, stainless steel cylinder that had killed sharks. It didn't look like much of a door key, but it would have to do. As the hot water beat on his shoulders, he inspected his chest and found a grapefruit-sized bruise. Every deep breath produced a sharp pain. David dried with the bed sheet and then ripped it. Exhaling completely, he used one strip of the sheet to wrap a long truss that firmly held his ribs and midsection. Then he loaded half of his ammunition into the power head and removed the safety pin. A second strip of sheet was wrapped around the small cylinder to give it an inch-thick skin. He then wound another piece of the white muslin tightly around the foam rubber taken from his pillow, making a mitten for his left hand.

David's nerves were on edge as he waited to hear the sound of an outboard pulling away from the L'Attrapis. He again inspected every detail of the small cabin for anything that could be improvised into a weapon. The bath mirror was actually a reflective plastic embedded into the wall. There was nothing that he could break to make a sharp knife. The round, spray nozzle extended from the far wall of the shower on a short length of pipe. His injured ribs ached as he struggled to loosen the chrome nozzle from its connection beyond the wall. Finally, it gave and unscrewed. He tied the showerhead and pipe to the remaining sheet strips.

\\\\\\\\

Palmer wrapped four sets of lead-weighted dive belts around Mike Post's body while Mullen levered the legs of the corpse away from the small, gray inflatable's side.

"I know this ain't the best duty we could have pulled, Tony, but we got to pay attention to every detail. We got to get rid of this evidence. This guy wasn't such a bad Joe." The short man chuckled, "Hey, we'd have done the same thing, fucking that little chimp, if we'd had the chance. Like they say, sex these days can be a death sentence." He laughed again, wrinkling his nose. "Funny how a person shits themselves when the reaper grabs a hold. If I'd have known we was going to kill this poor bastard, I would have starved him for a few days rather than put up with his rotten stink."

It was a dark eight PM, with a half-moon to rise in the coming hour. Dressed in black combat fatigues with their faces blackened, Palmer and Mullen disappeared into the night's horizon. The quiet, twenty-five horse Honda outboard easily pulled the three men to the outside of the reef. When the lights of Petit Martinique disappeared, Palmer took the engine out of gear, lit a cigarette, and inhaled deeply. As he exhaled he murmured, "God rest." A quiet grunt, punctuated by a splash, was the teacher's only ceremony. Much lighter, the dinghy quickly accelerated, then banked through a close turn and sped for the far shore.

The lights from the L'Attrapis guided them back to the inlet passage though the reef. About a quarter mile off the village of Eastern's shore, Palmer reduced the dinghy's speed. The taller man racked rounds into the chamber of his Mac 10 and nine-millimeter pistol. Palmer had explained his fears, and discussed a reasonable plan of attack with the mute.

They shut off the inflatable's engine and tilted it up a short distance from the sandy shore. They coasted to the beach, slightly south of the cottage where the thick fringe of sea grape trees hid their approach. The two-man team pulled the rubber craft into the branches. They didn't bother to tie the bow line for a quicker than usual departure.

Palmer straightened and rolled his shoulders to crack his neck. It was stiff from the weight of the ammunition he carried on his chest. He had a sawed-off, seven-round, pump shotgun slung across his back and an automatic pistol in a shoulder holster. On his web belt was a CO2 powered tranquilizer pistol, sistered with an extremely sharp, thin-bladed knife. If experience had taught him anything, it was not to be caught short of bullets or weapons. Since the woman had displayed the jewels, he felt they were expected. Hopefully, she wouldn't anticipate such a quick visit. Palmer would have loved another dose of nicotine, but knew he couldn't take the chance. The taller man had his ponytail concealed under a dark, knit, watch cap. He offered the short man a yellow-wrapped piece of chewing gum as they moved forward.

The seagrapes parted at the edge of the sandy beach road. They were standing about two-hundred yards away from the cottage. It was a familiar location from where they had previously watched Warner. The white truck wasn't visible next to the small, darkened house. Maybe the blonde hadn't been lying when she said she was going out to dinner. Palmer thought they might get lucky, and the blonde bitch would be somewhere else while they did their work. The best-case scenario was for them to be inside, already in possession of the loot, when she returned. He planned to sting her with the tranq gun and then drag her back to the boat. They'd have a private celebration during the passage to their next destination.

He smiled, and unconsciously rubbed his crotch. Even though he was against a white man mingling genetics with inferior races, the black bitch they had on board excited him. More than once, he'd encountered a smirking Tunaman at her cabin door. The boss knew everyone's price, and bargained extremely well. He'd probably fed the gullible black slut the usual routine. Palmer could hear the bald man telling her she'd become one of his gang after this escapade. He pictured the big bald man coupled with the black, wild-haired woman. He smiled and rubbed his crotch again, wishing the blonde would return.

Mullen flattened his huge frame to the ground. The big man silently edged to the left in an attempt to get to the rear of the small cottage. He had to cross the unbroken length of almost a football field, without being recognized. Any other evening, a similar venture would have been simple. Today's misadventures had put everything in a new perspective. It was a hurried plan. The night was starry and the mosquitoes weren't the usual swarming vampires. Mullen lurched forward, sprinted the distance, fell flat and hugged the dry, sandy earth at the edge of the withered corn stalks.

He clicked his Mac 10 from single shot to automatic. The big man waited for the designated signal from his partner. Nothing appeared out of the ordinary at the small, West Indian cottage. This was the fourth time they had approached the place at night.

The shorter man weaved his way along the dark border of the seagrapes until he was directly across from the cottage's porch. As he'd done on the night of Richmond's showdown, he stayed motionless for fifteen minutes. He waited and hoped to spy any movement, which never came. Palmer signaled a quick double flash from his small penlight. He knew his partner was watching as he crept up the small wooden porch steps. He'd watched this cottage so often during the past months, he almost felt at home. He wasn't certain if he was sweating because of the heavy clothing or from nerves. His teeth chewed the gum and painfully scraped his upper lip. He tried to contain his breath as he listened for any noise inside. Only a few dogs barked in the nearby village. A pair of bright auto lights crossed the shadow of the hill toward Hillsboro.

The tall, pony-tailed man saw the signal flashes and approached the side door of the cottage. The doors and windows had been left open. To the tall intruder, this either proved stupidity or a belief in the fellowship of the locals. The pony tailed man smiled again at the inane thought as he entered the darker void. After waiting a minute for his eyes to adjust, Mullen crossed the kitchen and checked the bathroom while his partner quietly spun through the living room.

The house was small. There was basically no place to conceal opposition except the closet they now approached. Together, the duo entered the bedroom from separate doors. It was obvious the blonde had moved in, since her luggage was stacked to the left of the closet. Palmer lifted his right arm, just barely visible in the darkness, and Mullen knelt to aim the machine gun at the closet door. The shorter man stood with his back against the wall to the right of the door, between the closet and the entrance to the bathroom. Cradling the shotgun in the crotch of his left arm, he grasped the knob and pulled open the closet door.

The wooden door swung and bounced against a suitcase, but nothing moved inside the small closet. It was almost pitch black. Palmer snapped on his penlight, and whispered the taller man closer. Mullen slung the Mac 10 around his neck. His free hands cleared the rack of clothes. Everything was dumped on the floor. The big man easily snapped the wooden closet rod out of the way. Palmer clicked off his penlight as they stood motionless and listened. Nothing seemed out of the ordinary. Somewhere in the distance, a baby cried.

Mullen stretched upward with both hands and then cautiously slid the plywood ceiling panel to the right. His friend clicked on the small beam of light. The big man pointed to the rear wall and Palmer nodded. Mullen fully extended his big frame, as he groped with his right hand into the overhead void. First, he heard a thud, followed by the feeling of being pinched. It was then, Mullen created the most violent scream possible from a tongueless man. A bloody, handless arm was withdrawn into the small beam of light. The bulky man couldn't do anything except howl and clutch the wrist spewing blood. The shorter man realized what had happened seconds too late.

The big man's body burst backward out of the closet and bowled him over. Palmer instantly righted himself near the outer bedroom door and pumped seven deafening shots into the wall above the closet. Then he grabbed the penlight from the floor to examine his friend's wound. A split second later he was spun against the wall, dropping his shotgun. He felt the shot before he heard it. The bullet had caught him in the left upper chest, just inside of his shoulder holster. He unsuccessfully tried to reach for the pistol as he crumpled to his knees. His mind raced, but couldn't comprehend the situation. He was too old to get shot, too smart, and always too ready. Palmer's left side was becoming numb with shock. Pointing that small flashlight had been the dumbest thing he'd ever done. That was his thought as he collapsed.

The big man urgently wrapped one of the shirts from the closet around the stub of his arm, twisting the sleeves into an inadequate, makeshift tourniquet. Mullen grabbed the short man by his collar and supported him in a cradle against his right hip. It was only the strength of his now handless arm that held his friend tightly. The pony-tailed man kept a wall to his back as he moved toward the front door. With a groan, he propped his smaller bearded friend against the wall as he prepared to make the run to their boat. Mullen pushed the stub of his right arm firmly against his thigh trying to reduce blood loss. His left hand pulled the machine gun from his neck. He fired a burst into the darkness beyond the porch where he believed the shot that hit Palmer had originated. He thought again, swallowed dryly from the pain, and pitched another burst above the closet to the unseen enemy who had cleaved his hand.

It seemed every dog in the village was now barking. The recent rise of the half-moon produced long, vague shadows. Mullen knew he could make it back to the L'Attrapis and get help. He just knew it. Briscoll would take care of them. They had good medical equipment on board. He just had to make it to the inflatable. That's all. Just get there — and then he and Palmer were home safe.

This time, it was at a hell of a cost. There was no visible enemy to make pay. But someone would pay for this. They'd come back and torch the whole damn island. Mullen tilted his head back, trying to regain some self-control by taking quick, deep breaths. It didn't work. Clumsily, he inserted a new clip into the machine gun.

The tall man pulled off his knit cap, and wrapped his good left arm through the automatic rifle's nylon sling several times to help steady and secure it. He reasoned there was no point in staying a moment longer in the cottage. By now, the locals would have alerted someone — and even the nigger immigration agent couldn't be paid enough to forget or hide this. He rose to his feet, and half carrying, half dragging his limp friend, he moved as fast as possible across the porch. Ponytail flying, the big man leapt down the three steps, landing on the road. A light at the far corner of the cottage roof suddenly beamed, outlining the intruders' silhouettes.

Mullen instinctively whirled and again the area was dark after a rapid accurate burst of bullets. Yet, before he could recoil and start to the beach, three shots stunned him. The first bullet ripped through his left bicep. The big man managed to hold his automatic, but dropped Palmer and spun in the direction of the shot. Before he could raise the small machine gun, another bullet caught the same shoulder. The third round to his abdomen brought him to his knees. Mullen coughed blood, as he toppled backward.

Brave villagers started their vehicles and headlights began to search for the source of the shots.

Amy, clothed in dark jeans and a dark-green sweatshirt, slumped against the left wall of the cottage. Perspiration flushed away the bug repellent she had applied for concealment under the front porch. Her chest heaved as she gulped breaths. The night had drained her strength. She had planned everything perfectly. Amy had expected, but hoped it would not climax with a gunfight. From her position under the porch, she had watched one shadow skirt along the beach road and then walk directly above her as he entered. When she knew both were inside, she'd crawled out, and shot when the small circle of light became a target. Next, she'd ducked and waited at the corner of the house in ambush. Bill had moved the switch for the porch light to that corner of the house, to surprise the intruders when they departed.

The guerrilla tactics Amy had learned in the Naval Academy's classrooms had controlled the evening's events. It was obvious the enemy would come. She had wagered two things. First, the opposition would not respect her as an opponent. The second was that David was still alive on the motor yacht. Once they had seen her jewelry, David would be interrogated and forced to disclose where the valuables were hidden. It was a risk that placed David and the island woman, plus Bill and her, in grave danger. It was also the only certain way to quickly bait the rats to her trap. She wasn't sure if Bill could help her do it. She wasn't sure if she could do it. And she never thought these men would be so well armed.

Bill volunteered, more from manly courage than reason. He was just small enough to squeeze into the crawl space above the bathroom to provide quite a surprise with a cutlass. Besides, he had never fired a gun, while she was well trained. She had warned him of the type of armed men they were facing, but she didn't fully explain why anyone would sneak into the cottage and put his arm up into the ceiling. The short West Indian had spent an hour in the afternoon sharpening the long cutlass blade with a file. Bill was convinced the voice of the man he'd heard order them to leave the big motor yacht was the same person who had questioned him about the Century — which had begun all this nonsense. When the ceiling panel had moved, Bill trembled from fear. He struck once and hard with the cutlass. If a head had popped up for a look, Bill would have split it like a ripe melon.

Amy didn't budge from her cover. She held the pistol firmly in both hands, ready to fire. Perhaps, there were other accomplices waiting in the darkness of the trees. The two men, who lay crumpled in the road, didn't stir as a vehicle pulled close. About fifty-feet away, a truck stopped as soon as its headlights played on the two men and the stream of their combined blood. Even though a voice hailed her name, Amy stayed hidden. She'd learned that trusting the wrong people could lead to grave disappointment.

Four young West Indian men, dressed in khaki work clothes, jumped out of the truck's bed and cautiously approached the bleeding men. Two of them picked up large stones for weapons and babbled incessantly with rapid animated movements. The closest man kicked the machine gun away from the larger body and then grabbed the weapon. The opening of the truck's front doors followed loud beckoning shouts that it was 'okay'.

Amy recognized Hope and Wendell, the old man from her boat ride to Carriacou when they crossed in front of the headlights, but she still didn't come out of the shadows. Instead she retreated, crossed the rear of David's house, and entered through the kitchen door. The Walther pistol went into the pocket of her jeans.

Bullet fumes clouded the rooms with a smoldering smell. Amy flicked on every light as she went through each room. The place was in shambles with chips of plaster littered on the floor, mixed with the expended shells. Blood puddled through the bedroom all the way to the front door. Her heart sank as she looked up to the wall above the closet that had been shredded by the shotgun blasts.

"Bill, Bill," she first called timidly and then screamed, "Bill!" She ran to the closet and looked up into the darkness — only to be driven back by the shock of seeing his smiling, gray-bearded face.

"Me alright, little girl. How's 'bout yous?" He asked as he situated himself on the rafters to drop down through the opening. "Did yous get shot? Did dose scum bums get away?"

"No." Amy cried and buried her face into his shoulder as she hugged the old man close. "I'm all right. I saw the wall and figured they'd gotten you."

"Well, me give that bastard too good of a whack when he push up. First shot went through the wall and blows outs the roof. So I roll back as far as I could and squeeze to far edge where the roof joins the outside wall. Shots going above me." He pulled her arms from around his neck. "Me embarrassed, sees a, well, me kind a pissed me self from being 'fraid," Bill added sheepishly.

Amy laughed nervously. Then Bill joined with her, until they both roared hysterically. She sank to the bed. "Never expected this on my vacation. I feel like I could sleep for days." Then, she started to weep.

"Never thought I'd have to shoot someone."

Suddenly, a khaki-clad youth armed with the Mac 10 jumped through the front door, waving the gun. It was one of Hope's boys who had been filling the boat with diesel. His father followed him into the smoky room.

"Whoa, Clement, don't be pointing that thing this ways," Bill ordered. "After tonight, me had 'nuff of guns for a lifetime. Pray my ears quits this ringing 'fore me hits the grave. What bring yous here?" The young man slowly walked through the house, scouting for more villains.

"What bring us here, you old coot!? Dumbest question I ever heard. Me and Wendell was sitting, playing a good game of dominoes, when all this commotion, like firecrackers, breaks loose," Hope explained.

Wendell walked into the room wearing only a white T-shirt and blue printed boxer underwear. "Apologize for my bloomers, Dearie, but we came as soon as we heard. Hope says 'that's some fireworks goin' on down by de beach', but I watched 'nuff movies to knows gunfire when I hears it." Pointing to Hope, "He was telling me 'bout all de goings on wid dat big yacht anchored out dere. And how's youse thought dey had kidnapped SP, Raymond Dubois' eldest girl, and a school teacher, and was holdin' dem."

Bill grabbed a printed shirt from the floor and covered his wet crotch. He spoke as if the words couldn't come out fast enough. "Well, that's what was about to happen here. Those bad guys was gonna kidnap this little girl — and God only knows what they would have done to her. So what's the outcome with them?"

All watched the lights of the truck turn and head back through Eastern. Allister Hope looked around at the damage the house had suffered. "Both of those bad guys are still sucking air. My boys threw them in the bed of the truck after stripping all those weapons." He casually pointed to the dark handle of a pistol protruding out of his front pocket. "Miss, I was real worried that something you did today might provoke such an incident. But truthfully, I never expected such mayhem, with guns and all."

Wendell continued, "Hope was keepin' an eye turned to dis beach when all dat shootin' broke loose." He made a comical figure, pretending to shoot a machine gun. "We jumped in the truck as soon as first shot broke de night's peace. Dem guy's was after sweet little you? Well dearie, I guess you got a better protector in Billy boy than I ever expected. The crew will take 'em to the clinic and keep watch on 'em until de police come. Don't 'spect dose two are gonna make it beyond Hell's Gate before morning, considerin' all de blood splattered round here. Goodness, you are gonna have some cleanin' up to do. Say, why don't you come back to Top Hill wid us? Promise you'll be safe up there. After a couple sips of Jack Iron rum, you'll forget 'bout all of dis and sleep like a baby."

Amy's body was still quaking with tears from a combination of fear and self-reproach. Although she had been well trained, she never thought she would have to use it. But she consoled herself that the two men deserved their fate. The three older West Indians standing around the bed stared as she regained her self-control and wiped her nose on the sleeve of her sweatshirt.

"No, I can't leave David out on that yacht. I know he's alive, and with what just happened, he'll be in mortal danger." Amy used the bed sheet to wipe her eyes. "I have to get to him."

"Yeah," Bill agreed, feeling courageous, "Yeah, this all about saving SP, Feliza, and the teacher."

Hope said, "Let me help."

"Me, too," Wendell chimed.

CHAPTER EIGHTEEN

When night finally arrived, darkness did little to repair the horrifying events of the day. The outboard started and signaled the beginning of another dreadful episode as the inflatable dinghy slowly pulled away from the yacht. It was that sound that David dreaded as much as he anticipated. Poor Mike was probably being delivered to a watery grave. Amy might be destined to a worse fate, still to be decided by these three lunatics. This disaster was his fault, and it didn't seem as though there was much that could change the situation. Somehow this madness had to be stopped. Mike had paid the ultimate price. Feliza and Amy were still prizes held for the ransom of pure greed.

David wouldn't know his fate until Mutt and Jeff returned. Briscoll still valued him as painful entertainment if he had lied about the location of the hidden gold. David's self-respect had disintegrated with his courage after witnessing Mike's murder. Nothing now mattered except saving the two beautiful women whom he had inadvertently involved in this deadly fiasco. Both women had been manipulated by his unfaithfulness. Guilt from this indiscretion provoked his determination beyond all common sense.

The clock was no longer ticking. Time had run out. David grabbed his makeshift arsenal from the bed. The showerhead tied to the sheet was looped over his shoulder. He slid his right hand into the foam and tightly secured it with the strip of sheet. Momentarily, he reconsidered using his left hand to detonate the power head against the door's locking mechanism, but decided he'd have more strength and accuracy with the right. If the power head misfired and crippled him, his suffering would only endure until his captors returned.

Prayer had never proved to be a viable alternative, but without options David hypocritically begged for help. His breath came in gasps as he plastered his body to the wall beside the door. He turned his head away and buried his face against his left arm. Three times he aimed the stainless-steel cylinder at the scratch he'd made on the door. Holding his breath, he uttered one last pledge to anyone listening, concentrated, and slammed the power head with all the strength he could gather.

The back of David's neck burned and his ears were almost deafened by the explosion. The impact had numbed his hand and the power head clattered to the floor. A pungent smell of gunpowder filled the small cabin. The mitten was now smoldering, but had proven to be a good idea. His right hand was sore, yet still attached with all five fingers. From what he could judge, the bullet had passed through the door about an inch above the mechanism. He quickly reloaded the weapon with clumsy, stunned fingers.

Whoever was still on board should have heard the first shot, so every second that passed was priceless. With his remaining strength, he slammed his last bullet and something produced a loud, metallic clank from inside the door. But the door still didn't open. Terrified, David cursed at his ineptness and swore either his shoulder or the door would break. He hurled his body at it repeatedly until something nosily clattered. The door opened suddenly and he tumbled through. Like a drunken man, he staggered to his feet and rocked down the corridor.

Three steps later, he stopped and realized he was being a fool—rushing to a confrontation with a better-armed adversary. Briscoll undoubtedly heard the report of the forty-four caliber shells. Hell, if he hadn't, he had to be as deaf as David now was from detonating them. His audible world was only a high-pitched hum. His ears, shoulder, and hand rang with the same type of numbing buzz. The wall supported him as he sighed to regain composure. David still had his last weapon, the showerhead sling, and was ready for a bald Goliath. If he continued moving to the left, it would dump him into the main room, where he could meet the master, or make a final break and swim to shore.

That final break should be without Feliza, but he couldn't do it. First greed, now guilt controlled his actions. David turned and slowly walked to the right in an attempt to cross another corridor to the hull where Feliza was kept. They were never permitted to see each other's accommodations. It seemed reasonable the opposite hull had a mirror image holding cell of his. David's only option was to try every door he passed.

The first hatch opened to a storage room, and then David tried a door locked by a code keypad. It must have been empty since there was no answer after pounding loudly with the showerhead. The next door led to a stairway that went down to the engine room, but he couldn't hear or feel the vibration of any diesel motor. He crept down a few steps, stooped, and looked over the top of the huge, green twelve-cylinder engine. The motor didn't radiate any heat. His ringing ears did hear the racket of a wrench being dropped behind the generator at the rear of the room. The three Asian crewmen babbled over a collection of dismembered hoses and fittings. The chef, Conrad, and the other two men were greasy and dripped sweat. It seemed as though they hadn't heard his two blasts. Maybe he'd had some luck and the separation of the hulls had insulated his loud escape. It seemed everyone would miss dinner tonight.

On his way out, David tried to lock the working boys inside, but with a wheel lock on each side of the door, it seemed impossible. At the end of the hallway was a left turn that led to the portside hull. He hurried past a lavatory, the galley, and then the entry to the upper deck. He began to realize the dimensions of the L'Attrapis. His time aboard the yacht had been limited to only three areas: his room, and the inner and outer lounges. He found the portside engine compartment empty, but with the generator operating. Being without time or tools, he dropped the idea of sabotaging it. The next two rooms he encountered were locked. David knocked and neither friend nor foe replied. The expected mirror image of his room was unlocked and empty. After discovering another lavatory, he found he had returned to the quiet dining room. He had missed something, so he retraced his steps.

David quickly discovered the stairway to the upper deck hid a right turn that he hadn't seen in his rush. He climbed the stairs, turned a corner, and found another set of doors. Unless he was disoriented, this cabin looked towards the bow of the yacht. Over the sound of a distant fan, which pushed the air-conditioned breeze, he could hear faint music through the first door. Ready to swing his half-assed bolo, he opened the door to find a comfortable, but empty room. A tasteful double bed, definitely not a bunk, took up most of the floor space and faced to a large, curtained window. The music originated from a rack of electronics just to the left of a large mirror, which could reflect the bed or the view, whichever was deemed more entertaining. Suddenly, the door he thought was a closet, opened, and a very wet, naked Feliza appeared. She hummed to herself as she applied a large, thick towel over her splendid curves.

"Let's go. We've got to get out of here. Quick, before the two goons return," David said softly and touched her arm.

Feliza's jaw dropped. She looked at him like he was a ghost, both shocked and frightened. "David, how, ahh, how did you escape your room?" She hesitated nervously and ran her fingers through her voluminous mane. He had expected one of 'those' welcomes — where the passionate female prisoner wraps her arms around the hero and crushes him to her for a kiss. Instead, he got twenty questions from a towel wrapped model for hair-conditioner.

"Come on girl, there isn't much time. You saw what those monsters did to Mike. Grab something to swim in and we're out of here," he spoke quickly.

"It's not going to be that easy, David," Feliza calmly replied.

"Listen, Feliza, I could be swimming half way to Eastern by now, but I couldn't leave without you. Especially since it's my fault that you're involved in this mess. Has the strain been so bad you can't figure it isn't safe here?" He thought perhaps the terrifying incident of Mike's demise had scarred her emotionally and she wasn't reasoning with logic. David threw her the white tank top and red shorts that lay on the corner of the bed, but she let them fall to the floor.

"David, I don't know," Feliza returned in her whiney, little girl voice.

"Don't know what, Feliza? Time has run out and this is our last chance to escape while our hearts are still beating. Come on." Nothing he said seemed to faze her. Maybe she'd suffered a nervous breakdown from the violence and being treated like a caged animal. David crossed the few steps and wrapped his arms around her. Her back seemed cool, and she shuddered to his touch. Then, as her head rested on his shoulder, she began to whimper. It was a soft cat-like purr that ended in his name. He thought that she was finally returning to reason.

In a whisper, she said, "David we can't."

"What? Don't be absurd. Can't what? Can't get away from the murderous criminals who have been holding us hostage for weeks? Can't what, Feliza? I don't understand what's holding you back?"

"David, you go. Get out of here quick," she mouthed.

"Too late, Mr. Warner." Briscoll walked out of the bathroom, soaking wet, probably from the same shower as Feliza. He'd had enough self-respect to take the time to wrap a towel around his plump midsection. "Mr. Warner, one of us has very bad timing."

"Why you!" David stammered through a jolt of hate, fear, and jealousy. He rushed forward with his arms outstretched to throttle the baldy. His mind created a vision of what gross atrocities Briscoll must have forced Feliza to endure, while he was penned on the other side of the boat.

"Ahh, ahh, ahh, puleese, Mr. Warner, puleese don't precipitate another exhibition of your innate stupidity." The bald man raised his left arm, which was very well prepared with an automatic pistol. In a quick move, his right hand grabbed Feliza by the hair and jerked her backwards, toward him. "Mr. Warner, I am truly aghast, that you would enter a lady's boudoir unannounced and unexpected." He shook Feliza by the hair. "He is unexpected, isn't he?"

The look of dread and fear invaded her large brown eyes. "OK, Briscoll. You win. Let her go. You have me to play your games of pain and doom with. Let Feliza go!"

"Always the perennial gentleman, David Warner, extraordinaire, yet unfortunately nearsighted and dull. Otherwise you would have noticed the difference between yours and this young lady's physiology." Feliza was trying to relieve the pressure of his grip in her hair by grasping his hand with hers. "I suggest you sit down or I will most assuredly shoot you — then you will fall down."

David sat on the cabin floor and Briscoll released Feliza, who quickly put on the clothes she had dropped. Briscoll pointed to David's coil made from the strips of sheet. "Mr. Warner, what is that supposed to be? On second thought, don't explain. Drop that roll of rags and just push it behind you. Miss Dubois, please be so nice to tie your friend's hands behind his back." Feliza complied and bound him tightly. She made the knots much more secure than he would have imagined or desired.

"What shall I do with you? Mr. Warner, I had hoped we would become friends. After all, we share numerous likes and dislikes. We both abhor senseless violence and," he pointed the pistol at Feliza and motioned for her to come closer, "we both are weak of flesh, especially nice soft, brown, sensuous flesh. Isn't that right?"

David couldn't answer as rage drowned his brain. Briscoll kissed Feliza passionately while he continued to stare into David's eyes. "We've even shared some of the same pleasures." He patted her butt and said, "Go into the bathroom, fix your face, and do something to control that hair while I talk to your ex."

Feliza retreated without a sound. "She is a remarkable woman, quite remarkable, almost verges on civilized. But then if she were fully civilized, she would hold no interest. Correct? Civilized, as your friend Amy? Once they are house broken and predictable, they no longer have mysteries." The big man pulled on white linen pants and a shirt — and then sat on the far corner of the bed. "Is that what happened with you and that luscious blonde? Does Amy no longer have any secrets? That's too bad, really too bad. Once you know everything about a lover, it's the same as rereading a favorite book to try to find something you overlooked. You read it too quickly and discover nothing. That is, unless you are very lucky, or the book is excellent. I'll wager blonde Amy is as excellent as this dark island animal. In fact, as soon as my comrades return, we'll put both women to the test. It'll be similar to the pink rabbit that keeps on going and going in the battery ads. We shall see which one of them keeps moving her delicious butt the longest." Briscoll smirked.

"Briscoll, why? I mean you certainly have enough cash, toys and prestige? You have a lifestyle and freedom almost anyone would envy. Why cause all this pain and agony?" David kept working the wraps on his hands with his thumbs and could slowly feel it loosening.

"You see, Mr. Warner, oh the formalities between men who have shared so much. Let me call you David." He rested the pistol in his lap and relaxed to the discussion. "It is amazing I am involved in such chicanery. You are correct; there is no logical reason for me to continue in what must be considered a criminal enterprise. Surely you realize my associates, Palmer and Mullen, are not of the same cut as myself. But I am truly addicted to the stimulation of adrenalin that my lifestyle produces. Sincerely, I can't quit. Recidivist, that's me, a repeat offender."

"Briscoll, I can understand the thrill, but what about the pain you cause? You didn't have to kill Mike. Why?" David asked.

He turned toward the bathroom door, almost absentmindedly, "Feliza Dubois, please finish quickly. Now David, you want a hard, logical reason why I had your friend murdered before your eyes? Why?" His voice rose. "Because I could!"

Briscoll laughed demonically. "You truly are an ass. People want power, only to assert it. How would anyone have known Superman had great strength, if he hadn't lifted that locomotive? The adrenaline and the money are nothing without the power of indifference we wield to compel our fellow man. You are at a severe deficit, David. If the roles were reversed, wouldn't you love to kill or maim me? Of course, you would pull the trigger, or sink the knife not only because you hate me, but also because you can. Those bizarre, serial criminals who commit those hideous crimes do it because they can subjugate another human being to their will, if only for a short time. I had you enslaved for weeks. I must say, it felt good." The bald man glanced to the bathroom, "Very good."

Feliza reentered the room, apparently with everything under control. Her hair was brushed and pulled into a large knot at the rear of her head. Briscoll continued, "But what am I going to do with you, David? If I shoot you now, where you sit, that would make quite a mess. I think I'll wait for my associates."

"So, Palmer is right about you never getting your hands dirty." David uttered without realizing he was egging him on to shoot.

The bald man racked a cartridge into the chamber. "Oh, David, don't push this situation," Feliza sighed.

"So Feliza," David nervously replied, "You seem very comfortable with this pig. Decide to stick with the winners?"

"No, David, it's not that at all," her voice drifted off.

"No, David, it requires something you don't possess: common sense," Briscoll chided. "Miss Dubois realizes this is the least of all the evils. Did you ever read the fable about the man that is confronted with three doors, and at least one has a tiger behind it? Accessing your present situation, there are tigers behind every door. The best policy would have been to not open any and just jump overboard."

Saying that, he rose and pushed Feliza ahead of him out of the room. Briscoll bent, checked David's bonds, and then knocked him unconscious with the butt of his pistol.

Bill unfolded his aching body from the couch. The shock of his part in the evening's events had drained his energy. The older man was visibly upset as he stumbled in a stupor, trying to deal with his close call with death and the injury he had caused. His gray-bearded face tilted to stare up at the bullet holes in the partition where he'd hid. He shrugged his sagging shoulders, crossed himself, and said 'Thanks'. The small cottage was in tatters, but he carefully padded his bare feet through the debris, brushed plaster chips from the cooking stove, and boiled a pot of coffee. Almost the entire village of Eastern had been attracted to the cottage for personal inspections of the most exciting night in the village's history. Yet Bill was alone. A cloud of sorrowful detachment settled as he poured his first cup.

Amy had gone outside to use the mini pocket-telephone she carried. Bill couldn't understand how a little thing like that could reach all the way to the United States without wires. Hope and Wendell walked with her to where SP's truck was stowed under a tarp next to Summer Breeze. The two old friends headed to Western Bay to get Allister Hope's speedboat. They had no plans to stop at government headquarters to report the incident. That could involve hours of answering questions. Hope mentioned that he expected to pass the island's officials bumping to the scene in their official, dark-green Land Rover.

Bill chose to stay behind at the cottage, alone with his thoughts. He watched as the numerals on the digital wall clock changed to a two-inch-tall number twelve with two zeros. It had been a long day and for Bill, the night seemed to stretch on forever. There wasn't much left to do except get out to the motoryacht before it pulled anchor and escaped. It was time to finish this mess. As Bill poured a second cup, it dawned on him that no policeman, especially that Richmond boy, had made an official appearance. It wasn't like that prim-and-proper glory-grabber not to be at this scene with a photographer. Bill reasoned the starched shirt must be off-island and would kick himself for missing all the excitement.

\\\\\\\\

Standing next to David's wooden boat, Amy tried to conceal the quaking fear in her voice from her father. Her call had begun by telling the Admiral how great she felt on Carriacou. Yes, she was tanning gorgeously and had finally relaxed. But when her father asked about David, the walls that had constrained her nervousness eroded and produced a tide of tears. Completely out of character, Amy tried to describe what had happened between long, deep sobs.

"Daddy, it was horrible. These men have kidnapped David, and, and…they tried to kill me!"

Her father questioned, "These are local people, Grenadians, who tried to kill you?"

"No, Dad!"

"Who then?" He had squeezed his fist so tightly that the nails dug into his palm. "Who's chasing you?"

"Dad, I don't know. I just met them today." She stopped to wipe her eyes and wipe her nose. "They are rich white people, probably Americans, on a big motoryacht. They're doing something illegal and I think David found out about it — or at least, they think he found out."

"Is David there with you now?" Her father patiently asked. That question brought a deluge of tears and choking sobs.

"No, Daddy, I haven't seen David yet. I think he's locked up, a prisoner on this big yacht."

"Amy," Her father sat straight up and wiped his mouth. He poised the receiver between his shoulder and ear and started scribbling on a message pad. "Amy, are you sure about that? I mean, are you certain David is being detained against his will?"

Through more sobs she struggled, "No, Daddy, I can't be sure because I haven't seen him. Nobody else around here has seen him for weeks. David disappeared with two other people."

"Tell me, Amy, who are the other people?"

"One is a school teacher, a man, who is supposed to be an American. The other," she hesitated because she knew what reaction would come, "the other is a local woman."

Her father swallowed hard and said, "Amy dear, you aren't jumping to conclusions because David ran off with another woman, are you?"

"Daddy!" she yelled, gulped air and tried to regain composure. "Tonight I shot two men who would have killed or kidnapped me. Believe me, Daddy; this is serious! I wouldn't have called, but I don't know what to do." She started to cry.

"Baby, what's happening? Did I hear you right? You shot two men?

Where? I mean exactly where are you? Tell me," he persisted.

Amy shivered a couple times — yet managed to blurt out the continuing story of David's treasure hunt and kidnapping, the powerboat, and the gold. As she heard herself, it sounded so fantastic. She wondered how all of this could have happened within six days.

"Amy, I want you to get out of there now. Get control of yourself and get to a secure place. I'll call the Embassy in Grenada. This Carriacou Island is near Grenada, isn't it?"

"Dad," She swallowed hard. "Yes, Carriacou is close to Grenada, but I can't leave. All that's happened tonight has put David into more danger. There are men here with me who are willing to go out to the boat to free him and his friends."

"Amy, I don't want you to be further involved with this. I'll call the Embassy this moment. If I understand what you've just told me, you shot two men, but you haven't seen or heard from David. Those two men are from a wealthy American's yacht, and they invited you aboard today, but you didn't see David. Where did you get the gun you used to shoot them? You certainly didn't travel with a firearm, did you?"

"No, Daddy, it was David's gun. I found it where he had it hidden."

"Amy, this makes everything worse. You take someone else's gun and shoot two men for no apparent reason? Young lady, please heed my instructions and get your behind out of there as soon as you disconnect."

"I could lie to you, Daddy. My cell phone batteries are getting low. I'd better go. I love you, Daddy."

"Wait, Amy…Amy?"

Admiral Whistlow reclined against the heavily padded leather back of his desk chair, sighed, and looked blankly around his study at his framed service memorabilia. It was eleven-thirty on the worst night of his daughter's life. The worst night she had shared with him, anyway. The story was incredible, almost to the point of unbelievable. Almost, but not quite. Amy had always been level headed — just as David Warner had always been responsible. He paused and again sighed deeply, debating the depth of his daughter's shocking situation. Wetting his lips, he pushed ten digits.

"Ralph, Chuck Whistlow here. Sorry to disturb you at this hour of the night." Ralph McPherson was his department's liaison with the State Department. "I have a real problem that requires your immediate attention." Admiral Whistlow explained the circumstances, and what he felt was necessary to limit the fallout.

It was not reassuring to be told by the voice on the other end that when a U.S. Naval officer from the Academy shoots a foreign national on their soil, it instantly becomes an international incident.

"Admiral, I'll call the Chargé d'Affaires in Grenada." McPherson reassuringly said. "I'll follow by a fax of something about U.S. Naval personnel missing while on vacation. I'll make certain they keep everything quiet on their end. We'll get a lid on this quick as possible and get your daughter back to the good old USA."

As Admiral Whistlow replaced the phone to its cradle, McPherson looked at his watch and dialed another ten numbers. He knew he'd be up all night cleaning up this mess — or CNN would have a field day.

\\\\\\\\

More confused than relieved from the conversation with her father, Amy stood below Summer Breeze and watched the shimmering mast light on the big motor yacht. Everything seemed peaceful under the half moon. The big, bald owner would expect his men's return. It was time. Hope's son, Clement, approached, walking like a third world revolutionary with the machine gun dangling from his shoulder.

"Miss, I got their dinghy. It was right down the beach. What do you want to do with it?" he inquired.

"Well, I think I should return it." Amy looked at the three groups of people standing in the cottage's front yard recounting the evening's events. She motioned Clement to the side door.

"My father gave me orders not to let you out of my sight," the young West Indian replied. "He said I mustn't let you go anywhere. He's coming around in his boat and we should wait."

Bill was slumped at the table when the two entered. Amy tried to hide her teary, red eyes from the bright ceiling light. She found her bag, disappeared into the bath, wiped her face, and applied some make-up before reloading the PPK. She rejoined the men looking fresh, and then amazed her onlookers as she changed the clip of the machine gun and proceeded to load the pump shotgun. Her assailants had come with enough ammunition to wage a serious battle. It was a good thing they didn't have the brains to go with the weapons. She staggered, realizing how lucky the good guys had been.

"Look, I have to get going. That yacht's going to expect those two goons to return. I can do this alone. This will be dangerous," Amy sighed.

"Well, Amy, me coming with you. Yous don't mind if me take that shotgun? It's the only thing me could hit something with." Bill yawned, stood up, and stretched as if he were headed for a morning of boat building.

"Miss, my father says I shouldn't leave you. But we is supposed to wait for him." Clement smiled with sparkling eyes as he lifted the Mac 10 from the table. Amy showed him how to load it and put it on safety before they headed to the dinghy.

"Clement, we'll probably meet your father on the water out by the yacht. It will save time," Amy directed.

Everyone got wet feet pushing the inflatable from the shore. The night surface of the still Caribbean water was crisp as thin, clear plastic. The dinghy in motion merely crumpled it. Everyone sat on a pontoon with their weapons on their laps. No one spoke, either because of fear or concentration. Bill steered toward their destination at less than half throttle. Even Clement knew the two men now at the clinic were expected to return to the yacht moored a half-mile in the starry distance.

The L'Attrapis was dully illuminated with the usual cabin lights barely glowing through the heavily tinted windows, but the bright halogen anchor light on the radar mast beamed across the bay. Amy wondered what reception awaited them. Was bald Briscoll sitting on deck, ready? Had he heard the four bursts of gunfire hours ago? If he'd been watching his comrades on the shore as expected, he'd be waiting with everything possible to his advantage. From their one short conversation, she intuitively knew Briscoll would be running scared. The two who had come ashore were well-kept bodyguards. Without them, he'd have to search for courage.

The engines still might be clogged from Bill's putty job hampering an escape, Amy thought, but Briscoll would have probably been inside. He didn't seem like the type to sit outside alone on the deck appreciating the constellations. The three captives would be secured below deck and that meant they probably hadn't heard the shots. There might be more opposition aboard than anyone had seen. That was her big worry.

Bill guided the inflatable in close to the bow of the motor yacht, shut down the engine, and let the momentum glide them to the hull. He smiled when he heard no engines, only the generator running. With a quiet "Shush," accompanied by a finger to Clement's lips, Bill directed the tall youth to quietly pull the dinghy along the hull with the flat palms of his hands. A loud, deep squeak echoed as the rubber boat rubbed against the polished, white finish of the bigger craft. The three waited a few minutes in the shadows before moving closer to the stern.

Bill silently belly crawled across the L'Attrapis' diving platform, carefully moving the shotgun a few feet at a time. He scurried his short frame into the darkness at the far starboard corner. Clement followed the older man's example and pasted his back at the near side of the main doors. Amy wrapped the dinghy's line to a cleat and climbed onto the small rear deck. It took only seconds for her to regain her complete balance. Both men watched, as she seemed to be relaxed, running her open fingers through her blonde hair and then shaking her head to toss it. Seconds after primping, Amy surprised everyone by opening the door to the yacht's salon. Her right hand, inside her front right pants pocket was wrapped around the Walther pistol. With her finger on the trigger, she casually strode into the room.

The bright, recessed lights were intensified by the white room and blinded Amy for a second. In a few blinks, she saw Thomas J. Briscoll was certainly surprised by her sudden appearance. The man sat, dressed in white, at the head of the long table. The overhead lights exaggerated his already expansive brow. He sipped a cocktail from a tall tumbler. There was a plate of sliced cheese and crackers close to the dark-skinned woman to his left, who sat wide-eyed in amazement. Her tawny features were emphasized by the small, white tank top she wore.

That must be the bitch, Feliza, Amy thought. This is pretty good treatment for a hostage.

"Excuse me," the big man uttered. "Amy? It is Amy, isn't it? I do remember inviting you, but that wasn't until tomorrow night. What exactly are you doing, bursting onto my boat?" Before he uttered those words, he knew something had happened to his two friends. He could feel it, something bad — perhaps terminal.

"I'm here to take David Warner, Mike Post, and this woman, if her name's Feliza, off of the L'Attrapis." Amy spoke much slower and softer than her temper desired.

"What? That's absurd. You must be confused. I don't know this Warner, or Post," Briscoll rattled. "But if you went to all this trouble to visit, sit down and I'll get you a drink. What would you like?" He seemed about to rise.

"Actually, I'd really like it if you just sat there." Amy pulled her pistol.

Briscoll rubbed an itch near his nose. It could have been a sign of nerves. "Now you are giving me orders on my own boat? Young lady, you definitely are an aggressive American female, but you have made quite a big mistake."

In a blurring movement, the barrel of Briscoll's Glock automatic appeared against the dark woman's cheek. Feliza's head was cocked awkwardly away from the weapon. Her toothy mouth hung agape, but the expected scream stayed stifled in her throat. Briscoll coiled his left arm around her neck and tugged her out of the seat.

"I think I'll do exactly what I want. Better yet, you'll do what I ask. And I'll ask only once. This is what is called checkmate." The young West Indian woman hung limp in his grasp. Even though the white man was taller, he crouched enough to make her a very good shield.

"Oh," was all Bill said as he came through the door, followed by Clement. Both men had their rifles aimed.

"So, the Carriacou cavalry has arrived! Hah! Black men, barefoot with guns! You just have to love the Caribbean. Well, gentlemen, this is exactly what you must do so this situation doesn't get these two women killed. Put your weapons down. If you shoot at me, unless you are spectacularly accurate, this young, native lady is going to bleed profusely. However, my first shot will go directly into Amy's stomach; my second will go into Miss Dubois. This nine-millimeter bullet will guarantee each a slow, painful death from loss of blood. Before I pull the trigger for a second shot, one of you two men will fire, trying to stop me. You will only do more damage. Now, put down your guns."

Amy spoke, "Briscoll, I know you have David and Mike Post on board. Feliza, say something! Try to defend yourself."

The young West Indian woman collapsed to hang limply in the bald man's grasp. Her face contorted as her breathing became difficult. Then her nostrils flared as the grip seemed to relax enough for her to suck air.

"This young lady is of the same breed as your cohorts. God gave these island creatures little ambition beyond the will to exist. They will squirm and turn rather than confront a situation. This is the home of 'not my job; let someone else do it'." Briscoll flashed the black automatic again. "Isn't that right, gentlemen? Put down those guns or you will have many sleepless nights remembering your mistake. That is, if you live through the next few minutes. And please consider my beautiful boat, on which you now stand, has a white interior that will be splattered with blood. Even the best cleaning company in the world will have a difficult task bleaching the stains!"

Young Clement appeared thunderstruck and rooted as a monument to indecision with the small machine gun leveled at the scene. He shook his head as if breaking a trance and looked at Bill for direction.

The older man never acknowledged as his attention was focused on the white man who had such an insulting mouth, yet definitely the upper hand. Of course this was unexpected and confused Bill's plan of pumping off a few rounds into the interior of this plastic boat, easily rescuing his friends. Bill thought he had been called a creature. This white man had no feelings for the girl or for any of them. He'd shoot, plain as day. Bill knew he couldn't take a chance of being the cause of harm to Bernie's niece. The gray-bearded chin was moving up and down as Bill rapidly sucked his lips. He lowered the shotgun and placed it on the white floor. Without looking, he could hear his friend's son follow.

Amy didn't turn because she knew she'd been bested. The men behind her had succumbed to rational self-preservation, rather than let this showdown simmer for a few minutes. She lifted the pistol to classic target form hoping to pick off the bald beast hiding behind the curls. Then the Glock followed suit, leaving the side of Feliza's head to aim at her.

"Aren't you a bit unprotected, Amy?" Briscoll seemed to laugh. He knew he had her and fired a round out the door. Unshaken, Amy held her pose as she heard both men scramble behind her, their retreat accompanied by the sound of splashes. "Seems your compatriots have abandoned their cause. I strongly suggest that you do the same."

Amy didn't flinch. From the corner of her eye, she saw movement as the interior starboard door slowly opened. Two small, Asian faces, stacked vertically, peered through the widening crack. Swinging Feliza as a doll, Briscoll shouted, "Conrad and company, your contract of employment is hereby terminated. Get your yellow carcasses off of my boat. Now!"

Lurching into the room, the men bolted for the outside and dove into the night.

"Again, Miss, I implore you to follow the admirable trait of intelligent retreat. Do not consider this a cue for the performance of a feminine heroine."

Amy didn't offer a reply, but instead concentrated on regaining self-control by regulating her breathing. She tried to think calmly and analyze the mess. It was another car crash moment — when every action slows to a crawl and one can witness the approaching doom. Amy watched for Briscoll to make an unlikely mistake. All of her actions that night would be considered serious mistakes unless this man was stopped. The only possible tactic was to aggravate him into a foolish move. Perhaps that's what Feliza was waiting for. If only the native woman would struggle and draw the bald man's attention.

"You realize your two hired assassins are gone, perhaps dead?" Amy asked. "That was very stupid sending them straight into the trap I set. I guess it was your idea since you are the great, exalted mastermind. Yes, Big and Little fell without too much of a problem. They didn't even smell the golden dagger. You know about that fantastic piece, don't you? What I want to know is, how you are going to drive this floating monstrosity without a crew? Your engines are running properly, aren't they? Don't have a little problem with them overheating, do you?" She taunted the man she could barely see behind the woman's curls.

"Enough! Drop the pistol or I swear I'll shoot you in that nice, tight belly. You somehow tried to plug the inlets of the diesels, but were off a slight bit. You stuffed whatever it was into the generators' intake ports. It was almost effective — but not quite correct. We could have departed. Nothing you did kept me here. It was that coin and ring. Once I saw that such extravagant items existed, Ms. Dubois was pleasant enough to expand her original list of discoveries." Briscoll shook Feliza like a rag doll. "She related there was yet another item of considerable worth." He shook her again. "Wasn't that nice of her?!"

The desperation was evident as the bald man tried to scoff. "Seeing you come through my doorway, I realized my friends must have met a morbid fate. You are a much worthier adversary than your paramour, Warner and company. Yes, your lover is aboard, slightly indisposed. Now, let us return to the issue at hand. Drop that fucking pistol or I swear I'll give you another navel!" Briscoll screamed from behind his human shield. He lifted the dark girl from the floor and gave Amy one hope of shooting her opponent's very visible feet. Amy knew it would take a miracle shot and was not worth risking the chance. She refused to lower her weapon knowing he would probably shoot her out of frustration to avenge the loss of his cronies.

\\\\\\\\\

David had heard most of Briscoll's threats since the Asians had abandoned ship and left the companionway door ajar. His brain ached from a likely fractured skull. The hair at the top of his head was matted with sticky blood. He had returned to consciousness to find himself bleeding, face down on the corner of the bed. Briscoll probably placed him that way so he wouldn't bleed on the carpeting. He must have thought he had whacked David's noggin hard enough to keep him unconscious until the next day, if he ever awoke. The sheet wrapped around his wrists finally stretched and gave way after five temple-throbbing minutes of successfully playing Harry Houdini. The bedroom yielded no other weapon than his good-old sheet-and-showerhead combination.

He rinsed his hair and turbaned his head with a ripped bath towel before leaving to attempt to move a few markers to his side of the board. The commotion was only evident when he got to the starboard companionway. The L'Attrapis was very well insulated for sound. As he turned the corner to the salon, he saw the three Asian men squatting near the door — eavesdropping and then suddenly rushing forward. David could hear the bald man's mouth bellowing, but couldn't discern the words until he came closer to the door. His expectation was to see Mutt and Jeff displaying their new loot, but as he peeked from an almost invisible angle, he was shocked to see a duel between Amy and Briscoll, with Feliza caught in the middle.

This couldn't be happening, David thought. Amy was standing with his pistol poised as if she were about to practice at the academy range. David almost cried out her name. He hadn't seen her in months, but here she was, beautiful, now blonde and well-tanned. He wanted to run out, grab her, and disappear. His heart ached more than his head. She had his pistol pointed at Feliza. What had he done to these two women? Both of his loves were in Briscoll's sights.

As each of the three combatants concentrated on their immediate situation, David crept a few yards back down the hallway and slid up along the outside wall so the door protected him from their view. He thought about using a blind-side tackle on the big man, but he could react with a blast that might hit either woman. Briscoll stood sideways to David's position. Silently, he neatly uncoiled the sheet strips and stood behind the slightly opened door. This was the payoff, a home run in the bottom of the ninth. The line would either work to lasso his armed hand or distract the gunman enough to permit Amy a chance to fire or escape.

At that moment, he didn't know what recesses of his mind held his confidence or had even created his maneuver. Holding the end of the sheet in his hand, he allowed the weighted end to pendulum back and forth until it became a 'now or never'. He flicked the makeshift line out with the same skill that wins stuffed animals at carnival games. This was just slightly more serious. David almost laughed at the absurdity. The pain from his head was intolerable as the white cloth paid out and hit the big man's arm. David jerked hard to flip the sheet strip to cross itself around Briscoll's arm. That pulled the gunman off balance. One shot went wild as David dove forward and used his shoulders in a clip against the back of Briscoll's knees. That toppled both Briscoll and Feliza in a backward arc. Amy didn't budge as she watched the antics.

The three of them tumbled into a squirming ball on the cool, white floor. Feliza wrenched free of the neck grip and rolled to her right. David struggled for the pistol with his left hand and swung his still numb right into several rapid punches, but only one or two actually hit their mark. The

Glock barked three more times, but luckily, no bullet found a human target. Another punch was enough to crush the bald man's nose. The barefoot island girl sharply kicked his hand, releasing the automatic pistol. Then, she scooted across the floor to grab it. Finally, it was over and only heavy panting could be heard. Briscoll was finished.

It seemed both women had been hypnotized by the melee. Amy's eyes blinked David into reality seconds before she spanned the distance between them. He straddled the bald man's arms with his knees and was very tempted to pummel his face into obliteration. The exertion and excitement had blood wetting his neck from his head injury. With the increased throbbing at David's forehead, he was in dire need of a serious pain reliever when a soft hand brushed the swaddled, red towel from his head. Amy's tearful face filled his vision. Her lips quivered.

"David," was all she said before pulling him close. As their bodies touched, her control broke and sobs wracked her torso. Briscoll tried to advantage the moment and roll him off, but Amy swiftly swung the pistol and scratched his fleshy cheek.

Still sobbing, Amy managed, "You're both lucky men." Sprawled on the floor, the big man was very attentive because the small automatic was rigid on a spot between his eyes. The room suddenly smelled as if Briscoll had had an accident.

Amy kissed him. "David, I was so worried. This has been a dreadful time. I missed you so much." Turning her glance downward she continued, "And you, Mr. Big Shot Briscoll, I swear to God I would have shot you before giving up this weapon. I should shoot you now and have this mess completed. But I won't. Do you know why, Mr. Big Shot? Because they don't hang criminals in Grenada anymore. The prison is medieval and you'll spend the rest of your fat-ass life doing serious penance."

David kissed her this time. "I'm not so sure about that Amy. This monster had Mike Post strangled in front of us. Mike was a government schoolteacher. That, plus the Embassy could push for an example to be made since Mike was also still a U.S. citizen. Briscoll, I don't think your money will do you any good now." He fought the urge to punch him again.

"My turn," Feliza said from behind him. She wiped David's neck clean with the tail of the towel, to Amy's obvious frown of disapproval. His stateside friend moved away, but didn't lower the pistol until she saw that

Feliza had a bead on Briscoll. David's lovely island friend signaled him to get off the prostrate torso by inserting her free arm under his right arm. He assumed she wanted some payback, so he relinquished the position, sank into a chair, and hugged Amy.

Feliza knelt close to the big man's head, brandishing his Glock pistol. "Puleese tell me, baby," she mimicked, "where you going now? Paris? Buenos Aires? Bangkok? Huh, big spender, Mr. Money Man?" She slapped him hard. "So, I'm just a dumb island girl bred to be your female slave? So much courage that you shit yourself! You are nothing without those two hired animals." She laughed, put her lips close to his ear, and said something the others could not quite hear over our close breathing.

Feliza replaced her lips with the pistol barrel. David believed she was going to pull the trigger and reasoned with her against doing it. "He's not worth getting dirtier over, Feliza. We've been through a lot already. The authorities will take care of him."

"He's a pig, David. I say butcher the porker. He's going to tell the authorities about the shipwreck. Then all of our asses will be in the fire. Let me shoot him now. I'd really like to get this white boat all red with this fat man's blood. Where's the treasure you took from us, Briscoll? At least I can get that back!" She screamed and kicked him in the side. Feliza kicked him again before Briscoll gasped the location of the safe. It was in the same room, hidden behind a mirror, beside the television above the bar. David's head pained too badly to rise from the chair.

"Feliza, I'm Amy," She made the introductory effort now that her tears had subsided.

"So?" was the almost snarling reply. "If you want to do something, see if this bastard's telling the truth. Get the coins." Feliza was pumped up, completely opposite the shell of a woman David had found in the bedroom a short time ago. She was in control again. This is the trait he'd always liked.

Amy placed the Walther on David's lap before she proceeded behind the bar to punch in the combination after Briscoll pointed to the spring latch that held the mirror. The darker lady had to apply her pistol to the bald man who was now on all fours struggling to regain his anything-but-regal composure. He coughed out the numbers. The combination took three tries and his back took the same number of good punches. Finally, it opened. The safe was not small, maybe one cubic foot. David could see stacks of currency through his pain-blurred vision. Amy shuffled through its content, finally producing a thick, dark leather bag that made a familiar sound when the snaps were released. Briscoll's back sank lower when he heard the rattling of the coins.

"What else is in there, Amy?" Feliza asked quite cordially. The dark woman approached and kissed his cheek. "I'm sorry, David." She grabbed the unprotected pistol from his lap. Amy started to recount items, but then began to comprehend one gun was pointed at her and the other at David. He felt his sphincter muscle tighten.

"That's the way it has to be, boys and girls," Briscoll declared breathlessly as he wavered on unsteady feet. He kept coughing to clear his throat. From his rear pants pocket he retrieved a white handkerchief. First, he wiped his head before it became quickly splotched with red from his face. "Whew, that was exciting, wasn't it? Wasn't it?" The sarcastic remark was met with silence.

David first looked to a condoning Feliza and then to an appalled and frightened Amy. "What? How?" Was every bit of the vocabulary he had available in that instant.

"As ever, David Warner, the eloquent spokesman of such intellect." Briscoll stretched in a brisk, leisurely manner and proceeded to rearrange and tidy his clothes before approaching the open safe. He tended to his numerous aches and pains, punctuated with grimaces. Feliza kept a watchful eye on David, smiling as though they were flirting in a restaurant.

"Yes, David, you have a fine woman here," Briscoll pointed toward Amy, "quite worth her salt. And another lovely specimen a few shades darker, worth every bit of her hot pepper. Salt and pepper, Warner. Salt and pepper!" His voice rose to almost a shriek. He grabbed the leather pouch, pushed Amy out from behind the bar, and emptied the remaining contents of the safe into another suede bag. He coughed again and spat into his now saturated handkerchief. "Your salt lady has cost me a fortune. Her actions have completely undermined my business, killed my friends, and truly cost me the L'Attrapis, as I'll have to leave her. It's a bit too gaudy and princely to make an adequate escape to freedom. Yes, Amy, you luscious blonde bitch."

David rose until Feliza put the larger Glock against his bareback. Briscoll grabbed Amy by the arm, lifting her elbow to emphasize a point.

"Girlie, you should be shot for brutalizing my two best friends. They don't make men of such caliber any longer. Palmer was a creative sort, while Mullen was forced to be the brawn. I hope their end was swift and merciful. Was it?"

"No, not quite." Amy's stare toward Briscoll revealed no fear. "In fact, they may still be alive and suffering. The big one lost his right hand. Had it cleaved off, clean as a whistle. The short, mouthy one never got to stick a tranquilizer dart into anyone. I think I shot him four times. They were dumb, but I have to say, they weren't even in your league of stupidity, Briscoll. If I were you, I'd be plowing this barge with the engines wide open. Everyone knows about the L'Attrapis and will be expecting it at whatever port you choose. Now who's the intellect, baldy?!" Amy was irrationally shouting into his face.

To Feliza, who was holding both guns leveled in a true gangster pose, Amy said, "What did this leeching creature offer you to switch sides? Money? How much money is it worth to reside with human pestilence? Feliza, you have to realize, these three monsters have existed in similar violent circumstances years, maybe decades, before kidnapping you on Carriacou."

Feliza stood calmly, paying no attention to her white counterpart, and simply asked Briscoll if he had everything and was ready to go.

"Yes, and no, but shortly. You see, Warner, your cunt here fails to understand you were set up. Yes, yes, yes. Set up!" He paused, "Shall I tell them darling, or would you care to?"

"Let's just go, get in the Donzi and disappear. They don't need to know our business." With a wave of the Walther, Feliza feigned away the big man's advance to secure one of the pistols. She wasn't going to split her power and double her chances of getting shot.

"Not yet, darling," Briscoll drew out the last word. "Not until they hear our side of the story. Amy, I'm sure you find David handsome in some very wholesome, boy-next-door type bullshit. But he's not attractive or extroverted enough to have made the coincidental meeting and court the most beautiful woman ever born on this backward rock. David, you actually believe Ms. Dubois just came over to my side? Try again and reminisce to the beginning of your affair with Feliza of the woods. Bet you didn't know that's how Dubois translates in French. A beautiful woman swims to supposedly 'save' your very much not-in-danger boat, and suddenly you become the benefactor of romance, sex, and a working business partner. Warner, you are so naive. If a marksman could shoot your dive boat, why didn't he wait until it was occupied? But then again, Palmer and Mullen didn't even know about the private arrangement between Feliza and me. They followed orders and being ignorant of this situation, they couldn't divulge pertinent facts or complain. That's why they shot her with a tranquilizer at your house, idiot!"

Briscoll paused to cough again and survey the three faces. Madness was enveloping him. The depth of the present situation he'd always planned against was pushing him over the edge. "Amy, did you know your white knight in shining armor was living with this excellent specimen for weeks before you arrived?" He almost giggled, "You wouldn't suspect it from looking at them now, but I'm certain they indulged in carnal acts. Actually, he's a very gullible man when he is getting a certain appendage pleasured. He is also very stupid not to run — or, rather swim away when he had the chance. He feared this beautiful woman would suffer. In reality David, she was suffering through multiple orgasms every night. After you were locked in, so was I," he laughed.

Briscoll posed with his hands on his hips and continued his exposé, "In fact, if I may be so bold and forward, Feliza Dubois and myself also indulged in many carnal acts. But that was months before she returned to this island of her birth. You see, I hired this aspiring, bushy-haired, unemployed starlet one night on Sunset Boulevard to portray a role and she readily complied. Hollywood was just minutes away, but she could spend a lifetime waiting to make the proper connections. Then, this astounding female revealed she was from a Caribbean speck, which held more of my interest. She decided to join this subterfuge since it returned her home and paid extremely well." He laughed uproariously. "And as you can see, there is always a chance for rapid advancement. Hell, she started last year and already she's second in command. Not bad for a street walker."

"Enough! Let's go. If she did shoot your bodyguards, somebody official should be arriving by dawn," Feliza ordered. "I'm about tired of hearing you run me down. Chill out and grab the goodies or I'm going to leave your bald ass behind!"

"You wouldn't leave me behind. I'm your savior." Briscoll tried to curtsey, and stumbled. "I'm the man who took you off of the streets of Los Angeles, remember? But then again, you can take the whore from the streets, yet you can't take the streets from the whore. Isn't that right, David? You should know. Did you really imagine this almost feline creature learned all those talents at finishing school? No, not at all. She learned those sweet, passionate abilities when school was finished." He turned to bow at Feliza again as if he was drunk. "What are those two beautiful sisters you always talk about, doing? Are they as popular as you are, my lovely Ms. Dubois?"

"Listen to me, you fat, bald bastard! You helped me get out, but I swear, don't push me now, of all times. This is nonsense to stay here and chat," the West Indian woman spat the words.

"Well, my dear, sweet Feliza, give me the pistols and I'll remove the remnants of this mess before we disappear into the night."

Amy was still behind the bar and David could read that her mind was working on a possible escape attempt. She was watching the debate, waiting for the correct moment to take the advantage should it be given. His head pounded with every heartbeat. Feliza displayed a side so far unseen. His ego never suspected her to be anything but genuine.

"Give you a gun? Get real! You don't get a thing until I'm safely on dry land at another island as far away as possible from Grenada. You think me stupid, or what?"

Feliza knelt. "David, you are sweet and I really did care for you. But he's right; I truly love crispy Ben Franklins more than anybody or anything. Hey, we, you and me, worked for this loot. I get this, and you get the stuff you kept. Sounds fair to me." She kissed his cheek while rubbing the barrel of the Glock on his chest. "Remember, half of some is better than all of none."

"Wait a minute, you get this and he gets that? What do I get?" Briscoll stood at the bar, pouring a straight gulp of bourbon while holding the bag of coins.

"You get to live beyond this moment," Feliza said seriously and fired one shot into the mirror behind the bar. Amy ducked and Briscoll dropped his glass of liquor.

"Thomas, consider your options. I really don't need you to drive the speedboat, but I'll take you along for your plastic credit cards."

Briscoll muttered under his breath as he shuffled toward the double entry doors.

"Amy, I sincerely thank you for keeping a cool head and not shooting me to get at that fat bastard. Sorry how this all worked out, but hey, you get David, right?

"I don't understand," Amy replied. "That man has abused you. Let the authorities have him."

"That's easy for you to say, white, big city, American woman." Feliza was just beginning and dropped into the local accent. "I'se is just a po' island gurl. Dose au-thor-ities," she dragged it out, "will hang my tight little ass out to dry long wid 'im." Then back in stateside lingo, "And where will you and lover boy be? Not here, but back in the good-old USA. This little dark child's got nowhere to run to unless I run right now."

She followed Briscoll, but turned, "Yes, he did abuse me. He was one of the hundreds who have advantaged themselves upon me. I don't expect you to understand any of this, because you weren't only raised a thousand miles different from here, but thousands of dollars better. You never had to be abused to survive. Yes, Amy, when you are poor and dark skinned, all kinds of vermin try to suck you dry."

"Well, my jungle queen," Briscoll smiled and spoke near the entry of the room. He tried to retrieve the machine gun from where it had been dropped. "Then you must also be a breed of vermin, because you've been sucking me dry."

"Go on, Big Fella, go for it," she taunted and then smashed the window of the left door with a bullet. "Enough!" she shouted, "Not another word, Briscoll, or you'll be bleeding worse than you already are."

"Well, my sweet chocolate drop, I do believe it is to our ultimate benefit that these two be put out of their misery. As successful criminals impart, the dead can't testify. Puleese, let me shoot them, puleese," The bald man begged.

"No, and say nothing more about that." Feliza flashed David that 'hungry' smile and winked as she looped the Mac 10 over her shoulder. The beautiful woman waved and blew a kiss as she walked onto the diving platform. "Loosen the bow line while I start the Donzi."

CHAPTER NINETEEN

Night enveloped the unlikely, unlucky pair as they passed through the double doors to the rear deck. Feliza started the Donzi's twin engines as Briscoll loosened the lines. Whiteness emanating from the yacht's interior lights was in stark contrast to their dark deeds. Her improbable, slightly rumpled partner stood on the diving platform as if waiting for a taxi. Briscoll hulked, holding both lines while awaiting his next instructions, seemingly unconcerned with the haste necessary to complete a successful escape. At her signal, he jumped onto the speedboat, dropped the lines, and settled into the passenger seat much the same as a child obeying his mother.

Feliza was in her unrivaled glory, finally in control of her own fate. The automatic Glock spent another bullet to pierce the inflatable dinghy. She then stuffed the pistol safely between the seat cushion and her thigh. The small Walther pistol was held firm by the elastic of her skimpy, red shorts. Her comfort had been sacrificed for the security of sitting atop the bag containing the safe's contents. She pushed the throttle lever forward gradually until the deep-vee hull began to plane and cut the smooth nighttime surface of the sea.

This had been Feliza's playground and she could find the reef's entrance easily under the half-crescent moon. Her body swung slowly to the left, eyeing the man who had caused so much turmoil on that island. The village would never forget this night's events during her lifetime, but hopefully they would overlook her part. She was tempted to shoot Briscoll and toss his bleeding body to the sharks, but again decided it would be wiser to use his funds and the connections they could buy as long it was safely possible. When he became unnecessary, she'd feed him to the legal hounds. She could keep her tarnished soul clean of breaking the Sixth Commandment.

The big Yamaha outboards pushed the dark, unlit Donzi with relatively little noise at what the speedometer said was twenty-five. In response to a flick of a toggle lever, the trim tabs pushed the bow down and maybe gained a few more knots while creating a bigger rooster tail of spray behind the boat. To her rear, Feliza could see many of the homes of the village with lights gleaming at this late hour. She reached for Briscoll's arm and read his glowing watch dial, which showed the time to be after midnight. The fuel gauge pointed to full. That much gas could get them at least to St. Lucia, where the big international airport was isolated at the southern tip. With a few clothes bought in Vieux Fort, and the passports she now sat on, they could be anywhere in the world the following day. The usually slow Grenadian police would waste time checking within their own borders before notifying other islands of the problem.

With one hand Feliza pulled her hair free, and the breeze did the rest. This might be the last night of her curly locks, she thought. Soon, she'd have to change her appearance, maybe even shave her head. After the sale of the coins and jewelry, she could afford a wig in every style. For once she'd have enough money to be free. 'Buy her freedom like a slave girl,' she mused as her thoughts went to each sister and the interrogations they might face due to her actions. She'd have to get word to them and Aunt Bernadette that she was alive. This was the second and final time she would be forced to leave Carriacou in a lurch. The first time she'd left on the spur of the moment at midnight after a raucous party. It seemed like a good idea at the time to sail away with a German, but he dumped her when he got to Miami. The contests to win the attention of a man in Florida were more crowded than in Mt. Pleasant, Carriacou.

The girls of South Beach were so sophisticated and well-dressed, Feliza couldn't compete. Her talent at sex was the only raw material she could market. A small bikini clothed her and truthfully advertised her attributes. Her road through America had been walked first on the east coast resort beaches and then along the streets of California. As the insanity of her life increased, the first dreams of finding an adoring husband dissolved to the hope of obtaining movie roles. Men had passed with the years. The few good ones couldn't or wouldn't try to embrace her traits for survival. At twenty-eight, love now seemed impossible. David was probably the last man with a good heart she would encounter. No, she smiled to herself, she'd played him by the hard, not the heart. Still smiling, she nodded to herself, knowing there would be more.

From the north, two close-set piercing white lights rocketed towards the L'Attrapis. Feliza reasoned Richmond wouldn't be anxious to incriminate himself by calling the Coast Guard, so it must be a private boat checking on the blonde American woman. What a joke! Dear, sweet Amy arrives, and the island rolls over and begs to her commands. The Americans might make another invasion of Grenada while David rode off into the sunset with that blonde pampered bitch, but Feliza was certain he would always remember the incredibly exciting times he'd shared with this island girl.

The Donzi kept well beyond the range of those headlights, skimming to the east. She had fished this water with her father as a girl and reasoned the sea's night surface to the east, outside Petit Martinique, would be nearly as calm. Her pursuers would expect her to go west and seek the flat, placid lee behind the cays. The approaching boat wouldn't be able to hear anything over its own engine. The Donzi's only tell-tale reminder was sparkling phosphorescence lingering along its wake. She still had a quarter more throttle.

\\\\\\\\

Allister Hope guided his Formula to the portside of the L'Attrapis. He gunned the engines in reverse to close the gap using the half-sunk gray rubber dinghy as a fender. His older companion jumped to tie the lines. They both approached the open doorway to the boat's interior with caution. From the water below the diving platform, they heard a whistle. Bill and Clement bobbed out from under the fiberglass ledge.

"What you two doing swimmin' in the bay?" Wendell asked.

"We ain't swimmin', we'se escaping!" Bill reported, climbing the stainless ladder.

"Escaping what?" Hope asked.

"Dad, it was mean! I mean, they was mean!" Hope lent his son a hand to get up on the deck. "The bald man was going to shoot us, the women, everybody! You should have seen how he acted like he could just put a bullet in each of us while sipping a drink. I mean, he was like some kind of devil," the teenager rattled.

"Clement," Hope said sternly, "I asked you to stay with that blonde woman. Where is she now?"

"Dad, I think she's still inside. I know I should have stayed, but he was going to shoot. I know now I don't have it for no gunfight. Cheese on bread, it sure ain't like them movies on TV. That blonde woman, she must have been through all of this before." The young man talked so fast he was almost out of breath. "Like I say, she stood right there looking that bald man eye to eye. He hid behind that pretty woman who works at the Old Fort. We heard some shots, some other noises, and then someone just took off in their speedboat heading out of the reef. You must have passed them."

Already in the big, white meeting room, Wendell called, "It's okay. The Amy girl and Mr. SP are here. Jes' look a bit worse for wear."

Allister Hope entered, walking carefully to miss the blood and broken mirror scattered near the bar. David was cradled in a chair while Amy daubed his bloody head with some of the same vodka he was ingesting for pain relief. Amy was visibly exhausted and her hands were trembling.

"They just left in the small boat," Amy said, exhaling a deep sigh.

"We'd never find them tonight. Anyway, that's a job for the police. I think we should leave them well enough alone and thank our blessings our side had no fatalities," the gray-haired West Indian captain reasoned grimly.

"The school teacher, they suffocated Mike Post, the pony-tailed school teacher from Dover this afternoon. He's dead! Gone," David gulped out. It was very difficult to face the fact Mike had been dropped into the sea somewhere that night. He could only see Briscoll's round face grinning in delight at having both the girl and the money. "Let's go after them. By morning they'll be almost impossible to find."

"Tonight we would be chasing them blindly. Too tough to locate," Hope replied as he removed his ball cap, wiped his forehead, and settled into one of the chairs at the table.

"I think we can find them easily on radar. Can't be very many boats moving at high speeds at this hour of the night," Amy reasoned.

"Sorry, honey, my Formula didn't come equipped with radar. Don't tend to operate much at night. Even with one of those fancy stainless arches that gets in the way of everything, the boat's too close to the water for radar to be much good," Allister surmised.

"Well, I wasn't counting on yours. I was counting on this luxury yacht having the best radar money could buy," was Amy's retort, as they all suddenly caught the same idea. David led the way as they moved to the steering station.

Pain was roaring through David's head after he climbed the one flight to the pilot house. Three well-padded chairs were evenly spaced on pedestals behind an instrument console. Overhead hung a series of four video screens. One blue-backed screen labeled the anchored position while another indicated what they wanted. The radar's circular sweeping motion had a range of thirty miles and showed a small craft just to the southeast, almost rounding the closest island, Petit Martinique.

"How far are they?" Hope questioned.

"If I'm reading these distance rings correctly, they're about four miles away, headed to windward," David said as he ripped the towel that had been his turban bandage into a single headband. "How much horsepower do you have?"

"About five hundred, maybe a bit more. I don't know, I can really stretch her out," Hope answered. "But, Hell's Bells, they could change course at any time and we'd be chasing our own tail out there."

Amy reached for the VHF radio microphone that dangled next to the center seat.

"Not if someone stays here and radios you position and course changes. Mr. Hope, you should be able to catch up to those outboards in a few miles," she pleaded.

Without any further questions, Allister Hope agreed only because he thought Amy would stay aboard the motoryacht and give directions far from harm's way. As they headed to the rear deck, she successfully argued her place aboard the Formula, transferring the navigating duties to the duo of Bill and Wendell. Wishing to shut her up, the gray-haired man resolved she would stay below in the bow once they encountered Briscoll and Feliza. Clement grabbed the shotgun off the floor, and brought it along even though he realized it was empty of shells.

The Formula's diesels were still running. After a quick radio check with Bill on the L'Attrapis, they entered the race. Amy worked the radio while David sat in the bucket seat trying to convince himself his head no longer hurt. The power of positive thinking lasted until they hit the first small wave. He pulled the towel headband bandage tighter and wished for a bottle of aspirins and some strong liquor to wash them down.

As the Formula raced to full speed, David yelled at Mr. Hope, "Maybe we ought to be running without lights?"

"No way. I want them to see us coming. I think that small boat has twin one-fifties, which I can catch easily. My tankage is two-hundred gallons with a range to Martinique if need be. We have to catch them before they get close to the smaller St. Vincent Islands north of here. Clement, boy, you keep a sharp lookout for fish trap buoys. One of those trap lines catches in a prop, and they'll be all the way to Havana before we get up and running again," the father ordered. Allister, Clement, and Amy stood peering into the night.

It only took seconds for the Formula to pass the reef. Instead of going east in the chase, Hope swung the wheel to the left and they headed north. The Grenadines were his waters and every few minutes he would turn, looking at the islands' silhouettes to mark navigation between rocks, sand bars, and reefs. The cockpit was more than twenty feet from the slender-pointed bow. Surrounded by a sturdy windscreen, the passengers were never wet by spray. David guessed they were doing about sixty. He'd often viewed speedboats and seen a couple of race matches, but this was his personal first going an exceptional speed on the water at night. He shuddered, but realized they couldn't have a better skipper. God would have to help them, though, if they were to avoid hitting something like a floating log. The halogen bow lights barely illuminated what they were just about to pass.

According to their trackers back on the motor yacht, the Donzi was making a wide arc around the east side of Petit Martinique: a path much rougher than what they had to contend with at present. To close on Briscoll and Feliza, they'd have to race to the north end of World's End Reef and then cut eastward. A long boat like the Formula could roll and run with the waves coming from the northeast hitting its beam, while a smaller boat would be very uncomfortable, especially at high speeds. The Donzi couldn't turn west until the reef ended, as it formed a barrier to the north from the small, one-town-island of Petit Martinique. If they decided to head south, they could make Grenada. That would be an improbable route as the immigration personnel at the one-and-only airport would be on the lookout for a mixed couple. David chuckled to himself at the thought of describing them as a 'mixed couple'. Feliza and Briscoll couldn't possibly be more different in every way except for their love of wealth.

The half-moon was falling in the western sky as the good guys passed Palm Island's small silhouette on their port side. These waters were dangerous, filled with jagged, half-submerged rocks, but Allister Hope never reduced his speed. He stood stalwartly grasping the stainless steering wheel as the moment gripped him. By the reflection of the dashboard lights, David could see Hope's face. It may have been the force of the wind, or just basic good conscience, but it definitely wasn't fear that shaped his mouth into a tooth-grinding snarl. His son wore the same grimace.

Amy held the radio in one hand and gripped David's thigh with the other, locking herself into position. Every few minutes she would carefully turn to check if he was still conscious. His right hand had drifted down to her fit behind and relaxed in her pants rear pocket. An occasional, gentle squeeze let her know he was feeling fine and getting better. She met his first signal with a quizzical smile. In the not-far, distant future, he knew he'd be doing some serious explaining.

World's End Reef is just east of the Tobago Keys where thousands of cruising yachts have dropped anchor to experience pure, middle-of-nowhere solitude. David shut his eyes, concentrating on a scene of sailing Summer Breeze through the Grenadines. What they'd just covered in ten minutes could take hours under sail. He felt the boat bank in a right turn and grabbed Amy around the waist for a brace as he craned his neck, staring forward. Ahead, a cluster of sailboat mast lights hardly swayed in the calm protection of the semi-circular reef.

The sound of the inboard diesels changed from a roar to a higher whine as the skipper pushed the throttles another half-inch forward. Hope had kicked in the turbo chargers now that they were moving outside the area of reefs. Their ride got bumpier as they moved headlong into the oncoming seas. The bow lights showed a few white-capped wave tops.

Amy held the radio to her ear and then pulled from David's grip to get closer to the captain. "Hope," she shouted, "Bill has both boats on the screen and suggests we should point a few degrees south. They are just off the north point of Petit Martinique heading due north."

To David's amazement, Hope slowed the boat and cut the lights. After coasting a hundred or so yards, they sat rocking back and forth. "We'll sit and wait for them. They have to come by here. They'll meet a bad end if they try to cut west too soon." He stooped into the forward cabin and returned with a big, orange, plastic box and a large, chrome hand-held spotlight that plugged into the dashboard cigarette lighter. "Make yourself useful. I know it works, so don't try it until I say." He handed the spotlight to David. "This is what airplanes use in the dark to see the landing strip. Amy, when they loop back into our path, I want you below. No discussion. Even there won't be too safe if they can shoot straight. SP, I don't need to tell you to turn that big light off if they start shooting."

Clement took the orange box and moved to the stern. It was an official, metal, pistol flare gun that could shoot one phosphorous shell. "Boy, don't use that unless we is in really close. This isn't about using a flare for seeing them; this is about hitting that boat with a firebomb. These flares are supposed to be so hot they'll burn through fiberglass. You got three chances, so put the other two shells in your pockets." The elder West Indian kissed his own hand and patted the cowling of his boat. "I love you baby. Try not to catch any of those lead pellets that might be flying. That goes for me and you three. Stay down and Amy, you stay out of sight. Let's pray they aren't expecting anyone."

The radio cracked again with Bill providing an update. "They're close, maybe a half mile south," Amy reported and everyone went silent as those words directed their attention. David's black, plastic wristwatch had 1:16 on its face. It didn't quite click to 'twenty' before the chase continued.

Hope pushed the Formula gently into gear and then shoved the throttles forward. His night vision on the sea was good. It took another half minute for David to see the glow of the spray rising at the stern of Briscoll's boat. It was about four-hundred yards away. They closed that distance quickly. The Formula was headed south and then arced north. This maneuver permitted the smaller boat to take the lead.

"They'll be pretty comfortable by now, thinking they've left their payback, way back. No need for them to watch to their stern and they certainly won't be listening. SP, turn on that light when I tell you. Clement, duck down and keep your head below the gunwales. Amy, get below," Hope directed. David was surprised when she gave no argument. Hope demanded a bit more power, and it came in a surge that made David sink deep into the padded seat.

The Formula moved to draft into the smaller boat's wake. Seconds later, the skipper nudged David's arm and he switched on the spotlight. The nightscape transformed instantaneously under the light's brilliant beam. Feliza emerged into sight. She stood behind the helm, with her hair billowing like a black, bubble helmet above a bright-orange life jacket. Startled, she jumped momentarily losing control as she recognized her pursuers. The Donzi veered to the right. Briscoll's bald head turned and he raised a hand to shield his eyes from the search light. David could make out exaggerated movements with that same arm after Briscoll realized justice might be closer than he had expected.

It was a dangerous maneuver for Feliza to hold the wheel as she twisted to fire the Glock. Two orange flames spurted from the pistol in her right hand. Even though the shots weren't close, David cut the spotlight.

The skipper yelled, "Keep that light on them boy, until I say otherwise. Don't worry, that girl couldn't hit a house while rocketing along in that boat."

Again, the beam of light revealed Feliza trying to shoot, but the empty Glock was tossed. She crouched low as the small speedboat snaked to the left, using the following sea for a push. That turn also helped the pursuers. Finally, the Formula started to pull up to within twenty feet along the Donzi's port side. Feliza made a deft, dangerous attempt to turn into them as David blinded her vision with the spotlight.

The captain shouted to his son, "Clement, shoot! Try to hit the side of that boat!"

The flare erupted in a white blur that just passed above the topsides of the fleeting craft. Clement stumbled backward from the concussion of the shot, but quickly cracked the pistol open to reload. Briscoll was screaming something unintelligible at Feliza, whose lithe body was rigidly facing forward. David saw her reach for the machine gun and hand it to her fat, bald partner. Allister Hope watched every movement in the opposing boat and instead of darting the Formula away, he swung the wheel to starboard and closed the distance.

Clement responded to his father's next command with a blazing second shot that hit the near side of the Donzi and exploded a white-hot hole about a half foot in diameter amidships. That flare, coupled with their encroaching wake, threw Briscoll backwards, and the Mac 10's first burst traced straight upwards to the starry night sky.

"Kill that light. Let them cool for a moment," the skipper said evenly as if he'd just been out on a charter rather than being shot at by a murderer.

"Clement boy, grab those fender lines from the compartment. After you reload, trade the gun to SP for the light. I want you to hang on tight and blind them. Be careful; if you haven't yet gathered, this ain't play. I don't want to have to explain to Mommy why there's an empty seat at the dinner table. I'm going to pull up and cross in front of them. That fat boy won't be able to shoot over their own windscreen." He pointed to David, "Use all that Navy training and put our last shot through their glass close as you can to that driver. I'll make a big wake, and Clement, you listening boy? 'Cause this is real important."

"Of course," Clement said between heavy breaths.

"You drop our two sets of fenders right in front of them and we'll hope that Neptune and Jehovah shake hands and tangle those outboard props. We don't have far to travel before we're back at the Tobago Keys." The khaki-sleeved arm pushed the throttles to full power. "OK, here we go!"

The Formula rocketed back to port, shrinking the gap between boats in seconds. At first, it looked like they were going to collide, but Hope kicked up another wave that shook the Donzi. He pulled the big boat hard to port and ran so close he could see beads of sweat on Briscoll's face in the spotlight. Briscoll tried to shoot, but his unsure footing, combined with the recoil of the machine gun, made accuracy impossible. Fast, very fast, the Formula pulled ahead. The excitement had erased David's headache, and he leveled his arm against the windshield strut, waiting for the perfect shot. Clement kept the light trained as they got about a hundred feet ahead.

Hope steered hard to the left, and then quickly back to the right — running so close it seemed like the boats would collide. David saw Feliza grinning as he heard Hope order, "Shoot, SP, shoot! Clement throw!" David fired to see the trail of the flare skip once across the top of the Donzi's bow and slam into the windscreen glass, exploding into white light just inches away from a vacant steering wheel.

The small, white boat, still in the spotlight, launched to the left after hitting the wake, and perhaps the series of connected floats. Hope cut their speed. They watched the Donzi go out of control, spiraling into an arc about twenty feet above the water. Briscoll's arms fluttered. He was thrown over the side as the pilotless boat righted itself before slamming to the water sideways. Feliza was nowhere to be seen. The L'Attrapis' tender had its wheel cocked to port. The still running Yamaha outboards caused the boat to swerve into a tight, erratic circle. Briscoll might have still been alive when the bow hit him. Everyone swallowed hard at the vision of punishment the sea had paid to this villain.

The Formula rumbled at idle as Amy crawled from the forward hatch. "Over?" she asked.

"Mostly," The skipper answered as David watched the waters and hoped for a survivor. Clement crept to the bow and prepared to jump to the other boat while David scanned the light over the again tranquil surface. But then the smoldering Donzi straightened its course. The trio exchanged a look of amazement when a tuft of black hair rose behind the steering wheel. The pursuers had no more weapons, and all of their tactics had been viewed.

Hope shook his head as he pressed to follow. "That girl is amazing. She knows she's on the losing end of a finished game, but she ain't about to give in or up. Damn though, she ought to know better being out here. The reef is up ahead. I'm going to force her once and for all. This is cutting into my sleep time. Tomorrow is going to be a long day of questions and yawning answers."

"Be careful; she might still have my pistol," David warned. Feliza never once turned toward her pursuers. The nose of the Formula came within a meter of the target's ragged stern quarter. She had her boat flat out, but there was no way she could pull away. It was a hopeless attempt to extend her freedom. A green light amid the Formula's gauges flashed a depth alarm and Hope turned his Formula sharply as the Donzi sped directly into World's End Reef. David watched a slender, brown body dive away before the protruding coral ledge shredded the boat's bottom.

According to his digital, this misadventure had taken only twenty-five minutes and claimed two lives. David shuddered and pulled Amy close. It was a shame to see such a beautiful woman as Feliza consumed in such a pointless accident.

There wouldn't be much worth salvaging from the Donzi. The force of the collision had ripped off the transom with the motors. It wouldn't sink as it was wedged high and dry about thirty feet from the outside of the reef. Feliza's body would stay close.

Hope shielded his watering eyes as he crossed himself. He edged his boat in close. While David turned the spotlight across the wreckage, Clement crawled over the reef to inspect inside the boat. He'd been given instructions to search for a brown, leather bag and the woman that was carrying it.

"Must have been thrown clear," Clement yelled after he'd checked a few places.

David mused to himself that the sea had reclaimed the treasure of the Century. They slowly reversed from the wreckage on the reef to search for any of Briscoll's floating remains. David stood on the seat and cautiously moved the beam of light, trying not to miss anything that might need a decent burial. The Formula turned and started to chug slowly retracing its path to the east, when he saw something white on the dark surface. It was two of the white vinyl-inflated fenders that Clement had thrown.

David's heart jumped when he realized the orange of Feliza's life jacket was wrapped in the line. She was motionless. The floatation vest held her face above the surface. Amy held the light as Clement dove in and swam her close enough for Hope and David to pull her into the boat. With four pairs of attentive hands, the island woman was laid comfortably on the rear carpet. Amy screamed for all of them when she discovered a pulse. David suffered the dark irony in his attempt to revive Feliza; kissing life back into a woman who had admittedly used him — and doing so in front of a woman who had risked her life to save him. Plenty of forced breaths finally caused Feliza to vomit seawater.

David was becoming optimistic.

The dark woman still had her share of the gold strapped around her narrow waist. Using Navy field techniques, Amy found no broken bones or obvious injuries. One of the boat's beach towels made a good blanket, which Amy used in an attempt to make Feliza comfortable on the return trip.

They found Briscoll's body and lashed it on top of the Formula's stern platform. It would take a lot to explain away this night.

Bill and Wendell spent a comfortable night in the air-conditioned pilothouse of the L'Attrapis. They were happy to stay on board the motoryacht and not have to deal with enlightening the authorities who would be crawling around in search of evidence and information on the three foreign criminals.

Only three, because Mr. Hope took David aside after they had put Feliza to bed in the ruins of his cottage. It was three in the morning and only pure necessity was keeping them awake.

"You know SP," Mr. Hope said when they were out on the small porch, "seems like everyone took a beating tonight. You got a split head, two or three are chatting unsuccessfully with St. Peter as we speak, and that girl from Mt. Pleasant is going to awaken to a Hell storm. I think there's more to your kidnapping than I'll ever know, 'cause I don't want to know. That's your business and none of mine. But, is that girl in there going to pay?"

"What do you mean?" David asked.

"Well," He paused to yawn, "I thought that you and she were kidnapped together, but she escaped in the Donzi with the big fellow."

"Oh," David began to understand the conclusion. "Yeah, well that bald guy had us both and took her with him. That's how it was."

Hope took his cap off and ran his fingers through his short, gray hair. "SP, you've been on Carriacou for a while and can see that everyone is just about getting by. Oh sure, there's some, like me, luckier than the rest, but most people here are living very basic lives. That girl in there is one of us. She may have been away, doing 'whatever'…" he emphasized the 'whatever,' "but she's still a local girl and I would personally hate to see that beautiful young thing grow old in St. George's prison. Did she harm anyone?"

"No," David rubbed his nose to see if it was growing longer. "No, she really didn't harm anyone. The story is exactly what I said. Briscoll took her as a last hostage, but there's one more thing, Mr. Hope, you don't know. Richmond, the immigration agent, was in with them. He shot the teacher in plain view and was going to kill us. I could say more, but who am I going to say it to? Know what I mean? If he's the one that leads the investigation…"

The island gentleman cut him off. "Not to worry. After she called her father, I used Amy's fancy phone to call my family in Grenada. Now none of us have to worry about Carriacou's finest causing problems for anyone other than himself. By first light, there should be a contingent of the Coast Guard and every other bunch that wants to get in on the most exciting time since Reagan sent in the Marines. That boy Richmond always looked too good. I figured he must either be already getting gifts or waiting for the right time to collect them. Either way, his time is up. Guess that's why we haven't seen him."

Again, David looked at his watch and said some sort of good night. Hope turned to go to his truck, which carried Briscoll's body. Clement, his sleeping son, was slumped behind the wheel. "The word from the clinic is those other two died. So, it is just our story and," his arms swept around David's small cottage, "this mess to prove you was attacked. Just our story..."

"Okay, Mr. Hope. I got it." David returned inside as he pulled away. Amy had shaken the plaster chips from the couch cushions, and was curled in a sound ball of sleep. The other female was sleeping peacefully in the center of David's bed. They'd take her to the clinic when she awoke. He hoped the next morning would come very late — and said a prayer of thanks it was coming at all. He passed out as soon as he laid his still-aching head on the kitchen table.

\\\\\\\\\

Uniforms with guns filled the next morning. Admiral Whistlow had built a late-night fire under the embassy, and forced the local American Foreign Service personnel to either cheerfully accompany the Grenada police to Eastern, or be transferred to Mongolia. The Grenadian Coast Guard provided transport and set up a blockade around the bay. Briscoll's crewless yacht couldn't leave. Mr. Shremshock, the Chargé d'Affaires, had probably begun daubing sweat hours before landing on the beach at eight in the morning, with a Lt. Commander Nichols of the Grenada National Guard in tow.

Shremshock waddled onto David's porch with a friendly hand extended, but the other hand put a finger across his lips to mean 'silence'. "Good to see you again, David." He spoke with a rolling-eye familiarity. "Sorry, it is under these circumstances. We got a call from Washington early this morning and I responded directly because of its serious nature." His voice emphasized 'Washington,' 'directly,' and 'serious'. David imagined it was all for the benefit of the Grenadian in the pressed green uniform who had followed him through the door.

The dusty street between the beach and cottage was filled with people milling around. As David gave his statement, Amy and Feliza showered to make a graceful entrance. They told the same story, with a consoling Shremshock repeatedly mentioning Amy was the daughter of a U.S. Navy admiral. Feliza played on the Lt. Commander like an orphaned niece tearfully telling her uncle of a bad date. Every important head was nodding in agreement and seemed genuinely convinced. Both of Briscoll's men had taken the elevator to Hell and eliminated any other perspectives. Feliza and David implicated Officer Richmond in Mike's murder. Lionel Richmond had vanished from Carriacou — apparently heading for a safer place to spend the bald man's bribe money. Too much bad publicity would evolve from a soured government official for Grenada to search for him. If they happened to find him, he'd plead guilty at a quiet trial.

Prim and proper Allister Hope and Bill Steward stood behind the account and filled in any remaining doubts. By noon, everyone who had investigated, participated, or lived in Eastern were all smiles, sipping cold beers bought by the American Embassy. The now famous, successful gunfight by Old Bill and the young American blonde woman against the professional, hired killers was a celebrated holiday. It was time for a rest.

The Coasties wouldn't have to leave home to chase someone, risking a sea battle. Instead, they scoured the reef and shoreline unsuccessfully for Mike's body. The police could return to relaxing under a fan at headquarters after demolishing an international kidnapping, smuggling, and white slavery ring. They had done it without the assistance of the FBI or Scotland Yard. The courts wouldn't be tied up with an expensive trial and no bad publicity would hit Grenada. In fact, Shremshock intimated that the Grenada Coast Guard was the grateful recipient of two small, but very fast, drug interdiction boats coupled with ten thousand gallons of fuel. So, it was, as they say, a win-win solution.

Photographers captured and catalogued the damage within David's cottage and then the entourage moved to the L'Attrapis. The girls and David feigned trauma and didn't submit for photographs.

Bill, with Allister and Clement Hope, became celebrities, filling the pages of the local newspapers. Briscoll and his boat became notorious. His body was the only one claimed and shipped to St. Petersburg, Florida. Probably after several political gatherings, his motoryacht would be auctioned for a high bid if the Prime Minister couldn't discover worthwhile reasons to deem it a governmental necessity. Probably the U.S. Chargé would also get some use out of the boat.

The three Asians from the L'Attrapis swam ashore, but found nowhere to hide. The boys had entered legally and only faced deportation. They stated no connection existed between them and the misdeeds of the others. Again, an evil white man had taken advantage of both yellow and brown third-world people. The only English speaker, Conrad, acknowledged and detailed their story. The three were quickly permitted to stay on in the Caribbean at a reasonable salary as the yacht's maintenance crew rather than return to the slums of Manila.

A few of the authorities lingered before boarding the second Coast Guard cutter back to the relative fast lane of Grenada. The local clinic spared a doctor and nurse to give the battered three from the beach cottage a complete check and suture the gash in David's head. His headache finally waned.

After the story had been told, what seemed to be thirty or more times, David and the two women followed the shade to a completed Summer Breeze. It was his first chance to study Bill's accomplishment and the tool for his next escape. Everything looked perfect from the white bottom to the varnished mast. David was feeling the three cold beers that had almost quenched his thirst and his belly was full of the food the villagers had brought.

Exhausted, both physically and mentally, the three sat in a group not destined to become a 'ménage'. Amy burped and leaned against his right shoulder while Feliza quietly relaxed against the ballast stones they had raised. David joked and laughed that with the perfect publicist, these two girls could become famous as the 'Salt and Pepper Crime Fighters'. Feliza was in a mood and didn't think anything was funny. Amy was in a trance.

Word had been sent to the Old Fort that Bernadette's favorite niece was safe and sound. Another night of recuperation was in order. Six eyes were closing as the sun once again caressed the peak of Top Hill. David met the most comfortable bed he could've imagined with a folded blanket on his clean-swept living room's wood floor. Almost comatose, he slept the sleep of the near dead. Amy had the couch berth and Feliza sprawled unconscious across the bed.

Something clattered to the floor and forced David's dismal return from dreamland. He jumped up, once again unsure of his surroundings. He heard more bouncing and knocking before he walked over, stunned to see Amy and Feliza wrestling in the shambles of the bedroom. The wall digital warned it was just the beginning of morning. Dull, gray darkness outlined the white window frames with the sunrise's faint glow.

Amy and Feliza were both poised to strike again when David grabbed their attention by shouting, "Whoa!" Neither moved except to take deep breaths. "What's up? Feliza, you look much better than I would have expected. I thought you'd have slept for at least a day."

"I would have, David, if you and your bitch hadn't hid my belly bag," Feliza screamed.

"I was just trying to keep us all from going to prison, you dumb ass. You whale on me after I saved your fucking life," Amy was enraged. "We should have left your ass floating for fish food, you ungrateful, evil bitch."

It was the last 'bitch' that put them back into the fracas. Feliza had the upper hand until a flip, a shoulder roll, and a throw dislodged her. Finally, Amy had the darker woman on her stomach with both arms pinned behind her back.

"David, tell your white cunt to let me go," the dark woman cried. "Jesus Christ, you are breaking my arms. Stop! That hurts!"

"Listen, and understand," Amy put her face close to the other woman's cheek. "You would be dead. And the way I look at things after your little confession, you should be. But I have nothing against you. David is the one that you hurt the most."

"You listen, white bitch. I could have wasted you, or given the gun to Briscoll and been on my way to Timbuktu leaving you to make large, red puddles. Now, you're stealing my gold and I'm headed for…." Feliza started to sob in a new tune. "I know you saved me. Do you realize how hard it is to thank people who know you were against them? David, can you ever forgive me?"

Amy twisted Feliza's still-confined arms until Feliza straightened. "Forget that, 'can you forgive me', bullshit, you heartless, greedy bitch. You were headed out of here first chance you got to escape. Now, don't go devout on me. David might be moved, but we both know exactly what part of him would be moved. Don't we? Now, tell me how sorry you are."

Feliza spit. "Fuck you! You two are made for each other. You know that? Made for each other! David's so naïve and you are so foolish. Like I give a royal damn what you do, or how you feel about me. Go to Hell white girl. Go straight to Hell! I might not be in line for a Sister Mary Teresa medal, but at least I'm only trying to get by as best I can through this miserable life."

Amy released her and pushed the dark woman's face forward onto the bed. Feliza never stopped talking, "This is something. I finally get a real break and now I'm going to probably be shafted out of my rightful share. You and lover boy here are headed for fame and fortune. Maybe someday you'll understand what it's like to be born to a place like this. They say Carriacou means 'island of reefs', but I think it means 'dead end'. You white people come here because it is so simple. You bring air conditioning, hot water, TV, stereo, and transport to make yourselves comfortable. It wasn't here before you. Why? Well, that's because we can't afford to live any other way. Look around, see a McDonalds anywhere? Then look at Mustique filled with rock stars, and where am I born? The most backward place in the Caribbean, Carry-fucking-coo. You vacation, lie on the beach reading your beauty magazines on how to have a better orgasm while we eat cornmeal or rice. Then you go home, but we are stuck never getting what we dream," Feliza moaned.

"Not my fault. Could chock it up to 'God's good grace,' but you have neither goodness nor grace — and you don't know God," Amy managed to get that out before Feliza sprang at her again. This time, the local girl took a few good punches, but landed a good kick of her own. David would have tried to end the brawl, but he couldn't get between them. He positioned himself and pulled each by the hair to separate them — but only succeeded in getting multiple well-deserved slaps across his face from each combatant.

"Stop it! Now!" David shouted as each woman continued to twist and flail her arms. "Now! This is crazy. I haven't had a good, sound sleep in weeks, always wondering if Mutt and Jeff were going to kill us. Finally, I get back home and have my sleep delayed by a catfight. Now, stop it! Feliza, no one is going to rob you of anything. Personally, I thought the split you offered on the boat was fair." He released both the blonde and black locks.

"Settle down!" He managed to utter before a huge yawn conquered his face as he walked to the closet. After a slight jostle, he retrieved the heavy brown suede belly bag and threw it on the bed beside Feliza. "Take it. It's yours. You earned it."

"What's that supposed to mean, I earned it?" Feliza grumbled.

"Well," David hastily fought to say the correct thing so as not to offend or throw them back into a clawing battle. "Well, you really found the wreck and dove it up. Feliza, you risked as much, if not more, than I did. Go on, take it, but be careful selling it. This gold could still make trouble for you. If you peddle it properly and invest conservatively, this could last you the rest of your life. We know there are still a lot of artifacts along with the bronze cannon hidden in the smuggling compartments of the L'Attrapis. Once 'the powers that be' discover it, there may be more questions."

"Who the Hell are you, Merrill Lynch?" Feliza snatched the bag from his hand. She cocked her hip and snarled, "You talking I should peddle this? Nah, I done wit 'dat!"

Amy stood with her back against the corner as if waiting for the referee to signal the next round. The dark girl unzipped the belly pouch and dumped the contents on the ruffled bed. Coins, rings, chains, and jewelry spilled noisily into a small pile. She looked up at David and Amy with gleaming eyes. "What about the rest, the dagger?"

"Wait a minute," Amy started.

"Bitch, you've got no part in this," Feliza cut across. "This is mine and David's."

"I was hoping I'd get something out of this mess besides a reputation and a story to tell," David remarked.

The island woman continually ran her fingers through her hair as she counted and stacked the silver and gold coins. She laid out the jewelry in the manner of a fashion store display. Then, she dangled the emerald ring on the gold chain and coaxed herself into a trance as she watched it swing back and forth.

"Look," Feliza spoke with her back to David and Amy. "I'm in debt to both of you for not only saving my life — but for not turning me over to the police." A slight, barely audible whimper shook her bare shoulders. "I know I played you along in the beginning, David. In California, Briscoll told me he was coming to the Caribbean with a chance for me to make breakaway money. He gave me five thousand up front and promised a thousand a week, plus a share in something he knew was here. I could return home being the little island girl who everybody would remember, 'returned home successful,' even after her daddy drown. Do you know what that felt like? Coming home with some money?"

"I'm not lily white, but I'm not a thief," Feliza hesitated, "or a killer. He paid me to be his private ear on this rock until his boat got here. He sent those two morons to get information from Bill Steward, but instead set his competition in motion. When I heard Bill had taken a beating, I should have split then, but it was only a beating." Her head slumped forward. "Only a beating. But I should have known if they were playing that way in the beginning, what to expect at the end. I played you in the beginning, but David, I really did fall in love with you. It was my type of love, though, for a man who wasn't my type. You are way too good for me."

The dark woman still hadn't turned to face them. She lifted the stack of gold coins and dropped them, listening to them plink back into a pile. "Any-way," she lifted the necklace from the bed and turned, "As you say, I'm not good and don't know God, but I know when I've been cut a break, a huge break. I try to pay my debts." She rose and stood facing Amy. Her soft brown eyes welled with the tears that slowly overflowed down her cheeks. David almost thought the fray was going to start over, but she slowly raised the gold necklace with the ring as a pendant and draped it over Amy's head. The tears came faster.

"I know my life's not worth much," Feliza choked, "but I hope this can slightly repay your kindness. It's a kindness I've never felt before, during this life." Now both women were crying, and then collapsed into a clutching embrace. "Take better care of this guy than I did," Feliza directed at Amy, who was staring at David. "Tomorrow, I'm headed back to Point Pleasant and my aunt. By the end of the week," she wiped her eyes, smiled, and dropped into the local jargon, "dis guryl is gonna be dancin' someplace else." She did a little twirl, threw her arms around David, and smothered him with a solid smooch.

"David," Feliza whispered, "I still love you — and you'll always be my dream guy." She kissed him again and whispered, "The sex was great." His left ear lobe got a bite signaling that everything was finished.

CHAPTER TWENTY

Weeks passed, but the village of Eastern never returned to its previous, peaceful tranquility. The small community was busy making business. Tourists vacationing on the big island of Grenada now visited the small Carriacou fishing community to view the scene of the famous gun battle. T-shirts had been printed with caricatures depicting two local, older, gray-haired West Indian men brandishing machine guns above the statement 'Eastern Keeps Its Own Peace'.

The Main Street Disco had concocted a commemorative drink composed of vodka, tamarind juice, and bitters, called Blood on the Sand. A Hillsboro computer entrepreneur had issued post-cards and posters from copies of the police photographs of that morning's grizzly scene. He had also published a booklet with information on the past and present history of the Century.

The shipwreck's salvage contract was awarded by bid to a Canadian company. An archaeologist from Texas A&M directed the operation, but little of value, other than historical significance, was found. The supposed seven boxes of gold remained lost.

The artifacts that had been concealed on Briscoll's yacht were displayed at the small corner museum in Hillsboro. The few valuable items were exhibited one afternoon a week at the vault of the National Investment Bank. That same institution was successfully merchandising one-year discovery shares in the Century's salvage company. The bronze cannon was resurrected to boom the start of the First Annual Century Yacht Race.

Boat charters for fishing and diving were more frequent. Allister Hope was the Grenadian government's overseer of the recovery of the wreck while Clement Hope had made a good business taking tourists diving near the wreck site. A new thirty-eight-foot Bertram sport fisher had been added to their marine stable. Residents spoke of little else since that fateful evening. It was some time before conversation topics concerning the drought, elections, and cricket matches regained prominence over the murders. The story played and replayed across Caribbean radio and television talk shows,

— always keeping the American villains in the forefront.

As tales of the wreck's supposed treasure unfolded and white slavery at the hands of mercenary assassins intensified, representatives of various international publications motored along the small island's dusty roads. They interviewed and quoted everyone: from teachers who eulogized Mike Post's efforts, to the replacement immigration officer who claimed he didn't know anything about his predecessor.

Now famous as 'Wild Bill,' Bill Steward remained silent, took a break from boat building, and stayed close to his home at Top Hill. A little bit of celebrity went a long way, as he received letters and phone calls from relatives and friends who had left the little island years before. It had become difficult for the bearded man to enjoy a quiet evening sipping Jack Iron rum while playing dominoes at his favorite shop, without being pressured to rehash the account. However, Wendell took up Bill's slack and only required the purchase of a drink to relate his and everyone else's part.

The enhanced reputation of the Old Fort Restaurant and the town of Mt. Pleasant also attracted more travelers who wanted to absorb some real-life Caribbean romance. Bernadette curiously had enough money to hire another waitress and a cook so she could manage and converse with customers while she reclined, well-dressed, in a large, comfortable easy chair. Her mysterious but notable niece, Feliza, had vanished — supposedly to pursue a film or modeling career.

The U.S. Naval Communications Division donated ten modern, slightly-used computer systems to the Eastern School. The new study department was created and named in honor of Mike Post.

Rochelle matured quickly after the events of Mike's death were publicized. Amy became her champion and mentored the young West Indian girl to the possibility of a future education and career in the United States Navy. The owner of the island's heavy machinery company donated the services of a crane and truck to haul Mike's landlocked sloop, Outpost, into Eastern where it resided as the island's museum.

The gaunt cows were still thirsty, and corn stalks and pigeon pea bushes shriveled in the heat. David rebuilt and repainted his beach cottage sky blue with white gingerbread trim. His landlady, Luella, installed a fence around the lot with the beach lane chained off-limits to questioning travelers. Still though, impolite wanderers shouted at the rarely visible occupants for conversation and autographs. Amy had extended her stay to unwind from saving David's life. Bad dreams, which she refused to communicate, interrupted almost every night's sleep.

Leaning on her prop posts, Summer Breeze waited under tarps until the inquisitive fervor diminished enough to permit a launching party. The launch finally took place on an April Saturday with beautiful weather and just enough wind to almost erase the heat. The hundreds of guests kept silent as a goat was slaughtered for good luck and Priest Paul delivered a short prayer and blessing before he splashed fresh blood on the white hull. Men, women, and children from Carriacou and Petite Martinique helped push the sloop into the bay and to her mooring.

A loud cheer, followed by booming Calypso music, echoed across the beach village to Top Hill and was followed by the delicious aromas of the ensuing, massive barbecue. Plates of chicken with macaroni pie accompanied bowls of deep-green callaloo soup. Heineken and Carib beers chased gulps of golden, overproof Trinidian rum. Women chatted in small groups, yet kept a constant eye on their young children swimming and frolicking at the edge of the calm water.

This launching was Eastern's second most remembered event of the year. The American Embassy rented the L'Attrapis, brought an entourage of notables, and covered the extra expense for public relations to restore the tarnished American image. A talkative, red-faced Shremshock prepared a huge pot of spicy Caribbean fish gumbo and a bigger barrel of rum punch. Everyone danced on the sandy beach until they collapsed either from exhaustion or over indulgence. Amy's father pulled a few more strings and got her an extended, six-month leave of absence due to psychological stress.

Unhappily for him, her island fame had spread to the international tabloids, but so far, no one had extracted a first-person interview from an immediate family member. After seeing a few news photos, Bob Guiccione had offered six figures for her to pose for Penthouse. Amy was flattered, but quietly nixed the proposal using her active Navy status as an excuse.

After she and David had several heart-to-heart talks, they set their own course for a future together. Their portion of the treasure had been transferred to a stateside attorney friend who slowly disposed of it through a New York auction house. The golden dagger and mirror brought enough after commissions that, with the proper investments, they could live adequately without having to contemplate anything but future destinations. They'd managed to create two trust funds. One was for Bill's daughters to get an education if they chose; the other was to enable Bill to teach his boat-building craft to students from other islands.

These good deeds didn't erase the effects of David's greed. It certainly didn't halt or even slow the momentum of Carriacou's change. They had caused something to go awry in the machinery of time. He had sought refuge on Carriacou from a hectic nonexistence. Instead, until they sailed away, they were prisoners of their notoriety. Bill had accurately predicted the distasteful changes that the treasure spawned.

When Amy couldn't sleep they'd take long walks along the side roads of Carriacou. At dawn one morning, they were strolling on the deeply rutted road behind Indigo Bay, in an area called Anna's Retreat. Swinging their joined hands as they walked through the quiet lane, he related the story of the two sisters' school with the pigpen.

They followed a narrow footpath, which led away from the beach, and suddenly they came upon the ruins of the indigo factory. The walls had withstood two-hundred-and-fifty years of tropical climates, economies, and governments. This abandoned, shady plain was one of the most water-rich areas of the island. Huge, green-leafed mahogany and tamarind trees towered over the fields that had previously grown plants processed to obtain the blue dye. The eerie, two-foot-thick walls of the stone structure, perhaps three-hundred feet in length, could have been an ancient cathedral or a castle. It was still early in the morning. Land crabs rustling to their holes were the only things, other than them, moving around the structure. The ruins were far from the closest homes, so they didn't have to listen to any disturbed yard dogs. They rested on a fallen stone column.

"Isn't it amazing how they built things to survive? What country constructed this place?" Amy asked.

"Probably the French since they controlled Grenada for the first hundred years, but the real development was under British rule. This place might have been leased to Danish or Dutch trading companies," David answered.

"Have you ever been up here before?" Amy inquired.

"No, I was pretty occupied before you came." He leaned over and gave Amy a deep kiss.

"Oh!" David exclaimed.

"What?!" David's sudden outburst startled Amy. She looked around nervously. "What's wrong, David?"

"Oh, um, I was about to say that I'd wanted to come here since Mike had showed me a rubbing of a rock carving."

"From the Indians?" she asked.

He sighed, knowing they were about to visit a sensitive subject. "He thought it was from the survivors of the wreck."

Amy wet her lips, kissed him, and smiled. "David, we can talk about that, it's not taboo."

"I know," was his reply, "but I don't want to stir the memories of everything that has upset you."

"Oh yes, but I'm getting over it. Dad wants me to sit with a service shrink and pour out my soul. Sleep's coming easier, but I realize it will always be there. I'm not ashamed of what I did." She stood and walked on.

"I'm the one who's ashamed. None of this would have happened if I had minded my own business. Should have quit when I had the chance," David sighed.

"That's bullshit, David, Monday morning hind sight. I don't blame you for trying to live a dream. Come on; let's see if we can find this carving." Amy pulled him after her.

"You might not blame me, but I am sorry for putting everyone through all of this. Greed is the deadliest of all the sins."

"David, shut up, and please quit apologizing. It seems like all you do anymore is say you're sorry. What happened, happened. Today will become tomorrow's past. That's just the way it is. Nothing we can do about it except to feel blessed and enjoy our time together. We both know we are lucky to have so many great tomorrows looking us in the face."

A big sigh escaped him. "Mike said the stone was so big it couldn't be moved. The indigo farmers had to cultivate around it. It should be visible."

"Let's split up. You take this side of the building and I'll take the other." They parted with another kiss.

The trees blanketed the soil with shade so there was little of the usual thorny underbrush. David's steps were slow, as he kept looking in every direction. Finally, he saw the large, gray boulder at the edge of the trees.

Retracing his steps, he hailed Amy and they examined the carving.

"Do you think the four mutineers carved this inscription?" Amy inquired as her finger traced the letters and the date of 1699. "How would they get all the way back here? Why would they go to all of the trouble of carving a piece of evidence that would prove they had survived the Century's sinking?"

"Mike didn't know and there's been no reference to this carving in any account I've read or heard. He said he'd dragged an old metal detector across this entire field without any success, except for finding rusted nails."

"This rock seems inconsistent with the rest of this level field. If you look, the trees are arranged in rows like hedges. The slaves must have cleared the fields. This rock is big, but I'm sure it could have been shattered to use for building."

"Ahh, I'm not so sure. Slave labor on such an arid island must have been a dry Hell. Remember, all picking and planting was done by hand. Perhaps the plantation manager felt it wasn't worth the effort. Maybe they thought it was a tombstone. Who knows?" David answered.

"Can't be many people who knew it was here. From the looks of things, we're the only visitors this place has had in a long time. I don't see any of the usual signs of goats or cows."

"Not much for them to eat here in this shade. They'd rather raid present-day farmers' gardens. No sign of the usual empty beer bottles either."

She returned to tracing with her finger. "Wouldn't it be great to be a true psychic and be able to read the story by merely touching it? What do you think this means?" Amy's index finger followed the design beneath the date. "The four lines that make what looks like two triangles joined without a baseline."

"Well, speaking of baselines, it could almost be a baseball diamond," he paused.

"A diamond, that makes sense. Maybe they hid the jewels here. That's why a metal detector wouldn't pick it up. Maybe we should…" Amy suggested.

"Let's go," he interrupted her and turned to walk.

"Okay, you're right, David. Enough is enough. But don't you ever think about what happened to the treasure? I mean, the salvagers haven't found much. Crisscrossing the shipwreck with all that sophisticated equipment has brought up only a few iron cannons. They've dredged a barge full of sand for a few gold coins. I don't think it was ever there. What do you think?"

David was now hurrying back to the lane. "Amy, I don't think much about it anymore."

"Come on, David, you have to have thought about it!" She stopped and stood with her arms on her hips. "You mean, you've been able to just put it out of your mind? I'll never believe that!"

After clearing his throat, he turned and kissed her. "You are the only treasure I want."

"That's the right answer to that question." She kissed him back. "But don't you ever wonder?"

He wondered all right, all the way while walking back to Eastern. It was almost ten by the time they showered, did all the things that they had to do, and finally started breakfast. It seemed their few friends knew they were the most available in the late morning. It was now almost a tradition to chat over coffee. The bell rattled from the new gate.

It was Bill looking sheepish behind a pair of big sunglasses.

"Hey, what's dis guy gotta do to get a cup of coffee?" he yelled from beyond the fence.

"Be right there, Billy." David unfastened the chain and shook his hand.

"Where the dogs?" Bill asked as his head swiveled around.

"What dogs? What are you talking about?" David was puzzled.

"Me hear last week that people bothering so bad that yous bought two of them mean old pot hounds," Bill answered.

"No, in fact, things are almost quiet again."

"With fence like that, nobody think a sweet couple lives here. Anyway, me come by to find out what wrong with Summer Breeze. She leaking?"

David made a hurried look at his boat floating easily on the water. "She's still showing a lot of the water line. You think she's leaking? I'll swim out."

"Well, dere gots to be something wrong if you don't wanna to sail her. Me figure that you think she's gonna sink and that's why you haven't taken her out, but once," Bill said.

"Oh, Bill, I just haven't been in the mood. I know the boat's perfect. When we took her out after the christening, Summer Breeze sailed like a dream. Life hasn't been real dream-like lately. You know what I'm saying, buddy? Amy's hasn't been sleeping well. Me either."

"That makes three of us. That's all the better reason dat we go sailing. Hell, when me was a younger man and things got in too close, me just hop down to the water, hoist the main sheet, whether day, night, or in between. Yes sir, SP, ought to goes on a little sail. Me be your charter captain, cruise 'round all little islands 'tween here and Grenada for a day or two. Be good for you to practice and get feel of her. In that piece of water, there's plenty of different winds, tides, and strong currents." Bill was successfully selling his own brand of a seamanship course.

Amy joined with a cold beer for Bill. He tried to resist and opt for a hot coffee, but easily settled for the cool, brown bottle. Amy sipped her own and said, "Bill, I think you are absolutely correct, one-hundred percent. Summer Breeze deserves to have the dust blown off. Let's do it, Captain Bill. Let's go; we all could use a bit more salt water than what we get in our daily swims."

"Yous gets 'nuff privacy to go to the beach? Really, without no one taking your photo or asking dumb questions about how's that feel; how you do that; you don't look like that type of guy; you don't look that dangerous; or, oh my, where do you hide all dat meanness? Me get that sheet all the time. Pardon my French, Amy, but it's 'bout to drive me crazy. Me build boats forty-five of me sixty plus years and now all they want to know 'bout is a cutlass and a shotgun." He finished the beer quickly. "Ain't telling you two nothing that you don't know."

"Okay, okay! I apologize for not paying more attention to my pride and joy," David said as he handed him another cold beer. "Day after tomorrow we'll take off. That'll give me at least a day to get the beer iced to keep the crew happy."

"Oh, maybe me cutting yous across? Yous two don't need an old man like me. Yous probably thinkin' of going out by yous own selves. Me could just loosen the lines on Moriah, but tell you true, me just don't feel like sailing nowheres alone. Cecilia and girls gots no interest going out in a boat, less it's a cruise ship." Bill stared down at the floor.

"No way, Bill," they said almost simultaneously. David continued, "I'd really like to have you at the helm to show me how to make Summer Breeze perform."

Bill's head rose slowly and showed a broad grin. He slapped his knee and said, "Good, that girl built really strong and she ought to go to wind real fine. We can tweak her mast with the running back stays."

"So, where will we go?" Amy inquired.

"'Tween here and Grenada dere's 'bout a dozen islands. Can sail 'round, drop the hook a couple of places. Sail down to Gouyave or Grenville in Grenada if yous wants. Just be nice to get out of here for a while. Plenty of secluded bays to swim and fish. Bring that diving stuff and me knows we can get lobster for dinner."

"Sounds good. We'll go to the market and I'll make plenty of sandwiches," Amy added. "Bill, have you ever been down to the ruins at Indigo Bay?" She looked directly at Bill and never glanced to see David's disapproving frown for bringing up the subject. "We walked down there this morning."

"No, me never been down there, too many jumbies," the old West Indian man shrugged.

"Jumbies?" Amy asked.

"Yeah, that place gots the jumbies. Yous know, jumbies, ghosts, or spirits. Nobody me know goes back in there. They too scared," Bill reported. "Why yous ask?"

"No reason, buddy," David tried to change the topic, but Amy brought it back.

"We walked through the ruins and found a rock with a carved inscription," she said.

"Maybe was an old tombstone. In old days, they buried family close to home. Could be original Indians done it before white people come here," Bill replied.

"No it's not like that; I think it has something to do with the shipwreck."

"Wait a minute! Me don't wants to hear no more 'bout that boat. That already caused too many problems. Me promise everything holy, if ever me got out that mess, me never do nothing so stupid again." He gulped his beer and a second later he asked, "What's the rock say?"

"Mike said he found it years ago and showed me a photo and a charcoal rubbing. Today we happened upon it," David interjected as Amy rose to get another round of beers. She also returned with a pencil and paper.

"Here's what it looks like. Maybe you've seen something similar somewhere else around this island?" Amy asked Bill as she copied the inscription. Bill stood so he could peer directly over her shoulder as she shaded the design.

"Me would 'member if I seen the name CENTURY carved somewheres. No, never nothing like that, but me seen that design at the bottom before. Where de hell did me see it? Me no know. Member thinking it so peculiar. Give this old man a few minutes and it will come."

David wanted this subject to end and be forgotten, but Amy kept plodding on her inquisitive route while tapping her foot to an unknown rhythm — like it was the countdown on a TV game show.

Bill announced, "Nows me knows. Me and brothers were drift fishing down by Kick'em Jenny and went ashore to bottom fish. Yeah, that's where me see it. Carved right there plain as day." He parted his hands to demonstrate the carving was bigger than a foot across. "Yes sir, it's on a big, flat stone just 'bove high water mark. Recollect thinking, how somebody had such a great job going to every island and carvin' its name. Now me realize how dumb that was."

"Carving the name? I though you said you found it on Kick'em Jenny?" Amy continued her questions despite David's unvoiced objections.

"Amy, you probably don't know, but to the south of here is an underwater volcano named Kick'em Jenny, after a female donkey, 'cause it can be so stubborn and can be bucking at any time. Where me seen the inscription is on Diamond Rock."

As the words escaped Bill, the room went silent. For a moment David could picture the devil rubbing his hands and whispering, 'I'll get them this time' — and he knew what was coming next.

"So, this Diamond Rock is close?" Amy gave her total attention.

Bill looked up at David without the smile. "Sorry, SP, me mouth just starts moving. Sometimes too fast. Gets head of the brain."

A loud sigh rushed out of David's pursed lips. "Not a problem."

"Amy, 'bout two hours by sail from here. First rock pile you come to down the west side of Carriacou."

Amy sat straight up, "Will we be fighting the current to get there from here?"

"Depends on tide, but probably not. Seems its always running that way," Bill noted.

"So, the pirates or murderers from the Century would have had no problem getting there from here?" was her next inquiry.

"Like me say, depend, but they was smart and in no hurry. They wait 'til conditions was right. Guess they were sailing in a small, twenty-some foot, flat-bottom lighter."

Amy rubbed her jaw. "Why did they name the rock Diamond? Just suppose those who named it saw the carving. Will we be passing by there on our sail?"

"That's up to SP. His boat." Bill shifted in his seat.

"Yeah, we'll go there if you want," David replied.

"I want," Amy said.

"Got to get going." Bill rose to leave. "SP, sorry for blabbing so much, but me can't drink beers in the daytime," Bill apologized as David walked him out.

"Like I said, Bill, not a problem. Come here day after tomorrow with a smile and be prepared to teach me all the intricacies of sailing these waters. Smile buddy; we are going to have a great time." David patted him on the shoulder.

"Think you told me that before, but me come smiling." Bill turned and shuffled down the beach lane.

Returning to the cottage, David found his better half waiting shirtless in the living room. "Thank you, David." Amy pulled him close. "I want us to have a little adventure."

He knew this was intended to compete with memories of Feliza. "We can putz around Diamond and maybe we'll find another clue." She unbuttoned his shirt and rubbed up against him. He didn't have to wait until they went sailing to smile, but he could still imagine the devil rubbing his hands together.

\\\\\\\\

Summer Breeze was ready for a trip when Bill appeared on the beach at eight on their designated morning. Amy had stowed all their supplies and was reclining on a cockpit cushion in her delicious, yellow, one-piece suit. Dolly would stay on the mooring and they'd paddle a small inflatable when they went ashore. David winched the wire halyard for the gaff-rigged main, then dropped the mooring line, and ran to raise the genoa. It was good practice if he ever had to do this alone. As a precaution, David had the Yanmar diesel running in case things got too close.

The wind caught the sloop and spun her slowly to a portside tack. A few minutes later, Bill directed David to sheet in the genny and they ran down through the inside of the bay. Their course was set to go out through the reef at Kendall, the furthest passage to the south. Large, dark shadows of coral heads littered the bright-green water that churned under the keel.

David must have looked worried because Bill commented, "Don't fret SP. There's plenty depth here and been through here so many times, me could 'most do this in the black of night. Be in open water soon."

Amy took a deep breath. "This is the vacation I've been waiting for. Thank you both." She gave a blushing Bill a lipsticked smooch on his hairy cheek, and then stood on the high side hanging on the port stay. After passing between the dark brown cliffs of southeastern Carriacou and the protruding reef, Summer Breeze heeled further over as she caught fresh air. Bill let her fall off just a bit as they headed to bluer water. The boat felt perfect. The three of them alternated at the helm, tacking back and forth, and trying to determine how well the boat pointed to weather. The sloop reacted excellently at each maneuver. It felt really good to hear the shouts and childish laughter the morning's sail evoked.

After forced tacks and jibes, Summer Breeze effortlessly followed the sea to Diamond Rock. This was not a pile of rocks like Bill had described. Diamond was a huge, dark-gray monolith that the volcano had thrust starkly from the depths to about four-hundred feet above the sea's surface. The boat's arrival disturbed the birds that stained its rocky crags white. The depth sounder showed the bottom ran at about two-hundred feet until they were in close. While they circled, Amy checked its surface as much as possible through her binoculars. Just one day away from Carriacou had brought out a different woman, cheerful instead of thoughtful.

Diamond Rock appeared almost impenetrable. A small pebble ledge that faced nearby Isle de Rhonde was all that could suffice for a landing spot. They dropped anchor on the small bit of lee side, enjoyed a restful lunch, and snoozed in the afternoon heat before paddling ashore.

"We won't stay here tonight, will we?" David asked Bill.

"Nah," he pointed to the closest island. "The underwater shelf is too narrow to lay an anchor out very far. Wind liable to swing round and in too close while we'se sleeping. Right round that point on Isle de Rhonde is a pristine hooking ground. Water clear and fish plentiful. Can get a fresh dinner anytime. Only take fifteen minutes to gets there."

Amy anxiously untied the rubber boat from the foredeck and pushed it over the side into the water. She equipped the raft with a shoulder bag, a water bottle, and most importantly, one of the metal detectors.

"Oh no!" Bill rolled his eyes while helping David paddle.

"Oh yes," Amy countered, strapping on a dive mask with a snorkel before rolling out of the small boat. She swam and explored the underwater terrain while the men pulled their craft onto the small shore. Bill and David decided to follow her example and cool off by sitting in the calm water.

Once they were banded together, Bill used Amy's mask to splash water on a big, dull, yellow stone. Water settled into the indentations of rock. "That's almost the same carving you drew," Bill confirmed.

"Looks like there's something else carved down here." Amy delicately splashed and rubbed the stone. "Looks like an arrow pointing up with a number twelve. Might be seventeen or nineteen."

Bill dropped some more seawater, and they all seemed satisfied that the mark was a twelve, but twelve what? Amy clicked on the detector, but nothing reacted to her search. They guessed at this inscription's significance.

"You can't deny," Amy said after she removed the detector's headphones, "that this carving is connected to the one in Indigo Bay. One led us to the other." David sort of drifted away, watching his white sloop reflect on the water while Bill just sat rubbing his hairy jowls as she continued. "It must be from the Century. You two have got to give me that much." Amy was excited.

"What do we think the number means?" she asked.

David offered, "Could be meters or feet. Maybe latitude. Twelve degrees latitude is close to here."

Bill sat for a moment, deep in thought and then concluded, "Steps.

Ain't it steps that they used when they buried treasure?" Amy and David smiled at each other. "Me no know. Am I pronouncin' it wrong? You knows, steps. Twelve steps is what me think it means. Twelve steps, that direction."

Amy kissed his cheek again.

"What's that for?" he asked.

"For being so brilliant," she started looking around. "Doesn't seem so steep that they couldn't have brought the boxes up one at a time. David, you are about average size. Take a dozen steps."

The same feelings were flooding his body as months ago when he first recognized the beams under the coral head. Knowing that outcome, he wanted to balk, yet couldn't.

The twelve steps carried them to another landing above the beach. Bill used the water bottle sparingly to daub at the surrounding rocks, but nothing appeared.

Amy tried the detector again to no avail. "It has to be here! Why would someone go to all the effort carving two designs that lead nowhere?" David recognized the frustration in her voice.

"Gots to agree with you. Feel how hot it is. Right now we sweating when don't have to." It sounded like Bill was complaining. "But we'se here for fun. Whoever carved dat was on this rock for a purpose and guarantee wasn't no local. Seen some of carvings that Indians did 'round Carriacou. They is scraggly things with lines going everywheres. If this from a fisherman, believe me, would be only initials. No, whoever crawled round here was someone with some learning. They knew how to lay this out. To me, this is too smooth to be scratched by a rock on a rock. No sir, someone took hammer and a cold steel chisel and carved that. Amy, you right, this means something, but where's the answer?"

No one spoke for minutes. David took his time and walked up and down the path, looking behind small trees, moving stones that lay close to the area. His inspection found nothing that remotely looked like a chiseled character.

Finally, they sat on that small ledge pondering the next step. The ragged cutoff jeans Bill was wearing were still wet from wading and when he rose, David noticed they were muddy. Cursing, he headed back to the water to get a rinse. Then, it became evident.

The mud he wore was an accumulation of fine, powdered dust from the rock. That made it almost impossible to tell what was mud and what was solid rock. They each took a good drink of fresh water from their bottle before David used the remainder to attempt to wash away the years of accumulated mud cemented to the slight terrace. He had to refill the bottle, along with Amy's mask, three times. They scraped the mud with a stick before the next carving appeared.

Again, it was an identical diamond shape. This one had an arrow pointing to the left with the number twenty. Each of them looked at the bleak, brown stone that lay to that direction. It seemed to be a sheer face slanting downward at about forty-five degrees. David went first and measured the distance. Amy followed with the detector. She picked her way slowly, always careful to place each foot properly on a firm rock. A few times, she almost lost her footing and had to drop the detecting rod to grab a scrub bush for support.

The incline of the smooth surface didn't provide much traction, nor did the surrounding area give away any clues until Amy clicked on the machine. Her face beamed as she knelt to get a better balance to swing her detecting arm. "It's here! Something is here under this! I don't know what, but the detector's buzzing away!" She moved the rod slowly to determine the boundaries of the hit. With a soft stone she scraped a circle and then drew cross hairs to pin point the middle. Being above the water, the sensor unit wouldn't display anything positively, since it wasn't plugged into the diving helmet. David listened and could tell it had hit something big.

Amy leaned back quietly, starry-eyed in amazement. They both listened to Bill, who was just wheezing one deep breath after another. "Back to the drawing board," David said.

"What?" both answered.

"What cartoon character was it who said to put on your thinking caps? That's what we need now, some more of Bill's island logic." David offered.

"What yous mean, logic?" Bill sounded annoyed.

Amy was attentive as David explained his rationale. "Bill, you are accustomed to this climate and what people can easily accomplish. There doesn't seem to be any easy way to place whatever is here under this slab of stone. My thoughts are, they put it here to return for it later." Amy agreed while Bill returned to chin rubbing. "So, what's the answer? We still got more than two hours of light to figure out how they did this three centuries ago."

Bill spit. "Answered yous own question SP. If it is the men we think came off the Century, then it was only a handful. To me, that rules out brute strength. Ain't never cool here, so less they had slaves, no hole was getting dug in dis stuff. Bet on a cave. They knows something before about this place. Maybe anchored here or something, but they didn't bring whatever is now under us to here by no accident. Whoever they was must knowed dis made good place for stashing something."

Amy sat, quietly staring at the ragged shoreline of boulders thirty feet below. "I think they put it in a cave," she spoke quietly.

"Where's the cave?" Bill looked around. "Me no see no cave."

"I do," she answered calmly. "We are sitting on it."

Amy was as brilliant as she was beautiful. The obvious conclusion had eluded David. Worrying about the consequences of future and past actions would later become his only plausible excuse. He laughed out loud. "You got it, darling!" David slipped and would have fallen to a serious injury if she hadn't grabbed his arm to steady him. "Thank you for everything." He crawled to plant a serious kiss on her waiting lips.

"Bill, do you think you could go back and get the five-gallon bucket we use to wet Summer Breeze's deck?" Without a question, he turned to carefully retrace the path. "Grab the biggest screw drivers you can find in the tool locker," David added.

"Screwdrivers? Want Phillips or flat?" He muttered and then said, "I'll bring some beer, so it don't go to waste."

Amy and David, equipped with sticks and water bottles, scratched the perimeter of the fallen ledge. "I think they put everything under an overhang and then caused it to collapse. A naked eye couldn't tell anything unnatural happened here. Those boulders below made me think," she explained. "These guys probably had a barrel of gun powder and knew how to use it."

By the time Bill returned, they were ready to make the first beers instantly disappear. They'd dug along the edge of the table-sized slab to find it was about a foot thick. The metal shafts of the screwdrivers made easier work of the hard-packed earth. Bill kept dropping a bucket with an attached line and pulling up a few gallons of water at a time until they'd washed away enough sediment to reveal a small crevice.

"What we do now? Me no know. Sure enough, this thing too big for men to lift. Can't see how we could get more people 'round here to grip and lift. There just ain't enough good footing. What yous think?" Bill directed his question to his companions.

"Physics," Amy responded. "Physics and gravity. We dig on the lower edge and hope that by the time the sun sets, we'll have enough out of the way so this slab will slide and fall to join its relatives down at the water's edge. Let's start digging at the center and we'll work out to the edges. That way, it shouldn't shift with us in front of it. That would be a definite no-no," Amy directed and then went to work. Bill retreated to the sloop for more refreshment. He returned as they were clearing the last dirt to reveal a clean, unobstructed front. Unfortunately, the stone's massive weight kept the rock in place.

"Brought only physics me knows, a lever." Bill proudly displayed David's blue crowbar. The West Indian distributed icy-cold Heinekens, and then computed the dimensions of the slab, approximately sixty-by-forty inches, about a foot thick. With some effort, he found the upper edge against the hillside and inserted the bar. He pulled so hard his eyes seemed to bulge out beyond his bearded cheeks. Bill tied the bucket's line from a good-sized bush to a suitable rock, providing a handhold to grab in case someone slipped. Greed had them within its grasp again.

They took turns grunting and groaning until a tricky combined effort shifted the slab a fraction of an inch. From then on, each bite of the crowbar slightly moved the boulder. A nearly full moon was creeping into the eastern sky as the large rock finally slipped and toppled to the waiting sea below. Their sweating efforts had cut fingertips, sunburned backs, and coated them with a thirsty dust; yet they were still driven by the over powering desire to see what had been hidden. A couple of coughs and a lot of sighs signaled a pause in their activity.

It was Amy's curious energy that found the surface of the first of eight steel chests. After she silently swept the years of dirt from the lids, Bill and David managed to duck walk them down to the beach one at a time.

"Bill, I think we ought to pry open the first one. That way, if there's nothing in it, we can leave the rest," David proposed.

"No way, SP. Dere ain't nobody that dumb or cruel, to go to all dis trouble to hide empty chests. Anyway, don't feel empty at all. Fact, it feels like it's about to give me a hernia. If we open one now, we might all have a heart attack and that'd leave it all for whoever comes next. Nah, SP, me vote to ferry each back to Summer Breeze before we do anymore prying." Bill wiped the sweat that was dripping into his glowing eyes.

"I second that!" Amy shouted.

It took hours to move the eight chests. Each rusty box was bigger than a cubic foot and made from quarter-inch-thick iron secured by a single padlock. They had previously thought one chest had burst at sea, but their findings argued otherwise. Two cases unquestionably weighed less than the others. They estimated the weight to be close to the same as that of a big sack of cement. The inflatable could only carry one at a time without risking ripping out its flexible floor. The trio struggled to get each box up and over the gunwales of Summer Breeze. Bill fastened two canvas sail bags to act as a gasket to prevent scratching her new paint. He and David pulled attached lines while Amy pushed from below.

It was nine on a tranquil evening before they settled into the corner of Corn Store Bay at Isle de Rhonde for the night. Little conversation had passed between them since their energy had been drained. Beers and Amy's sandwiches were passed around the cockpit, which was now packed tightly with rusted iron boxes. This moment had all the elements of a dream from which they would eventually awaken. Until someone pinched David, a smile would stay plastered across his face.

"What do you say to a toast, fellows?" Amy raised her green bottle. "Here's to the three stumble-bumming lucky musketeers."

"Me no know what that mean, so me say me favorite thing. Here's to those that wish well, all the rest can burn in Hell."

The bottles clinked again as David muttered, "The rest are already burning."

They had gone to all the effort and found what they'd been searching for, but then, rather preposterously, lounged around before opening the boxes. Maybe it was out of fear of failure, fear of success, or fear of what success might bring, but they dawdled. They took a refreshing swim, dried, and waited while Bill plugged in the cockpit light he'd installed.

It was good they had waited. Amy used two screwdrivers to simulate a drum roll while Bill placed the lip of the crowbar into the ring of the ancient padlock and broke it with his remaining strength. The square lid had to be wrenched to open on creaky hinges.

The shock from seeing all those gold coins almost sent them into convulsions. Thankfully, there were no other boats in the bay to hear their loud roar. Silver and gold coins filled six chests — and a seventh had a startling array of jewelry. The eighth had been sealed with pitch. It was half full of silver coins and held a fragile, yellowed journal.

"Wow, wow, wow!" The bearded man shot out of the cockpit clapping his hands. "Thank you, Lord. Thank you Lord! SP, me never thought those treasure stories real!" Bill bounced around the boat, swinging from the stay wires to the safety lines while dancing a type of West Indian, gleeful jig. He finally sank, worn out, and sat with his back against the cabin wall. "How 'bout that!" He kept repeating as he lifted handfuls of the coins. "How 'bout that!"

Amy smiled, quietly searched the jewel box, and quickly adorned her deeply tanned throat with an exquisite diamond necklace. Regally arrayed, Amy was quite a picture. Again and again, she dripped loose rubies, sapphires, emeralds, and pearls onto her towel-wrapped lap. Giggling, she dug through countless gems and pieces of jewelry until she discovered a withered, rotted leather bag. Carefully prying apart the remnants of the pouch, she displayed a huge diamond ring, as big as a cherry, pretentiously woven among the golden arms of three reclining, naked women. Whistles and exclamations applauded her as she nervously placed it on her thumb and extended her hand.

Two Heinekens later, Bill curled into a snoring ball. The two sail bags adequately covered their find. A contented couple, Amy and David, chatted for a bit while they snuggled on the bench behind the helm. Exhaustion soon drove them to sleep where they fell, drunk on beer and wealth in Summer Breeze's cockpit. Their dreams that night weren't any better, nor were they any worse.

When the next morning came, they were still at a loss for words and sat just staring at each other over coffee. Their muscles ached, but without any doubt, they were rich — filthy rich. Carefully, they moved their wealth, hid it in the cabin's salon, and quietly returned to Carriacou.

A forever-grinning Bill used the excuse that the pressures of his island notoriety had become too great and that he was sailing with David and Amy to Florida. To Cecilia's protests, Bill promised to send for her and the kids if he didn't return within two months. They stocked Summer Breeze with everything from necessities to delicacies. Without any hoopla or fanfare, they hauled anchor to inconspicuously island hop north. Seven weeks later, in Fort Lauderdale, they sat around the table in a newly purchased condominium sipping more chilled Heinekens. Their smiles hadn't faded.

Amy resigned her commission and cut her father's dismay short by sending her parents on a golfing excursion to Scotland. That happened after the wedding. Bill was David and Amy's best man. Bill returned to Carriacou, and with assistance from a mysterious, but never-seen investor, constructed a huge boatyard where he and his daughters' husbands work to this day. No one really understands why he's still grinning. They all lived happily ever after — and Summer Breeze still cruises the Caribbean.

CHAPTER TWENTY ONE

The brittle yellow pages of longhand stored within the iron box, which had been sealed with pitch, unveiled the final days of the Century. It required weeks of studying the text under a magnifier before Amy could render this translation:

27th August of 1699

Who ever is to read this, know it was penned by Peter Strickland once a good sailor easily tempted to a bad end. Forty-two days after the schooner Century left Portugal on an ill last voyage with a crew and passengers numbering sixteen. Of those only three still breathe. Captain William Zane may be the devil hisself caused the others to meet a foul end of poison. Cooky Gunness mixed the evil meal as we stopped on the windward side of this isle bounded with reef. Those were sleeped to the sea and we laid the ship to rest theyre also. Not before taking this of the jews gold and burying it neath the broade rock.

It was four that divided one lot that was in this verie case. Gunness was killed by the devile Zane before he sailed alone to Hell I hope. If not theyre yet I

hope to pierce his blackest of hearts. Mate Allsop and I

are condemned souls for this foulest of deed. Zane could not parry we two and left us without direction and a bunged vessle to live out our days on that dismal lonely place.

Allsop craft a next bottom to our vessle and we assigned the gold from that sad graveyard. If you have found these casks then we are done for. If we do not put Zane to a sharpe point he will never recover the jews gold that have sent our souls to burn. Better tidings for you have now found it.

ABOUT THE AUTHOR

Ralph Trout is the quintessential Caribbean cowboy. His life has been an adventure from sailing and sport fishing charters to successful treasure finding. THE WRECK is the second of many novels evolving from having lived and worked throughout the Caribbean for thirty years.